THE CHRONICLE OF THE DEWNAN

This
SACRED
LAND

PART 1, THE RETURN OF THE PRINCE

TIM
BAGSHAW

@iamselfpub
www.iamselfpublishing.com

contents

Maps:

Chapters:

Ocean And The Pretan

Tamara in the land of the Dewnan

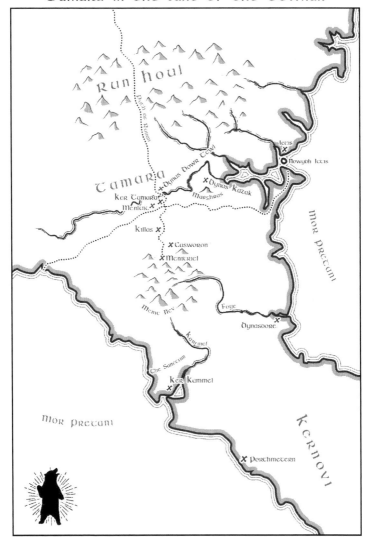

Run houl

Dreth an Ruunn

Tamara

Dynas Dowr Teom

Ker Tamara
Menlor

Dynas Kazok

Marghros

Ittis

Newyth Ittis

Mor Prettan

Killas

Casworon

Menkriel

Meme Nev

Foye

Dynasdore

Kammel

The Sanctum

Ker Kammel

Mor Prettan

Kernovi

Porthmetern

Menluit and the Twin Forts

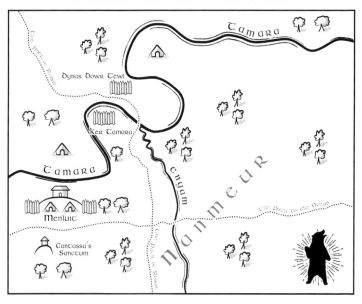

The moons of the Dewnan

Loor Bleydh	*Wolf Moon*
Loor Tewedh	*Storm Moon*
Loor Plansa	*Planters Moon*
Loor Tevyans	*Growing Moon*
Loor Skovarnek	*Hare Moon*
Loor Golowan	*Midsummer Moon*
Loor Medh	*Mead Moon*
Loor Barlys	*Barley Moon*
Loor Trevas	*Harvest Moon*
Loor Helghyer	*Hunter's Moon*
Loor Owrek	*Golden Moon*
Loor Derwenn	*Oaken Moon*

For Penny, with love.

Absence of Evidence is not
Evidence of Absence

beholden to caesar

ante diem X Kalendae October, AUC 697
Consuls, Publius Lentulus Spinther, Quintus Caecilius
Metellus Nepos

Terror and panic filled the air, corrupting the brightness of a crisp autumn morning. Women wailed and babies cried inside the Aduatuci citadel. Men, the few that remained, ran from building to building, trying to rally any who would listen for one last stand. But it was futile. Their last, best hope had already come and gone. The battering ram was at the gates and all feared the fate that awaited them.

'Where is father?' Valis cried. 'Why does he not come to save us?'

Eight summers old, with short-cropped blond hair and blue eyes like hers, the boy looked imploringly into his mother's eyes, as he stood in the middle of their small roundhouse at the centre of the oppidum. Alarm was on his face and in his tremulous voice. She had no answer for him except the truth.

'Your father is dead, Valis. Cut down by the Roman warriors, along with the other men of this tribe, in their final brave attempt to preserve our freedom.'

An old man sat on the bench opposite her and tried to be positive.

'Sumela, there is still hope! See, I have my short sword. I will defend us against these Roman thieves and vagabonds. They will not take me down easily.'

She breathed in deeply and shook her head slowly and sadly.

'If you say so, father.' She looked at her son and smiled gently. 'So you see, Valis, it seems there is hope yet, grandfather will protect us.'

Suddenly, there was shouting outside and her neighbour called through the door.

'Sumela, Sumela! They are in. They are coming! We must go; there is protection in numbers. We must all gather together.'

Sumela's stomach tightened and she tried not to show her fear, controlling her body from trembling for Valis's sake. Yes, protection in numbers, some would be picked off, but others might survive. It was harsh on those taken, but for Sumela and the Aduatuci who remained, it was all they had left. She strapped her sword belt to her waist, knelt down to kiss her son, and tried to look as reassuring as possible as she said, 'Father, come on. We have to go now.'

The old man slowly got to his feet with a stiffness of movement that belied his fighting assertions of moments before. He followed his daughter and grandson out of the house. Now the noise intensified; the street was full of running people.

'Where is the gathering?' Sumela called to several who rushed past her, while she held firm to Valis's hand. Nobody answered her and instead just looked at her, dread in their eyes, seeking desperately to get away from the Roman plunderers at their backs. Their attackers had broken through and were spreading out through the oppidum, encircling them and consuming everyone that stood in their way.

'We will go this way,' she said to Valis. 'Father, try and keep up.' The old man grunted something in response, but she did not hear what it was as she pushed along with the fleeing crowd, frantically looking ahead for any sign of a gathering of the remaining few Aduatuci, ready to submit and beg for mercy.

Between the buildings, they ran. After a few moments, Sumela looked back and, as she did, her father tripped while trying to maintain the pace. Losing his balance, he fell sideways into a narrow passage between two roundhouses.

'Valis, we have to go back. Grandfather has fallen. Hold tightly to my hand.'

She pushed her way through the oncoming crowd, which flowed like a storm-swelled torrent surging to destruction, and pulled her son into the alley where the old man lay sprawled on the ground.

'Leave me, Sumela. Leave me. There is no point now; go, seek safety if you can find it.'

'I will not leave you. Either we stay here or you get to your feet.'

'I am scared, grandfather, help us!' The full realisation of the terror overwhelmed the boy and he looked despairingly into the old man's eyes.

The father looked up to his daughter resignedly, exhaled, caught his breath and pulled himself up.

'This way,' she said and led them down the narrow passage. 'We will try and find a path through, away from the push of the crowd.'

'What about safety in numbers?' her father called after her, but she was already running.

And then it was too late. Sumela and Valis ran out of the other end of the passage and straight into two Roman legionaries. One grabbed her arm, while the other wrenched Valis from her grip and slapped him across the face as he screamed. The boy fell to the ground. Sumela called desperately to him, 'Keep still, Valis. Don't move!'

Both legionaries pinned her hard against the wall of the roundhouse. She could not understand what they were saying, but their intention was all too clear; with manic grins and lecherous eyes, their rough, battle-stained hands began to pull at her clothing and press and grab at her lower body.

But, in their haste to violate another of the oppidum's women, they let their concentration drop, and so did not see the onrush of Sumela's father – not until one of them convulsed as a short sword incised between his ribs.

The other, who had slapped Valis, let go of Sumela and drew his weapon to take on the old man. Sumela swiftly drew her sword and, as the legionary lunged at her father, thrust her sword into his back. Both legionaries writhed on the ground, but there was no time to think, as others ran towards them from different directions, shouting in their Roman language.

'Quick Valis, father, over there; the stairs to the battlement. It is our only chance.'

Up the stairs they went, Sumela and Valis first and then her father. Out onto the battlement, they ran. Others of the tribe were there, but now there were Romans coming the other way.

'Come on then. You are not done with the warriors of the Aduatuci just yet!'

Sumela stopped and turned to see her father charging back towards the Romans at the top of the stairs. It did not last long.

A sword through his ribcage disabled him, and then, without a second thought, the oncoming legionaries pushed him over the battlement – there was a pause before a sickening crack was heard as the bones in his frail body split on the rocks below.

'Father!' Sumela ran back, but there was nothing that she could do, for him or for herself.

The others on the battlement were herded away, but it was her they were after. They knew what she had done and now she would pay.

'My son,' she begged, 'do not harm him. He is innocent. Let him live, please...'

'Mother!'

Valis tried to reach her, but the hand of a legionary came across his face, and then, for one last fleeting moment, his eyes met hers. 'I love you,' she mouthed. 'Be brave...' And then he was gone.

Now they all closed in for their pleasure, frantically she tried to struggle, but the end was inevitable, and when the dagger came, relief was all she felt.

***

Julius Caesar watched as the ram struck again and broke through. The gates swung open and the mass of waiting legionaries twitched like a giant predator anticipating the surge it would make towards its intended prey.

It was the end of the campaign season and his men had been granted an unexpected reward today and for this, they applied themselves with a fresh zeal. The Aduatuci leaders had reneged on his terms and attacked the besieging legions in the night. The sortie had been strongly repulsed and perhaps four thousand of their best warriors lost. Now his men had broken down the gate and would enter the citadel and take prizes at will until the Pro-Consul's cornu sounded.

At the command, the legionaries rushed forward. A thin line of defenders stood just within the gates, their swords drawn and crudely made shields deployed, but the forces they faced were overwhelming. Gladius and pilum ran through them, a brief red fountain glistening in the morning sun before they disappeared beneath the trampling boots that squelched through the defiled, blood-soaked and broken bodies in search of a live victim. But the legionaries had not come to kill. Not this time, unless in self-defence. The commodity was far too valuable for that. Instead, instructed by their leaders, they had come to take, indulge and sell.

More of the Aduatuci appeared on the battlement, women and children amongst them. They were running and then, the first of his men appeared in pursuit. An older man, slower than the rest at the rear of the fleeing group, turned and raised what looked like a cooking knife in an attempt at resistance. He was of little value in the slave market and so one of the legionaries drove his gladius into the old man's ribcage. As he lurched forward, a woman, his daughter perhaps, holding her young son's hand turned and ran back towards them in despair.

The legionaries bundled the old man over the battlement. As he fell with a thud and crack on the ground, the woman looked over and cried out at the contorted body below. She turned away and they were on her, pulling at her clothing. Some of it came free, exposing her shoulders and part of her upper body. As she tried to resist, her son cried out, and he was quickly muffled by a firm hand. Then, the legionaries forced her below the wall, while others gathered around.

Caesar watched on, taking it all in. The continued spoils of war drove the legions forward and contributed strongly to the maintenance of discipline and order. Many of the recruits were petty criminals; taking and abusing was in their nature, and if they were to continue to work for him, their base desire needed feeding. The bond between him and them grew ever stronger and their collective adventuring brought rewards and built their experience and their loyalty.

'Dominus, the Massaliot merchants are here; all is prepared.'

Interrupted in his train of thought, Caesar turned, acknowledged his Centurion of the Pro-Consul's Guard, passed overall command to the Legate of the Xth Legion, Titus Labienus, and walked back behind the lines, accompanied by the centurion to the large tent where he held briefings with the legates and senior tribunes. As he entered, two men, both Greek merchants from Massalia, stood to greet him. The first, fat and perspiring like many of his kind, carried himself with a self-assumed air of importance as he stepped forward to speak.

'Pro-Consul, I am Peneus of Massalia, senior partner in the Massalia Galliki merchant company. You are a valued client and we are pleased to offer our service to you again.'

The man was all bluster and obsequious arm waving, but Caesar's face gave no sign of emotion as he cursorily glanced at the second merchant.

'Gyras, you are welcome. Your grain supply to my legions continues to be of great service.'

The second Massalian merchant bowed briefly but honestly. Following the Pro-Consul's lead, he felt it wise to betray no further emotion.

For a moment, Caesar said nothing and stared coldly at the fat merchant while, even here, well behind the front lines, the pain and anguish in the Aduatuci citadel offered the backdrop to the discussion to come.

'Yes, Peneus, I asked for the senior partner of your company to attend me. We have done business before, of course, although you and I have never met. No doubt, the strain of a long ride was too much for you on previous occasions.'

The Greek offered a shallow bow and with a further unctuous smile, delivered between two ruddy plump cheeks, said, 'Caesar, dominus, it is our company promise to serve our customers and all their needs, and if they ask for it, to attend them personally. We were delighted to handle the merchandise gained from your last campaign and shall be pleased to serve you again.'

Briefly, he glanced towards the noise from the citadel.

'Your company promise, to serve?' The Pro-Consul stared towards the merchant. There was an unmistakable look of contempt on his face, but Peneus did not seem to see it.

'Always, dominus, and we are ready to do so again…'

'And to gain… from your "customers"?'

There was a slight flicker of unease in the merchant's eyes, but he persisted with his line of response.

'Dominus, we take our small gain, but it is our customer's interests that come first.'

Caesar had heard enough.

'Peneus, let us not waste any more time, your company owes me a lot of money from the slaves of the last campaign. When will you pay the full amount owed?'

There was menace in his voice and Gyras shuffled nervously on his feet as he watched his fellow Massalian's reaction. There was only one response in his mind: *apologise, blame it on an administration error and pay Caesar now or at least guarantee that the funds will be with him as soon as possible.* Peneus, with a carefully constructed look of concern, however, chose a different response.

'Caesar, Dominus. We have paid you in full. The market was deflated at the end of the year by a glut of goods, slaves and metals from Asia. We got the best price we could. Now, the market is returned, I am confident of a better price, and these Aduatuci are so strong and tall, and their women feisty, more reliable than the Germani. They will sell well!'

The Pro-Consul continued swiftly.

'Peneus, I am reliably informed that the price you achieved was far better than you have informed me. I ask again, when...'

Peneus cut in, now fully sensing the mood against him, his eyes moving erratically as he sought a plausible reason for his deceit.

'Why would we try to deceive? I assure you, all that was owed to Caesar was sent to Caesar.'

The Pro-Consul's shift to outright anger was instant and alarming.

'You lie, even here in Caesar's tent, you continue to lie. I have had you watched Peneus. Three new villas in Massalia and your farm in our Province; it has been an exceptional year for you, even when the market has been so deflated.'

With sudden desperation in his voice, Peneus sought a way out.

'Dominus, let me go back to Massalia and investigate further. If the money is owed, I will ensure that it is paid as quickly as possible.'

Caesar's firm, calm glare returned as quickly as it had gone.

'I cannot allow that. I will recover what I am owed by my own means. I do not like people who steal my money and an example must be made.'

He stood aside and the centurion sprang forward, his gladius quietly unsheathed while Caesar spoke and thrust it deep into the Greek merchant's expansive, protruding belly. Peneus looked down and then up, rooted to the spot in his terror. Blood trickled from his mouth, while a deep red stain quickly spread across his mud-spattered tunic.

Caesar held his glare while the centurion held firm to the hilt of the gladius, ensuring he had penetrated completely.

'You see, Peneus, when you deny me my profit, you deny my men their profit as well. They have lost good comrades, borne great hardship to spread the glory of Rome, and will not tolerate a fat Greek thief like you stealing their rewards. Your body, returned to Massalia, will serve as a warning to others. I will take all that you own as recompense. Your family will be homeless and without any funds – all because you thought that you could deny Caesar.'

The centurion released his grip and withdrew the gladius. A whispered incomprehensible word, one final attempt at protest, came from Peneus's mouth as his head gently rocked. He staggered and fell backwards. Blood oozed from the incision, cascading down his belly and formed a growing pool between his legs while he lay on the ground, involuntarily twitching as his life slipped away.

Gyras tried to stand as confidently as he could. He knew he had done no wrong, and had met Caesar before, and discussed his trading journeys with him in a friendly manner. Still, he looked nervously at the Pro-Consul, ready to attempt a defence if needed.

'Gyras, it seems you are the only merchant left to deal with our soon to be gathered new harvest of slaves. Are you able to take on the contract?'

Relief coursed through him and he switched easily into a discussion with his client.

'Dominus, I am, but I will need to make arrangements. Will your men be able to hold them while I send word for assistance?'

'Gyras, I will do better than that; I will detail whatever men you need with commands to remove them to Massalia. There you will make appropriate arrangements, and when the trade is completed, come to me in Ravenna, when the worst of the winter has passed. There you will be able to confirm the profits that we have made, before discussing another matter I would like your help with.'

'Dominus, I will proceed with the arrangements immediately.'

the tempest's due

The small boat lurched to the left as the next wall of water caught and lifted its stern. Jolted from their seats, drenched to the bone and very cold, her crew gripped their oars and grimly regained their position, praying silently for mercy from Ocean's spirits.

How long had this been going on? Most of them had lost all sense of place and journey, rising and falling steeply, as roll upon deep roll buffeted the boat, thrusting it forwards, backwards and sideways, pushing the boat and its crew to their limit.

Here, sky met sea in a tumult of noise, confusion and all-consuming terror. The thunderous wind; glowering, impenetrable darkness; and deafening resonance that beat upon the water drained the crew's confidence, while the ever-present swirling and flying spray, which helped to fill the boat despite their constant bailing, brought a growing sense of foreboding and impending doom to all those within.

They should never have set out.

She was made of oak with tall sides and high stern and prow, combining seven oar positions on either side. There was a single mast one-third of the way aft from the bow, held firm by forestay and backstay. Normally, the yardarm supported a single sail of treble-stitched animal hides, to withstand strong winds. Tonight, however, it was furled and firmly tied to the mast at dusk, with the weather change clear for all to see as Sira Howl, the Sun Father, hidden by building cloud mass, descended to walk in the underworld.

In the centre of the boat, a large, hide-covered hatch led to a low storage area packed with trade goods and gifts, while at the rear, a large and extended steering arm provided a rudder of sorts, giving crude steerage in all but these most exceptional of circumstances. Underneath, a shallow keel allowed for Ocean sailing, but also for penetration along the river valleys, rias and estuaries through which she sailed and carried her cargo, between the lands and territories of the Ocean People; and often on rugged, challenging seas. She could withstand storms and return to safe harbour, but tonight was different; the violence of Ocean's spirits pushed this most sturdy of craft to its limits.

The boat rested for a moment on the crest of a wave.

'Pull hard, pull!' roared the coxswain at the right bank of oars in front of him. 'Balance us!' he bellowed to the opposite side as he and the helmsman hauled the rudder arm. The boat pulled back to the left and careered headlong into the valley of the wave, which crashed and flooded over the bow.

'Forward, two oars, bail! Get the water out!' yelled the coxswain.

He stumbled forward to give help and closer direction. As he stumbled along the boat, he swung his head around, weighed down by sodden hair and roared, 'Stay where you are; keep weight in the rear.'

In the stern, next to the helmsman, a young man, eighteen winters old, observed the coxswain's actions. Taller than the rest of the crew, he was slender in build with intense dark blue eyes and long blond hair, and his mannerisms, in spite of the storm, marked him as different in origin from those around him. His height gave him natural authority and his countenance, even at his young age and drenched as he was, made an impression. The crew looked to him for confidence and reassurance. He understood this, knew his role and stood with purpose and conviction, determined to keep his balance. He wore close-fitting flax linen trousers and a heavy cloak that covered a long tunic, all soaked through. Many of the crew had beards and long moustaches, but his face was clean-shaven.

Breathing heavily, exasperated and increasingly desperate, the coxswain returned and balanced himself beside him. He was shorter, stoutly built and at least ten summers older. The darkness of his face indicated regular engagement with the elements and now rivulets of rain ran down it, past intense, dark brown eyes that worked feverishly, taking in all aspects of their situation, considering the possibilities.

Against the din, he shouted, 'We cannot stand this much longer! Ocean batters us and we gain water faster than we can get it out, particularly below deck.'

He paused to catch his breath before continuing.

'When the storm blew up, by my reckoning, we had made good progress, but now Borum, his winds and Ocean's spirits connive to drive us to unseen land and jagged rocks. It is a day and half a night since we left the beach at Ynys Carreg Goch. Soon, I am sure soon we will approach the haven at Porthmetern, but to do that safely we must be able to see…'

His voice trailed away as he fell sideways and struck the right wale with his shoulder. The forward rolling wave had absorbed the impact from another, causing the boat to lurch again.

The young man staggered across the deck, placed his arms under the shoulders of the coxswain and pulled him to his feet.

'Maedoc! Are you hurt?'

The coxswain held the wale for support and looked down to his feet. For a moment, pounding water, wind and darkness drowned all hope in his mind. Should he confess to the Pryns that they were doomed and had no hope if this continued and that actually, they were gradually sinking?

'Maedoc – can you hear me?'

Still, he looked at the deck, his shoulder aching and the storm roaring. The crew held their breath, waiting for a response as they tried to steady the ship. Slowly, he moved his head from one side to the other. No, he – they – were not quite finished yet; his calculations, despite the confusion, told him they must be close. He had promised the King that he would fetch the Pryns and return him safely, and with him, the gifts from his hosts: the work of Demetae and Ériu goldsmiths was sitting in the hold, adding to the weight of the boat, helping to drag it down. He knew the King and that he would await the gold as keenly as he waited for his son.

Secretly, quietly, he had also promised *her* – the real proponent of this journey – that he would bring him home, ready to be educated for the trials ahead. They were close now, he knew it, but some force, some demon, worked against them. He would not concede to the Ocean's anger – or to whatever, whoever manipulated it. Not yet.

'I am not hurt, just bruising.'

He raised himself, and pushing away from the wale, turned and brushed past the Prince, their eyes meeting briefly in acknowledgement as he raised his head.

'I must get back and hold the steering arm... or we are certainly doomed.'

The young man's kin in Demetae – land of the dragon slayer, across the Mor Pretani – had insisted a small band of warriors, friends and acquaintances accompany him. They rowed the ship now, or tried to, alongside the small crew, coxswain and helmsman who had sailed the boat to Demetae. A small entourage for a young man of high birth returning to his homeland after summers and winters away; and yet, despite their warrior status and the Prince's high birth, it was Maedoc who commanded the ship.

A man of humble birth, born and raised in a small round by the estuary of the river, Heyl Kammel, on the coast of the Dewnan tribal lands, he had entered the service of the King nine summers ago and quickly shown himself capable, adaptable; a man who could be trusted to resolve a problem. He had learnt the refined speech of the men and women of the court, the ruling elite, in his desire to progress and had risen in the King's esteem accordingly. His ability with boats – particularly his capacity to take command and find his way, even when out of sight of land – had marked him as different from the other servants. He had crossed to Demetae on a number of occasions, and even on the darkest nights, in the midst of a storm, he knew where he was going. He had worked hard to get his position, and resolution returning, he would not give in now. Besides, in the few days, he had spent in Demetae, waiting for his young charge to prepare, they had struck up a friendship; he liked him. It was his duty to see him home safely.

The Prince looked to him, admired his determination, but could see he needed help and acted on his position of authority.

'Maedoc, I will help Cass steer. If we are close, unfurl the sail, the wind is behind us now. Let it help by driving us to the shore. Can we take the middle two oars from either side? Set three of them bailing and put a man on watch as high in the prow as he dares to climb – any sign of land or rocks, he must shout as loud as he can.'

The coxswain looked into his eyes, nodded and went forward before barking out instructions.

'Cass, move your grip lower, I will hold the top end.' Gripping the steering arm tightly with one hand, the young man paused to wipe rain and bedraggled hair from his face before holding firm with both.

The wind, with the aid of the bulging sail, dictated the boat's forward movement, but the two helmsmen gripped tightly and did their best to keep control. Then, as the Prince held firm, Cass leant forward and spoke as confidentially as he was able to in the surrounding tumult.

'Can ee hear it?'

'Hear what?' the Prince shouted back.

'Cryin', on th'wind?'

'Cass, it is the wind in the backstays. Concentrate – we must hold this steering arm firm.'

The Prince re-established his balance as Maedoc supervised increased bailing. There was definitely less water in the boat, and the lookout in the prow peered determinedly through the darkness. *Perhaps, even after this battering, all would be well.*

As he stared, he paused. Could he hear something?

Foolish! How could it be? Wind and ropes, certainly in this storm, made strange noises. He was exhausted and his mind tricked him. The crew furtively looked up at him. Glances between them told him they heard it too. He redoubled his expression of purpose, gripped the steering arm and, as he did, became aware of a darker line appearing at the furthest extent of his vision. *Was that…?* As he peered forward, he also saw a faint flickering light, slightly to the left. Yes, it was a light, maybe a beacon. *Land at last!*

'Cass, I see the shoreline. Can you see that light, ahead and to the left?'

'I zee it, my Lord: beacon o'some sort. Appen tiz a warnin'.'

The Prince called to the nearest oarsman, 'Deri, go forward and fetch Maedoc; we approach land.'

As he returned, Maedoc breathed heavily as he shouted above the wind, 'Karrek Guilan over there, beyond Porthmetern. We must use our oars fully now if we are to reach land safely. We approach the mouth of Heyl Kammel. Nearly there now, one last effort.'

He moved closer to the Prince's ear.

'Ocean's spirits play with us. They mean to take us if they can, but the voice,' he nodded his head meaningfully, 'yes, it argues for us and should not frighten us. Come on! We must not lose control.'

The crew heard the voice and felt the threat of the approaching shore.

The young man was determined to remain confident and for all to hear it, even through the storm. 'Maedoc, I hear the voice too. It works for us, but if we lose control now we will certainly founder. All must be strong. If the spirits work against us, they will sense our fear and take it as a sign of weakness. Childhood memories tell me, too, it is my father's land we approach. Let us pull for shore!'

The Prince spoke with assuredness and authority. The coxswain bowed his head in acknowledgement. Ahead, the line of cliffs parted for the entrance to a small estuary.

Maedoc, still with inner strength, turned and roared his commands, 'Hold firm to your oars! We must clear the headland first and then the estuary will be calmer. Come on, lads – nearly there. One last big pull and then we can rest.'

***

The acolyte clambered along the coastal path, head and body bent against pouring rain and a gale so powerful she used her hands to crawl, gripping the ground, holding on as she negotiated narrow parts of the path, trying not to slip, and not daring to look down at the rampant, pounding sea below. Her reddish-blonde hair flew wildly around her head and her cloak pressed tight against her body. In this way, she battled along the path.

She had come from the house of the priestess, the sanctum, a sacred place built on a distinctive outcrop of land, sticking out into the sea. Two hills were on one promontory and close by, but separated by a narrow passage, another rock reared from Ocean's depths. To the determined eye, the hills had the appearance of a two-humped beast with its head sticking out of the water. A sea serpent, a spirit from ancient days, tamed and harnessed to the land.

Here and along this ragged coast carved by the elements, the priestess of the Ocean People, supported by her acolytes, spoke with the spirits, defended men's souls and, on this night of all nights, in the midst of the raging storm, stood firm and pleaded for mercy.

Finally, the acolyte reached the highpoint she aimed for. Here, the path turned inland to follow the entrance to a river estuary, falling away as the high cliffs descended to fields and a rocky shoreline. The headland stuck out its ancient rock, exposed over an age immeasurable by wind, rain, salt water, and here, in a crevice protected marginally from the onslaught of the storm, a fire burned brightly; a beacon to guide frightened souls and their boats from troubled waters.

'My lady, Ryd has come to The Sanctum. He says a boat has been sighted trying to enter the estuary. He did not like to disturb you.'

The priestess stood rigid, close to the fire, staring with wide blue eyes towards Ocean and darkness. Tall and thin, with long blonde hair flecked with grey at the crown blowing freely, her gaunt, stretched body reached towards the deafening black void. Her mouth moved slowly, with conviction but with no sound, or at least none evident above the roar of the storm. She made no reply.

The acolyte tried again.

'My Lady, there is a boat at the mouth of the estuary.'

Still no apparent recognition.

'My Lady...'

'I know that they are here, Elowen.' The priestess's forward stare remained as she took a small step backwards to re-establish her balance. She spoke again, just loud enough to be discernible. 'I see them. They are strong and react with great bravery to Ocean's tests. But it is all in vain; the boat is doomed, the spirits are hungry and sacrifice is called for.'

She turned and spoke agitatedly to Elowen.

'There is more than the spirits and their quota of souls at work here. A promise has been given, by whom I do not know, but they know of our quest. All of this...' She gestured wildly behind her, her hair spiralling upwards in the wind. 'It is for him!'

Her voice trailed away, a flicker of pain passed across her eyes and she closed them. Almost instantly, they were open again.

'Go back to the house, Elowen. Leave me! I must use all my strength if we are to stand any chance of averting disaster.'

'But, my Lady, the storm… I have never known such a storm. We are all concerned for you.'

'Go, Elowen. Go and tell all that I remain strong and determined, but I must concentrate. Go!'

Reluctantly, Elowen turned, pausing only to look into the darkness and where she imagined the boat to be. Her lips moved silently in a prayer for deliverance before she returned along the path, occasionally looking back to see the priestess standing firm, looking down towards the mouth of the estuary.

***

The crew stuck doggedly to their task. In sight, but not, it seemed, in reach of salvation. Now there were other voices on the wind; cackling and wicked laughter as waves crashed on the unforgiving shore and Ocean's spirits broke free.

They heard the wave before they saw it, a gurgling, gobbling approach, recognisable, even in the cacophony of the storm, as a harbinger of doom; one of Ocean's fell creatures, as old as the Earth Mother herself, sent from its deepest depths to collect the Tempest's due.

Maedoc and the Prince saw the panic on the faces of the crew and turned to see the approaching wall of water. Both turned back instantly.

'Row, Row hard! Come on, boys; row as hard as you can, together. Come on!'

It was too late. The wave was upon them, turning the boat sideways, pushing it towards the rocky shore and engulfing it. The cargo shifted and the boat tipped and capsized while all those within spilt into the expectant, hungry sea, tumbling uncontrollably into a churning mass of grey, green and white. The spirits, just below the surface, pulled gleefully, tugging them down as the crew grasped frantically at air and water. Some tried desperately to clutch the sides as they went into the water, but the boat rolled over on top of them. The mast, sail and rigging collapsed as it struck jagged, teeth-like rocks, hidden in the waves, snapping at their victims; and all around them, the storm roared its delight at their capture.

A second wave, even larger than the first, approached and turned to white at its crest as it thundered towards the rocks and rode with ease over the top of the boat, consuming, mauling and scattering all those who still struggled. Screams of terror preceded its final towering death roll before it consigned the boat and her crew to their fate, weighing them down and confirming their watery end.

Dragged under the boat, the Prince was disorientated and frantically sought the surface. He saw faces and tried to swim towards them, but then, a force – an underwater current – pulled him away into deeper water and the faces faded. He found the surface but in the dark could see no one else. The shouting was fading. Panic began to grip him. Despite the strength of his young body, the weight of his clothing dragged him down. Another breaking wave came over him and his head sank. He raised it again, pushed upwards and grabbed a gasp of air as the wind roared and spat around him. He sank again.

'*Take off your jacket and cape, discard your boots and throw away your sword.*'

The voice was firm. *Was it Maedoc?*

'*Swim; throw it all way, let it go!*'

He knew he had to do it, even discard his sword. Did he say that to himself or was there somebody near? He struggled again to raise himself above the surface, cleared his long hair from his face with a firm jerk of his head.

There was nobody there.

With a kick to maintain a brief balance, he discarded all but his tunic and inner trousers and sank again in the water exhausted from the effort.

***

'*Meliora… Meliora can you hear us? We know you can. Answer us, conqueror and tamer of serpents, mighty priestess and apologist for men.*'

She would not respond to their mockery. If she concentrated, kept her mind on the boat, she could see it clearly; she could save them, or save some of them – save one of them.

'Meliora, why are you trying so hard?'

She sensed the indulgent, sardonic smile.

'It is pointless to expend so much energy, you know it. After all, we do so enjoy our conversations. We really wouldn't want you to tire yourself out.'

The intensity of the laughter was too much and she swayed for a moment as her concentration fell. She knew it was pointless. A bargain must be struck – it was the only way. She had tried, but now she must concede to the inevitable before it was too late.

'Meliora.' No longer the faux laughter, the voice came back clear and strong. *'We are promised a rich offering and we have them… we have him. What can you possibly offer that would make us give back this gift? Give it up, Meliora; accept their fate. The storm brings us souls – there is no difference here.'*

Who had made this offering?

Urgently, she used the fullest power of her mind, audible only to her and her tormentors.

'I can bring you other men, twice as many men. If you let this boat safely to shore.'

'What, more of your criminals? We don't want them. We have too many of them. This cargo is special. We know it. Word has reached us, and good men are hard to find. We shall have our due.'

It would not be long before the crew were lost. Desperately, she struggled once more to see them. Was she too late already?

'All right, no criminals, captives; a person of good standing if you will let them go.'

'Who, Meliora? Your conscience is clear with the criminals and the enemies of your people; who will you bring to sacrifice? You will not be able to find enough good people to replace the crew of this ship. So who shall we save, Meliora, and who do you offer to replace them?'

She took a deep breath and cast her eyes sadly to the ancient rocks around her. She had known this was coming, as soon as she had seen his likely fate. How else could she confound the forces of darkness that conspired to extinguish this last great hope of the Ocean People? Even greater storms than this were gathering. In what other way could she bring him safely to shore and honour her promise to her friend?

She paused before replying.
'I will replace him.'

***

The trauma of the storm, the shock of entering the water and the effort of staying afloat were all taking their toll. All sound of his comrades had gone and he felt very tired. He had to get ashore, rest his legs, and place them on something firm. The shore seemed very far away. Could he do it? Had he the energy to get that far? He closed his eyes to sleep as his muscles relaxed and he sank back into the water.

For a moment, his childhood returned and his mother smiled as she stood on the bank of the river calling to him. *Artur, use your legs and arms to push hard, use them to bring you forward. Now you are swimming. Good boy!*

The warmth of her smile suffused through him. Her praise motivated him. She nodded now to his tutor, waist deep in the water, following alongside the young boy. *Come in now, Artur, that is enough for today. Bradán will help you.*

The boy swam to the bank supported by his tutor.

Now come here and let me get you dry. What a clever boy, your first real swim! I'm so glad I came today. His mother gave him a quick dry with the cloth and held him in front of her. *Remember, Artur, we are Ocean's people and one day you will do great things. It is your destiny. But Ocean and her spirits both give and take – and the day may come when you need to swim. Practice now, regularly, every day with Bradán. Do you understand?*

He nodded in response.

She wrapped him in the drying cloth and held him close. *I am very proud of you, Artur.*

The Prince kicked hard for the surface, and using his arms, brought his head clear of the water and there, only one wave crest away, was the remains of the mast. With all his remaining strength, he kicked towards it.

***

The horse hesitated again and reared slightly, snorting, braying nervously as the roar and whining whistle of the gale rose to a new pitch of intensity, bombarding all his senses. It tugged furiously at his mane, pummelling his body and now, borne on the driving rain, he detected the distinctive smell of salt water. He could see little, but with his rider on his back, he slowly picked his way to the crown-topped summit of the sacred hill of Menit Nev.

Horse and rider were as one, companions from an early age, with a deep understanding and trust between them. That was why he braved this deafening cacophony and cautiously but resolutely carried her to the summit in this terrifying, storm-tossed night.

On Steren Uskis, my brave friend, nearly there. Can you see those rocks ahead? Let us aim for them. They will provide some small shelter from the wind as we look towards Ocean.

Rider and horse had been here on many occasions and she fully understood the relationship between this special place and the distant coastline, even on the blackest of nights. Menit Nev, the hill of heaven, dominated the land. Ocean's people venerated it and had constructed barrows and great stone alignments across the high land which focused on it. It lay beneath the lights of the ancestors, the stars, the mother bear, the warrior and the one fixed star that guided them – all invisible tonight, but constants in an otherwise uncertain and fragile existence.

Protected from the worst of the wind and rain by the hood of her cloak, her head was only just discernible. Despite this, two slate blue eyes sparkled clearly and distinctly from within and, as horse and rider reached the outcrop, they focused intently on the purpose of this journey, achieving contact with the distant events that she sensed were reaching a conclusion. With all her ability, she channelled her mind towards the familiar point, the high cliff at the head of the estuary, indiscernible in the storm, but still reachable with concentration and a practised application of her mind.

Meliora, if you can hear me through this tumult, what news? Has he come ashore?

There was no reply. She tried again.

Meliora, what can I do, I received your message of his approach, how can I help?

Still no reply. She paused as the horse steadied himself against another powerful gust.

Meliora, I came as soon as I heard, but it will take too long to come further, what can I do?

Faintly now, falteringly, she could hear a quiet, tired, familiar voice responding.

He will come ashore, madam... I have their agreement... terms are agreed.

The gale bore down on her senses and she could only faintly hear the reply of her fellow priestess. What she could hear filled her with foreboding.

What have you done? What have you agreed? Meliora, tell me.

No going back now... all settled... do not worry...

The voice trailed away, lost again in the surrounding chaos.

Meliora, please, tell me what you have done?

There was no further reply. She tried but she could not re-establish contact.

Desperately, she urged the horse back down from the hill in the direction of the distant promontory where Meliora was making her last stand. The rain began to ease, and with it, the first hint of light as Sira Howl, walking again in this world, brightened the sky behind her.

***

'My lady, Ryd has come. A man has been found on the beach, we believe it is Pryns Artur.'

Elowen had scrambled back along the path at first light to find the priestess with her back against the rocks. The rain had stopped and, where the fire had been, grey ashes swirled as the wind caught and deposited them in crevices on the cliff's edge and away across land and Ocean.

'Is he alive?'

'Yes. The men bring him on the cart. We expect them at the gate soon.'

The priestess raised her body away from the rock and smiled resignedly.

'Elowen, I will stay a little longer and recover. Make sure he is comfortable, let him sleep and then we will send him to his father.'

'Meliora, we are waiting. You know the consequence of betraying us. Those that you seek to protect will not escape if you go back on our bargain now.'

'I will not break my bargain!'

Her response was firm and filled with exasperation but remained inaudible to the younger woman who saw only a tired pause in the priestess's response.

Meliora spoke again. 'We have worked hard to bring him safely to shore, my friend. Make sure that he is well looked after. We have said he is of great importance – all of the portents say so; take all steps possible to protect him. Is that clear?'

'Yes, my Lady.'

'Do not forget the ring. He must leave here with it. Morlain will tell him more and the fates will ensure that he finds his way to her. It is our job to ensure that he comes ashore. The ring must come into his possession and he must look after it and protect it.'

'My Lady, I am clear on our task; you have told me often. We will clean him and ensure he rests and we will have everything prepared for you to hand over the ring.'

Meliora did not respond immediately and appeared lost in thought as she looked out across the emerging landscape of the early dawn. She spoke again. 'And Elowen…'

'Yes, my Lady?'

Her eyes softened as she looked affectionately at her acolyte. 'Thank you for your help with this. It is what we are here for, to engage the spirits and protect our people, where we can – particularly when they hold our future in their hands.' She smiled. 'This is what we do. It is our purpose.'

They both looked out across the estuary, lost for a moment in their own thoughts. Wave tops drove towards them, still cresting white as they approached the battered shoreline, and gulls and choughs fought doggedly against the wind as they worked their way around the nooks and crannies of the promontory.

Eventually, the priestess spoke again. 'You are my best pupil, Elowen. Remind me: how long have you been part of this house?'

Elowen looked at her mentor with unease. She appeared deflated, resigned. Perhaps it was just the exertion of her night's work, maybe, but there was something else. She knew the priestess too well.

'My Lady, this is the tenth winter since I entered the house.'

'That is right, of course – that year of great storms, a little like tonight – and in the days, moons and seasons since, you have learnt well. Your knowledge of this land, Ocean's ways and the stars is very great – nearly as good as mine.'

She took a deep breath before continuing.

'Elowen, at the end of my tenure, you will lead this house. I have made it clear to all that I choose you to be my successor. You are the strongest; the spirits will talk to you and you will converse with our sisters elsewhere in this land. They will all need your strength; difficult day's approach, I am sure. You will need to work together.'

'But my Lady, why should we anticipate my succession, nothing…'

The priestess turned sharply towards her and interrupted the startled reply.

'But that's just it, you see, Elowen – we never quite know, actually, how Fate will deal its hand when we might be called to face danger, put ourselves at risk or events conspire to take us on a path we did not expect. Today, tomorrow, three winters from now, we just can't tell.'

She paused and gently shook her head.

'The young Pryns, of course, will learn this in the days ahead, and he will need all the help that can be found.'

She looked old now, worn out from a night of exertion and intensity. With resignation, she said to Elowen.

'All I am saying is that you must carry on our work and ensure our sisters remain strong and able to guide and advise the men and women of this land. The spirits of Earth and Ocean are strong. The people will need our help.'

She smiled as reassuringly as she could and straightened her back to stand tall.

'Now, I will remain and rest a little longer, take in the fresh, clean air. Go back to the Sanctum and await the arrival of the cart. I will be along shortly.'

Elowen looked at her with concern, but understood that further discussion was not required and reluctantly began her return along the path.

A little way along she turned to look back. The priestess was still standing on the promontory. Through the gloom of the early dawn, it was hard to tell, but she appeared to be smiling as she raised her hand to wave. Before the path dipped away towards the sacred compound, Elowen looked back again. The priestess had gone.

***

Meliora stood on the edge, buffeted by the wind and looked down to the boisterous sea, breaking on half-submerged rocks. The sky brightened as the new day began to establish itself. She thought of her first day as a very young acolyte, unaware and carefree. She had worked so hard to support her priestess. From her, she had learnt to channel her conversation with the spirits and control her gift and had blossomed, matured and shown that, despite what others might say, there was much more to her than her ability to talk the language of the spirit world. How happy she had been.

'Meliora you must join us now and then your young protégé will not face danger at our hands.'

She thought of her mother and father; how from a very early age, they had known there was something different about their daughter. Her periodic trance-like states from the moment she could walk, murmuring in a language nobody understood. Many in their ignorance had said she was simple, mad and others had whispered that she brought danger – an emissary of the spirits sent to select victims for sacrifice – and her ramblings were evidence of conversations with the other world. Her mother and her father had said different, had been brave in their defence of her and, as the whisperings grew, had brought her to this house and asked the kindly old priestess to take her in, to take care of her and properly channel her gift and instruct her.

'Join us now, Meliora. Join us before The Father rises fully with his light of the morning. In His great presence, you may

recant and stand back – and if you do, your young friend will face mortal danger whenever he journeys on Ocean.'

Meliora stretched her body and stood tall to face the wind. Her tiredness had gone and her grim but determined countenance heralded her intention. She took a deep breath, closed her eyes and stepped forward.

foResisht and destiny

Julius Caesar pushed his chair back from his writing desk. He had sat there all evening since an early working supper of fried veal with honey and eggs, enjoyed with his Legatus and Senior Tribunes wintering with him in their quarters and townhouses on and around the Pro-Consul's Ravenna estate. Embroiled in the details of maintaining control over the newly conquered Belgic tribes and consolidation of all of his Gallic achievements, their time together had passed quickly. Now, on this cold and misty evening with the light from the wick of his desk oil lamp fading, his mind turned to the campaign season ahead.

Towards the end of the Belgic campaign, he had sent Publius Crassus with the VIIth to reconnoitre and winter in Atlantic Gaul, amongst the Maritime Tribes, The Andes, Venelli, Veneti, and others. The young man had proved an increasingly able Legate and soon sent word that the tribes had submitted to Caesar.

He had also ordered Decimus Brutus to the Pictones tribe, allies of Rome at the mouth of the Liger, one of the great rivers of Gaul to oversee the assembly of a new fleet of ships, capable of sailing on the Ocean into which the river flowed. Initially, the mission would be secret, at least to his Roman audience, until he was ready to reveal his intention. Then he would look to young Crassus for a suitable act of provocation that legitimised his attack. The new year had begun and he awaited news of Brutus's arrival and the commencement of the work.

All Gaul had yielded to Caesar and he and his men would continue to assert the power and glory of Rome; and yet, he needed more, something else, to impress and astound with its sheer audacity. All winter it had been in the back of his mind, a final crowning flourish that would upstage and improve even on the exploits of Pompey, his fellow Triumvir, in Asia and with the Cilician pirates. He would catch the imagination of the ordinary Roman citizen and achieve a new level of triumph. His thoughts turned to the Veneti. He must control or destroy their famous fleet. Nothing in Gaul should detract him from his purpose or threaten him from the rear. So, one step at a time, he would gain control of the Veneti and then move on to even greater triumphs.

As he dwelt on these matters, Caesar could hear a shuffling of feet and muffled voices in the corridor. A knock and the door opened to allow the centurion of the Pro-Consul's guard to enter.

'Centurion, what is it? It grows late.'

'Dominus, Gyras the Massaliot is outside. You asked me to inform you as soon as he arrived.'

Caesar's eyes sharpened as he stood up.

'Good, bring him in.'

As the Greek entered, Caesar took in again his appearance. Small and stocky, around thirty years, with thick black hair and a rugged dark complexion. Gyras was not overweight, but clearly enjoyed his food, suggesting relative wealth. He entered confidently, an independent man, at least in his own mind. Still, he followed the formalities and expressed humilities. No sense starting off on the wrong foot, and however wealthy or successful you were, it never paid to offend the Pro-Consul. He had seen where that could lead, so he bowed before greeting Caesar.

'You look well Pro-Consul. It gives me great pleasure to attend you again. In Massalia, we continue to rejoice in your victories and the pacification of the barbarian threat!'

He paused to beam broadly, before adopting a more business-like expression.

'I trust you were happy with the arrangements with the Atuatuci slaves, the fee that you have received?'

'Gyras, I am pleased with the arrangements, my faith in you has been repaid. What news from Massalia? Pompey's men, I hear, have been in the city again. I assume you have been talking. Can I offer you some wine and something to eat?'

Gyras stood back, gave a further small bow; but responded confidently.

'Dominus, I thank you, some wine would be good, and yes, Massalia has achieved a further agreement on corn supply for Rome with Pompey's envoy. It will be finalised soon.'

'Good, I am sure that you and Massalia will do all you can to help secure the corn for Rome.'

Gyras bowed his head in acknowledgement before the Pro-Consul continued.

'I have other matters I wish to discuss. I recall our dinner and conversation in Ianuarius over a year ago. That is why I asked you to attend me when the Atuatuci trade was completed. Please, sit, take refreshment and then we must talk quickly. I have a busy day tomorrow and must rest.'

Gyras removed his cloak and sat on one of the low seats stretching the length of three sides of a low table that dominated the centre of the room. He drank wine and took different meats and bread. Caesar, sitting opposite looked at him intensely waiting for him to finish. Gyras felt the pressure and understood the desire to engage and discuss beneath the veneer of hospitality. He swallowed the last morsel, sat back and waited for Caesar to speak.

'I will come straight to the point. When we met last winter, before the trade of the Atuatuci, you told me of your dealings with the Veneti and other tribes of the Maritime, on the far side of Gaul, of how you trade with them, source goods and materials from them. Is that not so?'

Gyras knew the Veneti lands, had travelled there, but they were many leagues distant from Ravenna. Had Caesar not sent a legion to the area? Surely, his scouts would tell him all he needed to know. A glint in the Pro-Consul's eye as he looked intently at Gyras suggested there was more. What did he want?

'Yes, I have traded with the Maritime tribes. The Veneti, in particular, have great ability with ships on the Ocean. They command their sea lanes and charge a large toll for safe passage. They bring goods and produce from Gaul and Pretanike to the mouth of the Garumna and to Burdigala, to the Massaliot and other merchants. Although,' Gyras hesitated, 'the trade has been much diminished in recent times.'

'And Gyras, you are a great traveller and like to engage your sources and customers; so would be ready to travel again to the land of the Veneti and other places, perhaps, if Caesar asked you to?'

Gyras warmed to his subject and reacted to Caesar's praise of him.

'I like to go to my sources, form a relationship, understand them, and have confidence that they will provide my clients with goods that they will be happy to receive. Gwened is their main town. It is not a typical Gaul or Keltica town but instead a fortified settlement on the coast, with inlets for their fleet. They have places of worship for their gods on small islands and coastal promontories. I engaged one of the Princes of the ruling house and formed an agreement for his men and mine to meet at Burdigala each summer trading season.'

Caesar leaned forward and looked straight at him.

'Gyras, because time is short, I will speak candidly with you. I have opened up all Gaul for trade, bringing opportunity to the Massaliot merchants and our other friends and allies, but I still need to know more about the land and its people, and I am interested in the Veneti and Pretanike, as you call it. What can you tell me about the fabled land across the Ocean?'

Gyras shifted uneasily. Familiar with Caesar's sudden temper, he ventured a more guarded response.

'Only what I hear from the Veneti merchants. I have not been there. Pretanike is the source of tin, traded by Hellenes, Phoiníkē and others. They produce particularly fine dogs for hunting, good meat and slaves, of course, and these have all passed through my hands for clients in Massalia and into Italy and Hispania. Merchants also talk of silver and other metals, although I have never handled any.'

He brightened now at a sudden recollection.

'The works of my compatriot Pytheas provide insight and valuable information for those contemplating a voyage to Pretanike.'

'Yes, yes, I have read *On the Ocean* and very interesting reading it is, Gyras, although many doubt its descriptions and indeed the veracity of your compatriot's voyage.'

Emboldened by the conversational response, the Greek responded with more confidence.

'I am just a proud Massaliot. We are explorers and traders, descendants of our forebears who first came to Massalia. I believe, in time, others will show the impressive nature of his journey and the importance of his writing. If I were to travel beyond the land of the Veneti, I would use the example of Pytheas to guide me.'

'Gyras, it is interesting you say that. I have asked you here to request your help. I want to know more about the Veneti and their links with Pretannia. I would like you to follow in the footsteps of Pytheas and go there. I need reconnaissance and detail of where might we bring a legion ashore. Will the land sustain us? How well equipped and prepared are the people? I believe you are the man to help me to answer these questions. You are, I know, a trusted friend of Caesar who will never divulge our conversation tonight and who wishes to support him in his intention to control the barbarian threat and open up more of the land for commerce, for the benefit of the people and friends of Rome.'

The Pro-Consul paused, his penetrating eyes narrowed and brow gently furrowed.

'I can trust you, can't I, Gyras?'

The Massaliot coughed nervously.

'Dominus, of course, you can trust me. Have I not proven so in all of our encounters, in all of our dealings?'

Caesar continued to look intently at the merchant before replying.

'Yes, you have; and hence why it was you and your knowledge that I asked for, why it was you I trusted with the Aduatuci. You are a man of experience and gravitas who is prepared to travel quietly and independently. But, my friend, these are challenging times, it is through strength and knowing who our friends are and who our enemies are that we shall prosper and move forward.'

He looked now at the merchant with complete conviction.

'Gyras, I want to be clear with you, as my friend. I intend to deal with my enemies quickly and by this means, my friends and I will prosper. In Gaul, I have fully demonstrated this, I think you will agree?'

The threat could not be clearer – you are with me or you are not; I have the power to deal with dissent and bring ruin to those who oppose me.

He understood it and had seen it enforced first hand.

There were others in Massalia, who privately and quietly spoke for Pompey, but there was something in the eye and manner of the man who sat opposite him that told Gyras he would not fail, and that nothing would stand in his way. The future of Gyras, merchant of Massalia, his business and family, was here and now. He sat up promptly and responded in a tone that suggested he was surprised at the question.

'As I have, I hope, made clear, I and my kinsmen are in awe of your achievements and know that ultimate victory will be yours. With your leave, I will rest and depart at first light.'

***

The Prince opened his eyes. As he touched them cautiously, the familiar smell of animal skins and furs came from beneath him. His eyes moved from side to side, up and down, assessing his surroundings. An arm's length above him, a thickly-thatched roof met a wattle and daubed wall. The roof then rose away in a conical shape, held in place by rafters of elm leaning gently towards a central meeting point. Supported by concentric staves, it reduced in circumference up to the apex of the roof.

An unseen open fire warmed his face and he heard a gentle bubbling coming, he assumed, from a bronze cauldron. Common to all such roundhouses, this stood on a tripod astride the fire. The aroma of cooking meat and herbs wafted through the room. He felt hungry. The floor of the house gave an earthy smell, mixed with the thatch of damp straw. It must have rained while he slept. Smoke from the fire filled the air, escaping the building by permeating the thatch or through an open door. As he lay, it wafted sideways with any movement in the house or a gust of wind that made a foray through the door or gap under the eaves. He was warm, wrapped in a woollen blanket, comfortable with his head resting on a cloth duck-down pillow. He lay and listened to the rhythms of the house, content with sounds of cooking and the supportive, quiet movements by persons unseen in this familiar domestic setting.

He turned slightly and tried to tilt his head sideways to face the fire, and as he did so, something in his mind moved also and a realisation began to build. He was not where he thought he was, wherever that was. His stomach tightened. This was not right – laid down, wrapped up. His eyes moved furtively. Where was he?

In his position, close to the wall, he could hear the wind blowing outside; the cries of gulls and what sounded like waves. He must be close to the sea.

Suddenly, and without warning, it all came back to him; the turbulent water, surrounding and smothering him, a pounding wind and desperate shouting. His body was taught as he gripped the blankets that covered him. He breathed heavily and his stomach rose and fell with increasing rapidity.

'Maedoc,' he called out forlornly.

They had all been swept overboard and the boat had sunk beneath them, driven down by the towering, relentless waves. He had swum to the mast. He could not remember seeing anyone after the boat had capsized. Where was everyone else? He could remember nothing after the mast.

As his mind worked through the events, he became aware of someone behind him. He tried to raise himself quickly and turned to see a woman who was sitting contemplating and watching his actions. Older than him, she regarded him in an unemotional, detached way. He had come ashore and been brought here. Perhaps this woman was a servant, charged by his father with helping those who needed to rest and recover?

She spoke with a surprisingly authoritative tone for a servant woman.

'You are safe; relax, raise yourself gently. We will bring you some food from the pot and something to drink.'

He raised himself to a low sitting position, and then turning, rested his back against the wall. He stared at the woman seated in front of him, before slowly breaking off a piece of bread to dunk into the broth placed before him. 'I am Artur ap Mawgan,' he said, 'and I seek the hall of my father,' before eating again, aware now of how hungry he was. After rapidly chewing his bread, quickly slurping his broth and gulping a first drink of the beer, he said, 'Where am I, how did I get here? Are the rest of my crew here too?'

She stared back at him. He had been through a very difficult experience, but he looked terrible; tall, yes, but thin and gaunt. On his arrival at the house, the acolytes had cleaned him and put him to bed. His hair still looked like a storm-ravaged hayrick, but he had rested well. Still, even after a day's rest, she did not believe him capable of lifting a heavy sword, let alone wielding it in anger.

'*Meliora, I have followed you in everything, trusted your judgement but was your life really worth sacrificing, for this? What chance have we if this is our best hope? He is still a boy and I do not believe him capable of battle, or that any battle-hardened warrior will follow him.*'

Her reply was functional, bordering on harsh.

'I am sorry but I believe they all perished. Manawydan and Ocean's spirits have taken their due, as they must, it seems. A number of bodies have been found. It is unlikely, I think, that anyone else will have been spared – including, I am afraid, Maedoc the coxswain. I have no word of him.'

For a moment, the stern expression subsided and sadness passed across her face. The Prince, disconsolate, did not notice. Instead, he looked at her with anger in his eyes.

'You must send men out to search again. I demand it! If I have come ashore, others may also. Come, I will lead the search.'

He tried to stand, but his legs gave way and he fell back on to the bed. Slowly, he managed to sit up again and she said, 'You have slept well but you are still weak from your ordeal. You must continue to rest and spend a further night in this house, I think, if you are to recover some strength. Prince Artur, the men of this house are searching still and I am told that your father's men also search all the coasts and inlets. All that can be done is being done to find any further survivors.'

He pushed his hair from his face and leant forward. 'You have spoken to my father or to his men and you are charged with caring for me on his instructions? He has come to see me?'

'My name is Elowen and we have met before. You were a young boy and I a young novice acolyte when I last saw you, ten summers ago, when you went to your mother's people in Demetae. You have grown, but your boyhood features are still very recognisable.'

How would he have reacted if she had said banished? Thrown out by a father who, in his devastation, had lost all reason, placing blame on an innocent child? She chose her words carefully.

'You are close to one of your father's halls. He took up residence several days back. In eager anticipation of the arrival of your boat and its cargo, I am sure.'

She paused for a moment and stared intently at him.

'I do not act on his instruction unless I wish to and neither he nor his men will come here to look for you. Although no doubt by now, he is aware that you are safe within the sanctum. My lady, however, lit a beacon to guide your boat and warn you of the treacherous rocks. She anticipated your arrival and called for your safe delivery. The men of this house found you and brought you here.'

The image of Meliora's body, bloody and broken on the rocks, stranded by the receding tide, flooded back into her grieving mind. For a while, she had been distracted, but now the image returned with full force.

The men had called for Elowen and she had known before she got there. Still, the sight had removed her strength, and she had fallen to her knees as the men looked on and bowed their heads. Meliora knew these cliffs and rocks intimately; even in the midst of atrocious weather, this could have been no accident. Her friend was stronger than that, capable of withstanding even the greatest of doubts. It could only then be some form of offering, some exchange for him. Why else would her mentor, and the spiritual leader of the house, have done this?

The Prince looked at her grimly. 'Yes, I remember now; there was a light away to our left.' His gaze drifted towards the far side of the room. 'We all saw it.'

Silence fell between them. Ocean's sounds filtered through the walls and the cauldron bubbled over the fire.

The young man spoke again.

'A lady, you say, who called for our delivery – a priestess then – and you, an acolyte, are one of her followers? Where is the lady? My men thought they heard a voice on the wind but surely not in the roar of the storm?'

He laughed in spite of himself.

'Of course not, but I must thank her at least for trying.'

Elowen looked away. She had to temper her disappointment and her indignation at this statement, but he was making it difficult. She had promised Meliora that she would work to protect and guide him, but that was before she knew her friend

45

would sacrifice her own life to save his. If she had to talk to him, guide him, at least he should be clear on some facts.

'Yes, a priestess, a very good one, and she struggled through the long night, great darkness and the terrible storm. She called to Ocean's spirits, pleaded with them to secure your safe arrival.'

Her indignation surprised him. Who was she? If she knew him, why treat him like this? He was a Prince of the royal house. 'But madam, her struggle was in vain, I think – my friends and crew seemingly all lost and I washed up half-drowned, lucky to be here.'

'You, my Lord, are lucky to be you, but you are not lucky to be here. You were saved from the tempest when all appeared lost... saved by her skill and sacrifice, which she gave alone.'

He snorted contemptuously and leant forward to pick up the beaker of beer.

'I don't know what you mean. Where is the priestess?'

'She is dead, broken on the rocks, consumed by Ocean's spirits and do you know why? No, of course, you do not – safe and secure in your arrogance, no doubt. Dead so that you may come ashore alive and fulfil all that is prophesised.'

Her words had a clear hint of mockery, and then she said, 'I assure you, she did not fail.'

Elowen looked away again to calm herself. She must be careful and must not allow her emotions to overwhelm her. She turned back and spoke firmly.

'Listen, young Pryns of the Dewnan, my friend and the inspiration for my work and my life gave her life to bring you here. Otherwise, you, like your followers, would have been lost in the midst of the storm. You are the "chosen one" and my lady, priestess of this house and a woman of character and intelligence, believed it sufficiently that she was prepared to offer herself in your stead. Looking at you, listening to you now, it is indeed even more difficult to understand why she would believe that; but for her, I will help you to recover and move towards your destiny. That is what she asked me to do. But you, young man, should show some respect.'

Regretting his haste, he spoke to her in a more measured, humbled tone.

'Elowen, forgive me, I spoke out of turn; I am still tired from my ordeal. I am sorry for the loss of your friend – but I can swim, when sadly many of my companions could not. That is what saved me. When I was a young boy, my mother ensured that I learnt to swim. She always said that one day it might save my life, and as in many things, it seems she was right.'

She responded quietly but with conviction.

'You were allowed to swim, Artur.'

Silence resumed between them. This was no good, she had to restore her balance, regain control and rise above argument. She was the priestess and had a task to deliver. Meliora had spent many seasons training her. She must not fail her now.

'Eat, drink and relax. I must attend to matters in the sanctum. Then I will return.'

She glanced to the serving girls standing in the shadows.

'We have prepared these clothes for you – while I am away, can I suggest that you change and wash your hair. It will help you if you use the warm water to loosen the tangle and the matting. We did not want to attempt that last night for fear it would wake you. I think you would benefit from more ordered hair. Ogma and Carys will help if you need it.'

She contemplated him again.

'I have been in my working clothes while I watched you, but I think it appropriate now for us to dress according to our status, at least while we sit at the table and discuss what is to come; you as the returning heir to the King of the Dewnan and me as Priestess of this house. Roles I suspect that are not without trepidation for both of us. Artur, you need to recover quickly now. Let us start as we mean to go on. I have things to talk to you about, things that you need to know; serious things. Please, wash and change – I will return shortly.'

When she returned, in place of the functional working tunic and trousers, she wore a dress of deep red, with a golden rope belt wrapped around her midriff and small shell-like gold earrings, which sparkled as she crossed the floor towards him. Her hair fell luxuriously down her back and her soft grey eyes looked more warmly upon him now; and she was not alone – two younger acolytes followed her, a few paces behind. Artur, cleaned and changed into new clothes, got to his feet, still stiff, and gave a low bow.

'Pryns Artur, will you sit at our table? We can talk and more food will be brought.'

She indicated to the other side of the house and a table made of oak. At its head was a distinctive high-backed chair, decorated with intricate carving to a level of detail that he had not seen in Demetae; the Priestess's chair was representative of the Dewnan and their connections with a wider world. She directed him to sit opposite and the acolytes brought more stew, but also fish, mutton and a bowl of last autumn's apples, shrivelled but retaining some of the flavour of the previous summer. They also brought bread, a jug of beer and juices flavoured with mugwort picked from the boundary hedges of the nearby fields, and fennel grown in the small herb garden within the sanctum.

How much older was she? Seven... eight winters, maybe? She had both presence and command and was not going to be interested in him just because he was a Pryns of the royal house. Still, he attempted to look confident and engaging.

She occasionally caught his glance and smiled perfunctorily. The arrogance of young men defied belief! Chastened perhaps by his inexperience and, of course, by his loss, he nevertheless believed in himself and that belief would only grow, she could tell that. Still, whatever he was thinking now, there were basic things he needed to know before he set out for an encounter with his father in the morning.

'Artur, it falls to me to begin to tell you of things that you need to know and begin to understand. I will start this task and then others will carry it on.' She ate a little meat and then continued. 'In the morning, you will see your father again and he will tell you that he has brought you back and that you should be grateful.'

She drank some mugwort juice, watching him closely for his reaction. Something in his eye suggested nervousness, some memory or a sense, perhaps, of his father's antipathy towards him. He said nothing and so she ate a little more and then said, 'How well do you remember your sister?'

He slowly chewed the food in his mouth, looking for a reason for the question in her eyes.

'I imagine Andras is much changed, grown to maturity while I have been in my mother's lands. I can still see her face, but she was always my big sister, six winters older than me. We were never close, as I recall, and although seasons – years – have gone by, I always felt she did not particularly like me, that she resented my birth.'

'Possibly, older children often feel antagonistic towards younger siblings, particularly if they have been the sole child of a marriage. Artur, Andras has your mother's looks, is your father's favourite and has his ear. She will not speak positively for you, I am afraid. It was your father's folly to listen to and act upon her thoughts, and of others within his circle, and send you away after your mother's death. Of course, his arrogance has allowed him to sustain his decision for a remarkable number of years, but he should never have sent you away; and he has always known this day would come and that you must return. And yet last night his extended folly achieved a catastrophic end and friends dear to both of us were lost.'

She put her beaker down and stared determinedly at him.

'I warn you now not to expect a warm welcome. He has sanctioned your return most reluctantly; but there is an even greater storm coming. Deep down he senses it, knows it, and although many argued against it, was persuaded to let the boat depart to collect you, that he should have his son and his heir close by, for whatever is to come.'

The previous night haunted him. He was unwelcome and his arrival had only brought death and destruction. He felt increasingly wretched and the warmth of her entrance faded from him. He was impatient now with her candour.

'I don't know why you speak in this way. Surely, the years have passed and however he felt before, now we can be reconciled, come together as father and son and challenge the enemies of the Dewnan together. Certainly, that is my intention.' There was a pause while they stared at each other across the table. Then, with a hint of petulance, he said more loudly than perhaps he intended, 'And I do not understand why, as you say, that I am "the chosen one", saved when all that I care about is lost.'

She would not respond to his temper and after a pause said calmly.

'You mentioned your mother earlier. She influences you strongly still, it is clear, and I can see her in you, although you look like your father also.'

For a moment, he didn't say anything and then said

'I see my mother in my thoughts and dreams, it is to be expected,' he looked at her now with renewed resolution, 'but I am a warrior of the Dewnan. I am here to support my father, despite what you say about him, and to do battle with our enemies.'

'Artur, there is nothing wrong with referring to your mother and I know that she influences you deeply. I knew her. She was a very fine, strong and caring person. Her influence on this land was deep and is all around us still. There are many who, even now, mourn for her passing, nearly ten summers later, and believe the land of the Dewnan is a darker place without her.'

The Prince looked back at her. She could see that she had touched a nerve. His head slowly shook and there was just a hint of moistness touching the edge of his eyes. He drank some beer, his hands shaking slightly, and he sought to moderate his erratic emotions, but after all that had happened, control did not come easily. As quickly as his irritation had grown, it subsided and now he sought to confide in her.

He put his beaker down and, more quietly, he said, 'I was there, do you know that? I remember little of my childhood, before Demetae, but I remember the day that she died and I always will. I should have done more. It will always be with me.'

'Artur, you were eight summers old, you would not have been able to resist the attack. Your mother knew that and you must know it now, older and more experienced as you are. You managed to escape and you should be certain that was what your mother intended.'

She allowed him to consider what she had said before saying, 'If you will, I would like to talk a little more about her. Did you know... do you remember, for example, that she was a great patron to this house and a close friend of my Lady Meliora? They believed that the land of the Dewnan, with the valley of Tamara at its heart, faces a great danger, one that has grown steadily over many years and is now virtually at our door. The threat comes from a great power. Not a marauding Estrenyon or Belgae war party that the warriors of this land can fight a never-ending war of attrition with; instead, a power much stronger, sweeping up from the lands beyond the Mor Pretani, confronting our cousins and consuming all that stands in its way. We hear of great battles in Gaul, defeat and slaughter, and the arrival of the Roman army on the borders of Armorica. You have heard of Rome, I assume. We face great challenges to our land and way of life. Your mother and Meliora anticipated this and now I, and all my sisters, believe we will be tested to our limit and that we must find a way to stand firm. They, we, believe that your fate, your destiny, is to lead our fight against this approaching storm and that in you we have the greatest chance of defence and repelling our enemies. And for that, they were prepared to sacrifice everything and to do everything in their power to ensure that you grew to maturity and were in a position to repay their belief in you.'

Artur looked at her and then to the fire, his mother's face clear in his mind, warming his thoughts as he took in all that Elowen said, 'My mother told me often as a small boy that I would do great things when I grew up. But surely, all mothers tell their sons that, if they care and love them?'

'Artur, old certainties are fading and a new order is approaching. If our people are to face up to that, they will need a strong leader who will take the fight to the enemy. Your mother and my lady believed from your beginning that you could be that leader.'

'And now they are both dead, your friend, my mother, and my crew and friends are all lost. It seems that many must fall by the wayside before this destiny that you speak of can even begin to be fulfilled.'

'Yes; but now your task is to ensure that the sacrifice they made is not wasted and you have much to do. You may believe that it is luck and chance that has brought you here, but it is not. This is a journey of many stages. Despite attempts to stop you, you are still on that journey because of the support of those that care. Andras has inherited your mother's powers, but not for good and not within the orders of the sanctum, but for her own ends, bitter perhaps, at her perceived supplanting by your birth. She seeks to persuade your father that this house and our sisters across the lands of the Dewnan are not necessary; that we are not the force for good we proclaim to be and that we represent something that has gone and is no longer part of the Dewnan. Again, you must draw your own conclusions on that, but I advise you to tread carefully in both your sister and your father's company.'

The crackle and spit of the fire threw warm mellow light amongst the shadows of the house and produced a gentle glow on Artur's face.

'Good people have given their lives already, Artur. Others are waiting for you, to help you face this great task, because they believe in you, even though they hardly know you; now you must endeavour to deserve and retain such honour.'

She rose from her seat.

'Rest now and sleep more, if you can. In the morning, we will remind you of the way to your father's house. You will need your strength for that encounter.'

He looked back at her with a firm stare, despite a sudden feeling of tiredness.

'Yes, I will need reminding. Elowen, I promise you, I will honour all of the sacrifices made, and although I do not yet know how, I will avenge my mother's murder.

***

The day was well established when the Prince stepped out the next morning.

The land tumbled through a mix of tussock grass and green and yellow lichen on grey boulders to a boisterous sea of deep turquoise and shades of green. Beyond, blackened cliffs, ancient and igneous, wrought in the furnaces of Mamm Norves's fiery beginnings, erupted and stood sentinel to Ocean and her pounding.

A fresh onshore breeze tapped and rattled at his head, caught and pulled at his hair, and drove a procession of high white clouds across a light blue sky. An occasional gull balanced on air currents, surveying the land and shore for opportunity. Crows, buffeted by the breeze, cawed to their companions, flapping their wings for purchase and shouting their views to the world and anyone who would listen.

Two earthwork banks crossed the entrance to the sanctum, topped by a palisade fence of sharpened stakes that separated the house and promontory from the coastal land beyond. At the middle point of the bank was a gateway, an entrance to the wider world and beyond. Cliffs, bright and fresh in the late winter sun, went straight ahead for a short distance before bending away, weaving in and out of multiple inlets and small bays, indenting the coastal relief. Artur turned and looked back over the top of the house to two distinct small hills, and a further high rock rising from the depths that was separated from the land by a small passage of water. On top of each hill, he could see grey stacks; protrusions of bare rock, ancient watchmen battered but immovable, guardians of the land, defiant against the swirling, insistent Ocean.

The morning work of the house was in progress and the people of the sanctum went about their work. Saddened and subdued by the sudden loss of Meliora, the household tasks still had to be undertaken; livestock needed feeding and clothing washed, while others came and went through the gate, attending to the sheep and cattle that grazed the small fields which spread away beyond the palisade and along the coast in both directions. The people were thin and pale. The end of the winter, with its chill nagging breeze and penetrating mists, when the storm was not raging, was the lowest point of the year. The food store was nearly gone and most of what remained challenged even the hardiest of eaters. Only the arrival of a half-drowned Prince, desperately in need of resuscitation, called for the use of the last remaining good food and drink. No one complained, all understood the importance of his life, but combined with the winter gloom and loss of the revered Meliora, none had reason to be cheerful, despite the rare brightness of a clear morning after the storm.

Artur watched them work. Something in his head said this was familiar, that he had seen it all before. Distant memories suggested earlier visits and an innate familiarity with the rugged and green coastal landscape.

From one of the smaller adjacent roundhouses, Elowen now stepped out, dressed in black and purple, marking her mourning and new position as Priestess. She turned and walked towards him, her long reddish-blonde hair flowing behind her as she faced the oncoming breeze. Her pale skin and lightly freckled face surrounded eyes the colour of the grey stacks, flecked with darker shades that brightened with her smile as she approached.

'Lady Elowen, I am grateful for your care and advice, but I think I must prepare to depart.'

'Yes, you must not delay any longer entering your father's hall. He will know you are here and grow pensive and agitated at your non-arrival.'

He looked away, was that irritation on his face? She hoped so.

'We have spoken and you must tread carefully, Artur; your father is a proud man. It will be difficult at first, but I believe you will come to an understanding with each other and there is more to your father than might first meet the eye. I spoke about him last night in a negative way. Always remember, though, that he loved your mother intensely. All that has happened since her death is a consequence of his inner anger and devastation at her loss – he has acted unwisely, been badly advised, but now you must allow him a chance to make the right choices.'

'Well, if I am to face that challenge and approach my father this morning, I need to know the way to his hall. There is much that seems familiar, but I am not certain which direction to head in.'

'Ryd here will guide you, and you are closer than you think; it is only a short walk over that hill. You will be there by late morning.'

'That close and yet my father, or his people, have not come to find out if I am safe, or to meet me?'

'We have talked enough now, I think; but suffice to say that the past dictates that he will not enter this house or its precincts. At the coming of the storm, he and his court moved from Porthmetern, where they had been in residence and had anticipated your arrival since the full of Loor Tewedh. Ker Kammel is more sheltered and closer to here and yet he will not come or send word to you, but expect you to proceed promptly to him. Be assured he will have been fully informed of your progress; and his impatience, driven by his perception of your lack of attendance to him, will be growing stronger as Sira Howl climbs in the sky.'

He nodded, and then asked, 'Did you say 'Loor Tewedh'?'

'A local term for the Dewnan, different to Demetae, I think. The moon of storms, one of the Father's twelve gilles, wanes and will return next year. Loor Plansa, fresh and revived, will give his signal to the farmers seven days from now; winter is nearly over and planting will begin. The first signs of new life emerge in the hedgerows and lambs grow tall in the fields.'

She looked aside to one of her attendants.

'We have prepared a new sword for you as you did not come to us with one. It was lost, I assume, in the turmoil of the sinking, but you must not enter your father's house without a weapon worthy of your status.'

'Thank you, Elowen. I think I did discard my sword as I swam.'

Artur took the scabbard, sword and belt.

'Ryd will now guide you to your father's house. I visit Ker Kammel at his bidding and unbidden and I am a regular walker of the lands in these parts. We will meet again soon.'

'Lady Elowen, thank you for all that you and this house have done for me; I shall not forget what you have told me and, of course, the sacrifice of your friend. I will do whatever I can to honour her bravery and struggle.'

She looked firmly back at him and returned a short flash of her eyes in acknowledgement.

'Artur, I have one more thing, before you go. Take this and keep it close to you. I think it will bring you good luck and maybe, even, provide inspiration.'

In his hand was a small ring. A band of gold with a worked pattern of gold meander around its outer circumference and an inlay of lapis lazuli, the colour of the sky on a clear summer's morning, full of promise and light. The ring radiated the intensity of its inlay and the warmth of its gold, sparkling in the morning sun, and drew them both to it.

'This is a fine thing,' Artur said.

'Yes, it is.'

The Dewnan and their agents controlled the trade in the movement of gold items from Demetae, land of the dragon, and Ériu, of golden fame, across Dewnonia and the Mor Pretani to Armorica, land of the Veneti, heirs of Venetia and beyond. Occasionally, a fine example of the work of the goldsmiths of Ériu passed across these shores, for trade or as an offering to Ocean's spirits, but this ring was different. The shank around its edges, moulded and shaped by many fingers, suggested great age. That it had seen and supported many lives in pursuit of their tasks and ambitions, and even with the briefest acquaintance, it seemed to offer a sense of tradition and precedence. Artur stared intently at it.

'There is great age in this, I think; it is worn with use around the edges here.' He looked up. 'My hand has a strange tingling sense… almost as if the ring is agitated, excited in some way. Where has it come from, and why is this for me?'

'It is a special thing, made many lives ago, far from here, and brought to these lands by the men of Achea. Artur, I only know a little and others who you will meet will tell you more, but I can tell you that this ring is yours. You are the ring keeper's heir, the intended next in a long line of ring companions, selected to share its existence. It is the ring of your ancestors, a link to those who have been before and all the way back to those who first brought it across the tempestuous and life-giving Ocean and have protected and venerated it to the point that it meets you here today for the next of its life stories; its next adventure. Artur, it is a great honour to be chosen.'

She smiled at his hesitant look towards her.

'Look… I think it glows more intensely now that it has found the one it has waited patiently for.'

There was no doubt it emitted something, a sense of bonding.

'Your mother was its last keeper and, as ring bearer, chose who the ring would go to next, and she is not bound to pass it on to her children. When you were a boy, she took several of my sisters into her confidence and was clear that the ring should come to you, and then she gave it to this house for safekeeping when she was campaigning with your father against the Estrenyon. There were many who loved and looked up to her in these lands and those who knew her well say that it supported her and that her wisdom shone even more brightly when she wore it. Some say that it mourned for her when she left it behind, but I think the wisdom it bestowed led her to leave it behind on her last journey. She intended it for you from an early age and knew that her stewardship of the ring was temporary. I know that, after your recent struggles and for battles to come, she would want you to have it now.'

Artur continued to gaze at the ring before wrapping his fingers around it and lifting his head to smile at Elowen. 'The stories of my youth tell of magical rings – but can it really have the powers that you describe? It is of fine gold and blue stone, but it is a man-made thing?'

'Maybe so, and I only relay what I have been told. I did not say that it was a magical ring; but I believe that a special thing, such as this, instils in its wearer a sense of well-being and certainty, knowing that you are the latest in a long line of ring wearers and that you, and only you, are the intended recipient. Perhaps that certainty and comfort will give you confidence over the difficult days ahead and belief to those around you.'

The ring glowed less brightly now, subdued in its lustre and sparkle. The priestess watched as he continued to examine the object.

'Artur, only you can properly determine the power that it has and it is yours to explore until you, in turn, must pass it on.'

He looked at her and nodded thoughtfully.

'Now, you must go, but before you do, I have one more thing to say. Be careful with it; it has come a long way through many generations to be with you. It may yet serve you well in difficult places, but do not show it widely just yet. Keep it close and protect it because others will also see it as a valuable, beautiful thing and will covet it for their own devices and pleasure. Draw your sword for a moment and I will show you how it will help to conceal the ring.'

She held the sword. It had a wooden hilt and grip and, at the pommel and guard, elaborate ironwork with decorative full moon roundels. All but one of these joined a matching roundel on the opposite side of the handle, secured by riveting. The one that was not, she took in her fingers and removed, although it was held firmly in its place by an inner ring or sleeve of metal that stood proud of the main guard. Once taken off, a small compartment opened up, just big enough to hold a single precious item.

'Place the ring in here, replace the roundel firmly. It will not come off. See, you have to grip it with purpose to remove it. Keep it safe in there and wait. You will know when it is right to wear it, others will guide you and, I hope, the days will come when you can wear it openly, but for now, it is my counsel that you conceal it, particularly in your father's hall.'

She handed back his sword. He was about to ask another question, but she spoke decisively. 'You must go. Ryd is here. I will see you again soon, Pryns Artur, but for now, goodbye.'

Artur followed his guide through the gate in the bank. After a short climb to the top of the first cliff, he stopped and looked back. The illusion of the serpent briefly appeared in his mind and the jagged grey rocks along the ridge of the nearest hill added to the semblance of a spiny tail, rising from the water and holding firm in the heave of the swell.

Elowen stood there, distinctive and tall, confident on the serpent's back, her hair billowing in the breeze. She had watched his progress along the path and now raised her hand to wave and he responded before turning and following Ryd along the path.

As he walked, Ocean, calm and playful below, belied her earlier aggression. Seals bobbed on her surface, rolling together in the building warmth of the morning and, occasionally, there was the rise and fall of black shapes – pilot whales exploring the coastal waters in the early spring sunshine.

the kins of the dewnan

'My Lord, Pryns Artur has arrived from the house of the Priestess. He asks leave to enter.'

'Oh, at last, he deigns to join us. Bring him in. Cadan, Goron, Withell, sit beside me and help me greet this errant son.'

The three warriors moved closer, anticipating the entrance of the new arrival. Other men, warriors and leading servants listened intently to the words of the chieftain or King, as he styled himself – the most prominent leader within the confederacy of the lords of the Dewnan. This was his inner circle, his most trusted supporters, his bodyguards, and when he needed it, advisors and confidants, all wrapped up in each other, brusque and arrogant in their own self-importance; leaders of the tribe, controllers of lives – answerable to no one but the King, and he only answerable to his own destiny.

Into this tight, exclusive group, Artur now stepped. The hall, constructed of a wooden frame with wattle and daubed walls, was different. It was not a conventional roundhouse, but instead, a rectangular building with clear corners and a vaulted ceiling, wooden beams and trusses covered with a roof of thatch. Artur's father had travelled in his youth to the lands across the Mor Pretani to Demetae, Ériu and Armorica, where he had seen buildings of a similar design; and then, when he had married his Princess, one of the ways he had demonstrated her place in his heart was by building this different, and for the Dewnan, imposing building. A mark of his own prestige and a hall fit for her and her place within his life and affection.

Across the simple earthen floor, several large dogs lay sleeping and a collection of spears and shields stood stacked against each other at one side. Beyond, an arrangement of tables led to a central prominent table, more substantial, weighty and cut whole from an ancient oak of the forest. A table fit for a leader and his warriors to sit at and discuss the challenges of their world. On the table were distinctive drinking cups for drinking wine or mead. Broad and shallow with symmetrically positioned handles, they were signifiers of the origins of the Dewnan nobility, a lingering reminder of greater days and regular contact with the distant warm lands and the Middle Sea, stifled now by the advance of the Roman legions.

The hall was dark around the edges, but lit at its heart by a central fire. Servants lingered in the shadows, waiting to respond to the needs of the King and warrior brotherhood. And not just brothers, women also stood here, the women of warriors – supporters of their men in every way.

Artur knew all about the halls of chieftains and Kings, understood the close-knit brotherhood, but there was something else, something different here and he knew it from the moment he entered the room.

'Pryns Artur-ap-Mawgan! You arrive at Ker Kammel at last. My men found the wreckage of your boat and recovered the bodies of some of your crew. We had thought you lost too, and yet here you are a full day and two nights later. Can you explain this?'

Artur stood before his father. Never as tall as Artur was now, but still, to a young boy who had idolised him, always a commanding and absorbing presence. Now, a yellow unkempt beard flecked with shades of grey and white framed a face of red, prominent cheeks below narrow, mocking blue eyes. His hair, brushed back coarsely, receded towards the summit of his head and he sat on his chair, his throne, a paunch in his belly visible above and below the table and his shoulders drooping. How could he have changed and aged so much in ten summers? Artur bowed before him.

'Father, I have come home to take the fight to our enemies and to do as you bid me. It was a terrible storm. We foundered on rocks close to here, in spite of the bravery of the crew. I do not know how I made it to the shore, but I have seen no other members of my crew since we capsized and the boat sank. Father, one last search should be mounted now, some of them may yet be found, stuck in some steep cove, unable to clamber out without assistance.'

As Artur spoke, a young woman walked to the King's chair, lent forward and said something quietly in the King's ear. Artur knew his sister, Andras, instantly. She had grown to full womanhood, and as Artur looked at her he saw, with her medium-length auburn hair surrounding a fair complexion and hazel coloured eyes, what he remembered of his mother. Mawgan turned to her as she stepped back and acknowledged her and she, in turn, looked towards Artur, raising her eyebrows quizzically and with mockery as the King turned to his son. Ignoring Artur's request, he addressed the hall.

'These are difficult days in the lands across the Mor Pretani. We rejoiced at the rout of the Belgae, but now the Romans threaten Armorica and our remaining trade routes. They will not stop, it seems, until they have murdered and plundered their way to the control of all Gaul.'

He paused and stared grimly across the hall. All stood and waited for him to continue. He looked again to his son.

'Strength and purpose is what we need, Artur; and yet you arrive quietly, unimpressively and alone after taking a full rest and respite at the house of the priestess of the serpent. I trust your dalliance with the ladies will not impede whatever support you are able to provide in the pursuit of our enemies. Pryns Artur, speak to me.'

Withering looks from around the room followed the King's stern glare. Artur raised himself to his full height and with determination, replied to the King.

'Father, I have trained and learnt and fought skirmishes in defence of Demetae, all so that I could return strong and able to support you in the defence of these lands. I hoped you would be pleased to see me alive after many years apart, and Ocean's spirits, it seems, require their sacrifice.'

The King was on his feet in an instant.

'I do not wish to hear of spirits – save that for your priestess. No warrior and dutiful son that I know of would have neglected proper service and homage to his father and his King. You should have brought yourself from the beach and been here yesterday.'

Artur stood firm.

'I did not bring myself from the beach to anywhere. I was brought – and I awoke in the house of the Priestess.'

'Do not seek to defend yourself, Pryns Artur, and do not argue with me. You have lingered longer than you should in that house and now you have much to make up for and prove if I am not to very quickly regret my decision to allow your return!'

Andras, from her position behind the King, regarded Artur with a stern, interrogating stare, before saying, 'Father, if I may, Artur was sent to our mother's family because he was the cause of great distress and because it was felt that his removal and education in the lands across the sea would be better for all. It is disappointing that his return has done so little to restore our faith in him.'

Artur looked to the King and said, 'Father, I can only say again, I am here to serve you and fight for you. I am not the cause of distress, but with your leave and by your side, I will take the response of the Dewnan to our enemies and all who have caused us distress, or intend to in the future. '

'Yes, well, we shall see. I am not optimistic, Pryns Artur, after such a discouraging start, but I do not wish to discuss it further now. Come and stand behind me, I have business to discuss. Keep quiet, listen and learn.'

After a large gulp of mead Mawgan wiped his beard, placed the cup back on the table, and again surveyed the hall.

'Where are the emissaries from the Veneti colony? Stand forward, state your business and the purpose of your visit to the citadel of the Dewnan.'

Two men stepped forward and gave a short bow. One of them took a further half step and spoke.

'King Mawgan ap Dhearg, Lord of the Dewnan, I am Callard and this is Loan. We bring greetings to you from Aodren of the Veneti, Lord of the Crossing at Pendre en Menluit, and Ker Tamara.'

Mawgan nodded casually. 'You are welcome. What do you want now of Mawgan ap Dhearg? I have allowed your Aodren increased concessions. You control all Tamara to Ictis, and the Veneti are my chosen agents of trade. I receive your payment, but you too have grown fat and wealthy on the commerce between the wharves of the twin forts and Ictis. What more do you ask of Mawgan ap Dhearg?'

Loan stood forward. 'My Lord, Aodren asks again for your assistance, to take the fight to the Estrenyons and to help us defend your borders. We fight and harry, cross RunHoul and the ancestral lands, and engage their raiding parties; but they increase in boldness. If we do not check them properly, before we know it, they will be on the banks of Tamara, threatening the heartland of the Dewnan and even the citadel of Ker Kammel will not be safe.'

Despite the emissary's earnestness, exasperation clearly weaved its way through his words. Artur watched with interest. Their deference, it seemed, was staged rather than real.

Mawgan stroked his beard and considered the emissaries.

'What has changed since the last emissaries were here? I told you then that I would not aid you in your slave capturing. I have an agreement of non-aggression with my allies the Durotrages. I will not go against that agreement. Bring me proof that the lands of the Dewnan are threatened. Then I will consider your request.'

Frustration passed across Callard's face. He stood forward again to support his comrade.

'My Lord, if I may be so bold. When did you last see an ambassador of the Durotrages at Ker Kammel? How can we trust them? Infiltrated by the Belgae and other Germani, their blood is no longer pure. Gawell cannot hold their confederation much longer and, one by one, the tribes and the great forts fall. We have picked up Belgae in recent fights in the lowlands beyond RunHoul. Defeat in Gaul does not seem to have deflected them from their purpose. What further proof do you need? The alliance with the Durotrages is dead.'

Many around the King reached for their sword hilts and drew them slightly from their scabbards. Mawgan was on his feet.

'You dare to come into my hall, to Ker Kammel, ancient seat of the Dewnan, and tell me, your High King, when my alliances are dead? I shall decide when such an end has been reached – not you, an emissary of a foreigner in these lands, however closely we may be related. I will tell you this. Others covet this trade, the metals of the valley and Kernovia, and the trade at Ictis, but I rebuff those approaches because of loyalty and kin. Do not make me regret it and change my mind.'

He glared at both emissaries.

'Take this message to Aodren. If he offers council he should bring it himself, not...'

The entrance door to the hall opened noisily and checked him as a tall authoritative man entered, followed by two men supporting a body straddled across each man's shoulders. The lead man strode purposefully to the centre of the hall, ignoring the approach of the servant who normally received new arrivals.

'Hammett, what is it?'

'My Lord, forgive me, I thought it important to come straight in. I have returned from the far side of the river. We have found more bodies and searched the sands, and were convinced of no survivors when one of my men saw a body amongst the rocks, almost hidden, where the river meets the Ocean. It is the coxswain, Maedoc, and he is alive.'

'Maedoc?' Artur's question was urgent as he stepped forward. Hammett, startled by the interruption and a stranger he did not recognise, glanced at the King.

Mawgan's anger with the emissaries, which had been halted for a moment by this new development, now transferred willingly to his son.

'Speak when I ask you to, boy, and not before!' Mawgan ordered, turning to his son with scorn. 'Return to your place and keep silent.'

He turned back to Hammett

'Has he spoken, a rich cargo was promised but I expect all hope of the gold is lost. Raise his head; let us see if he will speak.'

'He breathes but speaks unclearly. I think it is only exhaustion and rest in warm blankets by the fire will restore him.'

Hammett gently lifted the man's head to face Mawgan.

The coxswain looked narrow-eyed and exhausted at his King and spoke disjointedly. 'My Lord, all lost... so close.' His head shook slowly from side to side, as he spoke. 'Normous wave... tempest's fury taken its due.' He took a further breath and his eyes looked down at the floor. 'Even the Pryns... I swam until I could swim no more.' He lifted his head and looked at the King; there were tears in his eyes. 'I could not find him.'

His head sank again, he was muttering faintly under his breath.

'Nothing, nothing we... could do... could not find...'

'Maedoc!' Artur tried to say it quietly but failed. There was no response from the coxswain. Mawgan turned quickly to his son, but now checked himself. Perhaps the show of real emotion, the sense of the loss in the coxswain's eyes, gave him pause for consideration. Quickly he recovered his poise.

'Hammett, find somewhere warm for him and ask the servants to feed him. I think you are right; warmth and sleep will restore him and then, in the morning, we will ask for a better version of the sinking of the boat and the loss of my gold.'

Hammett gave direction to the men supporting Maedoc's limp and exhausted body.

'And Hammett, send for the priestess, something is afoot here. Let us find out why she contrived to keep my son so long.'

The King turned to the Veneti envoys with a stern countenance.

'We will talk again later. I think we have had enough of this excitement for now – I will retire while the servants prepare the hall and then we will eat. You are welcome to join us.'

Released from his father's command for the moment, Artur moved swiftly to support the men who carried a still mumbling Maedoc towards the kitchen building adjacent to the hall.

Watching him, a woman walked alongside Andras. Her hair, short and black, surrounded a sharp, intense face with high cheekbones and narrow piercing green eyes. She was of medium height, comparable to Andras, but thinner and with a pale white complexion that was accentuated by dark black eye make-up. Their eyes met and together they turned away from the main group and passed out of the hall. They walked to a far corner of the wall that surrounded the fortress, which overlooked the estuary, or heyl, below. Once confident they were away from anyone's hearing, they spoke quietly.

'My Lady, despite our efforts, he is here and now the coxswain also. What do you plan? Your father chastises him, but I fear it will not last.'

Andras did not answer immediately and looked along the heyl. Then she turned to her companion.

'Yes, Zethar, he is here. How were we to know the old priestess would throw herself onto the rocks? Their commitment to his safety is even greater than we had imagined. The spirits were enthused by our offer, but a priestess of the sanctum is surely better. As for the coxswain, I do not know how he found his way to the shore and, in spite of myself, I admire the determination that he needed to achieve this.'

'But how do we respond? Pryns Artur will grow in strength. He has courage – you can see that. He will gain the ascendancy and then you will be the daughter of the King, not his heir.'

'Thank you, Zethar,' Andras said with irritation, 'for stating the likely course of events.'

A gentle breeze blew around the fortress mount and, in front of them, seagulls argued noisily over some unseen opportunity.

'And where is my mother's ring?'

Andras looked up at her companion, stroking the fingers of one hand with the other.

'She and her priestess conspirators have prepared everything else. They will not have left that to chance. Do you think he has it?'

She took a deep breath and turned towards the arguing gulls and watched as one of them soared away from the rest with some item of prized capture held in its beak, the rest in pursuit. Andras, looking fixedly ahead, and again spoke slowly.

'It should have been mine. I am her daughter. It passes from mother to daughter. I am its rightful keeper.'

Zethar responded firmly, 'We have been through this on many occasions. The ring and its companions, wherever they are, are purely symbolic; a link to our ancestors, the men of Achaea, no more than that. We do not know if anyone has your mother's ring. It may have been lost.'

Andras looked at her grimly.

'I know. It is not lost. I watched my mother as a child; she placed too much importance on it. It has disappeared these last summers, but it is not lost. Symbolic it may be, but the wearer of the ring has significance. They inherit all that has gone before and men will rally to that if it's correctly used. Many will look for a sign of hope in the difficult days ahead. The ring could give great power to its wearer.'

'But still, my Lady, even if it is kept secret somewhere, we do not know where or who has it. I saw no sign of it on your brother and I watched him closely. Far better, I think, to focus on how we remove, once and for all, the one obstacle between you and your rightful position and authority in the lands of the Dewnan.'

The early afternoon sun sparkled and shimmered on the heyl and the first signs of an ebbing tide. Andras said, 'Yes, perhaps you are right. We have to find a way to remove him again, place him somehow in the way of danger. But how?'

'My Lady, would it not be easier to find a willing accomplice to remove him? You have gold and other wealth that you could use.'

'That is too dangerous; my association could be discovered. If I were implicated, it would create conflict and division. I work on my father; I influence his thinking and what he says, how he reacts to Pryns Artur. But I am sure his view of me would change if he found I was the cause of his son's death.'

'And yet you know that the priestesses, whenever they are able, seek to influence change. Your father has his reservations, but they have persuaded him to allow the Pryns to return. The High Priestess does not come here, she feels that she does not need to. She is clever, my lady. We must do more than watch and wait. They all work in support of your brother.'

Andras did not respond for a moment, but then smiled at Zethar as an idea entered her mind.

'Of course! Why did I not think of it straight away! Perhaps there is a way to take advantage of these emissaries from the colony.' Staring into the eyes of her companion, she continued: 'Can I persuade my father to send Artur to the Veneti? If he goes alone, or even with the coxswain, I am sure he will, in the way of all emotional hot-headed young men, get involved in their raiding and there is surely plenty of opportunities there for him to meet an unfortunate end.'

She looked at Zethar in a knowing way and Zethar smiled back. 'Yes, my Lady. The idea has promise and, of course, we still have our Durotrages contacts. I know they have growing links to the Belgae and both tribes are disgruntled with the actions of the Veneti men. We could disguise it with an effective ambush, with superior numbers.'

A frown spread across Andras's face. 'Of course, if he goes to the colony it will put him closer to her. She will influence him, but I do not think she will stop him from wanting to prove his fighting worth to his father.'

Zethar looked back at her thoughtfully, considering another possibility that could serve her purpose, as well as her companion's higher aim. 'My Lady, I think you are right; and perhaps, maybe, there is a way to prevent her influence from even beginning to work on him.' She looked intently into the eyes of the Princess. 'Seek to influence your father and I will send a secret message to those who can help us.'

'Whatever you plan, I cannot be implicated. But if you succeed, I will not forget it and I will ensure that your reward is significant.'

'Madam, I am grateful – but my actions are in pursuit of more than material reward. I seek real change and to maintain your rightful position as heir to your father's throne. Sure, you will need a man by your side, but we both know that you can manipulate him! You will bring a different perspective to this land and build a proper link with our friends amongst the Estrenyons. With powerful allies in the Durotrages and the Belgae, you will not need a ring to assert your power! Instead, you will be able to move swiftly to remove the priestesses and their foolish talk of purity, the Pretan and the Ocean Peoples, and our corrosive alliance with the men from across the water, whose influence diminishes with each passing year. The Pretani inheritance is fading fast. We need a new power in these lands. That is the only way to stand up to, or perhaps even accommodate, the Roman threat.'

For a moment, Andras looked back at Zethar with equal intensity before the sound of voices, shouting from the Hall, caused both of them to turn and look behind them.

Andras spoke again. 'Come, Zethar, you are right; we are not done yet and we have things to do and my father to influence. Let us return to the Hall. It sounds as if they are preparing to sit for the meal.'

***

Towards the end of the feast, Elowen, followed by two acolytes, entered with poise and confidence and walked the length of the hall. Her eyes never wavered from Mawgan at his table. The Prince, sitting at the end, watched the King and Priestess with great interest, drawn to her mildly challenging and assured progress.

Mawgan also watched, but Artur sensed that he was less impressed and perhaps even slightly wary of this new presence in the room. He hailed her as she approached.

'Lady Elowen, for I understand that's what I must now call you, I am sorry to hear of the accident that has led to the death of the Lady Meliora.'

She stood before him, acolytes alongside her, expressionless, looking straight ahead.

'My Lord, it was no accident, but you are right it is a great tragedy. Her wisdom and direction will be greatly missed by all who believe in a true and honest path.'

Mawgan stared back at the priestess, clearly considering what she might mean.

'Lady Elowen, so that I clearly understand, if it was no accident, then what are you saying? Is someone to blame for the death of Meliora?'

Her presence filled the room as she stood conversing with the Prince's father and it briefly appeared to Artur that she was the senior one, looking down on the King who sat before her. Did his father sense this too? He maintained an air of mild irritation, perhaps frustration, as he sought to gain the upper hand.

Elowen continued, smilingly resignedly as she responded. 'No one is to blame. Instead, maybe, it is fate and destiny that has brought about this unhappy event.' She paused briefly before continuing. 'However, my Lord, despite this heavy loss there are reasons to be positive, are there not? Your son has returned to you and this will strengthen your hand in the fight against the Belgae and Estrenyon, and the support for your Veneti allies against the Roman advance in Gaul. Be assured, they are coming our way, and I am not convinced that even the power of the Veneti and their ships will protect us.'

Mawgan ignored these final points and responded. 'I am glad you mention my son because I was about to ask how you managed to keep him from his father for a whole day and night. What sort of attractions did you provide?'

A ripple of quiet laughter passed amongst the nearest warriors, but Artur smiled inwardly as Elowen looked back at Mawgan, not with contempt but with a clear expression of pity.

'King Mawgan, your son was shipwrecked, found just alive by our men and brought to the Lady Meliora and to me. I am sure you will agree that it was in your interest that he was returned to well-being, ready to meet you properly this morning. The King sat back and surveyed the wider room before bringing his eyes back to look at her. 'Lady Elowen, you are newly installed as Priestess, so let me be clear with you from the beginning. What is best for my son is for me to decide and you will not interfere.'

His clarity had checked her. She conceded and made no response except to bow her head slightly in acknowledgement.

'Now, please, take a seat; another member of the crew has been found alive: Maedoc, the coxswain, who I entrusted to bring my son to me. When you have eaten, please look at him and ensure that all is well. It is probably no more than exhaustion, but I would welcome your opinion and any necessary remedy you can offer. Then, Lady Elowen, we will have a story, a tale of our ancestors. One from the beginnings, I think, from the elder days... Let us see if you can tell a tale as well as Meliora.'

As he spoke, her eyes flickered intensely. She said no more, but smiled politely and withdrew to a seat held back for her by one of the servants while the acolytes stood behind her.

Mawgan turned to acknowledge a servant and took more mead, before turning back to those around him at the table. He addressed his next comments to the Veneti emissaries.

'You spoke earlier of the Estrenyon threat, but what of Armorica? As the Priestess reminds us, it is only bad news we hear from that direction it seems. The Romans are on your borders. Are the rumours correct? Have you struck a deal? Our ancestors have stood up to the persistent Estrenyon, the Germani, and have halted their progress. A clear line of division exists and our friends in the Durotrages stand as a buffer between us. What of the Veneti, I say? Nothing seems able to stand in the way of the Roman threat. I hear of this great and powerful leader and how they do not fight in the way of warriors, but instead unleash a relentless wave of attack that is impossible to stand against. Tell me, what news from Porth Ictis and from across the Mor Pretani?'

Callard spoke first.

'My Lord, the Romans and their leader, Caesar, have progressed across Gaul and none have withstood their progress. Indeed, those that attempt it have fallen victim to the murderous force of his army; and he and they spare no one. Our approach, I believe, has been to seek a position of agreement with them. It seems that we cannot fight them on the land,' he leant forward for increased emphasis, 'but we are the Veneti, we understand Ocean and all her ways. A form of partnership will be sought; we who control the water and they who control the land.'

Mawgan looked away from the emissary, around the room and towards Elowen. 'My Lady you smile in disbelief, I think. Do you not agree with our Veneti friend?'

'Only, my Lord, that in all that we have heard so far about the Roman army and about this Caesar and his disdain for life and mercy; he does not sound like the sort of man who will be interested in a partnership. Control and the utter ruination of our way of life is his objective, I think, and I suggest it is folly to think otherwise.'

Loan spoke now.

'My Lord, I think that the Lady Priestess forgets that the Veneti dominate the trade routes, control the seaways. They may know how to fight a land battle, but they have no understanding of the Ocean and her ways. They will not overcome us.'

'And yet,' Mawgan responded, 'it seems their force is unstoppable on land, what is there to say that they will not be able to do the same on water? Nor are they your only challenge. What of the Curiosolitae? They encroach your command of the Mor Pretani and compete with you for the trade at Hengast's Fort? On a number of fronts, you are finding yourself in an increasingly difficult position.'

Artur, along with the rest of the room, listened intently to his father. In spite of his disappointment with Mawgan's welcome, the King's understanding of the wider world and tribal relationships was impressive.

Loan responded.

'My Lord, it is true, we face many challenges, but while the Veneti of Ker Tamara prosper, so do the Dewnan. We will meet this Roman general and his army and assert our tribe and pre-eminence over the lesser tribes of the Mor Pretani shoreline.'

Callard spoke in support.

'King Mawgan, we will stand firm, but we need all the help that we can find. Send men to the aid Aodren. Help us respond to all that threatens us.

Andras sitting one place removed from Mawgan now lent forward to speak. 'Father, I have a proposal.'

Mawgan nodded his head in acknowledgement.

'It seems a clear gesture must be made; an expression of support and an acknowledgement of need. Send Artur. He has done precious little so far to convince you of the worth of his return, but he is your son. Send him off with these Veneti emissaries. It can do no harm. He might do some good and learn how to fight like a fully-grown warrior, and he will be out of your way. Who knows he may even prove of some use! And if you do need his services, you will know where he is to recall him.'

Artur looked at his sister. He was beginning to understand the pattern here – and the obviously close relationship between father and daughter. He leant forward confidently in response.

'Father, I will gladly go to support our Veneti friends, I am ready to take the fight...'

His father was swift in his response. 'You, young man, will say nothing. Lately arrived and ignorant of much that we talk of. I am in no way convinced that you are yet deserving of the right to comment at this table.'

Artur sat back shaking his head. Elowen, however, feeling the need to break the pattern of exchange and sensing an unintended opportunity, now caught Mawgan's eye.

'My Lord, if I may make a contribution, I wonder if the Lady Andras has a point. Your son needs to quickly come to terms with your kingdom, reacquaint himself with it, the high lands and rivers and motivations of your allies. If only for a trial period initially, perhaps, it would make sense for him to go to the Veneti colony. Do you think this could help complete his education, perhaps?'

Andras looked warily at Elowen before acknowledging her support with a slight nod of her head.

Mawgan looked both ways along the table at priestess and daughter before replying.

'I will consider this. Lady Elowen, will you attend the coxswain, Maedoc? Goron, Cadan, Withell, please join me; I would have your opinion away from the table.'

***

A further building provided the kitchen at the rear of the hall. It was a short step to the door at the back of the hall, enabling quick service to the King and his court.

Cooks and servants bustled, preparing additional dishes; nuts from the winter store, sourdough bread and pots of honey, as a follow-on to the roasted beef, mutton and bean stew of the main course. The air was thick with smoke from the fire and a lingering smell of both cooked meat and human sweat infused to create an eye-watering, pungent mix of taste and endeavour.

In a quiet corner, but still feeling the warmth of the cooking fires, Elowen found Maedoc. He lay on an old leather cloak, covered by a thick woven blanket, his head propped up by a rough pillow. A bowl next to him showed he had taken some broth, drawn from the mutton stew. His belly would warm from within, along with the heat that surrounded him, and a half-drunk beaker of ale had probably served to calm him after his likely exertions before Mawgan. Eyes closed, he dozed quietly in the midst of the agitated activity all around.

Elowen took a blanket from the store pile, placed it on the ground and sat down beside him. She had drawn a bowl of warm water from one of the cauldrons and had mixed into it several sprigs of rosemary collected from the cooking area. Using a small, dampened cloth, she gently dabbed at his face and wiped across his forehead. Occasionally, she put the cloth back into the bowl, allowing it to soak in more of the herb-infused water, and softly stroked his matted hair and held his hand.

After a while, Maedoc opened his eyes and looked up at her.

'It is you.' A tired but warm smile of pleasure passed across his face. 'I thought I recognised the softness of that touch.'

'Hush,' she said gently, 'you need to rest and regain your strength. You have been through much, and I am enjoying tending you.'

He turned his head sideways on the pillow and, after a short pause, spoke again, bitterness mixed with sadness in his words.

'Elowen, that was no natural storm... such waves! We had no chance, I see that now, but we were so close. They took pleasure in bringing us so near, only to dash our hope, at last, on the rocks...'

His voice trailed away as Elowen quickly interjected. 'Maedoc, stop,' she squeezed his hand, 'there is great sadness, but good news also, which will aid your recovery. Come, let me help you to raise yourself up, take some more broth.'

Once positioned in a more upright position, she helped him drink from the bowl, and when it was emptied, she wiped his face and sat back beside him, looking with round, affectionate eyes as she spoke softly again.

'He lives, Maedoc. The young Pryns, he came ashore on rocks below Penn Tir and was found at first light yesterday. We tended him at the sanctum while he slept and rested. He entered his father's hall this morning.'

Moisture appeared in the corner of the coxswain's eyes. He said nothing, looking up at the low rafters. Eventually, he looked at her.

'I couldn't find him, Elowen. There was panic and shouts all around. I saw him go into the water and lost sight of him. I swam and looked, but I could not find him.'

He paused again for a moment as the confusion of the capsize flooded into his mind.

'I had come to like him and could not forget my promise to Meliora and Lady Morlain, who entrusted me to bring him home. I, a trainee acolyte. I swam until I had no strength left. I do not know how I found the shore, but I fear there will be few survivors.'

As she looked at him, a small hint of moisture also softened her eyes.

'Brave, faithful man, you could have done no more! You were asked to undertake the task, because who better than you? Who has more skill with boats and navigation? Who better to bring him home? Even Mawgan in his wretched acceptance of the need for his son's return acknowledged that there was none better than you for this task.'

She paused for a moment, still squeezing his hand gently, before continuing.

'But you are right, I am afraid. As far as we know, there were no survivors but you and him. You are also right, I am sure, that it was no natural storm. We were clear in our purpose to bring hope to these lands and to face the coming challenges, and that did not sit well with others, those who can converse with and encourage the negative spirits of the world.'

She stared at him for a moment, knowing that he would guess her meaning.

'And for that, they would sacrifice brave and hardy warriors – young, strong additions to the Dewnan fighting force?'

'Of course, they would!'

Incredulity sparked in her eyes before she remembered the lingering effects of his ordeal. She lowered her voice, but still spoke with purpose.

'They care not for the fighting strength of the Dewnan, but only their own position. I cannot prove it, but I am sure they seek an alliance with others to undermine us. We must defend the Ocean People and our way of life; there are enemies on our borders, but there are also enemies within. Be in no doubt, it is they who sought to thwart us with this mighty storm, but even they, I am also sure, will not have expected the sacrifices we were prepared...' her voice trailed away '...to make...' She paused again before looking intensely at Maedoc. '...To bring him ashore.'

He looked enquiringly at her before she continued, quickly and perfunctorily.

'Meliora, Maedoc, she gave herself, an even better offer to Ocean's spirits. She is no more, but he came ashore and our purpose continues without her.'

His eyes widened and a look of shock spread across his face. 'That is bad news indeed. She was so kind to me, allowing me into the sanctum.'

He looked down as thoughts of the priestess filled his mind. After a short while, he looked up again.

'If Meliora is no more, who is lady and priestess of the sanctum?' he paused, 'You?'

'I am and Meliora saw you as a worthy member of the priesthood; she had and would have continued to have great faith in you. We must thoroughly honour her sacrifice and pursue our objectives with even greater vigour. I have seen the Lady Morlain and there is more to tell you; but for now, I must return to Mawgan and hear his pronouncement on the Pryns's engagement with the Veneti.'

She stood and straightened her dress, brushing off the dust from the floor, and as she did, the Prince appeared behind her. 'Maedoc, already you look better, restored by the caring hand of Elowen I see. There is great sadness, by now you will know. I had to come and see how you were and with all that we have lost, it warms me and strengthens me to see you sat up and talking.'

'My Lord, I too am greatly heartened to see you although our losses are indeed great...'

Elowen caught his glance and then said, 'I will leave you, but be brief in your conversation now. The King will expect the Pryns in the hall when he returns.'

As she walked away through the kitchen, Artur sat down next to Maedoc.

'Wise friend, I am learning very quickly, Meliora and Elowen, of course, have already given so much, too much, and our comrades... and my father, well, it is not, at least yet as I might have expected, might have hoped.'

Maedoc, with difficulty, raised himself up a little further.

'No, I have often found that things do not turn out quite as I had expected them to, but I grieve for the loss of brave friends, what more could I, should I have done?'

'Nothing, you did everything that you could and more. We have fallen victim to a determined foe and we will be prepared for future battles. And, all that sail with you and I in future will learn to swim, I am determined on that.'

A grim smile of acknowledgement passed across Maedoc's face.

'But Maedoc, we are here and we will honour the loss of our friends by taking the fight to the enemy wherever he or maybe she appears. Will you come with me, will you help and support me? With you on my side, already I feel stronger.'

'My Lord,' he coughed involuntarily, 'It would be my honour and my pleasure and there is much yet to do, but you must go now. The King, as I am sure you now realise, has a short temper.

I would urge you as Elowen did to be back in the hall before your father returns.'

'Yes, I will go, rest now, we will talk again soon.

Artur walked back into the hall and stood beside Elowen as the King made his entrance and walked straight to her. 'Well, will the coxswain live?'

'My Lord, you were perfectly correct. He is very tired and needs to stay warm for the next few days, but then I believe that he will quickly recover. He is hardy! However, he is devasted at the loss of the crew. My Lord, he also regrets greatly the loss of the cargo. He, of course, remembers your particular interest in this. I hope I have done right in assuring him that great leaders understand Ocean's unpredictability and would not blame one individual for a lost ship if the cause of the loss was not within his control.'

'Hmm, I suppose so.' His hitherto harsh expression softened very slightly, 'Thank you.'

He turned and walked to the centre of the hall and addressed all within it who now gathered around to hear him speak.

'We have heard today further news of the troubles of Gaul and the threat that comes closer from the men of Rome; a threat that our kin across the sea believe they can withstand. We also hear again of a perceived increased Estrenyon threat; and then, in the midst of all this my son returns to me, alone and a little bedraggled.' He paused for dramatic effect, 'It has been an interesting day!'

There was another pause, as he surveyed the hall and those around him, before he brought himself to his full height and continued, 'The colony and our Veneti brothers ask for assistance, in anticipation that they will need it in the fight to protect my lands. My son, meanwhile, needs to prove to me, and all of us, that he has something to offer to the defence of the Dewnan. I do not believe we should yet call the lords of the Dewnan to a full council of war. I will, therefore, send Pryns Artur to help the colony and, in doing so, learn of these lands, engage with my people and lords of Dewnan.'

He looked determinedly at Elowen and then gave his son a short hard stare before continuing. 'But I will not let him travel alone. I am the King of the Dewnan and Pryns Artur, for better or worse, is my son. I, therefore, propose that a small group of similarly young warriors, rheidyrs of the Dewnan with aspirations and something to prove, replacing those lost to Ocean's rage, will accompany him. He and this company of warriors and their gilles will provide our initial contribution to this perceived threat; a small advance force demonstrating our concern. If the threat becomes more real, then I will reconsider this. Messengers will ride to all parts of my kingdom, to the Lords of the Dewnan, asking for volunteers, and when the rheidyrs are gathered, they will depart from here and go to the colony with the emissaries. The coxswain, I think, will also join the group as manservant to my son.'

He turned to face Artur and with a further firm stare he gave the briefest of statements: 'I will watch the progress of this mission with interest, but for now, that is my final word.'

He held his son's gaze before turning away and walking back towards the high table.

'Lady Elowen, let us have that story.'

He sat in his high-backed chair, while his closest supporters moved to sit around him. Elowen contemplated the King. Even she had not anticipated such a positive outcome from Andras's suggestion and had only gone along with it to remove Artur, for a while at least, from the stifling, critical atmosphere of this hall. So what had caused Mawgan to enhance her suggestion and create this opportunity for his son? Not his sycophantic inner circle, that was for sure – something else stirred within him. The memory of his lost wife and her advocacy of their son perhaps, or maybe, beneath all the rhetoric and posturing, a desire to find a way to help his son to succeed? Meliora would have known, but now she had to learn how to read Mawgan and understand him, but that was her challenge. This offered real potential: accompanied by his manservant and a small, swift-moving band of warriors, Prince Artur now had a chance to begin the pursuit of his destiny.

'As you wish, my Lord, and I will tell the story of our beginning and when the world was cold.'

'Thank you, Lady Elowen, we will enjoy that,' he said as he turned towards a servant to take a beaker of mead.

Andras looked at her father with surprise and poorly-disguised dismay. She had not intended this. Instead of her brother being lost in the midst of some futile engagement with the Estrenyons, he now had a chance to shine. She had worked hard to perpetuate her father's sense of Artur's blame for the loss of her mother and a hostile view of the Pryns within her father's hall. Yet, the priestesses had persuaded the King to allow her brother to return on some trumped-up notion that it was what her idolised mother would have wanted. The return of the little brother she had not asked for, who had always been her mother's favourite, and who, it seemed, still retained their mother's favour even from her place in the underworld.

She wanted more power, more than just standing behind the King offering comment, and soon. Andras could not put it off much longer, she and her father must find a suitable partner for her. A warrior and a lord appropriate for the daughter of the King of the Dewnan; it was far better to approach that while she was in ascendancy in her father's court, as a prominent member of her father's entourage, and not the sidelined sister put aside by her brother's return. She looked towards Zethar; would their contacts in the Durotrages and the Belgae be able to respond to this? She had to find another way to influence her father's thinking because the momentum, at least for now, had moved and her brother had his chance. She looked around the hall, feeling isolated and alone, and walked disconsolately back to her seat.

Artur, oblivious to his sister's deeper intentions, stood silently and watched his father as he walked away. He wouldn't trouble him with a response, an expression of gratitude; it almost certainly wasn't called for, and on the evidence of the afternoon, would be rebuked anyway.

He thought of his lost comrades. How he and they had fought a tempestuous, unforgiving Ocean just to respond to his father's call. He would honour them, prove himself worthy to them, and prove his father wrong. He was glad of the decision and pleased, he now realised, not to be staying in his father's hall any longer than he had to.

Mamm Norves and the Age of Cold

In the beginning, Sira Howl, the Sun Father, entered the sky, proud, strong and full of desire. He drove his fiery chariot across the heavens in search of companionship and a lover with whom to share his light and his warmth.

Mamm Norves, The Earth Mother, was beautiful and when he first saw her, he shone with all his powers, in awe of all that she bestowed, and courted her by telling stories, making her smile and showing warmth and caring as he danced around her.

Not a day passed without him bringing new gifts and looking for new ways to demonstrate his love for her. He helped her to dress in verdant greens and browns, the colours of the land and helped Ocean to drape her in deep blue. To him, alongside the daily pleasure of her beauty, she brought wisdom and humility.

Each evening, he left her to sleep and walked in the underworld, gladdened in his heart, and returned the next morning with renewed vigour and pleasure in anticipation of another day in her company.

Then, one morning, the Sun kissed the Earth in a way that he had never kissed her before. Her desire for him overwhelmed her and she kissed him back. As they came together, their passion for each other was of a kind never felt before, or since, and was of such power that great and momentous change was the only possible outcome. From the bubbling cauldron of their union and the intensity of their love for each other, new life, men and women, the children of the Earth and the Sun, the first-born walked across the land and sailed on Ocean.

The Sun and the Earth watched over their children and men and women grew and prospered. They lived with the land and all it provided. They did not take more than they needed and Father and Mother were proud of their children, nurtured them and helped them to grow.

As the years went by, however, these men and women, these first children, grew complacent and indulgent. They failed to honour the Sun, their father, and the Earth, their mother, and all they had provided.

Sira Howl grew angry, watching the actions of his children, and strong and fiery as he was, fully aware of his power and his previous benevolence, decided he would teach them a harsh lesson to show the importance of all that he and the Earth had afforded.

The Earth, aware of his frustrations and his intentions, came to him and begged him to reconsider. He, proud and determined once his decision was made, refused to listen and pulled away from the Earth. She, no longer resplendent in his warming rays, decided to act quickly as she grew colder and less able to support all of her children. The Earth gathered a small group of men and women, those who had remained faithful, respecting Ocean and the land.

'My Children,' she said, 'you must go now to a special place, beyond the Snowy Mountains, where it will be warmer, and raise your children there, and through the lives of many children, you must wait. Others will join you and you will grow stronger in your exile. Sira Howl will return, but go now, protect yourself in the valleys and the caves of my warmest parts and only return to these lands when he brings his light and the intensity of his love back to me.'

As she spoke, another group, from those who had failed to honour her and taken what they wanted without consideration of others, heard what she was saying and determined that they too would find a warmer place. They went away, not to the lands south of the Snowy Mountains, but to the vast flatlands far from Ocean. These people were clever, calculating and could not be trusted, but Mamm Norves, who sees everything, saw them slip quietly away and let them go. No matter how much they betrayed her trust and abused her, she could not knowingly harm any of her children.

Many years and lives of men then passed. The Earth grew cold and harsh as she withdrew within herself. Even in the protected lands, the chosen people found life difficult and they did not grow in the way that they had before.

Then, one day, Sira Howl turned back to Mamm Norves. He saw how she had diminished, how she was frail and unhappy without his love, and felt great remorse for what he had done and how he had distanced himself from her. He came close to her again and she warmed and grew brighter in the face of his renewed attention. As she did so, the barrenness of the land receded and her chosen people walked forward once more. Life, abundance and the vibrant colours of an earlier age returned with new vigour in celebration of her reawakening. She encouraged her children now to spread out from their refuge and explore new lands. New people had joined them in their exile and they stepped forward together, bright and optimistic at all that unfolded before them.

On one particular day, when Sira Howl shone brightly in the sky, the chosen people came to Ocean's wide expanse once more and she sparkled and glistened before them.

'My children,' said Mamm Norves, 'this is mighty Ocean, who you once knew so well. She will foster you and support you, my chosen people. But beware, in her vastness she will harbour good and bad spirits and she will grow and change as Sira Howl and I renew our relationship. Today, she sparkles with beauty; but it will not always be this way. Dangerous and capricious spirits live within her and they will bring great tempests to test you. Treat her with respect and understand her and she will serve you well.'

Ocean's people prospered and spread amongst the lands that surround her and along the great rivers. They hunted and sailed and lived in harmony with Mamm Norves and all that she provided. They were days of plenty and the people lived happily together.

As the seasons and the years passed, Estrenyons, descendants of those who snuck away as Sira Howl diminished, began to return to Ocean's shore. Mamm Norves perceived this and set aside land for them. They took this, but being greedy, they expected more and continued to move, taking more land. Like spoilt children, they demanded more. Sira Howl perceived their greed and his anger began to return. He burned more brightly than ever now, such was his frustration at what he saw.

Increasingly alarmed and realising that the Estrenyons would never stop on their own, Mamm Norves resolved to stop them herself. Once again, she called her chosen ones to her.

'My children, seek higher ground. Ocean grows: a great flood will spread across me and you must prepare.'

Then, because her conscience and compassion would not allow her to do otherwise, Mamm Norves turned to the Estrenyons and gave them the same warning. They looked at her and said with a sneer, they would not leave their lands; they had come this far and nothing now would make them return and give up what they had taken as their own. Saddened at their contempt and dismissive response, she, who had given them life, turned away dejectedly and left them to their fate.

When the great flood came, it came quickly. At first, the water trickled across the land. Soon it was knee deep. For those who remained, it was already too late. The Estrenyons, who had disrespected Ocean, were helpless. Finally, as Mamm Norves shuddered and shook, a great wave of water, that neither people nor boats could withstand, spread across the lower lands and *drowned all in its path. Ocean's people, the chosen ones, watched from higher ground as the lands they had walked on disappeared beneath the waves.*

Ocean, however, was still Ocean, just bigger, and once they had paused and thanked Mamm Norves for her guidance and her protection, the chosen ones returned to her and sailed, and traded upon her once more.

The few Estrenyons that had managed to escape from the great flood returned to their own lands beyond the great forest and did not come to Ocean's shore again until many years and lives had passed.

***

Days passed after the feast and the return of the Prince to his father. Loor Plansa, gille of Sira Howl, and one of the twelve guardians of the Earth while the Sun Father walked in the underworld, bestrode the heavens in his full, shining on the Dewnan and on a small, secluded roundhouse, deep in the woods of the higher Kammel.

Zethar rested on her lover's broad chest and then raised herself again slightly, allowing her small pale breasts and pert pink nipples to caress his mat of black curling hair and the moist entrance to her inner body rub enticingly along his firm and powerful leg.

A veneer of stern intensity could not hide the alertness of his body hair and arousal that transmitted from him as their bodies touched. It was having the effect she desired.

Earlier that evening Anogin of the Atrebates, a giant of a man, and his small band of warriors had arrived at her roundhouse. Travelling sundown to sunrise, remaining hidden by day, they had entered the land of the Dewnan, or Dumnoni, as the Atrebates called them. They crossed the high ground and Tamara the Dark River with ease, towards the setting sun. No one had seen the warriors or tried to stop them and, even in the midst of their passion, contempt was uppermost in Anogin's mind. The Veneti men could not be everywhere and they had travelled well away from the colony as an extra precaution, to a crossing high on Tamara. As for the Dumnoni, or "Dewnan" as they called themselves, and their supposed warriors, well, no doubt they slept in their beds unaware of the ease with which their borders and women had been penetrated.

This tribe, the Ocean People, were different from all the rest. They saw themselves as "chosen" and had grown ever more lax in recent years since the weakness of their Chieftain – who was not a King, no matter what he might tell himself – had been fully exposed by his sanctioning of women to positions of authority. These priestesses, their sorcery and corrupting influence, undermined the whole tribe. He had even allowed one of the witches to become his Queen!

The Atrebates were Belgic warriors; men of the land, not of the ocean, whose influence had grown in Pretannia over several generations. No corrupt influences weakened them; instead, they enforced a proper order and steady expansion, led by men, across all the lands they encountered.

Anogin, warrior and agent of the King of the Belgae Confederation, had nothing but disdain for these weak and lesser people and he would subdue them. If he wanted to enter their lands, take any of their women for his pleasure, then he would, before taking their wealth. That was how the Belgae warlords had first come to Pretannia with the German mercenaries, who were their wilder cousins from the great forest beyond the Rhenus. Small warrior bands had crossed the Germani Sea, slaughtering and butchering all those who stood in their way. They struck fear into the local tribes while the incumbent elite, who had grown fat in their complacency, were unable or too slow to respond.

That was how he would take control of the Dumnoni when his chance came. Then, when he was King, he mused contentedly as Zethar rose up and down with increasing vigour on his large and rigid manhood, perhaps he would propose an alliance with the Roman general. As the defeat of the tribes in Belgica had shown, resistance was unwise. Commios now ruled the Atrebates in Belgica with the support of Caesar and did well from that alliance. Quietly, Anogin admired Caesar and his ways. The alliance would surely work for both Anogin and the great man, and maybe the Belgae Confederation too as they pushed into Pretannia against the Cassi and Trinobantes. These tribes, on the far side of Tamesis, were a real obstacle to the Belgic takeover of all Pretannia, albeit they were currently embroiled in a bitter war between themselves. This was where the King of the Belgae focused, looking for opportunity, leaving this decrepit Dumnoni land to adventurers like him: acknowledged, but not openly supported by the King. He had been at it nine summers since that early chance finding of the infamous Dumnoni witch queen. It was a slow process, but he sensed that momentum was building and at least some of their women knew their place and gave a good fuck.

This was not his first visit to Zethar's roundhouse.

Caution was still called for, while the Veneti warrior merchants had their colony, but they weakened quickly now. Their days were over and with them the Ocean People. The Curiosolitae now dominated the trade at Hengasts and the Veneti clung to this last vestige of peripheral influence in Pretannia. Soon they would be pushed off the land and drowned in the very ocean they called their own. Compromised and weak, the Durotrages' King, Gawell, was already complying with the demands of the Confederation and now Anogin looked for new ways to undermine the Dumnoni.

Zethar's eyes narrowed with intensity, was his mind elsewhere? Not completely, the rigidity and size of his desire told her that. She rose above him and guided his entry into her. He felt good, she felt good. She looked forward to his periodic forays into the Dewnan lands. It must be at least six springs since they had first met and their intimacy had remained throughout. He got what he wanted and she enjoyed providing it.

However, she knew there was more to his forays than his desire for her. He and his men undoubtedly picked up slaves from the more remote settlements and took them back across RunHoul; and yet he seemed to know a lot about the King and asked more questions about him. She told him everything she needed to; about her relationship with Andras, and how it was vital she remained prominent in the leadership of the tribal lands after her father's death to ensure that the priestess order was removed. He made clear his contempt for them and so she responded, looking for a way to exploit this in her favour.

For Anogin, the point of Zethar was her connection to Mawgan's hall, to the famous Ker Kammel. That was why he was here. Mawgan, fool that he was, she informed him, believed there was still a "relationship" between Gawell and himself, the Dumnoni and the Durotrages. Gawell, plied with gold and extra amphora by his secret Belgae advisors, allowed him to think that in his official communications between them, while Anogin and his men probed for any weaknesses and opportunities as they arose in order to undermine the "King" of the Dumnoni and his tribal lands. The shag was just a bonus.

He drew himself up, kissed and caressed her nipples, removed Zethar from their coupling, lay her down, rose over her and re-entered, feeling her intensity and taking his own pleasure. She gasped as he thrust firmly inwards, his speed and power bringing them both to their climax.

They lay back on the bed of animal skins. As his breath returned, she rose again, leant over and stroked his black shoulder length hair.

'You are so strong, brave Belgae warrior! Your power stimulates and excites me! No man in these lands can match you; do not leave it so long before you return!'

He inclined his head towards her.

'So you have been seeking comparisons in my absence? How many Dewnan warrior boys have you indulged to draw this conclusion?'

His appearance was stern as he looked firmly at her. She wavered slightly in her purpose.

'None, why would I? You seem to leave it just long enough before I begin to despair of your return and can still remember your arms and power. While I wait for your return, I have no need for any other man.'

They could not renew their intimacy yet. Despite her desire for his body, she needed something else first. It would not wait and she must talk to him while she had him, subdued, under her spell.

'Anogin, I have thought of you a lot recently,' she smiled, 'more than usual, wondering how I might get word to you.'

'Oh yes, and why would that be?'

'Mawgan's son, Artur, I have told you about him, has returned. He is here now. Andras and I tried to prevent it by bringing calamity upon him and yet, with a sacrifice we did not anticipate, the mad old priestess brought him ashore. He lives and strengthens with each passing day. His father recruits a warrior company to support him from the sons of the Dewnan lords and then they will travel with a retinue to support the Veneti colony – and there he will encounter the high priestess. Her hand is behind it all, we believe, ensuring that the legacy of his mother lives. They set great store by him.'

She looked at him apologetically, betraying her nervousness at his likely response.

'Although, in truth, I am not sure why; he has nothing compared to you! Our project to remove the priestesses and establish a proper order is in great danger. Anogin, we need your help.'

He stared coolly and calmly at her. Their passion spent, she felt cold, drawing the furs around her.

'That is disappointing news. When will his retinue set out for the colony?'

'Soon. The Company began to assemble three days ago, when I was last at Ker Kammel. Each warrior brings his own small retinue, one or two supporters per warrior. They will be in excess of forty men when they depart, by the new moon at the latest.'

He had lost interest in her now. *Did she know?* Of course, she did not. She only knew what he wanted her to know. He had never described the detail of his quest, begun so well with a bit of luck. Mawgan's whore had been alone in the tent, virtually unprotected. The few guards were easily overpowered by his larger force. How typical of the lackadaisical Dumnoni and their slapdash Chieftain to gift him such an opportunity! He had enjoyed it, the chance to dispatch the infamous witch queen of the setting sun and remove her from the equation. The spirits, he knew, would show contempt for her presumption and the heresy she embodied by assuming influence in a world where women had no part, but compliance to the decisions of men. The thought of her eternal damnation pleased his thinking.

She had fought hard, mind, and it was only afterwards that he had found out her brat, Mawgan's heir, was in the tent also. The boy had made no sound. *He would not have lasted long if he had*, he thought grimly. Then Mawgan's party had returned and they had left quickly.

Unfinished business, and if the witch's spawn was back, something had to be done. Zethar was right. A new threat was growing.

***

Gradually, Maedoc's strength had grown. Brought to the house of the priestess, he had been watched over by Elowen and her acolytes. Now, as Loor Plansa reached his full and the first real warmth of the year filled the air, the Maedoc of old had returned, even if, deep down, a part of him would remain chastened and saddened forever by the experience of that stormy, fateful night.

Early on the evening of the full moon, he and Elowen sat high on a hill of the sanctum. Plansa's creamy orb, tinged with yellow and red by Sira Howl as he descended to the underworld, rose behind them. Beneath them, the sea bustled playfully in the last of the evening light, Frequent flurries of white crested the gentle, rolling waves and lines of underwater currents curved erratically around the inshore waters. They watched as cormorants and shags dived, disappearing into the water at speed before returning a little distance away, often with small fish or eels sparkling in their beaks.

He pointed out one such successful dive to her and, as he did so, she gently stroked his right leg and turned towards him.

'You look so much better, and there is colour in your face. Maedoc has properly returned, I think.'

'I do feel better today. I ache less and my mind feels clearer. This fresh but clean breeze invigorates me. I still feel such responsibility for those lives, and yet, I cannot help it, I feel the need to get going. I am just sitting around now, not doing anything.'

She searched his face, his eyes. His mix of responsibility and caring, along with his zest for life and his desire to be practical and do things, greatly appealed to her. She smiled for a moment as she contemplated these qualities within him. Then, something seemed to click within her. He noticed the subtle shift in her face, the tempering of her smile as she spoke again.

'I have told you there is no blame attached to you or to Pryns Artur for what has happened. You and he are the survivors of a determined attack by the others, the enemy; those who would restrict freedom, control thinking and control us! Both of you have foiled their intention – he through his undoubted bravery and the sacrifice of others, you through your own bravery, strength and determination to survive. You are right, you must move on, and there will more skirmishes yet before the real battle begins. We must face those small encounters in preparation for the great battle to come – and, of course, when I say we, I mean you, the Pryns and his followers, and the warriors that you will meet along the way.'

She paused for a moment and followed his gaze to the head of a seal, bobbing in the water below, conscious of them, staring back and seeming to listen as they talked. She continued, 'We do not face one enemy, but a number of forces that would destroy us. With a fit and healthy Maedoc, even in the face of great sadness, there is hope!'

His eyes widened as he laughed with great affection. 'You flatter me, I think, to aid my recovery even more quickly! I will play my part, but others will have the commanding role. I will serve wherever I can and you, of course, have already played a substantial role, and I am sure you are not finished with all of this just yet!'

'Perhaps so, but I do not flatter you. Already, you have played a prominent part for good in unfolding events and confounded the enemy with your tenacity. The Pryns looks to you. He may be impetuous and have the arrogance of a young warrior, but he is no fool and recognises a good man when he sees one. He will need your wisdom, friendship and knowledge of the lands of the Dewnan in the days to come. If you are ready, you must depart for the Colony. The young rheidyrs, the chosen sons of the lesser chieftains, are gathering at Ker Kammel, and we cannot delay our plans much longer. You must return to the Pryns.'

He looked away from her with a gentle smile now, gazing at some distant point, before turning back to her with a determinedly earnest face. 'You are right; I have delayed long enough. It has been many days now since Mawgan gave his direction. I will gather my belongings and depart before nightfall.'

Elowen looked back at him, expressionless for a moment, before bursting into laughter as he broke into a broad smile.

'If you are indeed fully recovered and must leave me, you will go nowhere this evening brave warrior of mine. We have a lot to catch up on!' her smile faded slightly. 'But, in the morning, the journey does begin and I do not know where it will take you but, wherever you are, I will be thinking of you, Maedoc, and waiting for your return.'

Her eyes fixed his for a moment before she jumped to her feet and looked down at him.

'Come on, we should eat; I can smell the cooking pot even up here. Let's go back down to the house and see what has been prepared for our meal.'

pROVOCATION

Publius Crassus, Legatus Legionis, commander of the VIIth Legion of Rome, stood before the large meeting table in the Legate's tent. Around it were the Primus Pilus and Pilus Priors, senior military commanders of the ten cohorts of the legion. Here also were the military tribunes, the quota of ambitious young men of Rome allocated to the legion. These were members of the leading patrician families and senatorial elite, placed with them to be involved in the affairs of Rome and its growing empire, and to gain experience. They discussed the issues of leadership and command, directions from the Pro-Consul, sourcing supplies to service the needs of the men and engagement with the surrounding tribes. They met four times a month and now an increasingly pressing matter was under discussion.

Crassus nodded and spoke to the legion quartermaster. 'Senior Quaestores, give your final assessment and recommendation please.'

'Dominus, we have a month's supply of corn left. On reduced rations, maybe a month and a half. The Andes tribe have provided all they can, and the supply from the Province has not been as reliable this winter. We must find new sources, send for additional provision, or engage the surrounding tribes. The reports I receive tell me there are substantial stores and the ability to supply the legion, in particular, with the Curiosolitae and the Veneti. These tribes have their own corn, as well as stores through trading with the tribes of Pretannia. It is their habit, I understand, to build sufficient stocks in the autumn to trade with surrounding tribes when their stores get low at the end of the winter and charge an additional premium. The Curiosolitae and Veneti, Dominus, is where I recommend we secure the corn.'

Crassus stroked his chin and considered the quaestores' conclusions. They needed a better supply line. Despite the achievements of recent campaigns, they were not yet in fully secured territory. He had sent a positive report back to Caesar at the end of the last season, and they held hostages from all of the principal tribes, as was the normal procedure, to ensure the tribes upheld their promises to Rome. However, he still felt it would take all of his and the legion's concentration to hold their position. A hungry legion of around six thousand men, all angrily demanding their daily food, was something he did not want to contemplate. Although, if the tribes would not supply what they needed and became belligerent again, he and the VIIth would be ready to confront them. Let them see how far that got them.

As quickly as it had arisen, the bravado in his thinking subsided and practical considerations reasserted themselves. He knew his father's position and relationship with his Pro-Consul had helped him become Legate at such an early age. It wasn't officially recognised – but Caesar was impressed with his performance and he did not want to jeopardise that in any way. He had received new communication from the Pro-Consul late yesterday evening, further confirming this and giving important new instructions. Engaging the tribes now could enable him to source new corn and respond to Caesar's latest directions.

'Quaestores, send back to the Province, and if our suppliers are failing, find new merchants to deliver to our needs. In the short term, however, we only have one course of action. I accept your recommendation that we must send envoys to the Veneti and Curiosolitae.'

Secundus Avilius, the Primus Pilus, looked at the Legate and allowed a slight nod of approval. He was, in effect, the senior military man. His cohort carried the Eagle into battle. His experience was substantial, and unlike the Legate and his tribunes, his family did not aid the pursuit of his career. Instead, he stood here through his sheer hard work, determination and, maybe, a little bit of luck on the battlefield.

'Crassus, Dominus. It is the correct approach, but we should proceed with care. These barbarians, the Veneti, in particular, do not see themselves yet as part of Rome. They are volatile, unpredictable and, I think, still believe that they can stand against us, despite their protestations of the autumn. I do not trust them.'

'Secundus, I agree, but we must be clear that the legion needs its supplies and we will have them; but preferably voluntarily with a sensible price paid.'

He turned to the rest of the table.

'Pilus, Tribunes, who should we send to talk to the Barbarian, persuade him it is in his interest to supply the Legion of Rome?' Crassus nodded at the Praefectus Castrorum, or Camp Prefect, Marcus Trebius Gallus. He was thirty years old, tall for a Roman and with thick well-kempt dark brown hair, despite the impending onset of middle age. Gallus was a veteran in the room, a career man with no wife, dependents or family to speak of, as Crassus understood it. He had given his life to the army. The Legate found him to be a good judge of capabilities and his name, which indicated that Gallic blood ran through him, meant he also spoke their tongue. He was a useful man to have under his command.

'Marcus?'

'Dominus, I believe we would all volunteer for this important task, but it is a challenging one and requires balance and judgment. The Veneti are haughty and self-important. We secure the corn first, with diplomacy, and then strengthen once the season begins.'

The Legate looked around the table and nodded at an eager young face looking back at him.

'Titus Silius?'

'Dominus, I volunteer to undertake one of these missions. The Praefectus Castrorum is, of course, correct, the discussion requires a balanced but firm approach and it is only we, your Tribunes, the young diplomats of Rome, who are able to undertake such a delicate but vital task. These are barbarians, of course. We will be firm with them and clear that it is to both our advantage and theirs that they should agree to supply us.'

Crassus looked thoughtfully back at the young Tribune. Confident in his position as a member of one of the patrician families, he was, nevertheless, eager to please and was always looking for a way to take on new duties and impress. He would send him and maybe he could deliver on several objectives. He might come back with the corn, or not, and that might yet be to their advantage.

'Very well, Titus. I would like you and Quintus to go to the Veneti. Their prowess on the Ocean and fleet of ships, of course, makes them of particular importance. It requires two of you,' he looked towards Gallus, 'and at least for the time being, we should take account of their assumed pre-eminence.'

Questioning looks passed between the Pilus, but Crassus ignored them and looked to Quintus Velanius, the longest-established Tribune and approaching the end of his three-year commission. Velanius looked to the Legate and nodded with stern acknowledgement.

'Marcus Gallus, you will go to the Curiosolitae and, while there, I want you to explore carefully how ready they are to provide further support to Rome. I understand that they and the Veneti are not close allies and, instead, seek to undermine the Veneti, most notably their trade with Pretannia. I think you will find they are ready to come to an understanding in the hope of realising a perceived future opportunity.'

'Dominus, I will explore that.'

'Good. Envoys take a small escort with you and depart at first light. We will expect you by nonae. Proceed with speed and due caution. Good luck to you.'

He spoke now to all in the tent.

'We will come together again when the envoys return. Titus Terrasidius, Marcus, Secundus, stay a little longer, please; there are additional things I would like to discuss with you.'

The rest of the men filed out of the tent, leaving the three senior men with the Legate.

'Gentleman, can I offer you some refreshment? Wine, perhaps? Some cheese, or meat?'

He signalled to the back of the tent, where a servant stood waiting. They moved to a smaller low table with more comfortable seats. Crassus urged them to sit.

'The response of the tribal leaders will be interesting. Marcus, our hostages are secure?'

'They are under strong guard.'

'Good. I expect the tribal leaders to see this as a commercial opportunity, but we can never be certain how they will respond. We need to be ready for a different approach.'

'Dominus, Crassus,' the Primus Pilus spoke next, 'This is an important mission. Is it wise to send Titus Silius? He is young, impetuous and haughty. Like the Veneti really, and I do not believe that they like haughtiness played back to them. I think they may find his youth a little insulting for such a serious issue.'

The Legate nodded his head gently as Secundus spoke. *Look for ways to provoke the Veneti*, those were his instructions. *Do not reveal your intention to anyone. It must look as if the conflict has happened through the actions of the tribe and that Rome is the injured party.* The communique from the Pro-Consul had arrived the previous evening and the eagerness, inexperience and obvious sense of superiority of Titus Silius was too good an opportunity to miss to enrage the Veneti elders and provoke a rash action that the legions of Rome could respond to. Sending the experienced Quintus Velanius would cover any impression of deliberate provocation.

'Secundus, you are right; he is a little impetuous, but he has to learn. That is why he is here. Quintus will provide balance and restraint. He is experienced beyond his years; and, of course, we need the corn.'

The Legate took a sip of his wine before continuing.

'I would like to discuss another matter with you all now. I received a further communique from the Pro-Consul yesterday evening and I would like to share some of its detail on a strictly confidential basis.'

All three nodded or inclined their heads to show they understood the need for discretion.

'The Pro-Consul has decided we must begin to take steps to counter the Veneti's dominance on the Ocean. If we are to control all Gaul for Roman advantage, we cannot allow the unchecked retention of a significant naval capability by one of the tribes that has submitted to our leadership. It is incompatible and so he has dispatched Decimus Brutus, who perhaps you may know, on a secret mission to the mouth of the Liger to prepare the ground for the construction and assembly of a fleet. I expect to hear from him in the next few days.

He will gather materials and commission local shipwrights. He will engage, secretly first of all, with the Pictones and Santones, who are loyal to us, offer a good price for the service of their ships and crew to ensure their continued loyalty, and begin the process of assembling the fleet. The Pictones and Santoni have no great affection for the Veneti, who overshadow their trade and charge them a heavy toll for passage on the Ocean. I understand that Brutus will take with him a small party of our own shipwrights and carpenters to oversee construction and he has agents in place in the Province ready to recruit experienced oarsmen as soon as it is expedient to do so.'

Secundus again was the first to respond.

'Crassus Dominus, it will not be long before word reaches the Veneti, no matter how well it is concealed.'

Crassus smiled back at him.

'Well, if it does, it does, but for a while at least, secrecy may aid the shipbuilding and prevent any pre-emptive strike.'

He looked now towards the Camp Prefect.

'I did not say this amongst the others, Marcus, but your mission is of critical importance. I do not expect Silius and Quintus to return,' for the briefest of moments he paused, 'with much. Take a full maniple to the Curiosolitae, an enhanced guard that reflects the "importance of our special relationship with them", but do not leave until Silius and Quintus have departed. Take suitable gifts and be clear that we want to build a relationship for the long term, to exploit "and dominate" the Pretannia trade together. Marcus, I am sure you will know what to say, how to enthuse them and how to achieve your twin objectives. In truth, I think they will be very ready to talk to you but, of course, do not forget that we must also have some corn!'

'Dominus, I will do my best.'

***

Mael, High King of the Veneti, tilted his head slightly backward to listen to the messenger, breathed in deeply and raised his hand to interrupt the conversation that continued around the table.

'My Lords, a small party of Romans are at the gates of Gwened. They ask leave to enter and say they have come to discuss trade and "friendship" between the Veneti and Rome.'

A collective widening of eyes and grumblings greeted the King's statement.

'Very well, Helori. Bring them to the doors of the Hall. I will tell you when we are ready to receive them.'

The steward went away and the King again looked at the table.

'Spring is coming. Their army camps on our borders. They have hostages from us but give no hostages in return. Their arrogance is tedious, overbearing and we all know they will not be content with letting us be. Their way is the only way, their culture the only culture, and they seek to infiltrate and dominate wherever they can.'

Grim but resolute faces looked back at him as he picked up his beaker and took a drink of the Massalian wine it held.

'Of course, if you do not accept this voluntarily, they will send the legion in to make sure you do. They are accommodating of those who submit, that is what they tell the world. Agree with their approach, be part of "the empire" and accept that it is they who will take the wealth and all the benefits that come from that.'

He looked determinedly around the table.

'We are the heirs of Venetia, and Ocean's people! Do we really want to submit to all of that?'

Multiple voices responded around the table.

'No!'

'We do not!'

'It is our land, our inheritance from the Lady Venetia of blessed name!'

Mael turned to Rozenn, his Queen, and her eyes, wide with affection, looked back at him.

The King's cousin, Erwan, however, stood up at the far side of the table.

'My Lord, we know the Romans talk to the Curiosolitae and that they continue their efforts to undermine and steal our trade with the Dewnan and with the Germanis at Hengast's Fort. The men of Massalia do not engage with us as they once did. The trade with the Middle Sea has diminished and now we watch as the tribes of Gaul succumb to the murder and butchery of the Roman legions. Can we really stand against their aggression?'

'Cousin, a trader from Massalia was here only recently. Is it not possible, now that the fighting has subsided, there is new interest there, something to build on?'

Erwan smiled resignedly.

'One swallow does not make a summer, cousin. Never was the old proverb truer than now. He is surely the first we have seen in many moons. I will not build my hopes upon it. The Romans will open wide, strong roads through Gaul. That is their way. It is how they control; and then the merchant wealth will pass along those roads to Massalia, the Middle Sea and to Rome – and will no longer think of the Veneti.'

The King sighed as he looked back at his cousin.

'Erwan, you describe a grim future. Will we not defend our Pretan heritage? Our ancestors were achieving great things long before any Roman. Should we succumb to their bullying?'

'My Lord,' the King's young nephew, Judikael, rose to speak.

'I entertained the merchant and assured him of our commitment to trade. I sent him on to Aodren at Pendre en Menluit in the land of the Dewnan. He looks for new opportunities. It could be a new beginning. Let us talk to these Romans, strike a deal with them; Ocean is ours and they control the land, outside of Venetia. We have talked about this before.'

The King watched as Erwan and others around the table shook their heads. His brother and heir, Perig, who had waited to hear what others would say, raised his hand to speak.

'My Lord, brother, although some may see naivety in Judikael's words, is there not something in both his and Lord Erwan's assertions? The Romans want to take our wealth and control all Gaul. Destroy, control and demand conformity is their way; but we have something the Romans do not. Our fleet and understanding of Ocean and her ways, provide us with an opportunity for dialogue and agreement, and if need be, the means to defend ourselves. They know that Ocean is not the Middle Sea with her tides, currents, great depth and the mighty balum beneath the waves, and they are wary. We are the heirs of Venetia, Ocean's people! We have friends and kin across the Mor Pretani. We can defend ourselves!'

The discussion continued for a little longer until Helori opened the door slightly and edged his way into the hall, closed the door behind him and walked around the table to the King.

'They are in the inner yard, my Lord. Shall I bring them in?'

The King turned back to the table.

'My Lords, they are here and so our discussion must end. Let us find out what it is they want. We will begin by discussing the people that they have taken from us. All winter we have shown our desire to live in peace, even though they are the aggressor. Our people should now come home. I will talk, let us maintain our discipline from this point onwards and not give them any unnecessary opportunity. Bring them in Helori.'

***

The King's steward crossed the yard to the dismounted Roman delegation. Quintus Velanius and Titus Silius, supported by a translator and their guard, stood ready to follow him. 'We will only allow the Tribunes with two servants or soldiers each into the hall. It is the Hall of the King of the Veneti and we do not allow armed groups into it, large or small.'

Titus Silius bristled at the perceived slight.

'We are emissaries of Rome, here to talk business. What do you think our intention is?'

The steward, with no show of emotion, looked straight back at the young Tribune.

'These are our rules, my Lord. You must abide by them or I cannot admit you and I must ask you to leave Gwened.'

'Who do you think you are? I am from one of the most important families in Rome. You are nothing but a lowly servant of a tribal King. I shall proceed...'

Quintus Velanius interrupted him, shaking his head very slightly at the translator, indicating he should not interpret.

'Titus, we are here to discuss business with our Veneti friends, let us honour their custom and proceed to our audience with King Mael. Let us not lose sight of our objective through unnecessary confrontation before we have even entered the Hall.'

Silius glared back at him for a moment before nodding his head in acknowledgement. Supporters were selected and the party followed the steward.

The contrast between the brightness of the day outside and darkness in the hall, mixed with the smoke of the fire at its centre, made it difficult at first to see ahead of them. Gradually, the interior of the hall, its wooden columns and timbered roof supports became clearer. They approached what looked like an open-ended table where a group of men, the tribal elders, sat waiting for their arrival, watching their entrance. The elders all had shoulder-length hair and long moustaches, typical of all the Gauls they had encountered. Interspersed around the table, there were also several women. As they came to a stop before them all, Velanius and Silius stepped forward to offer their greetings and state their business.

'King Mael, noble Lords, I am Quintus Mucius Velanius and this, my fellow Tribune of Rome, is Titus Laelius Silius. We are honoured to be granted an audience and bring greetings from the Roman Republic and its representative in these lands, the Legatus Legionis, Publius Licinius Crassus.'

As the translation was completed, the expressions on the faces around the table changed from impassive to irritation, and some even showed barely disguised anger. The King held his hand up, indicating that no one should respond.

'Velanius, Silius, welcome. I return greetings from the Veneti nation to you, guests in our lands. What is it that you wish to discuss with me?'

'King Mael, I thank you for your greetings. From our station in the territory of the Andes, our orders are to work with our tribal allies to maintain the peace in Armorica, but we cannot do this without an adequate supply of corn. We have come to you today to open a discussion on the supply of corn for the VIIth Legion of Rome.'

As the translator paused, uproar spread around the hall before the King, banging his fists firmly on the table, restored some order. Smiling, tersely, he addressed the Tribunes.

'Honoured guests, you will, of course, understand that it is difficult to hear a Roman talk of keeping the peace when the aggression of recent years has come solely from Rome and your leader's ruthless suppression of any who dare to oppose him. Tell me, how is that "keeping the peace"?'

There was silence around the table. All now stared back at Quintus, waiting for him to respond. It did not deflect him from his purpose.

'Honoured King, we are here to ask if you are prepared to supply corn to us. We are here to offer trade and a fair price to supply the Legion.'

'Tribune, you evade my question, but before we talk of trade, what of the hostages, that the Legate took from us in the autumn? We have kept to our side of the bargain, so now, before any other conversation can begin, our people must return to us.'

Quintus shifted uneasily. He could sense Silius preparing to say something, so spoke quickly.

'Noble King, the hostages are safe but I am not, however, here to discuss hostages but instead talk trade and the supply of corn for the Legion.'

The King gently stroked his long moustache, considering the emissaries, and said, 'You come to negotiate on essential food supplies but have not come with the ability to discuss what you must know is the most important issue to us. There will be no corn, no matter what price you are prepared to pay, unless we know that our people, kin of those who sit around this table, will be safely restored to us as part of an agreement to supply.'

Velanius was about to reply when Silius stepped forward.

'King Mael, we come in good faith to trade for corn. We are citizens of Rome and we seek friendship with the Veneti, but you will, I am sure, understand that a hungry army will not just sit and wait for a supply to arrive. Let us strike a deal now and keep the Legion in its base and look forward together to the spring and our blossoming friendship.'

A further ripple of angry murmuring spread around the table. The King breathed in deeply and addressed his reply to Velanius.

'Tribune, I advise you and your young friend against veiled threats. You are visitors here and respect is our due. If you are not prepared to give that you should leave now, with no corn and no expectation of receiving any from the Veneti.'

Quintus was about to reply when the King held up his hand to stop him and continued.

'We have quickly understood your purpose and I have stated our position in response. Let us retire to consider some more and then you are welcome to join us to eat and drink and we can discuss this matter further.'

At a nod from the King, Helori came forward to usher the Roman group out of the main hall to an adjacent guest room. Mael rose from the table and turned towards his private room. As he did so, Perig came alongside and spoke quietly as he walked.

'You have established the right position. You will emphasise the hostage point over dinner?'

The King smiled resignedly at his brother. 'Perig, what are we to do? We can tell them, no hostages, no corn; but as the boy has informed us, they will come and get it anyway, or at least try to. Are we to inflict the same misery on our people that has befallen all the others who have stood up to them?'

'I do not wish it, but when they have our corn, what next, our fleet? We must hold out for a fair settlement, trade as equals and the hostages come back to us.'

Mael sighed deeply as he walked ahead.

'Yes, brother, you are right, of course, but I imagine a similar position was "established" with them by other nations, a perception they would trade and negotiate as equals; but for us, we have conceded already, you see. They have our people, we have none of theirs, unless, of course, we seize these emissaries, but that would only inflame the situation further.'

He stopped and turned to his brother.

'Leave me now, Perig, please. Important decisions approach. I need to think. I will send Helori to look for you later, before our meal. We will discuss our approach more before we meet our guests again.'

***

As evening approached, the call went out for the King's closest advisers to attend him. Four stood before him now, Rozenn, his queen, Jodoc, the High Priest, his cousin Erwan and nephew Judikael. The King sat at a high-backed chair, arms resting on the table in front of him. The others, subdued, looked back and waited for him to speak.

'Where is Perig?'

Helori stepped forward from the door.

'My Lord Perig was called away to speak to his lead mariner and returned today to Gwened. I have asked his steward to direct him here when he is concluded.'

'Very well, no doubt we will find out more shortly. Rozenn, my dear, you said nothing earlier. It is unusual for you. What is your view?'

'My King, Mael,' she smiled at him, 'I do not give rash opinions and prefer to consider before I speak. We face a decisive encounter if we choose to retain our integrity and our dignity. They come to "trade" and yet will not pay our asking price, the cost of the corn and return of our people. It is clear from the way the older Tribune evades your questions this was never a consideration. They have decided what they will pay and I am sure whatever that is, it is a trifle to them. All they need is the corn to see them through to the campaign season and, probably, the return of their leader, Julius Caesar, the butcher of Rome!'

She scoffed and continued.

'If no hostages are returned and we supply them with corn and take gold from them in payment, we are complicit in their illegal war! A war prosecuted on a trumped-up falsehood that we – and everybody else they have trampled over – are in some way a threat to Rome or somehow in need of their "civilisation". So there you have it, their strategy; first to create anarchy and mayhem and then, ride to our rescue, "to keep the peace". I ask you! All we wish is to live alongside them with our own identity and ply our trade as we have always done, but they will not accept that. Caesar will not accept that, I am sure.'

Erwan caught the King's eye as Rozenn concluded.

'Cousin, the Queen is an impassioned defender of our nation and I pay tribute to her resolution and insight, but I return to the point that I made earlier. What are we to do if we do not supply the corn? The boy Tribune, who is surely a deliberate insult to you and to us, was clear and we know this; they will send their army against us, no doubt to avenge our supposed insolence. We cannot win! We should take the action that best protects our position, and that is not by seeking confrontation. Let us send the corn and then seek further discussion. Maybe Caesar will not return. If we can protect our position through the summer, there is a chance that other events will draw his attention away and the threat will diminish.'

'Hmm, Jodoc, you have also been quiet, what is your view? Refuse to deal on inferior terms or be resigned to make the best of our situation?'

'My Lord, as you know, my brother is with the Legion. We drew lots amongst us to decide who must provide the hostages, so I am torn. I do not trust them. The Legate should have called for a meeting personally but sends an underling and a boy. If we concede, they will keep coming back until their "empire", perhaps very soon, absorbs us and our heritage, our nation, will be lost forever.'

He paused for a moment, and with a hint of appeal, looked towards the King.

'But my younger brother, who I have such hopes for, is with them and because I cannot see how we will overcome them completely, I am cautious of impetuous action. We have the fleet and our understanding of Ocean and all her ways and with that, I think, we have a position of strength. We should listen more and send these emissaries back with our terms before we decide on our action.'

King Mael looked around them all, nodding his head.

'Jodoc, all of you, I agree with much of what you say, but I think the Queen is right, the decisive encounter approaches, I feel it. Anyway, we will go to the hall now. Let us see if they have more to say after their period of contemplation.'

***

The men and women of the Hall of the Veneti all turned as the King and his party entered and walked to the high table and began to move towards their own places on the lower tables. The Roman group, stood apart and nervous, were ushered to theirs, some to the lower tables but Velanius and Silius to the high table.

All stood, ready to sit when the King did. As he sat, he looked to Helori, flustered and in conversation with someone who he could not see by the main door. The steward looked anxiously in the King's direction before nodding, presumably at the unseen person, and walked hurriedly to the King.

'Helori, what is it?'

'My Lord, I apologise. It is Lord Perig. He says he must speak with you immediately about something that he has learnt from his ships' master. He says that it will not wait and he must talk to you, away from the Hall and before further discussion with the Roman party.'

The steward lowered his voice for these final words and then cautiously raised his head and looked away from the King in the direction of Titus Silius. Mael looked at him and followed his gaze towards Silius, before turning his head cautiously to Quintus Velanius. The older tribune, unlike his younger colleague, noticed the King's stare and looked back guardedly. The King quickly turned to Helori.

'Very well, send him through to my rooms and ensure wine and drinks are replenished for all in the hall while I am gone. Rozenn, Erwan, will you join me please?'

As the King stood, turned and walked back out of the hall, without any explanation, shuffling and muffled conversation broke out around the tables at this highly unusual turn of events. The military Tribunes, unable to follow the conversations around them easily, despite the efforts of the translator, looked nervously towards each other.

As the King entered his private room, his brother turned to face him. 'Perig, what is it. We will be making our guests nervous. I hope there is justification for this.'

'Ample justification, I assure you. I have just concluded a discussion with Corentin, my senior master. He returns today from a short voyage to the mouth of the Liger. While the ships unloaded and took on new goods, a Pictones approached him. The Pictones, as you know, have a close relationship with the Roman occupiers. It seems this man, however, is unhappy with this. He believes the Pictones have conceded too easily and yet is party to information about their collaboration.'

'Perig, please, get to the point. Our food is waiting. What has your man heard?'

'This senior Roman, I do not know his name, arrived at the citadel of the Pictones at the full moon. Immediately, he began a discussion to agree on the use of the Pictones fleet by the Roman army. He has also brought with him a small group of shipwrights. They intend to commission a sizeable fleet, comparable to our own. He believes that it will be ready to sail and they will be on Ocean by midsummer.'

For a moment, the others in the room stared back at Perig as he stared intently back at them. Finally, the Queen gasped and sat down, looking to the far side of the room.

Perig continued, 'Brother, my King, what other conclusion can we draw but that they intend to confront us, overwhelm us, control us?'

'Yes,' Rozenn interjected, 'and all they need now is some corn, some food to see them through to the campaign season, to keep them in good shape.' She stood up again quickly, 'Before they attack us and destroy everything that we have. Oh, Mael! The decisive encounter does approach. We must stand and prepare to fight. It is our only choice!'

She walked towards the door to the hall, before turning and waiting for the King to respond, but Erwan spoke next.

'Cousin, I have argued for a balanced approach to defend our position and avoid confrontation and yet, despite our hostages and the peace we have kept, it is hard not to conclude that they have simply bought our passivity to allow them to consolidate and attack us when the season returns. I feel a fool. I am with the Queen. We must take quick and decisive action.'

Grim-faced and determined, the King looked around at them all.

'Lord Erwan, do not concern yourself. We have been too inactive and that is my fault. Now I see what we must do. If they hold hostages from us, we must hold hostages from them. That is how we would have proceeded if it had been another nation of Celtica or Armorica and how we should have proceeded from the beginning with this Crassus and his envoys. We will return to the Hall. There is work to do. Perig, prepare the guards and wait for my signal. I do not think our guests will agree to a longer stay voluntarily.'

He strode back through the door and into the Great Hall, followed by Rozenn and Erwan. He signalled to the steward.

'We will have the food now please, Helori.'

When the meal was finished, and the cups and beakers of wine and mead had been replenished, the King turned to Quintus Velanius, while those around them sat back and allowed the two men to face each other.

'So, you have considered our price and enjoyed our hospitality, what is your position? If we are to provide corn for the legion, it is essential that the hostages we gave in good faith in the autumn are returned to us. Will this happen as part of our agreement?'

The Tribune looked back at the King, around the room and then back at Mael.

'My Lord, we have come to negotiate an agreement for the supply of corn to the VIIth Legion, not to talk of hostages, which is a separate matter for discussion only by the Legatus Legionis.'

'I see, then why is the Legatus not here? I am the leader of the Veneti nation, the matter under discussion is of great importance, and yet the Legatus sends you and this boy,' he gestured over his shoulder, 'to negotiate. Surely, he mocks us?'

Murmuring and angry whispers broke out around the hall and the members of the Roman party sat alert, uncomfortably waiting to hear what the Tribune would say next.

'Honoured King, he does not. We do not seek to mock you, only to agree on terms to supply corn to the Legion. We will pay a good price for whatever you are able to provide.'

The King listened to the translation, playing with his fingers on his beaker of mead, looking into it and swirling the liquid around within.

'Hmm, and why do you want the corn? What is your real motive? Will we see your leader, Caesar the destroyer of nations, in the land of the Veneti if we do not provide it?'

Quintus Velanius took a deep breath before responding, 'My Lord, I do not know if the Pro-Consul will return to Gaul. As I have said, the role of the VIIth Legion is to keep the peace, ensure safe passage and fair trading conditions for Roman and Gaul alike. To do that effectively, the Legion must be fed.'

He looked back as resolutely as he could at the King. Mael spoke again.

'Keep the peace, yes, that's right and yet word reaches me today that Romans have arrived in the land of the Pictones, at the mouth of the Liger, and are requisitioning ships and plan to build more to sail on Ocean and against the Veneti. Do you deny it?'

Gasps rippled around the room, and cries of 'No!' and 'the bastards!' and 'respond now!'

Velanius, stared wide-eyed as the mood rapidly deteriorated. 'I know nothing of a fleet or engagement with the Pictones.'

Things were going badly wrong. He had to calm the room and then they had to leave. There would be no corn supply from the Veneti. Then, beyond the King, Titus Silius rose. The disdainful, condescending sneer on his face did not bode well. Velanius's heart sank.

'King Mael, we are emissaries of Rome. We are here to bring the benefits of our civilisation to the peoples of Gaul. The Pictones are our friends and partners and we share an interest in exploiting the Ocean and exploring it. The Veneti cannot expect to have their dominance of these waters to go unchallenged. We have come to speak to you about the supply of corn, nothing else and we offer good payment terms, but if you do not wish to deal with us, we will leave now and engage instead with those who wish to be friends of Rome.'

The King looked towards the door where Lord Perig had slipped through and stood waiting, listening to the conversation. With the slightest of nods towards him, the King then turned towards the younger Tribune.

'You are a very disrespectful young man and you either lie or you are the puppet of others who lie and wish only the diminution of the Veneti nation. You are going nowhere until we can discuss hostages and the true intentions of your fleet. Lord Perig, guards, arrest these men!'

There was uproar as the doors swung open. Some of the Roman group tried to escape, but they were held by the guards or by others in the hall.

The guards brought Titus Silius around the table, his arms firmly held behind his back. He shouted to the King above the noise around him.

'You will regret this, Barbarian, and your insolence will be your undoing in the end. Rome will not suffer abuse from the likes of you!'

The King held his hand to the translator. 'I am not interested in the words of this boy. Put them all in chains and Perig, send one of them back to Crassus. You have heard my terms – our hostages and that fleet. When they are ready to talk, they can come back, but until then we will hold hostages of our own.'

He sat down. He knew what the young Tribune had said, or the essence of it, and despite the determination of the hostage seizing, a foreboding told him that they would indeed regret it. Beneath the table, Rozenn griped his hand and he turned to her, looking for reassurance.

She smiled back at him. 'You had no choice. We have to stand and fight and know that we have done everything to protect ourselves; all we believe in has gone before and has brought us to this point. We may yet be victorious! If not, better to be glorious in defiant defeat than skulking in acquiescence. Let us proceed with belief! We are the King and Queen of the Veneti. We shall stand proud and provide leadership to our people in these difficult days; and let us regret nothing.'

He smiled warmly now.

'Yes, you are right, of course, as always. Let us retire now to our chambers and we will rest in each other's arms, ready to face tomorrow and all the challenges that it brings.'

***

Marcus Trebius Gallus stepped from behind the screen when he was confident that the Veneti emissaries had departed. He had a good understanding of the Gallic language and understood the words spoken during the meeting between the emissaries and King Brice of the Curiosolitae. Velanius and Silius were hostages it seemed and the emissaries, on behalf of King Mael of the Veneti, had urged Brice to do likewise and detain him and his party. Had they noticed the much larger Roman contingent in the Curiosolitae port of Alet he wondered? He had brought a full maniple as directed by Crassus and a fight to overwhelm and detain them would not have been undertaken lightly.

What the emissaries certainly did not know was that he and the King had word in advance of their approach. They had agreed the position that the King would take and all part of their already agreed secret pact. Help Rome to overcome the Veneti dominance of the Pretannia trade and, in return, Rome would invest in the Curiosolitae, their King and in developing the Port of Alet. The tribe and Rome together would open up Ocean commerce and force the Veneti to accept a new way of doing things. King Brice, who had been trying to compete with the Veneti for years, found the offer too tempting to resist, but it was not time yet to reveal this plan. Instead, Gallus had advised that he should agree to the Veneti request and allow the Veneti to say that the Curiosolitae supported the Maritime tribes against Crassus. He, meanwhile, would send to the Legatus to assure him, no matter what he might hear otherwise, that the Curiosolitae were not in rebellion and were ready to stand in support of Rome when the moment was right.

The King smiled at Gallus as he returned to the room.

'They wish old enmity forgotten and for us to join as "brothers" to defend our position.'

'Yes, I heard, but we both know, honoured King, they wish to protect their own position most of all, to the detriment of the Curiosolitae and all that you have achieved. The world is changing. Old certainties are fading. You have seen how our leader, Pro-Consul Caesar, has carried all before him. He will not be pleased when he learns of this and I am sure will be back in Gaul as the season returns. With Rome, you can be part of that changing world, take advantage of a new order and build your prominence in the trade with Pretannia. Stand against it and you will share the fate of the Veneti. Oblivion will be your only companion. King Brice, I think you know this is the opportunity that you have waited for.'

'Yes, Gallus, you are right and you know that I am already convinced.'

The older man's eyes sparkled as he thought of the opportunities that lay ahead.

'Will you send to Crassus? I would not like false word to reach him before your dispatch.'

'I will take leave of you now, and send to the Legatus immediately.'

***

Julius Caesar sat down at his desk in his Luca apartments, smiling as he read the note from Crassus again, sent via the fastest rider available as soon as the young commander had heard of the hostage seizure and the Veneti embassies to the other Maritime Tribes.

The Pro-Consul had prepared a response, ready for collection and dispatch that evening. His instructions were clear. Offer nothing to get the hostages back. Caesar had business to conclude and then, with good weather, he would depart, gathering fresh forces on his way.

It could not have gone better, he reflected; and now it was time to deal with the arrogant Veneti, seize control of their fleet, remove that potential threat and firmly establish his hold on Gaul and the wealth and riches that came with it. Then, well, he had another target, and in pursuit of that, he was now awaiting a first report from Gyras the Massaliot.

Rheidyrs and Gilles

At the wane of Loor Plansa

King Mawgan's messengers travelled across the land of the Dewnan, seeking volunteers to accompany Prince Artur. All sensed opportunity, young men and their fathers alike. All knew that momentous events – the chance of battle, feats of valour and repelling the invaders – beckoned. None wanted to stay behind while the sons of other lords took advantage.

Varying distance to travel meant that the rheidyrs, warriors who travelled on horseback but fought on foot, gathered gradually and now, after nearly a full passage of Loor Plansa, the Company had come together.

Casvelyn, Brengy and Gawen were the first to arrive. They were tall and thin, showing the blood influence of the Estrenyon, but kin and loyal to the King of the Dewnan, riding along The Path of Ronan to rendezvous with their new leader at the King's great hall. They were from the coastal lands beyond RunHoul, intersected by small river estuaries, the sunken valleys of former lands. Here, people lived peacefully, fishing, planting their crops and raising their animals. The Durotrages left them alone, but raids by Belgae and Curiosolitae pirates meant that all three knew how to fight and defend themselves. Gawen was their leader, tall and lithe, straight and true, like the great bow and quiver of arrows he carried across his shoulders and back, and with which he had great skill and renown.

Kea, Briec and Tremaine were from the Kernovi, distinctive men of the rugged land of metals on the road to Belerion. This was a stark place of upland rough pastures, or goons as the Kernovi called them, and sea-battered, jagged ancient rock and cliff. Men fished and dug for tin, copper and other metals and brought them across Ocean or along an ancient path to Porth Ictis, while their lords derived wealth and importance from their trade. They were small and stocky, with a weather-beaten swarthy appearance, different from the other peoples of the

Dewnan family, and saw themselves as such, aligning with the King of the Dewnan for the sake of convenience and the barrier it would create against the Estrenyons, rather than from a sense of deep loyalty. Kea stood forward for the three, as the son of the most prominent lord. Confident and assured at first sight, he hid an inner torment. His relevance had been questioned by his father. As the middle son, neither his heir nor his favoured youngest, Kea was seen as expendable and the least likely, in his father's eyes, to assist the achievement of warrior renown for the King of the Dewnan and his heir. Kea, therefore, sought a new beginning, a new lord to follow, a chance to prove his worth, and set out with a desire to do things differently in spite of his father.

In their journey to Ker Kammel, the three Kernovi rheidyrs were accompanied by Silyen, son of Keneder, Lord of the Far Isle, who was custodian of the ancient burial place of Kings, beyond the land's end, facing the Ocean and their Pretani heritage. The waters between the Far Isle and Belerion were often treacherous, allowing the spirits to take lives with impunity. Some said the island was the ancient home of Manawydan fab Llŷr, guardian of the entrance to the underworld, and that he and his kind lived, even now, beneath the waves. Still, Keneder, who lived with Ocean's ways had come to hear of the return of the Prince and sent his son to be part of his quest.

Drustan was the youngest son of Idrus, Lord of Dynasdore, and younger brother of King Mawgan. His renowned fortress commanded the country around the estuary of the river Foye, which provided an alternative to Tamara as a route south from Ker Kammel for gold and other goods and travellers from Demetae and Ériu. Idrus had close links with both the colony and Veneti in Armorica, strengthened by their joint defence and protection of the shore. Artur and Drustan had recollections of each other from childhood, and as cousin and close kin, Drustan felt the affinity of a brother with the Prince. Following his father's instructions, he had joined the warrior band to keep watch on its progress, protect the interests of Dynasdore and pursue opportunities wherever they presented themselves.

Ambros and Marrek were men of RunHoul, over which Sira Howl returned every day; a place of scattered homesteads and small settlements. Men made a living from the land and tamed wild horses for sale in the valleys below or, more profitably, panned for metals in the govers or streams that descended from the high ground, gathering finds and transporting them along the Path of Ronan to the Veneti at Ker Tamara. Once, the higher ground had held much more, had been more productive and a centre of tribal hierarchy. Now, the hills had ceased to dominate the land and, instead, the coast and valley held the power. Still, the men and women of RunHoul remembered the ancient days in story and song, the great names, Venetia, Ronan and Ailla and amongst them. Marrek, in particular, was a singer of great repute. Encouraged by Ambros he had sung them on their way as they passed along the ancient path to the gathering at Ker Kammel.

Nouran and Gourgy had travelled the furthest, from the isolated northern hills called RunIska, where the lords gave nominal allegiance to the King of the Dewnan and courted the Durotrages when it suited them, ruling their own, inaccessible lands and valleys in their own way. Not even the legendary Pretani or noble Acheans had really penetrated here and it showed in the distinctiveness of Nouran and Gourgy's appearance and dialect, which was more like that of the ordinary people and the descendants of the old Dewnan lords. They had received a messenger from the King as a demonstration that he felt them to be part of his dominion. Never being ones to miss out on an opportunity for fight and plunder, they had selected two from amongst them and sent them to join the warrior band.

Finally, Tinos, Ryol and Lancelin, were men of the Great Valley, Nanmeur, which was the heartland of the Dewnan and Pretani heritage. Here, broad Tamara – the dark river, guardian and fertility of the land – gradually built in both volume and width as small tributary acolyte rivers joined her and swelled the short flow from the strategic crossing at Ker Tamara to the Ocean's meeting at Porth Ictis. This was a land of farms, rounds and small forts, joined by narrow intricate lanes and high hedgerows, where govers passed lazily through shady woodlands of oak, elm and ash. Here, cattle and sheep grazed in lush meadow and crops grew well with the plentiful rain and warm spring and summer sunshine. Lancelin, in particular, stood out from the three, as well as the assembled Company. His dark hair and skin, darker even than the men of the tin lands, distinguished him from the rest of the group. He had the look of a trader from the distant warm lands and the gentle smile of one who felt his own worth to be significant. He was often in Ictis and had close connections with the Veneti of Menluit and Ker Tamara. He now intended to use them to his advantage, to build his position within the newly formed Company.

After breakfast, the day after Tinos, Ryol and Lancelin had arrived, Artur called the rheidyrs together, who were attended by their gilles, or attendants. Artur, who had Maedoc at his side, was visibly younger than the rest, except for Lancelin and Drustan perhaps, but he commanded their attention nonetheless with his height and slender, almost elegant frame.

'Brothers, friends, comrades, you are very welcome to Ker Kammel, my father's hall, and I am honoured that you have chosen to travel from near and far to join me in the quest that lies before me. Where it will lead I do not know, but already I have come through a great tempest to be here, fought against a determined foe and now, with your support will go to our Veneti cousins and the defence of this land, which is sacred to us all. We are a small Company, but I believe that we can be a force that will add great strength to any whose fight we join. We are rheidyrs of the Dewnan and we will fight for our land and freedom against all who try to take it from us.'

He paused for a moment for effect, and as Maedoc counselled him, held the stare of those around the room. Some nodded gently, appearing to consider what he had said. Others, expressionless, looked back at him. They expected more.

'Loor Plansa diminishes and soon Loor Tevyans will ascend. We will journey slowly and build our understanding of each other. We head for Ker Tamara and the Veneti at Menluit. There we will take discussion with Aodren and his men, understand what they know of the progress of the Roman army, hear more of their encounters with the Estrenyons and agree our next steps.'

Lancelin leant against a post smirking, looking around as the Prince spoke. Artur saw this and paused. It annoyed him.

'Lancelin, have I said something that amuses you, why do you smile in that way?'

'Oh, it is nothing Artur, only that you seem very certain of Aodren's confidence and yet,' he laughed and looked around him, 'you have never met him and only lately returned after many years away from the land of the Dewnan.'

He paused for a moment looking around the group, continuing before Artur could respond.

'Forgive me, but word is that the confidence even of your father is uncertain, would it not be better if those of us who are more experienced went ahead to prepare the ground? I am confident, despite the difficult beginnings, I can achieve a positive reception for you with the Veneti lord. He and I are closely acquainted.'

Eyebrows rose and Kea, familiar with the type of disdainful response that Lancelin was trying to deploy, stepped forward with a quizzical look.

'Young man, you seem very certain of yourself. Are you confident of Lord Aodren's special regard for you?'

Artur moved to intervene, but Maedoc held his arm as he watched the faces and body language of the others in the room.

Lancelin openly sneered before replying. 'I am from the Great Valley,' his eyes widened as he stared determinedly at Kea, 'centre of power and wealth in all the lands of the Dewnan. You are from a...' he paused for emphasis, 'peripheral region. I do not blame you for not understanding the true nature of power and influence. The Company will benefit, I assure you, from my connections.'

Briec, Tremaine and their gilles all moved their hands to their sword hilts. Kea nodded gently, looking straight at Lancelin, eyes narrowing, as he appeared to consider his words.

'Ah, yes, now I see it, you are right, we come from the land of tin, stuck out in Ocean's midst, away from this mighty seat of power and Nanmeur the land of plenty.'

He turned away, and as he did so, Lancelin turned towards the Prince again and was about to say more when Kea spun round with sword drawn, and leading with his shoulder, charged into Lancelin, knocking him backwards, scattering those who stood behind him. Swords were drawn and Lancelin's gille jumped to his feet, ready to defend his rheidyr. Before he could draw his sword, others held his arms.

Kea pressed home his advantage and forced Lancelin to the floor, bringing his sword to bear, pointing it firmly at Lancelin's chest.

'I don't know how you respond to such as provocation in your "great valley", but in my "peripheral land", the insolence that you have displayed, both to your Pryns and to me, leads to a sound beating until the young man, because make no mistake, that is all you are, learns respect and gets to know his place. I give you warning, do not cross me again, boy, or I will ensure that beating happens.'

Artur moved across the room towards them and spoke now, sternly and with authority.

'Kea, take up your sword. Lancelin get up and apologise to Kea – what hope have we of facing our enemies if we fight amongst each other?'

Kea stood back and held up his sword, Lancelin got to his feet and dusted his clothing down. His gille, arms released, moved sullenly to the side of his rheidyr. They stood together now as the whole Company looked at them, waiting for them to respond.

'Apologise Lancelin and then we can move on.' The Prince was clear and confident now in his demand.

Lancelin looked resentfully around the room and brought his eyes back to Kea. 'Not peripheral or small. I was mistaken. Forgive me.' He bowed curtly.

'Good – and, Lancelin, let me be clear on this also. I am the leader of this Company, the son of the King of the Dewnan. Aodren will see me and talk to me, and he and I will reach an agreement on how we will work together, and form an alliance that will respond to our enemies with confidence and strength, and I do not need you to prepare the way for me.'

Artur turned now and addressed the Company as a whole.

'Prepare yourselves, we ride in the morning.'

The Company looked to each other as he turned and left, several nodded openly in approval while others spoke quietly, assessing their new leader. It had been a clear statement of intent and they all knew it. Even though others were sceptical of Artur's capabilities and his age, he had handled it well and confidence was increased. The Kernovi gathered around Kea, smiling and conferring, while Tinos and Ryol met Lancelin's grim gaze, shaking their heads. As Maedoc followed the Prince out, he met Elowen coming towards him.

'He strides with purpose. Is all well?'

'Very well, with a little help from Kea and an inept attempt from Lancelin, he has just overcome his first challenge within the Company.'

She looked at the Prince as he walked away, before turning back to Maedoc. 'I have news. My Lady asks that I accompany you until his first encounter with her. I ride with you in the morning.'

Unseen, he gripped her hand and smiled warmly.

'Good! And now we really do begin.'

***

By late morning of the following day, the Company had climbed away from the broad estuary by following the river back towards its source. The horses slowed to a gentle walk on the increasing gradient and narrowing path; and rheidyr and gille joined together in a tight group, talking and laughing, moving slowly along.

Above, the sky was a mix of blue and shades of grey as shower clouds passed over. Spring had come early and Sira Howl, when not behind a cloud, warmed their backs. A canopy of yet to leaf twisted brown and gnarled branches spread above them, while larch trees with emergent early leaves mixed with the tall young ash, rowan and short round hazel bush, to form the understory. The mature trees wore necklaces of ivy that were verdant and glistening now in the restored sunlight, and the older trees and half-fallen stumps, shaped by age and winter storm, gave forth contorted boughs, creating an intricate, disorganised mix of apparent arms. Each paused and held rigid before renewing their wild dance when the travellers had passed by.

Late snowdrops and an occasional early primrose appeared at intervals. Blackthorn blossom provided regular displays of white and the pungent smell of wild garlic, with a few of its own early flowers, wafted from the riverbank. Stretching away from the path, other saplings, such as spindly horse chestnut, straggled ramblings of holly and last year's fern leaves, added to the mix creating a dense concealing undergrowth.

Birds, busy with the tasks of the new season, sang all round and when the conversation paused, the rat-tat-tat of a woodpecker came faintly through the trees, out in the crisp early spring light, looking for larvae. Through it all, the river gurgled and chuckled as it descended the valley, pausing, meandering and occasionally rushing on, showing white tips as it crossed the prominent boulders in its bed.

Maedoc and the Veneti emissaries rode at the front, beside the Prince. Drustan and Elowen followed immediately behind, and the rest of the Company fell in line after them. In their midst, Marrek quietly sang a song to the spirits of the woods, to ease their passage, while Lancelin, still disgruntled with the outcome of the previous day's encounter, lingered at the back; his gille, agitated with his rheidyr, trundled along grumpily behind him, kicking stones into the undergrowth.

Maedoc spoke to Artur. 'The path is narrow here but soon it will widen for a short while before we turn and climb to the higher ground. We make good progress, but I think we will not reach Menluit by nightfall. With your approval, we will pitch camp overnight at the old fortress of Menitriel and proceed to the Veneti in the morning…'

Before Maedoc could say any more, Drustan, assuming his pre-eminence, cut across the coxswain and joined the conversation.

'How do you find it, Artur? This land that will pledge allegiance to you… is it not one of sudden contrast?'

Artur turned and spoke to him, loud enough for others to hear his response. 'Cousin, I remind myself with every step, the contrast of landscape between rugged coast and narrow green valley such as this. Even within a day's ride, the contrast is impressive and it is easy to forget the challenges ahead, with Sira Howl warming our backs and in the company of newfound friends.'

A loud 'ha!' came from the back, and Drustan and Artur turned to see Lancelin staring ahead with a petulant scowl. The Prince, again, spoke loudly from the front, taking care not to look back.

'Lancelin, we are to be warriors in battle, brothers together. You and I will need to defend each other. Let us forget our argument and move on as companions. Tomorrow, we will enter the Great Valley, Nanmeur, and you, Tinos and Ryol will be my guides, and I look forward to that.'

Quietly, audible only to those immediately in front of him, Lancelin responded, 'The pleasure will be mine, "my Lord".'

Along the line, the Company exchanged glances. His continued petulance did not sit well with the older rheidyrs. Those who knew him said that, in a tight spot, when they all needed to be together, there was no finer fighter amongst the rheidyrs of the Dewnan. He was brave and determined, but he had another side and his protracted sulk was becoming tiresome. Gourgy and Nouran, used to plain talking, dropped back and there were harsh words at the rear. Eventually, Elowen looked back to see the two men of RunIska ride forward and Lancelin looked upright and paler than before, but all the sullenness was now gone. Nouran and Gourgy, meanwhile, looked sternly at the road ahead. No one looked at Elowen and, instead, they all looked forward, expressionless, but everyone understood and Marrek continued his song.

After a while, Marrek paused mid-verse and spoke now out of curiosity. 'Pryns Artur, Ambros and I are proud to represent the homesteads of RunHoul, but none are here from Menitriel, the ancient seat of Kings? Why is it that this part of the Dewnan land does not stand with you?'

'Marrek, we will camp there this evening. Like you, I know little of our ancestors and their lives on Menitriel, or how they shaped this land, King Ronan's people. No doubt, Lady Elowen will tell us more when we have eaten.'

Elowen said, 'The land around Menitriel is not the land it was and few people live there. We honour the spirits on Menit Nev and across the sacred land, but homesteads are few and there are no rounds as on RunHoul. It was not always so. Our ancestors built their homes and farmed in these high and windblown places, but now there are no rheidyrs of Menitriel to join the Company.'

The conversation lapsed and Marrek did not continue his song. The path narrowed again, climbing above the river on their left. Deep in the woods now, the air was still and oppressive. After a while, they approached a large outcrop of rock that struck down towards the river from the valley side. Artur spoke to Maedoc and there was firmness now in his voice after the earlier banter.

'Something is not right. I sense it. There is tension in the air, danger perhaps. Do you feel it?' His eyes calmly scrutinised the rocks, paths and trees ahead as far as he was able. 'I am always wary of confined spaces, a legacy of the memory of my mother's murder, that awful day...'

He paused and looked back through the Company, but did not explain further. Others, those closest to him, watched him intently. They had heard what he said and with hands close to their sword hilts, waited for what he would say next.

'Maedoc drop back and prepare the rest of the Company, it may be nothing, but be ready in case. I will ride ahead with Drustan.

As they came around the outcrop, a large horse-drawn van was on the path, moving slowly in front of them. The van hugged the face of the rocky outcrop, allowing just enough space on its left-hand side for the rheidyrs and gilles to pass single file above the bank that now fell away steeply, down to the river below.

Led by Artur and Drustan, they all passed in single file and most of them turned to acknowledge the driver as they did so, but he averted his eyes, keeping his head hidden beneath the hood of his cloak, presumably still on his head after the most recent shower. He managed to keep the slow-moving vehicle close to the rock face of the outcrop, and an occasional, necessary turn of the head revealed a sparkling eye and a crooked five-tooth smile within the depths of the hood.

The path remained narrow and the undergrowth was even thicker than before. It seemed to be twitching as if alive, trembling – waiting. As the sun came from behind the cloud, there was a glint beneath the fern cover. Nouran, close to the back, was loudly telling the driver to take off his hood. They were nearly all passed, Lancelin and his gille, the last to come by.

The horses whinnied nervously, sensing the growing anxiety of each rheidyr, their heads tossing as their eyes anxiously surveyed the path and the other horses around them.

Kea, looking intently at the undergrowth, called urgently, 'Artur, ahead, look out... there is something in the ferns!'

The undergrowth transformed in an instant as at least thirty armed men rose and charged the front of the Company and then, suddenly and shockingly, the van disintegrated behind them;

its path side covering was torn away and wooden sideboard kicked out. A further ten armed men, who had been packed inside, surged from it, bellowing and hurling abuse and fell upon Lancelin, sending him tumbling from his saddle down the bank. His gille, turning in amazement at the transformation, fell immediately as an advancing sword pierced his body and ran through him just below his ribcage. It was quickly withdrawn as the armed men jumped down from the cart and trampled over him while blood sprayed like a wind-blown waterfall.

All of the rheidyrs preferred to fight on foot, but the horses were hard to control and so it proved difficult to dismount. The narrowness of the path, with the Company pressed by an attack from front and rear, also made it difficult, particularly in the middle as the horses neighed and whinnied frantically. Nouran and Gourgy, however, were close to the back with their gilles and small group of retainers. Always at the ready and used to the sudden appearance of bandits in the remote valleys of RunIska, they swung swiftly off their mounts, drew swords and turned to face the attack.

'What 'ave we here? Som'un wants to spoil our walk. We'm 'ave none of that. At em boyz!'

Metal clashed and rang with metal. The path was too tight to pull the shields from their backs and too narrow to do anything but fight close-quarters. Another retainer fell, cut through his belly before Gourgy, with a swipe at his side, took one of the attackers, and as he stumbled, pushed him back on to the other attackers, briefly slowing their onslaught.

At the front, the horses panicked and reared wildly. The most experienced of the rheidyrs held on, but some, including the Prince, fell to the ground. Those who retained their seat swung down and drew their swords. Instinctively taking responsibility, they faced the attackers. Casvelyn, Gawen and their gilles, led by a shout and a call to action from Maedoc, surged ahead of the Prince. Drustan had fallen also, but was quicker to his feet as they came past him. He ran to Artur and helped him to his feet.

'Drustan, I'm fine. Come on, our first challenge!'

They drew their swords and ran to support the fight. Artur, Drustan, Casvelyn, Gawen and their gilles, all now dismounted and began to drive a wedge into the forward attackers, parrying sword thrusts and pushing. Over the din, there was a shout from above and now the assailants pushed hard into the middle of the Company, holding off the majority and slowly surrounding Artur as Casvelyn fought to defend the rear of the group.

As the undergrowth parted, Elowen swiftly turned her horse and descended to the river, meeting Lancelin as he got to his feet from his tumble down the bank. She turned to face the fight on the bank, firmly controlling her anxious, wide-eyed horse and quickly realised the danger to the Prince.

'Lancelin, with speed now, redeem yourself with the Company. Casvelyn is nearly overwhelmed and the Pryns is in great danger. Show your renowned bravery and fighting skills, help Casvelyn, retrieve the Pryns and his companions. They must get out of that maul and withdraw to the river. Quickly, Lancelin!'

He sprang back up the bank, selecting his first target and, as he reached the attackers, cut a deep slice into the target's left leg. As his opponent fell, screaming in agony, Lancelin brought his sword up and down into the rear of his torso and out through his heart. He withdrew his sword. Then, with a swift parry, took down two more, with blows to the belly and head, as his third opponent stumbled. He jumped to the side of Casvelyn and together they took out two more of the attackers. Feeling the sudden depletion in their numbers, the surrounding maul paused slightly, and as they fell back a little, a sufficient gap opened for the surrounded to break out.

'Artur! Withdraw to the river, regroup at the river!'

As he called out, he and Casvelyn attacked either side of the gap and Artur, Drustan, Gawen and Maedoc fought their way backwards until they were free, and as they did so, turned sideways and ran towards the river with the Prince and Drustan calling to all of the Company to join them. Lancelin and Casvelyn, Nouran and Gourgy, leading the defence against the attack from the van. were the last to withdraw, slashing, shouting defiance and hurling abuse. Lancelin shouted to those around him, last of all to withdraw, 'To the river, we regroup at the river!'

As he edged away from the attackers, an arrow narrowly missed his head on the right-hand side, and as he looked up to the top of the rocky outcrop, he instinctively ducked as another flew over him, through the place where his head had just been.

Now Artur shouted, 'Lancelin to me, out of his range. Come quickly – we will cover you. Gawen, your bow!'

The Prince didn't hesitate to speak. 'Inspired, well done.' He was breathing heavily as Lancelin stood before him. 'A handy man to have around!' he paused, recollecting himself, 'but I am sorry, for your gille.'

Lancelin smiled grimly and turned towards the attackers gathering on the top of the bank. As he turned, he caught Elowen's eye and nodded his acknowledgement.

The rest of the Company and the Veneti gathered around them now, also out of breath, but adrenaline was pumping and they were ready for more. They had lost three – Lancelin's gille and two retainers. This was what they wanted, expected when they left their respective homes; fighting, winning and, wherever possible, treasure and spoils to take home. They were not likely to get much of that in this encounter, but they had the better of the first skirmish and they all knew it. The quick recovery from a potentially fatal situation had given them all a fillip. With their first test passed, and everyone now ready to resume the fight, Artur took the lead.

'Right, everyone, listen, we are not caught unawares now. We face them in a fair fight and stand firm here. They will charge down the bank, of course, but our sword skill and deployed shields will match them, to repel them or take them. Are we ready?'

They all roared back their approval and turned towards their opponents, hurling abuse at the attackers and encouraging them to come at them if they felt themselves worthy!

The enemy stood at the top of the bank, also needing to catch their breath, maybe surprised that the defenders had put up a strong fight. Suddenly, there was movement amongst them and a tall, imposing individual pushed them aside as he came to the front of the group. *He must be the leader*. He was certainly not happy with them. They had not achieved the quick conclusive engagement he had intended and now his black shoulder-length hair bounced vigorously as he gave orders. He had shot at Lancelin from the rock and now directed them for their further encounter.

Artur led the baiting. 'Come on, come on! We're ready for you now, Estrenyon scum! What? Not sure you can handle a fair fight? Run home and cower if you're not up to it!'

The Company had told Artur they were Estrenyons. How had they come so far into the Dewnan lands, so close to his father's hall? He stared intently at the black-haired leader. He would probably have to fight him very soon. He was considerably older; *at least ten years*, he thought. How was he going to overcome him? Tall, well-built and much bigger than those around him, he looked strong and experienced.

Then, a small beginning of remembrance began to build in Artur's mind. Had he seen him somewhere before? As he sought for more detail in his memory, Anogin, for that was who it was, turned towards him, catching his eye with a wicked, callous smile and a rise of his eyebrows as he stared straight back at him. Suddenly, in the midst of the bravado, Artur felt afraid. A childhood memory, a feeling of impotence, it all came flooding back.

That was who he was. He was there again in the trunk, listening as his mother fought off her attackers, determinedly, but in vain. There had been shouts, an initial scuffle outside the tent, just long enough to give him instructions and for him to execute them before they burst in. They had called her horrible names, leering at her and trying to rip her clothing, coming at her like bitter, angry dogs, baiting their prey. They had tried to force her to the ground, but they had not bargained with her sword skills. It was she and not his father who had taught him his basic technique. Then, the shout from a distance. Realising they did not have long, they all piled in on her, directed by the man who stood no more than a hundred paces from him now. Artur had watched it all through the keyhole of the trunk and watched her fall. He had wanted to get out, support her, but she had told him to keep completely still, to say nothing, no matter what happened. He always did as she told him.

As she fell, her face looked towards him as he watched forlornly, his eyes full of tears. Blood oozed from her as her attackers quickly left the tent kicking her as they went. He knew she was dead, but even in her final moment, she had composed a smile for him and a warm glow from her eyes as they gently closed before him.

Artur turned to the rest of the Company, his face full of anger and fury. 'Come on, we take them right now. Start as we mean to go on. Straight at em! Come on, for the Dewnan!'

He took them slightly by surprise, but only for a moment as they shouted their determined approval and followed him up the bank. Artur had only one objective, and now it was his turn to stare manically as he charged towards Anogin. The supposedly fearless Belgae warrior, perhaps sensing that he could lose everything – all his hopes and schemes in a very brief encounter with a now clearly angry and very determined young and perhaps stronger man – withdrew behind the line of his men. Artur incensed at what he saw and that his opponent would step back from the fight, came to the first of the Belgae with such determination that he dispatched him with ease. Another of the Belgae tried to charge at him from the left. Artur's left arm carried his shield and he responded to the attack by forcing the shield strongly at his attacker, fatally knocking his opponent's balance just long enough for him to bring his sword with his right arm around the back of his opponents shield and thrust it sideways through his ribcage. The man fell before him and the rest of the Dewnan, many of them far more experienced warriors than their Prince, impressed by this sudden burst of determined action, followed his lead.

The roles were reversed now, and even though the rest of the Belgae stood firm against increasingly overwhelming odds, it was a losing battle. Three more of the original attackers fell quickly and now their original contingent was down to half its size. In the midst of the engagement, Anogin withdrew gradually from the main fight. Two more fell to the Dewnan and now it was getting desperate. When he was a sufficient distance away, he produced a crude horn, blew it and shouted an unintelligible instruction. It clearly meant something to the Belgae. They stopped, stood back, turned and ran. Several of the Dewnan retainers gave chase.

Artur stood tall and shouted out to them. 'Dewnans, stop, to me. Let them go. They have at least shown courage and followed their instructions with determination even if their leader has not.'

He dug his sword into the soft ground and rested on his hilt. As the adrenaline dwindled, he suddenly felt tired and allowed his head to fall as he caught his breath, whilst those around him dropped to the ground, lent against a convenient tree or rested on their own planted sword hilt. Maedoc, having caught his breath, was the quickest to recover.

'My Lord, I suggest that we do not linger here. I don't think they will be back, but there might be others. The gilles and I will round up the horses. Let's break free of the trees and cover of the undergrowth, get to the higher ground while the light of Sira Howl is with us, camp on Menitriel overnight and then continue to Menluit and Ker Tamara in the morning.' Maedoc looked towards Elowen as he spoke and she nodded in agreement to his proposal.

Drustan said, 'The gille is right; let us head for the high ground. If there are more of them, the old fortress of Menitriel is more defendable. I hope, however, that only a small party could have successfully penetrated so far into our lands.'

Artur lifted his head and, rallying, stood and responded. 'I hope you are right, cousin; but it seems that our Veneti friends here should not be dismissed in their assertion of the threat.'

'I have never doubted the threat, cousin. At Dynasdore, we regularly repel raids. Belgae pirates are a constant menace.'

'Nonetheless, raiders it seems still get through, but we have done well today; our first engagement and we have shown that, with only a small amount of training, we perform well together.' Artur purposefully looked around at the whole Company. 'Thank you.'

Gourgy, sitting with his back to a tree, guffawed. 'No need to thank uz, young Pryns. We'z all 'ere for ar own interests as well as that oth' Dewnan. Warriors! Know ow to fight and take on these land grabbers. Roomer says ol' Durtorage's King has succumbed to 'em, an iz their vassal. So now they probe, look for ways to push inter ar land, take ar soil; like wormz diggin', wrigglin', unseen, searching for a way through. Pull out worms as ee cum ter the surface, I zay, and feed 'em t'crows! We'm ready for 'em. They'll not overwhelm uz, not wile Gourgy and Nouran stand an' fight!'

Artur nodded and smiled as he looked at Nouran and the rest of the Company, who were staring ahead in various directions, nodding in agreement.

'I'll tell ee somat else, young Pryns. If ee continue to lead as ee did today, uze shud 'ave no doubt of our loyalty. Great courage an determination, more, if I'm 'onest than expected, at least so soon. Even young Lancelin shown 'im might be o' some use.'

He smiled wryly and several of the others laughed. For a moment, a scowl seemed to have descended on Lancelin's face.

Casvelyn put his arm around him and squeezed him in his embrace. 'You turned the fight in our favour, young friend – well done!'

Lancelin smiled also now and the Company began to get to their feet.

The retainers dug a large shallow grave hidden from the path and dragged the bodies of the fallen Belgae and covered them over with earth.

They carried the two fallen retainers and Lancelin's gille to riverside shallow graves and covered them with stones gathered by the whole Company from the riverbed and its surroundings. All stood and silently bowed to the fallen.

After this, the gilles gathered the horses and the baggage that had been scattered in the fight, preparing for the rheidyrs to resume their mount.

Maedoc quickly brought his and Artur's horse under control. The baggage was intact and he escorted their mounts over to where Elowen remained sat on her horse. Holding Artur's on a long rein, he mounted and sat next to her, watching the rest of the Company prepare to move on.

'That was close – who were they? Belgae?'

'I don't know,' she said, 'but they had a clear intention to take the Pryns and there is significance in their leader. I am not sure what, but something changed Artur's stance. He saw something in that man that none of the rest of us did. No doubt it will become clear in due course. Thankfully, there is another side to Lancelin and his reputation has been justified.'

'Hmm, I will be happier when we are free of these trees. I did not expect to fight so soon and it will sit better with me when we can see all around us more freely.'

The Prince, talking with different members of the Company, turned now and walked towards them. He smiled acknowledgement at both of them, took the reins from Maedoc and mounted his horse. As he urged the horse forward, Elowen and Maedoc fell naturally in behind and the rest of the Company followed, gradually rising out of the valley. Lancelin, the last to mount, turned his horse and faced the small cairn that covered his gille. He nodded his head by way of farewell, turned the horse again and kicked on to catch up with the rest.

A short way along the path, hidden behind a group of trees, Anogin watched them leave. His company had scattered as they ran. It did not matter. They could find their own way back. He would return to his home and find replacements. He focused on Artur. How he regretted his missed chance all those years ago, but he would kill him. If he came from her, he was evil and Anogin knew he would remove him, consign him to an appropriate fate, as he had done with his mother. This so-called Prince of the Dumnoni stood in his way. A small victory today but Anogin would get his revenge. It was for everyone's good.

***

The last of Sira Howl's devotion for another day warmed them as he rode quickly towards the horizon behind them; and Loor Plansa, diminishing for another year, rode high in the darkening sky before them. His watch was nearly done. Soon, Loor Tevyans would replace him, new and vibrant for the year.

They had climbed gradually before crossing the lower slope of Menit Nev, the hill of heaven, guardian of the ancestors, and then around her sister peak, Bron Wennyly, hill of swallows, the herald of summer and long warm days, and steadily traversed the undulating high land that brought them now to a new vantage point. A shallow narrow valley spread before them with a path that wound across to a larger hill and, in the half-light, they could see rock formations, ramparts maybe. Artur, in the lead, kicked on.

They crossed a shallow gover and climbed to the summit and Menitriel, picking their way through strewn, weathered boulders. Ahead of them, finely balanced, were large piles of flattened stone, ancient sentinels perhaps, guardians of this ancient fortress with its crumbled walls. Artur rode up and around them; huge circular pebbles, skimming stones, stacked, abandoned, but ready for deployment at any moment; or a slingshot maybe, placed ready, ammunition for firing in a battle of Giants long ago.

Artur was the first to reach the summit and arrive at Menitriel, the long-abandoned fortress of the High Kings of the Pretan. Boulders and rocks lay all around, but a collapsing perimeter wall gave an indication of the former organisation here. In the distance, in the twilight, he could just discern more hills. They looked larger, more significant than the hill he and his horse now stood on. Then, between here and there, a broad expansive valley spread into the distance, shaped by Tamara. Far more than a river; a living flowing priestess of the land, bestowing fertility, supported by her tributaries, her acolytes defining and creating Nanmeur, the Great Valley at the heart of the land of the Dewnan. She grew in substance until she entered Ocean, offering a wide but intricate opening, allowing access for those who traded on it. A sunken valley swamped in ancient days but still penetrated daily by the rise and fall of the tide, controlled by the power of Sira Howl and his twelve gille Loors, the Dewnan believed, that mixed salt with the sweet fresh water flowing from the high ground and down through the valley, a potent mix, giving life to all who lived in Nanmeur. And all of it watched over from Menitriel, where the Pretan and the Dewnan had come together to create the seat of the first great Kings, founded on an ancient weather-carved rock, thrust upwards when Mamm Norves was born. Before him, smoke rose voluminously from freshly-stoked cooking fires lit in the rounds in the near valley, and, occasionally, a glimpse of flame and fire, licking the cauldron, bringing the evening meal to the boil, and all twinkling collectively like a constellation of flickering stars brought down from the heavens to shine out from the valley floor.

With a sideways glance at Elowen, who had halted her horse a short distance behind, Maedoc rode forward alongside the Prince.

'Nanmeur, Tamara's land and heartland of your people, she who is guardian and takes from and feeds both land and Ocean,' he gestured with his right arm, 'and our road and route to the outside world; to our kin in Armorica and to the men of Gaul and then beyond to the warmer lands.'

'And yet, despite its importance, my father allocates the management of the land and benefit of its produce and resources to another tribe, to the Veneti, from across the Mor Pretani. They are our kin I know, but why not control it ourselves?' asked Artur.

'The men of the Veneti have an agreement with your father and the other Lords and pay a large due, to gather goods and source metals and other materials and to transport them to the port of Ictis.'

'At least they have not taken our land and trade through war and battle and only with our consent. But still, why not manage it ourselves and take all of the profit?'

'My Lord, if I may be so bold, it is perhaps expeditious for your father and for the Dewnan to have friends like the men of the Veneti, despite what he might say in his hall. He takes his proper share of the profit; they have strength and their connections take our metals and produce to faraway lands. They have dominated the Mor Pretani for many lives of men and that may yet be to our advantage and, of course, they are our kin. We share origins,' Maedoc said, looking around at the remnants of the citadel, 'ancestors and stories of our beginnings, our past and ancient Pretan heritage. The creeping, encroaching Estrenyons are ever-present and who can guess at their next level of treachery? They are greedy and feckless. We have seen today that they will stop at nothing in pursuit of their aims and have no respect for boundaries.' He uncharacteristically spat on the ground at the side of his horse, disgust pronounced on his face: 'And then these Romans rampage in Gaul. All the reports say they show no mercy, Artur, so I expect we will need all the friends that we can get before very much longer.'

As the rheidyrs rode up to the citadel, the gilles and retainers scouted around the outer walls and a number now followed up behind, bringing firewood. As they had left the woods, several of the Company, led by Gawen, had tracked along deer trails and managed to kill two small roe deer with bows and arrows. After fires were lit in the shelter of several of the larger standing stones and a watch set around the outer tumbled ramparts, they gathered to talk and to roast the deer. Gazing out across the valley, Marrek sang a new song of high places and his home on far RunHoul, which was just visible, still in the distance. Some reclined on their packs, removed from the horses for the night, others stood, staring into the gloom of the evening and across the high land around them, consumed by thoughts of those who had fallen. Many were simply tired and happy with a large chunk of meat to chew on.

After a while, with his song sung, Marrek spoke up. 'Lady Elowen, we talked earlier, before we were diverted. What is the song of this fortress? Why did the people leave? What happened to them?'

Elowen looked back at him, her eyes keen in the firelight. She had tied her hair up for the ride, but let it hang loose now and it tumbled around her shoulders. She stretched out her legs, threw her now clean meat bone into the midst of the fire and smoothed out her riding dress, made from a dark brown coarsely spun yarn. As she considered her response, she dislodged the last of the chewed meat by rolling her tongue around her teeth behind her closed mouth. Before she spoke, she raised her right hand and removed the last difficult piece with one of her fingers.

'Marrek, I cannot tell you everything, and there are others who know more, can "sing the whole song", but the relationship between these hills and your home on RunHoul and Nanmeur has not always been the same. Gradually, over many generations, the Dewnan have claimed their land and built their farms – but before that, an ancient forest filled the valley. Men lived on RunHoul and Menitriel, farmed the land on the higher ground and hunted for boar and deer on the edge of the great wood. The people of both hills were the same people, ancestors of the Dewnan, led by the Pretan lords – men and women with distinctive painted bodies with intricate designs that had individual meaning, who came across Ocean and built their citadel here on Menitriel. They built a road to link Menitriel to RunHoul, through the great wood, allowing safe passage from all of the dangers and strange and powerful spirits that dwelt amongst the trees. The road is still there, you will travel along it tomorrow. The men of the valley call it the Path of Ronan. The Pretan called it Sawkerdh or "safe journey".

Marrek took in what she said and then asked. 'So are we Pretan or are we Dewnan?'

'We have always called ourselves Dewnan, but the Pretan influence in us is strong. Our ancestors dwelt first at Ocean's side.

Our affinity with her, as Ocean's People, our ability to benefit from the opportunities she offers is integral to our identity, as Mamm Norves intended; but the high ground is at the heart of this sacred land. The hill of heaven, the burial chambers of our ancestors and the land here on Menitriel, and around, has been important from the earliest days. Then, when the Pretan came, they took all that had gone before and made much more of it, here on Menitriel, on RunHoul and in the hills around Belerion, while developing the ports, trade and exploring new opportunities. They came across Ocean, and like all her people, followed Sira Howl and understood Mamm Norves, her deep and intricate workings and relationships, with land, sky and water. They saw the importance of Menit Nev and its position in the land, under the great stars of the heavens: the ancestors; the sailors' star; the great mother bear; Orsa, her son, and the mighty winter warrior. They brought new and wonderful things, built great stone temples and showed our ancestors how to farm the hills well. It was a golden age and there are many stories and legends; but, in the end, the warmth of Sira Howl faded and with it the glory of the Pretan. The high land could not feed its people and gradually they cut down the ancient wood, despite Ronan's promise – and the primacy of the Pretan across all the land faded. We still refer to our Pretan identity and heritage, of course, particularly with outsiders, and we are proud to carry their blood; but the hilltop settlements broke up and the people moved away from the hills and others came to influence the Dewnan. Over many lives of men, the valley became farmland and Nanmeur emerged as we see it today. RunHoul, greater in size and higher, retains settlements but here, on Menitriel, very little remains. Yet, once, this was the greatest of them all. The seat of Kings, whose influence dominated the lands around the Mor Pretani and far beyond – all the way to the great temples of Sira Howl – that are now in the lands of the Estrenyons.'

Silyen, from the Far Island, spoke next. 'Lady Elowen, when I was a boy, I always enjoyed the story of the Golden Pretani, how they first came across Ocean's wide expanse. My friends and I would often stand looking, imagining that we were the first to sight those sails, first to encounter the Pretani Prynses! Do you know the story? Would you be able to tell it for us now?'

'I know it, of course, and am happy to tell it, if you wish to hear it.'

The Company were happy and Elowen, her face aglow in the firelight, drew up her legs, wrapped her arms around them and began.

The Golden Pretani

Long ago, far away, on Ocean's far side, there was a golden city, resplendent in Sira Howl's warm light with fine, tall buildings, streets made of stone and surrounded by good rich earth.

The Pretan, masters of the land, were expert farmers, sailors and miners of gold. They grew plentiful food, made beautiful jewellery and sailed on Ocean as she lapped their shoreline, trading with and bringing benefit to all who they met. They honoured Sira Howl and Mamm Norves, knowing that it was their guidance and grace that allowed this good and plentiful life. Every morning they gave thanks for Sira Howl's return and praised him for the gift of another good day.

Venetia was Prynses of the Pretan, daughter to the King. One evening, as Sira Howl made ready for his journey in the Underworld, a vision of a great storm came to her, so terrible it would destroy everything they had built and held dear. Wind, tumultuous rain and mighty waves would consume the city of the Pretan. Nothing would stand in the way of such a terrifying and catastrophic tempest. Venetia was afraid but knew she had to act and so went to her father and his council to persuade them of the need to leave.

It was to no avail. They had withstood many of Ocean's storms, and Sira Howl had always returned and shone his light. Why leave their homes and their lands now? Venetia, however, knew that this was no ordinary storm; the clarity of her vision had been too strong and even the prowess of the Pretan would not withstand it. Repeatedly, she tried to persuade her father, but he could not leave.

Still, he loved his daughter, and in the end, said to her, 'Venetia, take boats, Ocean-going boats, enough to carry all who will follow you, and leave these lands. If you are right, go with my blessing and the love of a father who wishes you well, always. Seek new lands and carry forward the name of the Pretan. Go towards Sira Howl. If we have wronged him in some way, assure him of our reverence and our humility in his presence. Be kind and supportive to all that you meet and be the leader of your people I know you were born to be. If you are wrong, if it was just a dream and there is no storm, come back to your father and make him smile once more.'

Eventually, the fleet was ready. The Pretan loved Venetia and a large number of them chose to follow her. The boats had stores and as much gold, silver and precious stones that her father could provide, for use wherever they might make landfall. As they left the harbour, he and his council waved them goodbye. Venetia stood and waved back until she could see him no more. As she turned away, dark clouds began to gather, which grew larger, darker and deeper as the fleet sped away, driven by the freshening wind. The wind grew stronger and powered them across the ocean, but in the place where their home had been, now on the far horizon behind them, the clouds and the darkness concentrated their intensity. Venetia thought of her father and the people of the boats, thought of those they had left behind. They would never see them again.

The fleet sailed towards Sira Howl and his returning light. At night, they followed the ancestors, the stars, and when he strode forth into the world every morning, they sang songs of praise and gave thanks for his direction and life-giving light. Finally, after many days and many nights, they sighted new land.

They came on the soft blown breeze of a summer's evening, sails tall, broad and of many colours, bulging gently, cutting through the rise and fall of the waves with the sunlight sparkling on the water. The storm had faded and they had crossed the Ocean safely. In the calm of the evening, and with land in sight, they sang a song of thanks and joy for their safe passage and escape from catastrophe.

As they approached the land, the boats formed into the shape of an arrow. Venetia and her boat led the way and she stood tall and confident in its prow, pointing the direction for the rest to follow. In honour of their safe arrival, they coloured their bodies in many shades, as was their tradition on great occasions. At landfall, the people that they met expressed wonder at the multitude of colours, like a rainbow, that spread across the sails, boats and people, leading to gold and other treasures.

They arrived at an opening in the land, where Ocean and a mighty river met, and there was a great natural harbour. Here, they built a new city, in the image of the one that they had left behind, destroyed forever by the great storm. The metalsmiths and pottery makers that sailed with their beloved Prynses, who had delivered them safely to dry land, found a new passion for life and creativity. The metalsmiths made many fine things in gold and copper, while the potters made refined and distinctive drinking cups and brought new ideas to the people of that land. They had escaped the mighty storm and lived.

At first, they settled down and built a new life, alongside the people. Already, before the arrival of the Pretan, these people had forged connections across Ocean-facing lands, trading and building relations between them. The Pretan were small in number but impressive in stature. Tall and swift of foot, they hunted with bow, arrow and dagger, and were made noble by the finery of their clothing and the intricacy of their banners. Working together they built a lasting legacy for all of Ocean's people.

Venetia fell in love with Dalian, who had crossed Ocean beside her and shared her passion for voyage and exploration. To Venetia and Dalian, a daughter, Rosina, was born who, in turn, fell in love with Artrin when she grew to womanhood. To Rosina and Artrin arrived the blessing of a son, Olian. He was his grandmother's favourite because he was clever and strong and had the look of her father.

Venetia lived a long life, longer than any before, watching over her people in their brave new world. As she lay dying, Olian brought to her Eustacia, and as she gave their union her blessing, she said this: 'Dear children, my life on Mamm Norves is nearly over and soon I will walk in the Underworld with Sira Howl. Now it is your turn. We crossed Ocean's great expanse and built a new home, but the Pretan must go further, towards Sira Howl in honour of him. You, your children and their children must do this. The spirit of adventure and exploration is within you! It makes us different, we are the leaders and we must guide the people. Go now and think of me when he rises each day, and approach your day with hope reborn.'

Olian and Eustacia had two sons, Aleman and Thurien, and as they grew to be men, they showed themselves to be of Venetia's line, and their desire to travel, explore and spread the influence of the Pretan grew.

Olian summoned them both before him and said, 'I see your restlessness. I understand you wish to find out more and explore the lands of Mamm Norves. It is in the blood of the Pretan. Venetia, your grandmother of venerable name, crossed Ocean's vastness with a mighty storm at her back towards an uncertain landfall. With our people and those that we met, we built this city from which to spread our Pretan knowledge and culture. Sira Howl has guided us and kept us warm. Now, it is your turn to take the learnings and message of the Pretan to new lands. Aleman, my first-born eldest son, go towards Sira Howl and follow the land. There are tales of high mountains and great wide rivers. Cross them! Take supporters and our finest products with you and spread all that we know as far and as wide as you can. In doing this, be sure of your mother and father's love for you. We will think of you every day and send word to let us know where you are whenever you are able, and tell us all that you have seen and the progress that you have made.'

Next, he turned to his second born son. 'Thurien, you are my son and I am proud of you, as I am of your brother, but you have the appearance of our grandmother and it warms my heart to see her likeness looking back at me through you. She loved nothing more than to sail. Take boats from the harbour, gather supporters and explore the lands that Ocean touches. The people say they are the Ocean People, and that their kin spread far to the north across lands of forests, dragons and gold to the fabled northern isles, where it is much colder. Here, so the travellers say, at midsummer, Sira Howl is unable to walk away from Mamm Norves and all that she provides. Explore these lands, spread the word of the Pretan and send word home to your mother and father of all that you have seen.

'Go now,' he said to his sons. 'Take the message of the Pretan, let all who you meet, listen and benefit from all that we have learnt. Help others to make fine clothing, pottery, metalwork and jewellery and help them to design beautiful things. Then, when it is right, let the children of Aleman and the children of Thurien come together, far from here in a sacred land, and create a place of praise for Sira Howl that embraces Mamm Norves and will give great thanks for all that they have bestowed upon us.'

In this way, Thurien and his followers sailed to the land of the Ocean Lords of Armorica with their great stone temples, bestowing new and great gifts of learning and gold on its people. Here Thurien stayed and established his own great kingdom in honour of Venetia, from which he could explore the lands that Ocean touched. Still, to this day, the Veniti, descendants of this great coming together, show their gratitude to the Prynses Venetia and all that she and her people brought, and they too are great Ocean sailors.

The influence of the Pretan spread and they established themselves as overlords in many of the lands they visited, but they took care to embrace much of what they found. After sailing the ocean lands, Thurien and his followers settled and built a great centre of learning and praise in Armorica. Thurien fell in love with Galicia and they had three children, Leyon, Ronan and Aradia.

Ronan was strong and adventurous in the line of Venetia, and when he had fully grown and reached his maturity, his father said to him, 'Ronan, your brother, has returned from the copper mines of Ériu. He has spread the word and the learning of the Pretan and our supply is secure. Leyon is my first-born son and he will inherit the land of Venetia in Armorica. You must find other ways to make your fortune and to voyage, explore and spread the knowledge of the Pretan. Go to the land of the Dewnan. We have visited their harbours, traded for copper and found gold, but there is an opportunity to do more. The abundant waters of the Mor Pretani surround it, but it is also a land of forests and hills. Take your followers and bring the benefits of the Pretani to all that you meet.'

Ronan and his Company set out, made landfall and pressed inland, guided by the Dewnan. Following the river's course, they headed through thick forest. The land rose gradually beneath them until they could see, emerging from the trees, the sacred land of the Dewnan. In front of them, resplendent in Sira Howl's late afternoon light, Menit Nev, the crown-topped hill of heaven, rose up above the sylvan land and in full view of the distant Ocean. Ronan spoke to his followers. 'This will always be our beacon. On this sacred mount, we will join with the Dewnan and venerate our ancestors as others have before and, in turn, we will be venerated by those who follow as we walk in the Underworld under the glittering stars of the heavens.'

They surveyed the land all around them and then Ronan said, 'Now, let us make camp for the night, a place where we can give thanks to Sira Howl when he returns in the morning.' Thus, they came to Menitriel. Here, the weathered and stacked stones of the citadel and scattered remains of ancient battlements told of a race of giants, who the local people believed had once walked the land.

'Let us build out from here,' Ronan said to his followers. 'I can see far and I see the land that we will use. We will build houses and farms on these hills. We will be giants once more in the lands of the Dewnan!'

Gradually, the settlement and the Pretan fortress at Menitriel were constructed. Productive farmland spread across the hills around Menitriel. They used the stone that lay all around them to construct houses, stockades, roads and the great citadel of Menitriel, seat of Ronan, Lord of the Pretan and High King in the land of the Dewnan.

The wealth and prestige of the new settlement grew. Dynasdore was the port of the Pretan in the south and Ker Kammel in the north. Traders from across the Mor Pretani and other places visited regularly. They found gold, tin and copper, and shipped them to Armorica and Ériu, and made new and wonderful things in the land of the Dewnan. Ronan had answered the challenge of his father and the reputation of the Pretan spread to distant lands and more traders and emissaries came from near and far to visit Ronan in his golden land.

The great age of the Ocean People had begun.

pRIESCESS OF Ժamapa

The Prince and Maedoc, first to wake, had said farewell to Elowen. Both had tried to persuade he to stay, to continue their journey with them, but she had refused. They would meet again soon, she said, and then ridden away to the coast. While others packed the camp behind him, Artur surveyed the valley in the clearer light of morning and so had been the first to see the approaching party and had raised the alarm in case of further Belgae attack. They had, however, approached steadily and with no obvious intent of aggression. The Company mounted, or stood to attention in support as he had called for, but no one seemed threatened or concerned. They knew more about the new arrivals, it seemed, than he did.

As they came through the old gate, the leader came forward and headed towards him, head buried deep in a hood. The rest of the party, also hooded, rode large ponies or cobs, but this rider rode a tall, sleek and very different animal. He could not remember seeing a finer horse. Deep within the hood, the leader's two eyes sparkled as they reflected the rays of the morning sun, catching his attention as the horse and rider came to a halt before him. The rider crossed the reins, lent back and reached up to pull back the hood.

Despite his days with Elowen and all he had seen and heard, he was still surprised to see a woman sitting before him. The padded jacket she wore had not clearly indicated her feminine form; and even if it had, he was expecting a man. He had presumed this was a party from a local chieftain come to meet him as he progressed into Nanmeur, and so had not looked for anything to the contrary. She shook her head, loosened her hair and organised the hood behind her. Confronted by her now obvious femininity, he had to look back to see if anyone else was surprised. Some were, but clearly, most were not. They had met her before, he quickly realised. Some even appeared to give an involuntary acknowledgement and small bow in their saddle as she pulled hair away from her face, tugged by a gentle updraft of wind.

She sat proudly and confidently on her horse, as assured as any man. Her long dark brown wavy hair tumbled now down behind her back. Her face and skin were lightly tanned and downy in places, whilst her slate blue eyes suggested firmness and warmth; the colour of the ancient rock, infused with the influence of sky and Ocean. She wore, he noted, a sword at her side.

Conscious that he was staring without talking, as well his need to show leadership, the Prince said, 'Madam, I am Artur O'Dhearg ap Mawgan, Pryns of the Dewnan.'

Before he could say any more, her eyes brightened and grew in intensity as she replied, 'Are you? Good, then I have found the man I was looking for. I felt sure you would be here this morning.'

He sensed that she knew who he was, where he was going and all that had happened since his return. And now that he actually looked at her, Artur realised that he knew her too.

'Pryns Artur, my name is Morlain, high priestess of the Dewnan and guardian of this valley and its peoples. I have come to welcome you to the land of Tamara; indeed, to welcome you back to Nanmeur because, of course, you have been here before. You have come a long way and through great difficulty. I am very pleased to see you again.'

She tilted her head slightly forward to acknowledge his arrival and Artur, feeling on surer footing now, responded.

'My Lady, I had not anticipated you riding out to meet me. I am pleased to meet you also. I assume you have had word from my father and I suppose you must also know lady Elowen?'

She smiled at him before saying, at first dismissively, 'I have heard nothing from your father, and frankly, do not expect to, but yes I do know Elowen. We are good friends and she keeps me informed of your progress.'

She looked beyond him now, at the rest of the Company and spoke again.

'Now, it is still early, have you breakfasted? You have The Path of Ronan to ride before you reach Aodren's hall. Would you welcome some refreshment before you go? Eat with us first, share bread and fruit and a little meat. My acolytes and I would be very pleased if you would join us; and perhaps Pryns Artur, you and I can talk a little more and get to know each other.'

There was an assuredness and relaxed confidence about her; she was only a few summers older than him, but it made all the difference.

'My lady, thank you. Your refreshment is most welcome.'

She continued to look intently back at him. 'Good, and Artur, may I call you Artur? Please, just call me Morlain. It is the name I have been given for my life's journey and what I would far rather you called me.'

The acolytes dismounted and removed the food and drink from their saddlebags. Artur turned and nodded to his followers and they dismounted also, beginning to take the beakers of refreshing liquor and nourishing bread and fruit that the acolytes provided.

The Prince dismounted and Maedoc, alongside him, also dismounted and stood forward.

'Lady Morlain, I am very happy to see you again. Much has happened since we met at the wax of Loor Bleydh. I would like to tell you about my journey when you are able to listen.'

She swung down from her horse with ease and stood before him. She looked him up and down and her affection was clear.

'Proud, brave Maedoc, it is me, I think, who is more pleased to see you. I have heard of your heroic and determined attempts to find the Pryns and bring him to shore. You kept going until you had no strength left and with no thought for your own rescue. You must have impressed even Ocean's spirits. I know Pryns Artur will benefit greatly from your support and insight. I hope that we can both help him and his comrades in the challenges that lie ahead.'

She clasped his arms and Artur could see, despite the age gap between them, that her attention and words of support had a strong and positive effect on his friend.

Artur walked away as priestess and gille continued to speak. Then, when she and Maedoc had finished, Morlain watched as the Prince talked to the Company, who had gathered around, enjoying the refreshments, laughing over some point of debate; boys together, and several of them, including the Prince, genuinely not much more than boys.

Was this really going to work?

Her mind wandered to that first night Artur had come ashore. She and Steren Uskis, the swift star, Prince of horses, had galloped like the wind, in vain, to reach Meliora and prevent her from over-reacting. She had comforted Elowen at the discovery of Meliora's body and urged her to complete her friend and mentor's work. She had then seen him at his worst, barely alive, before the acolytes had begun the task of reviving him, cleaning and drying him.

Later, when they had met at the foot of Menit Nev, Elowen had expressed uncertainty about his physique, as well as his likely ability to lead men into battle. He had more presence now, even if his face still looked youthful, and he was not quite mature yet. It would not be long now, though, and he certainly looked strong enough; the product of the food of his father's hall, no doubt, and the natural ability of young men to recover quickly. Tall, compared to those around him, his long flowing blond hair and blue eyes also made him distinctive, and she noted how confidently he spoke with those around him. Was this to be her companion in the fight against the coming storm? Would he be up to it? He might, with more support and a little education.

She had agreed with Elowen that, while the Company gathered, recovering his strength was of prime importance. Elowen would add a little detail to what she had already told him, but would then leave the rest to Morlain. That started today. Already, events worked against her. She walked towards Artur, and as she approached, the laughter around him paused as the men of the Company turned to look deferentially at her. The Prince also turned to her.

'I am very sorry to hear of losses so soon in the life of the Company.' She allowed a brief glance at Lancelin, before resuming her attention on Artur. 'Yes, I pressed Maedoc for an update, but you dealt with the incursion, for now at least, which is good.'

'Yes' was all that the Prince said guardedly in reply; and so she continued, 'And then a reminder of our Pretani heritage.' Her face brightened and shone. 'Something for all of us in that: a song of illustrious deeds, a reminder of the importance of the bow and the arrow in our people's story – and, of course, all that it is possible for a second son to achieve.'

Her words suffused through them all, but Marrek, Gawen and Kia, in particular, felt the warmth of her smile, and their eyes looked at hers with an acknowledging smile. Then, she breathed deeply, adopted a practical tone and said, 'Artur, may we speak, away from the Company? It is important in the coming days that you and I get to know each other. A great storm approaches.'

Artur, conscious of the reverence of those around him, nodded and followed her as she turned and walked away. The noise of discussion and laughter began again behind them as the Company continued to eat, drink and enjoy the morning sunshine. Artur and Morlain walked along a narrow path between the heather and yellow flowered gorse. She unnerved him. Morlain was perhaps three or four summers older, no more than that; not as old as Elowen, and yet was high priestess of the Dewnan. Her confidence and the reaction of his men and, most particularly, Maedoc showed that she commanded their respect, even reverence. She stopped and turned to him.

'Artur, we are old friends. In summers past, we have shared company and games, although it seems that you have forgotten this as you have grown.'

Composing herself, she turned and focussed on a hill, prominent but alone in the midst of Nanmeur, halfway to the distant RunHoul. It was a distinctive feature, this singular hill, and, with Menit Nev and the citadel of Menitriel – features wrought in the landscape and on the surface of Mamm Norves. The reference points for a natural theatre of life, this sacred land where reverence for the ancestors and spirits merged with the conduct of daily life. Morlain stood in the midst of it all, inspired by what she saw and motivated to understand, interpret and protect all those around her. She readied herself to talk to him and explain.

'Let me come straight to the point. I am an optimistic person. I look for opportunity and the positive in all that I encounter, and I like to laugh! Now, though, there are serious things to discuss, if you will listen to me. I believe that we are all on the verge of great and imminent danger. You have heard something of the growing threat already, no doubt. What do you know?'

She saw herself as his equal, that was clear. As she spoke, the movement of her mouth, the intensity of her look and something in the wholeness of her face, triggered new remembrances, from the earliest points of his memory; from his childhood, before he was sent away. Morlain had the advantage on him because she knew more and had been wrapped up in all of the events and the developing situation over a number of years, while he had been closeted in Demetae forgetting much of what had happened before. Here was a chance to respond, show that he had at least learnt something since his return. He also looked out across the valley.

'I know of the threat from the Estrenyon. That is why my Company and I have come to help Aodren and the Veneti protect our borders. The Estrenyon tribes, as we saw yesterday, threaten the heartland of the Dewnan by raid and incursion. We will help the Veneti to protect the border.'

He paused, with the briefest of glances towards her, before continuing, 'And I know of the threat from the Romans and how, even now, they winter in lands close to our kin in Armorica. All I hear suggests that they are fearsome and merciless and that no tribe in Gaul has been able to halt them.'

She looked him up and down.

'Very good, a good summary. Let us walk a little further, although we should keep in sight of our respective followers. Let us consider other important factors.'

Despite himself, he could not help being pleased with her approval. She continued, 'Artur, it is the Roman threat we should really fear and for which we must prepare,' she paused to look pointedly at him. 'We have fought the Estrenyon for countless lives of men. We could, of course, live in peace with them, but they are not to be trusted. They have proved unworthy of trust, took our ideas and sought control and dominance over us. We should be watchful and I certainly do not underplay the threat they present because their leaders are vainglorious, avaricious and will stop at nothing in pursuit of their objective. The Belgae warlords are the most recent to come across the Germani Sea, as they now call it. They have built a strong influence over the Durotrages, and their trading centre at Hengasts Fort. They have now taken much of the trade of our Veneti kin and trade instead with their Belgae kin across the Mor Pretani, the men of the Atrebates and the double-dealing Curiosolitae in Armorica. They are only interested in wealth and domination. Durotrages, Atrebates, Belgae are all names that you will hear, but they will also face the Roman threat; their kin in Gaul already have, so I think we have less, on balance, to fear from them.'

She looked at him and he nodded to indicate his attention before she continued.

'We are different and have a different origin. Our lands may not cover what they once did, but as long as we hold RunHoul, RunIska and the coastal land beyond RunHoul, and they continue with their never-ending squabbles, we are relatively safe. Moreover, Artur, despite what your father and the lords of the Dewnan think of themselves, the Estrenyon lords look upon the Dewnan as lesser men in some way. Sure, they acknowledge the zenith of the Pretan influence and its importance to their story, but they do not hold to the Pretan line any longer. As more Estrenyons, including the men from the cold lands, have crossed the sea to the land that once was ours, so their reverence towards the Pretan inheritance has slowly decreased to nothing. For them, power and prestige is found where the Germani Sea is narrow and access to the world beyond is at its easiest.'

She looked across Nanmeur. Her face was agitated as she rolled her tongue around the inside of her closed, determined mouth. Morlain breathed deeply as she composed her thoughts. Then, without warning, she snorted contemptuously before turning back and said, with great passion: 'And let them think that! We do not need or want them here. Ours is an ancient land and we an ancient people. We fight for simpler things, dignity, honour and freedom!'

Her eyes and the intensity of her stare held him to her.

'Artur, they have taken much that we hold dear. In honour of Sira Howl, our ancestors built a triumphant progress, The Path of Ronan, all the way to the great stone temples, surrounded by a land of plenty. The Estrenyons saw this and coveted it. At first, we did not know this and we trusted them, but more came and then more. Once, we were one across all of the land, Pretannia – the Ocean People, led and inspired by the sons and daughters of Venetia and Ronan, who owned all of this land as far as you can travel. But the newcomers began to take what was ours, to push us back and still they push us, insatiable in their desire to have and to control. We hold RunHoul! It shields Nanmeur. They will come no further.'

She stopped to let him take in what she had said and regain her calm and poise. He stared back at her and said nothing but her emotion and her vigour impressed him.

'However, the Romans are rolling relentlessly across Gaul. They have wintered on the borders of Armorica, threatening our Veneti kin and all that remains of the proud Pretan heritage on the other side of the Mor Pretani. Nothing has stood in their way. Some brave stands have been taken and wounds inflicted, but that only ensures retreat and a more vicious, and merciless response. The men of Gaul are paying a heavy price for defending their land and way of life.'

She paused, conscious that she might be saying too much too quickly.

'They are organised and clever to a degree that many in these lands or even the Estrenyons will not be able to understand. They have great wealth and forces at their disposal. I understand that they dominate large areas of the warm lands and can bring great resources to their armies and their campaign. An empire bent on destruction, murder and the slavery of all who dare to stand in their way. Artur, I am sorry to be so gloomy, but it seems clear that it is going to take quite an exceptional act to stop them.'

'So why are you telling me all of this? Are you saying that I have set out from my father's hall to prove myself, along with all who travel with me, only to face certain defeat and an inglorious end? From all I have seen of my father since my return, it would not surprise me if he had knowingly sent me on this fool's errand, expecting no chance of success. And why are you so intimate when it seems, in the end, there is no hope?'

Her eyes widened at this unexpected show of boyish petulance and her warm smile returned as she looked at him, before calmly saying, 'Artur, there is always hope while those of us who have brains in our head and the wit to use them, maintain the desire to stand up for what we believe in. If we live by the grace of Mamm Norves and the guiding light of Sira Howl and are determined to stand firm... My words only relay reality, which you will need to fully understand if we are to achieve anything.'

He noted the "we" as she paused before continuing: 'Also, was it not you who only recently came away from seemingly certain death because of your bravery and determination to survive? So perhaps, it is possible to overcome inevitable defeat and fight against a premature end? Artur, in the near future, the Dewnan will need a leader who has this type of determination, a leader who does not know when to give in. Could it just be that you are the right man, who has arrived when you're people need you most?'

Did he feel better for her praise? Yes, but his father was the leader of the Dewnan – and Meliora's sacrifice had saved him.

Morlain continued.

'But I'm getting ahead of myself. I am not sure exactly how it will happen, but before much longer, perhaps by Loor Golowan or Medh, the Veneti will encounter the Roman army. Because of their skill with boats, they may well make a better job of their defence than others have, particularly in waters they know so well. The Roman force comes like a boulder down a hillside, unstoppable and destroying everything as it goes. How it will fare in Ocean's embrace is still unclear. Your father, of course, has sent you to support the Veneti colonists in the valley. They and their brothers and sisters in Armorica are proud of their heritage, our shared heritage. It is hard to believe that they will simply stand by while the Roman army overwhelms them. When that happens, Aodren and his followers will go to their aid. You, who are honour bound to assist them, are going to find yourself involved too. So you see, considering the scale of the threat and what you are walking into, my recommendation for urgent preparation seems wholly appropriate, does it not? That would be the case even if we had only just met – although, actually, we haven't. This is more of a reacquaintance, I would say.'

She was irrepressible. It was almost as if she was inside him, rummaging around, trying to find something.

'Yes, perhaps it does, thank you. So how do we find out more? How will we know what is happening in Armorica? Are we receiving regular reports?'

'The Veneti come and go across the Mor Pretani. Other traders come to Tamara's mouth and occasionally venture further. Porth Ictis is alive with information. I have my contacts and Aodren, of course, will have messengers relaying information regularly. You will hear more from him and those that surround him in the coming days.'

There was a protracted pause and then she asked, 'What do you think of the Nanmeur? It is a fine sight, is it not, on a morning like this?'

'Yes it is,' he said perfunctorily and then quickly added, 'I have much to learn, I know, and quickly it seems if I am to play my part in these coming events...'

His voice trailed away and silence fell again between them.

He is worried by the thought of the challenges ahead, she realised. *Why wouldn't he be?* Simple honesty she could deal with.

She spoke again, but now with renewed confidence. 'Artur, I love the valley. I have grown up here and I think that you will grow to love it too as you become reacquainted with Tamara and the woods, fields and hills that she has forged and fashioned for us.' She smiled and raised her eyebrows in a form of appeal. 'The Dewnan fight for each other and our homeland and all that you see is at the heart of that homeland. This valley, its richness and its colour defines us and I, at least, think it is worth fighting for.'

Her eyes surveyed all that she could see, as she considered her words and noted features in the landscape and sights that were familiar to her. She turned to him, determined now.

'Artur, there is something else. The Dewnan are the chosen people of Mamm Norves. We have what we have by her good grace, guidance and protection. We do not have the arrogance and greed of Estrenyons or Romans. Sure, we need to make a living, buy and sell; there are leaders and followers amongst us, some who have more than others do, but we all fight for each other when we need to and ensure that all have the basic requirements to live. I think, and you may consider this foolish, that our belief in this is central to the defence of Nanmeur and the land of the Dewnan. Why say different when it is true? Our kin in Armorica, Venetia's people and Demetae, the descendants of the dragon slayer – the Dewnan are better people than our enemies and we must fight to protect ourselves against the corrupting influence of those who would control us and exploit what we have for their own selfish gain.'

It was worth fighting for, he could see that, even if the odds appeared to be against them.

'And then there is one other thing that marks us as different, and better than them...'

She hadn't finished.

'For many generations, and as inheritors of Venetia's legacy, we have believed in the equal importance of men and women in deciding the future of this land. We are not perfect, and some men amongst us do not enjoy a strong argument with a woman on matters they consider that they are only capable of deciding on. The prominence of women in the priesthood, in particular, makes us distinctive again and emphasises why we are different, even from our kin across the water. Your mother, most recently, and her predecessors ensured that this continued, and now I intend to do the same and ensure that it continues going forward. In honouring both Sira Howl and Mamm Norves and their life-giving strength and collective wisdom, how could we do differently? From what I hear, these Romans and certainly the Estrenyon do not agree with our tradition. They assert that women should play no part in the governing, protection and spiritual direction of their lands and should merely be adjuncts to men. They control their women and use them as commodities, all draped in jewellery and fine clothes, to buy favour with others and arrange marriages for the advantage of the male-dominated world they live in. They think this is perfectly natural and the correct order of things and use violence and force if anyone dares to challenge it. We do not do that. So again, our traditions are different and the lands that we live in, the valley, the high land and the rugged coast all encapsulate our distinctiveness. We must fight to protect it! We are a dwindling force that is pressed more and more. The Durotrages lands, for example, would rather simply concede, it seems. A future defining moment is coming, Artur. We can either take a stand to hold the flood back, or be overwhelmed and consumed. All across Gaul, this is happening, even now.'

Of course, he would fight to protect the Dewnan and their traditions, that was a given. Surely though, she was going too far. His confidence grew a little as he responded to her deliberately forthright assertion.

'Morlain, there are some things, I think, that men do better than women. We are warriors while women are spiritual, perhaps.'

She smiled at his burst of confidence. Now he was beginning to find his feet, she thought.

'You are right, of course, men fight wars,' she responded, catching and holding his gaze. 'Although,' she added, grasping her sword hilt firmly now, 'be assured I can defend myself if I need to. I am not in favour of war and fighting, but on occasion, it is unavoidable. That is the way that it is. I only assert that, in the lands of the Dewnan, where women of prominence influence our culture, our present and our future, we are all the richer and stronger for it and are not subject to the grasping, self-indulgent men of the Estrenyons and these Roman aggressors.'

Maybe she was right. There had been prominent female influences on his life who he felt great reverence towards. He looked back at her for a moment and then replied, 'So how will I and a small group of companions defeat this unstoppable force? You like to see things positively, Morlain, and I will go down fighting, of course, in defence of the Dewnan and all we stand for, but it is hard to be optimistic given the facts that you have told me so far.'

'Artur, it is not just about you or your companions, but perhaps more about how you can influence events around you and seize opportunities presented. And Artur, you will also have me. Although you may not think so now, I believe you will begin to see that as a strong advantage.'

She let him consider that point for a moment.

'And Mamm Norves, the ancestors, Tamara, the spirits of land and Ocean and her spirits, should we not appeal to them?' he replied. 'That is where you come in? Already, the Lady Meliora has sacrificed her life to ensure my safe arrival. What are we doing to seek their support?'

She looked plain-faced at him now, avoiding any comment on Meliora or her actions and continued her point further. 'Artur, we have defended our homeland through many lives of men. We have expanded and contracted the land that we have ruled and yet our homeland, the lands of the Dewnan, have always been defended and we have done that through the collective force of generations of our ancestors working for us and in defence of us. Spirits are important but, Artur, it is belief that matters: belief both in yourself and that you are not alone, belief in what you are fighting for and the desire to do the right thing to defend what we stand for. Achieve that and the spirits will be with you.' She smiled again now. 'And I will do my best to ensure that support.'

She looked across to the rest of the group.

'Look, the group is breaking up; you must go very soon. One more thing before you go: the ring that Elowen gave you... you still have it?'

He looked at her. There had been dialogue between them then, or had Elowen been acting on instructions? His hand subconsciously went to the hilt of his sword.

'Yes, of course, I do.'

'Good and you have told no one that you have it?'

'No. Are you the person who will explain why I must be so secretive?'

'Artur, unfortunately, I must go, but I will tell you more soon. We will meet again in Aodren's hall, but listen now very carefully. The power of our ancestors is in this ring and its companions. It is one of a family of four. Along with our own abilities and our desire to make change happen and to defend ourselves, they offer us hope and show that there have been others before us who have fought and defended our lands and our way of life. In these rings, they have invested their spirit and their determination to support all who come after them.'

Maedoc walked a short distance towards them and called, 'My Lord, we must move on if we are to reach Menluit before nightfall.'

Morlain looked urgently at Artur, her eyes alive and alert as she held his attention. 'And do not mention the rings in Aodren's hall, do not talk about them or intimate in any way to anyone about them. I will explain when we meet and can talk again. Will you promise me that you will say nothing?'

'I have made that promise already to Elowen and kept it. I will say nothing.'

'Thank you, we will speak again soon. Goodbye, Artur.'

'Goodbye, Morlain.'

The stranger at the crossroads

The Company came together and steadily descended from the height of Menitriel. A light breeze blew and the warmth it brought spurred on the spring in Tamara's awakening valley. The Path of Ronan led them through the contours of the land, where earthen and stone banks were imbued with the outpourings of generations of windblown, animal-spread plant life that separated the road from the surrounding fields. Here, yellow clusters of primroses were common, mixed with the occasional campion and speedwell, and along the bank tops hawthorn and bramble combined to create a dense mix of growth and a natural hedge that was yet to leaf. Within it, blackbirds busied themselves, looking for a mate and feeding on early grubs and shoots, while argumentative extended families of sparrows reasserted their territory along the hedgerow. Occasionally, overhead, tree branches interlocked. Waking from their winter slumber, branches and limbs stretched and shook in the warmth of the breeze, preparing to embrace the new season and all that it offered.

Along the Path of Ronan, the Company rode and now rounds, protected farmsteads and fortlets began to appear with increasing regularity in the productive heart of the land of the Dewnan. They paused briefly at the entrance to one such settlement, Dynas Killas, to acknowledge the sentries' challenge on the road and greet its lord, a direct descendant of the old peoples, the ancient and original Dewnan, whose fort it was. His sentries quickly informed him of their passing, and in his haste to greet the Prince and his Company, he had walked out, despite his advanced years. Surrounded by a small entourage rather than mounted on his horse, he greeted them now and the retainers brought more refreshments, which he insisted the Company took before they moved on again.

'Pryns of the Dewnan back among us, eh? Yer father's messengers announced it so and just when we needs it, young fella! Rumour wuz you wuz lost forever,' he said, trying as hard as he could to stand upright on a small stump in front of Artur.

The Company exchanged glances and half smiles as they brought their horses around behind the Prince to listen. All of them, the sons of prominent lords of the Dewnan, were of a different pedigree, but they recognised the old man for what he was.

'An weez met before when ee was a littl'un, travelin' this way with yer mother, may the spirits bless er. Ee look rather like er now yer fully grown.'

A wistful smile came across him as he slipped into a mild reverie, speaking almost dreamily. 'A fine an wise lady. Kind words an good deeds she brought to all the families of the valley. Warm arts and contentment for all she met.'

His eyes sharpened as he looked again at Artur. 'Sorely missed in these parts.'

Then, gradually, another thought occurred to him. 'Lady Morlain, iz 'er worthy 'eir mind to my way o' thinkin' – an yer mother would say the same. She gwain by early, with a cheery call for Ol' Killas, 'eadin' for the goon.'

The Prince's smile wavered for a moment, but Maedoc leaned forward saying quietly, 'He means the high ground; Kia's kin use the term goon. You will hear it said here in the valley also.'

The Lord Killas took another balancing step, and with it, a more serious stance as he felt the need for a more worldly conversation.

'But, my Pryns, these iz worryin dayz. Stories we 'ear from ar neighbours and travellers on the road. Ole Valley's alive with talk of storms an Romins and their barbarity, and 'ow it cannot be long before they come in our direction. Thank Ol' Norves for the Mor Pretani, I say. First line o'defence is it not, against all that 'appens in Gaul and Armorica – and Mamm Norves knows what beyond that. O'course,' he nodded towards Callard and Loan the Veneti emissaries, 'our Veneti friends and their boats will protect uz; so weez doubly blessed.'

He paused for a moment, staring at Artur and then hastily collected himself, looking to those that surrounded the Prince.

'And now you're 'ere, with the beginin' of a loyal, peraps elite, followin'?' he liked the sound of that. 'An' I see that young Tinos, Ryol are with you, and Lancelin; well then, there's 'ope for us yet, I think!'

Artur gave a small bow as he sat upon his horse. Killas was level with him, standing on his stump, so Artur had not dismounted, but was increasingly conscious of the need to move on.

'My Lord, I am very pleased to meet you, but we must move on; we make for Pendre, Lord Aodren's hall at Menluit. I am learning much as I go and, from all that I hear, the need to bear arms together in our defence may come sooner than we think. May I rely on your support?'

The older man, full of bluster and indignation that the question should need asking, raised himself to his fullest height and looked Artur straight in the eye. 'Killas and iz kin baint aveered of no Romin and uz 'l swing our battle swords fer yer come what may!'

His hand went to the hilt of his sword, he drew it with difficulty and made to swing it with a call of support to the Prince, but in doing so managed to totter backwards off the stump and only just kept his balance.

His men rushed to support him, but he brushed them away and steadied himself with two hands on his sword hilt. There were a few muffled giggles behind Artur, which he checked with a sharp rise of his hand, before he moved his horse forward slightly, in concern.

'Please, Lord Killas, we must preserve our strength for the fight ahead. Do not expend energy on such gestures; I do not doubt your support and I am confident that our swords will soon sing together and we will stand for all we believe in and hold dear.'

The Lord of Dynas Killas, bending over slightly, leaning on his sword, turned his head upwards and smiled at him, breathing heavily.

'I look for'ard to it, my Lord.'

And with that, they turned their horses and cantered on.

Now they entered rolling countryside; farmland with plentiful livestock and occasional crops growing. The land was cut into by small rivers and govers, acolytes of Tamara.

Settlements appeared regularly on either side of the ancient road; large roundhouses with extended families all in the one house, or groups of smaller roundhouses with linked kinfolk supporting each other, all surrounded by walls of earth and palisade fences. They formed a defence against the Estrenyons, deep within the psyche of the Dewnan, and occasional outburst of inter-family bloodletting for perceived injustices, and more functionally, the retention of livestock at the points of the year when it was necessary.

In the late afternoon, they came to the brow of a hill and an open vista before them. The land dropped gently away to a new lower level, forming a series of intimate folds, small deep-cut valleys in the landscape. Loan, one of the Veneti emissaries, explained what they saw.

'Over there, Pryns Artur. You can just see the smoke rise from my Lord Aodren's hall and then further around, amongst the dips in the land, is where the Path of Ronan crosses Tamara at the river port of Ker Tamara. It is a short ride now to my Lord's house.'

The horses descended the small hill carefully and kicked on towards their objective.

'And what is that hill, Loan? I saw it from Menitriel, I think, as it's prominent in the landscape. Is that a beacon on top of it?'

It dominated the land, reaching its height through a steady and majestic sweep upwards, causing a distinctive but gentle command of all around. As he looked, the beacon flickered and seemed to gain more substance.

'It is Marghros, sacred hill of the stallion, which is said to be the very centre of power in the land of the Dewnan.'

He allowed Artur to consider that statement before continuing.

'The building upon it, Dynas Kazak, is the sanctum of Lady Morlain, although she travels widely on her mount, Steren Uskis, to converse with the priesthood and the people. The beacon is lit when she is at home, watching over the valley and land of the Dewnan.'

The Company was straddled along the road. Rheidyrs and horses and gilles endeavoured to keep up, looking towards the hill, entranced for a moment by the flicker of the beacon. Artur thought again of his earlier encounter with Morlain; was she watching him now he wondered? It was not the height of Menitriel, but always there. Sometimes, it was briefly hidden, before always reappearing as they rode along. She had looked towards it, he now realised, as she spoke to him, for inspiration, reassurance, as a reference point perhaps.

Maedoc added to the explanation. 'My Lord, in truth, it is both a sacred hill and strategic vantage point. Pendre, Aodren's hall and Ker Tamara control the river crossing, a gathering point of goods from the wider lands of the Dewnan and beyond for shipment onward to Porth Ictis. But sacred Marghros commands the land and Ocean, the valley and high ground are all watchable from its summit.'

'Why is it called the hill of the stallion? Is there a connection to Steren Uskis?'

'I do not know exactly when or why it was given that name. The male horse is, of course, a symbol of our people and our Veneti kin and Steren Uskis, I believe, comes from a long and unbroken line of male heirs from the ancient days. Maybe it was because of them the hill was named this way.'

They descended into a small tributary valley created by Enyam, an acolyte of Tamara, and approached a crossroads, where a rider rode into view. He wore a dust-covered brown cloak, mud-splattered trousers and leather-strapped sandals. On his back was a light travelling pack and in front of him, across the horse's back, there appeared to be a fully-laden saddlebag. Rider and horse looked towards Ker Tamara. He seemed unsure and surveyed the landscape, or was lost.

Loan rode ahead of the party. 'You there, state your business.'

The horse and rider turned to reveal a man of middling age, around thirty summers old, with thick black hair and a rugged dark complexion. This was unusual in the wet and temperate land of the Dewnan, but not unprecedented. Loan and Callard were curious, but not yet concerned by the stranger's presence.

By contrast, the stranger could not help but look concerned upon seeing the group of well-armed local warriors. He responded to Loan's question quickly. He could converse in the common tongue of the Pretani, but his accent and the way that he delivered his response suggested had come some distance to be here.

'Hello, yes, hello – how fortunate you came along.'

He looked at several faces of the Company that began to position themselves and their horses around him. His first answer was important. He knew that situations could turn quickly. He had seen on his travels amongst the Celtic and Maritime tribes of Gaul how tempers could flare, converting an exchange of pleasantries into an unanticipated standoff.

'Honoured lords, I am lost. I seek Aodren's hall and the port of Ker Tamara.'

'I repeat, my friend. Who are you?'

'He 'ms a bloody foriner – you'll 'ave to speak slowly. I've heard em's a bit slow on the uptake.' Nouran's sardonic contribution sent a ripple of smiles around the Company who were staring intently at the rider before them. But the stranger understood, and despite feeling nervous inside and initially betraying his surprise, he sat upright and confident on the back of his horse.

Cautious and courteous, but undaunted he said, 'Forgive me, I am Gyras of Massalia, I have long-established links with your kin in Armorica and look for new sources of goods and materials and wish to discuss trade with Aodren.'

He had landed at Ictis that morning. The Veneti crew who had brought him had offered to arrange his passage upriver, but instead, he had been ferried across from the port to Tamara's far bank and then through a connection made there, secured a horse. The crew, loading their boat for a quick return, and others at the port had been surprised that he wanted to ride when a boat upriver was far easier. Having travelled a long way, however, he told them he now wanted to see more of the country and not to be restricted to the confines of a boat and the riverbank. They had not questioned him further and it had all been remarkably easy. If they were this compliant with him, what hope had they against a Roman legion?

Caesar had been clear: he wanted an assessment of the land that surrounded the river running inland from Ictis. A potential landing point for the Roman legions in Pretanike was what he sought.

"I need alternatives, Gyras," he had said, "more than one possible landing point, and these Veneti, supposed great sailors, place emphasis on this port, this Ictis. Even your compatriot Pytheas mentions it. I need to know more. They bring goods and materials from there. Is there a strong hinterland then that will support my legions? Does it provide entry to the rest of Pretannia?"

His plan was simple; ride inland as far as he dared to the inland port he had heard about, pick up any trade opportunities and return to Porth Ictis by boat, listening for comments and views to help with his report. Then, return to Gaul as quickly as possible and rendezvous with the Pro-Consul, wherever he and his legions were currently rampaging.

The road had been hard. In truth, it was no more than a track. More than once, he had slowed down to negotiate the deep mud and work around seemingly impassable sections. This was not promising as a route for an invading army, but then on many occasions, he had encountered similar conditions in Gaul and it did not seem to impede Caesar's progress there. A good harbour, a protectable disembarkation point and the food supply were the immediate considerations.

After the meeting with the Pro-Consul, he had proceeded to Burdigala and took passage on a boat to Gwened, citadel of the Veneti, before arriving in the third week of Fevruários. He had met again with his contact, Prince Judikael. Gyras had forgotten the vanity of the man, and how easy it was to manipulate his ego. He told him he sought new sources to strengthen the demand for Pretanike goods from around the Mesogeios, the Middle Sea, and he sought partnership with the Veneti to make the trade happen. Of course, Gyras never failed to travel with some especially fine wines in his pack, which always helped to soften any aggressive stances he encountered and eased conversation towards what he wanted.

Judikael had said to proceed to Ictis and then to Ker Tamara and Pendre, hall of the Veneti, at Menluit. Here, he was to ask for his cousin, Aodren, master of the colony and lord of the strategic crossing. To indicate his support and allow his passage, he had also provided a special gold coin, with the mark of Judikael on one side and the horse symbol of the ruling house on the reverse. All would then know that Gyras was passing through Veneti territory with his support.

It had been a difficult crossing and the skill of the Veneti crew impressed him. For all that, though, a small group of boatmen from the Curiosolitae tribe had laughed at his description of his passage when he reached Ictis on the early morning tide and queried why he had not asked them to bring him on the much shorter sea route from their home port of Alet. Only the Veneti took the longer route these days, they claimed, and the simpler route – their route – would soon dominate all trade with the island of Pretannia. He had determined to say as little as necessary and yet ask as many questions as possible. With luck, two days would cover it and then he could be on his way. He knew that Caesar, having commissioned him, would be waiting.

Maedoc pushed his horse slightly forward.

'You seem a long way from home, friend, in these troubled days? Where is Massalia exactly?'

'It is a great city, on the shores of the Mesogeios and you are right,' he smiled and bowed his head in acknowledgement, 'I am a long way from home. The men of Massalia are Greeks and traders, natural travellers and pursuers of opportunity. It is the very stuff of life! In my case, it is also the foundation of my livelihood. I said as much in my discussion with Prince Judikael only a few days ago.'

Maedoc was unconvinced but the name, as intended, meant something to the Veneti men.

'You know Lord Judikael?' said Callard.

'I do and he asked me to show this token as a mark of his support and encouragement for my journey here, and to reassure others that I met along the way.'

They all viewed the gold coin.

'Very well,' said Callard, 'you may join our party. We escort Pryns Artur of the Dewnan to a meeting with Lord Aodren. No doubt, he will be pleased to meet you both.'

Gyras bowed to Artur.

'My Lord, I am honoured.' Artur silently returned his bow. Released for the moment from the questioning of the others, the Massaliot noted the distinctiveness of the Prince. Taller than the rest, even when sat in his saddle, there was something different about him, despite his youth. Gyras observed people; it was part of his approach, his way of conducting business. He would pick out the potential decision makers, the ones who could influence the sale in his favour. The young man had presence and Gyras determined, as he brought his horse around to the rear of the group, that he would find an opportunity to talk to him and find out more about him for Caesar. But maybe also, he thought, for some future opportunity of his own.

At the front, Loan turned to Artur, who rode forward now with Maedoc. 'Pryns Artur, if we had carried on the Path of Ronan, we would have quickly come to the port and the crossing, and beyond it Dynas Dowr Tewl, the twin fort to Ker Tamara on the far bank, but now we head directly to Pendre. It was built separately, away from the twin forts by Lord Aodren's grandfather when our colony first came to Nanmeur, as a mark of our arrival in these lands, and a hall was built to match those left behind in Armorica.'

The Venetian turned to look for a moment at the Greek, who looked around him with great interest.

'It is odd,' he said quietly, 'that our new companion came by road rather than river. It's far easier to come by boat and far less likely to get lost if your only intention is to talk to Aodren.'

He gathered his reins and turned his horse, ready to follow the short road to the citadel.

'No doubt my Lord will draw the same conclusion and get to the bottom of it.'

The road rose slightly before dipping again towards the base of the hill of the stronghold of the Veneti, now clearly visible up ahead. After a short distance, they forded a small gover, ascended the hill and continued, initially through woodland. The path climbed steadily, before they came out and into open grass pasture. The broad path to the citadel dipped again as it passed across this outer area, which contained a large number of cattle and sheep, before rising more steeply to the gate of the trev of Menluit.

As they approached, Artur noted how the land dropped away on his left, a broad sweep down to a line of trees, before rising again. Beyond the line of trees, to the right, he noted a small distinctive conical-shaped hill and a low wall on top of the hill, and within it was a small building on the crest. A light, just discernible in the fading evening light, flickered in the building. He watched intently as, fleetingly, it seemed to grow in intensity. Then, before he could ask about any of these things, they had passed between two tall heavy oak gates set in the earthwork bank, topped with the palisade fencing that surrounded the trev or settlement that, in turn, surrounded Aodren's hall at

Pendre. Ahead, Loan and Callard were dismounting and talking hurriedly to several others who held their horses for them.

'Pryns Artur,' Callard said, walking back towards them, 'it seems that we have asked you to ride with speed for no good reason, except to reach our destination. Lord Aodren has been called away unexpectedly to the silver mines downriver because of a dispute with the Curiosolitae traders. They grow increasingly belligerent and we must protect our position. When he received word, he felt he should attend in person. He sends his apologies and will not be back tonight. He has asked for you to be provided with every comfort of his hall and will talk more with you tomorrow.'

Artur dismounted and stepped forward while the rest of the Company gathered around him. Maedoc stood immediately to his right with his cousin, Drustan. Gawen and Kea stood close by and slightly behind on his left, and the rest of the Company stood in close attendance. Gyras the Greek, right at the back, took in his surroundings and quietly dismounted as the other's attention turned away from him. He busied himself with his saddlebag and covertly made a mental note of the defences of the citadel.

'Callard, it is no matter and, actually, it seems that much has happened since we left Ker Kammel only yesterday morning. I am pleased that we are finally here and can rest and refresh ourselves and then discuss our future actions with Lord Aodren when he returns tomorrow.'

'Very well, please follow me. Lady Gwalian awaits the Company at Pendre. She is Lord Aodren's daughter and will host the evening in his absence.'

They walked now through the outer buildings of the trev, a mix of roundhouses and rectangular buildings nestled around the main hall, distinctive to the Armorican elite and this outpost of the Veneti tribal elders that was positioned on the brow of the hill and home to Lord Aodren's close followers, his retinue and their families. As they walked, firelight shone out of doorways and the smell of wood smoke and food cooking dominated the air. Dogs milled around and several approached the party as they walked forward, wagging their tales cautiously and sniffing at them, assessing the newcomers. One of them, braver than his companions, suddenly barked loudly, delivering a warning which was then silenced by a stern unseen voice somewhere in the increasing twilight. All of the houses had open doors and, from within them, faces and figures were discernible in the firelight. Many looked towards them and came to the door to see the newly arrived party as it passed by. As they reached the last of these houses, a tawny owl called and swooped low in the darkening sky, beginning its evening search for food.

Pendre stood apart from the other buildings, separated by a low wall built of stone on the weathered natural feature of the brow of the hill. As they approached, two large wooden doors swung open and a small group came out to meet the Company. In the darkness, they carried torches to illuminate themselves and, as they approached, Artur saw that the lead figure was a woman.

She stood and bowed before him. 'Pryns Artur, I am Gwalian, daughter of Aodren. You are very welcome to Pendre, my father's house and to Menluit, citadel of the Veneti in the land of the Dewnan.'

It was not yet two moons since his return from exile and already he had met two distinctive women. Elowen had impressed him with her calm assuredness despite his unintended provocations. Morlain, irritatingly knowledgeable and organised as she seemed to be, had nonetheless further increased his confidence in himself, even if he was still to recognise that properly. But this was different.

Gwalian's broad and encouraging smile accentuated her chestnut brown eyes, enhanced by the glow of the torches, that shone brightly in the evening air. A straight, thin and elegant nose and engagingly small but prominent ears added to the immediate appeal of her face. Her straight dark-brown hair, cascading over those ears came down to just below her shoulders and she was at least half a head below him in height. It added to her attraction. Her slender body, tightly wrapped within a simple dark-blue dress, stressed both her femininity and her confidence in herself.

He was entranced, captivated and lost for words. She was beautiful.

For a brief moment, no one said anything. Gwalian raised her eyebrows and smiled expectantly at Artur.

Lancelin, at the back of the group, coughed and Gwalian moved her eyes towards him almost indiscernibly, before returning them to Artur. Maedoc gave a prod to the Prince.

Artur collected himself quickly and bowed before her. 'Lady Gwalian, I am honoured to meet you. I returned to this land in the final days of Loor Tewedh, only Loor Plansa has kept watch since then, and yet I am constantly surprised and excited by what my homeland has to offer.'

Her eyes widened as she smiled at him, taking in his clumsy compliment. 'You and your men are very welcome here.'

She bowed again, before half turning back towards the hall and gently gesturing with her hand and low outstretched arm. 'Pryns Artur, I have come to ask you and your Company to join us at Pendre's table. I am sure you are tired and in need of refreshment. Come and sit next to me and tell me about your experiences since your return, and then let us all drink to the defeat of our enemies and the kinship and the bond between the Veneti and the Dewnan.'

She had practised this statement and prepared it as a suitable welcome. Artur stared back at her as she spoke, absorbed in her face and its movement.

'My Lady, we – I should like that very much.'

'Good! You should also meet my father's steward, Winoc. He will be prominent in the discussions in the coming days.'

As she spoke, Artur became aware of a man standing to the right and slightly behind Gwalian. He stepped forward now.

'My Lord, I am honoured to meet you. But so few of you, or are you the advanced guard for a more substantial force?'

The Prince, caught off guard by Gwalian's beauty, did not have an immediate response and, instead, hesitated before responding more strongly. 'We are fighting warriors of the Dewnan and come to offer service in whatever way we can. If more are needed, we will send to my father for additional men.'

Artur could see the steward was unconvinced by his answer and made to respond, but Gwalian cut in.

'Winoc, Pryns Artur, can I suggest we save talk of numbers and strategies until tomorrow when my father returns. Let us eat, drink and get to know each other. Come!' she looked directly at Winoc, who nodded his head in acquiescence, 'Let us escort our guests to the hall.'

Callard called from the rear of the Company. 'Lady Gwalian, before we eat, on returning with Pryns Artur and his men earlier, we also found this man, uncertain which way to proceed, at the crossroads by the woodman's huts. He says he is from the warm lands beyond the Mor Pretani and he seeks an audience with your father on trade, and carries a token from Judikael as an assurance from Gwened.'

As Gyras came forward, she looked at him intently in the torchlight. Now stern and authoritative, she was her father's daughter, of the same blood, and she spoke for him in his absence. Showing her own confidence in her ability to lead, she took steps towards the Greek. He looked nervous, with the eyes of all upon him.

'We have not seen traders from across the Mor Pretani here at Menluit for many moons. I will leave it to my father to talk to you in detail, but I hope that your intentions are true. It seems these days that nothing but bad news comes from that direction, even if you do have the mark of Judikael.'

Gyras bowed low and said, 'Lady Gwalian, I am pleased to meet you and assure you that I am here with the intention of conversing with your father on sourcing goods and produce and conducting trade through the men of the Veneti and onwards to my city of Massalia, beyond the lands of Armorica and Gaul. Lord Judikael and I have worked together before and he has endorsed my journey again because of this.'

For a moment longer, she looked intently at him before saying, 'Very well, tonight you are welcome to join us in our food and conversation. Tomorrow, my father will want to know more about your journey and why you are here, but for now...' she turned away from him towards the wider group, 'let us all move into the hall and eat.'

She turned and led them in while Gyras briefly glanced to either side to assess if there was any additional reaction from those around him. But all seemed ready to ignore Gwalian's suspicions, at least for now, and instead focused on entering the hall, eating and, if they were anything like their kin in Gaul, drinking, he reflected. His body relaxed again and he followed the rest into the hall.

Behind him, unperceived by the Greek, Maedoc had watched his reaction with interest. He was a long way from home, that was clear. Even so, why the furtive glances? Was Gwalian right to be cautious? Was he hiding something? He followed the others into the hall. No doubt Aodren would find out more when he returned.

✶✶✶

Stars, sparkling like a canopy of infinitesimal flickering lights, spread across the evening sky as Morlain and Steren Uskis galloped along the road from Dynas Kazak, house and sanctum of the high priestess, atop Marghros, the hill of the horse.

Despite the array, the road was dark and increasingly cold under the clear and open sky. Her cloak was wrapped firmly around her now and the hood covering her head kept her warm and focused. A touch of frost in the air belied the warmth of the day and she gently cajoled her companion on, his head and mane responding to and reflecting the lights of the night sky, which guided them both with speed and assuredness towards their destination. The moon had not yet risen and only the certainty of Steren Uskis' movement and his ability to see clearly in the darkness had kept them moving forward at pace.

She sensed the need for a further quick meeting. How had it really gone on Menitriel? He had seemed reticent, perhaps irritated by her conversation and the issues that she had raised. She needed to see him again and stress the urgency of preparation. War was coming, she was sure of it. Not war in the way that they were used to; everything was at stake, everything was under threat.

As the two friends approached the trev of the Veneti with Pendre at its summit, she began to see the smoke of the settlement on the crest of the hill, rising and drifting lazily into the night air. They splashed through the gover that wrapped around the base of the hill and began the initial ascent. Slowing slightly as they crossed to the main gate, she smiled inwardly at the light shining to her left in the small house that he priestess had built on the distinctive conical of rock. The house, the sanctum, had been founded it was said by the ancestors of today's Dewnan as gradually as they had occupied the land away from the road through the woods between Menitriel and RunHoul. More recently, the house had grown through the endowment of the Veneti lord and his followers and now served the spiritual needs of both the colony and surrounding farmsteads.

Cantassa, the warden of this well-endowed house, and her small group of supporting acolytes were at home and keeping the light of the fire burning and the house warm. Morlain would retire there later to rest ahead of the morning and the returning warmth of Sira Howl and her next set of challenges.

Steren Uskis slowed quickly now and drew himself up sharply as they arrived at the closed gate in the palisade wall. As her horse turned sideways, she leant down to her saddle, drew a short but sturdy staff and banged loudly on the gate.

'Who bangs on the gate? State your business.'

'Sentry, it is Morlain. Please make haste; I come to converse urgently with Lord Aodren.'

***

The hall attendants ushered Artur and Gwalian to their places at the head of the large table that dominated the far end from which they had entered. This had been cut and shaped by the first Veneti colonists from ancient oaks that stood beside Tamara, direct descendants of Orsa's mighty oaks that had once dominated the valley. The table was not perfectly concentric, but it was effectively round, and in the soft smoke-filled light, allowed the Company and their Veneti hosts to intermingle and look around at the rest of the gathering. It created a sense of equality, togetherness and imbued a shared enjoyment of the company available and the food and drink to come.

They sat on simply constructed seats. These had been derived from much smaller tree trunks or substantial branches, each cut with a high back and with wool-filled cushions sown by the women of Pendre. As soon as he had sat down, Artur turned to look at Gwalian and again took in the pleasure of her smile and large brown eyes, which looked bright and alert, despite the soft light. Ready to converse and engage.

'How do you like our table, Pryns Artur? We are very proud of it. My great-grandfather and his men created it when they first came to Nanmeur. It is distinctive and allows, we think, for a collective conversation that is more open to all.'

'I have never seen such a table before,' he smiled. 'I like it very much!'

In the days that immediately followed this first encounter, he would never tire of turning to look at her face and would struggle on many occasions not to take another look, even when his attention should have been elsewhere. Artur had had his young man's crushes in Demetae, even the odd fumble and tumble in the long grass with local girls, which had led to more than, in his naivety, he'd intended. But this was different. His desire, to be with her, to listen to her and talk to her built strongly within him; and deep down his body stirred, desirous of more, if she would allow it, if she desired it too.

The noise of conversation began to fill the room as individuals engaged with those beside them and across the table. The attendants brought wine and mead and the first of the food dishes.

'Do you drink wine, Pryns Artur?' she asked.

'I have drunk it before, but it is not something that was common amongst my mother's people in Demetae. My father, I have seen, occasionally serves it in his hall.'

'Well, try this. I think you will like it.'

She reached for a jug placed in front of her and poured a dark red liquid into two wooden goblets provided for their use.

The thickness of the wine appealed to him and its warming, relaxing effect gave him reason to pause and look at the others around the table before turning back to Gwalian.

'It is good, I can taste blackberries and maybe even plums.' He laughed suddenly at his unintended analysis of the drink.

She took a sip and held her hand to her mouth as she laughed too. 'You're right, it does. Very good! Perhaps we are wine experts in the making!' She paused for a moment before saying, 'My father's men bring it up from Porth Ictis. It is from the warm lands, beyond Armorica, no doubt brought by traders such as our friend there,' she nodded slightly in the direction of Gyras, 'and it arrives here in large storage jars that the Greek and his kin call amphora. My father always has several wines in these amphorae available to him for his table.'

She took a sideways look at him and with a conspiratorial smile said, 'Maybe later we shall try some of the others.'

It was her turn now to look around the table, turning slightly away from him as she did so, sitting upright, not slouching, and holding her poise as she surveyed the assembled guests. Her prominent, fully shaped breasts were unavoidable to a young man's gaze, while her stomach gently rose and fell as she breathed calmly, aware of his attention and considering her next move.

Others looked towards her now as she was their host and the talk quietened in anticipation of some comment from her. No doubt some of them also took in her fine looks and enjoyed a moment, waiting for her to speak.

She settled her gaze upon Gyras. 'And so, honoured visitor, what brings a man of Massalia so far from home? And what of this Roman army and its infamous General? What news have you brought from the lands beyond Armorica?'

Gyras quickly put his goblet of wine down and wiped his mouth at the mention of his home city. He had not anticipated that her first words to the table should be for him.

'My lady,' he stuttered slightly, 'I am honoured by your attention and impressed that you remember the name of my home city. These are troubled days, what would you have me tell you?'

'Of course, I remember the name of your city. Despite what you might think, we are not all ignorant of the world completely. What is it you and your Roman friends call us? Barbarians! Just because we are not like you, it does not mean that you are better and that we are worse; or is it that I am only a woman in your eyes? I understand your people believe that women are of secondary importance to men?'

Despite her slight overreaction to the traveller's words, Artur sat and watched intently. She was the host, but the way she suddenly took confident command of the discussion was impressive and only added to his admiration.

Gyras sought to calm things with his response.

'Lady Gwalian, I simply meant that I have only mentioned Massalia once before and yet you remember the name of my home city. I am not sure I would have done the same if it was you who was visiting me and, therefore, I am bound to be impressed.'

She raised an eyebrow by way of silent quizzical analysis. 'No, I'm sure you wouldn't,' she replied.

She didn't trust him. There was something in his manner and he was too eager to say the right thing.

He felt the need now to say more. 'And are we friends of the Romans? It is true that Romans are regular visitors to my city, powerful Romans, but I do not believe in taking sides. I trade and seek to buy and sell goods for the benefit of my customers and my suppliers.'

Benefiting yourself most all, she mused, looking at him, her eyes bright and keen, studying the Greek and considering his response.

'Maybe, and yet you are the first trader from beyond Armorica that we have seen since last summer, at least. Why now, when the Roman general and his army camp on our borders? Are all the trade routes open again, or have they just let you through? Do you have any additional purposes for being here, I wonder?'

Despite his nervousness and her unsettling closeness to the truth, Gyras managed to deliver an assured reply. 'None, my Lady. I am here to meet your father, as directed by the Lord Judikael, and to discuss the opportunities for building the trading link between the Veneti, the Dewnan,' he nodded in acknowledgement towards the Prince, 'and Massalia.'

Drustan, with a short nod to Artur and to Gwalian, spoke for the rest of the table. 'So, what can you tell us of the Romans? At Dynasdore each new trader from Armorica brings more news of terror and murder and an unstoppable army. Tell us, what have you seen and what have you heard?'

Gyras took a gulp of his wine as Drustan spoke and paused before answering. 'I can tell you this.' He allowed himself a short pause, building the drama. 'The General, Caesar, is a very powerful man. He does not suffer those who oppose him for long; and you are right, he and his men, his legions, have been thorough, many would say ruthless, in the way that they have removed opposition as they march across Gaul. Many have lost their lives trying to withstand the most efficient fighting force in the world.'

His eyes now drifted back towards Gwalian and to Artur.

'If you will take my advice my Lord, my Lady, you will come to terms, because nothing can stop Caesar and the power of Rome. He has great wealth and to be part of his plan and the expansion of Rome brings with it many benefits.'

Lancelin, confident in familiar surroundings, grew restless as the Greek spoke. 'Benefits? Ha! What benefits? Eradication of our people and our way of life and our complete subjugation to the will of Rome? You sound too much like an apologist for my liking. They come to plunder, murder and control.'

Heads around the table nodded in approval of his response.

He looked to Gwalian. 'Where is the Lady Morlain tonight?' He quickly looked back towards the Greek. 'If she were here, she would tell you exactly what she thought of your benefits.'

Gyras smiled politely. 'My Lord, I do not support the Roman general and his advance or advocate one way of life over another. I simply state that his campaign has swept all before it and I see little reason to doubt he will continue to advance until he has completed what he set out to achieve.'

Tension was rising around the table and while some stared grimly at the visitor others, those of the Company, turned their heads towards Artur, waiting for him, expecting him to join the discussion. As he was about to speak he felt Gwalian gently grip his leg as she stared determinedly at Gyras.

Gyras, conscious of the rising anger in the room, faced the Prince, ready for the inevitable riposte to his statement.

Artur rose purposefully and directed his words first to the Greek and then around the table. 'Gyras, you are our guest and are welcome in these lands if it is trade only that you seek; but let me tell you this, if this Caesar wishes to cross the Mor Pretani and come to the land of the Dewnan, let him. We will be ready, and before then, we will stand together with our Veneti kin to defend ourselves against his unprovoked aggression. We will rebut this attempt to force the Roman way upon us, the proud and fighting Dewnan. We do not need it and have not called for it. When you have finished here, if you pass the General on your way back to Massalia, give him that message from me, Artur O'Dhearg ap Mawgan, Pryns of the Dewnan!'

The table as one, with the exception of Gyras, rose to shout encouragement and agreement banging fists and drinking vessels on the table in support. Gyras grimaced slightly as he nodded to the Prince amidst the enthusiasm and shouts around him. He had gone far enough and his conscience was clear, he had warned of the mortal danger they were in and of their impending doom. If this boy and his followers wanted to walk towards certain death, so be it. What else could he usefully find out now, and how quickly could he then report to Caesar?

As Artur sat down, he first turned to Maedoc who nodded in agreement, 'We will not concede to this tyrant. Well said!'

He turned to Gwalian.

'You are right!' she enthused, 'Let's take these Romans on. They have had it too much their own way.' Her eyes sparkled intensely as she stared into his, 'You could be the man to turn the tide!'

***

A gap large enough for Morlain and Steren Uskis to pass through slowly appeared as the lone sentry struggled to pull open one of the two heavy oak gates that allowed visitors into Menluit. When it was clear that the horse could get through, the sentry stopped pulling and stood to acknowledge the priestess.

'My Lady, I am sorry for my hesitation. The guard is reduced tonight and Lady Gwalian entertains at Pendre.'

He gestured in the direction of the hall at the top of the trev, which, even with lanterns lit, was now lost in the last of the twilight and a mix of smoke from evening fires and mist rising from the river.

'Do not worry. I know that you have visitors. I have come to see them also. I am glad there is somebody here to let me in!'

She urged Steren Uskis forward and they continued across an open space of land before reaching the main group of houses. Here she dismounted and whispered in the horse's ear as it bowed his head towards her. She turned to walk the short distance to the hall and he walked in the opposite direction to a large stone trough, drank and then continued to an area of grass where he ate and stood to wait patiently for Morlain's return.

The light of the cooking fires still shone out through the doorways and people could now be seen within, sitting around the fires, talking and eating. A sudden cry came from one of the buildings and a young enthusiastic call preceded the appearance of a young boy in one of the doorways. No more than eight summers old, the boy paused for a moment and then ran as best he could, hindered by a limp, towards her.

She stopped and turned towards him, smiled broadly and crouched down to his height as he approached.

'Calan, how good to see you! I see your leg is on the mend. How does it feel today? Are you still in pain? Or is it getting better? Let me have a look.'

She reached down, placed both hands around his left leg below the knee and gently tested its robustness down to his foot.

'Is better, ma'am,' he replied, beaming back at her now, 'I raced my brothers today.' A momentary frown passed across his face. 'They won, but I still raced 'em. I didn't 'ave to stand and watch!' A wide grin returned to his face.

She laughed. 'Excellent and well done!'

She drew him close to her and whispered in his ear.

'Now, will you do something for me?'

The boy drew away slightly, turned and nodded his head solemnly.

'Do not run again until Loor Skovarnek is new. That is the moon for runners! Then, when I have looked at your leg again, and if all is well, you can run a little each day. Do you understand? Let your leg build its strength gradually.'

Her eyes narrowed as she entrusted him with her plan. 'You and I will work on this together and in only a few passages of the moon, you will be able to race your brothers properly and you will win!' She looked deeply into his eyes. 'Will you promise me?'

For a moment, captured by her attention, he did not reply and then, with a serious and solemn face, answered, 'Yes, my lady.'

Her eyes opened wide as she grinned back at him, 'Good!'

'Calan, come on now. Leave Lady Morlain alone; she was on her way to the hall.'

The boy's mother approached them.

'My lady, he is on the mend, you see; and I heard what you said to him. He will take it steady until his leg strengthens. We are so grateful for everything you have done.' For a moment, her voice betrayed her emotion, 'We thought he would not walk again.'

'It was my pleasure,' Morlain smiled at the older woman and then down at the boy. 'Young boys are meant to run! I am glad to help. However, you are right; I must go. It was good to see you both, we will talk again soon.'

She clasped the mother's arm gently, smiling at her and softly tweaked the boy's cheek before turning away and setting off again towards the hall.

***

The excitement in the room following the Prince's defiance slowly subsided and as everyone's heads turned to the Greek for any further response, Maedoc spoke for the group.

'Tell us more of this man Caesar. What motivates him? What does he really want? To dominate our trade, through you and others like you, perhaps?'

Gyras recognised the distrust within Maedoc's question. He was about to answer when one of the large wooden doors at the far end of the hall was swung open by hall attendants and Morlain entered.

Lancelin stood as she approached. 'Lady Morlain you are here, come and join our discussion. We have looked for your arrival from Dynas Kazak all evening. Our visitor tells us that we must submit to these Romans. He says it is our only chance of survival. What do you think about that?'

Morlain walked to the table and took the remaining space directly opposite to where Artur and Gwalian sat. With a slight nod of the head, she acknowledged them both and allowed her eyes to linger longer on Artur. He saw it but looked away towards Gwalian, who smiled confidently back at Morlain.

'Lady Morlain, you are very welcome. Please, take a seat. The attendants will bring you refreshment.'

With a perfunctory smile and a mild sense of unease, which had nothing to do with talk of the Roman threat, Morlain nodded to Gwalian and sat down. The table watched her take a small sip of wine and waited for her to speak. She replaced the beaker on the table and turned to Gyras.

'We have not been introduced. My name is Morlain, priestess of the Dewnan. You have encountered the Legions? Total domination is their objective, I believe. Would you agree?'

'Madam, my name is Gyras of Massalia. I believe control is their objective – control of trade and all who conduct it,' he shot a quick look at Maedoc, 'and of the resources of all of the lands that they enter. They do not like opposition or disagreement with their purpose and I have said to your friends here that it might be advisable to enter discussion with them rather than oppose them.' He looked guardedly around the table. 'But I say this only by way of observation, based on what I have seen, rather than arguing for their cause.'

She nodded her head and looked around the table. Lancelin again caught her gaze.

'And we have said we must fight and take the fight to them.' He appealed to her, 'Surely that is the way to deal with this threat?'

She looked at him for a moment, considering what he had said, before turning towards Artur. 'And what does the Pryns of the Dewnan think?'

Artur looked around the table and then back again, concentrating strongly and purposefully upon her.

'I think we are the fighting Dewnan, and with our Veneti brothers, we must make a stand and repulse these people. Yes! I think we should take the fight to them. We are proud and brave warriors, inheritors of the Great Pretani, and we will show these people they are mistaken if they think they can treat us with contempt.'

He forms opinions quickly, she thought. For a man who was uncertain so recently, his purpose seems clear, even if it is misguided. Has he drunk too much wine? Or is there a more positive force at work on him? She looked at Gwalian, who looked back, awaiting her response.

Murmurs of approval spread again around the table at Artur's words. Morlain, with the slightest rise of one eyebrow, continued, 'You are right, of course. We have to stand and fight for what we believe in. However, from what I have heard, our visitor is correct when he says that we should not, in any way, take these people lightly. They are efficient and ruthless. Provoking a fight, unless we are confident we will win, would be foolish.'

Gyras nodded in approval.

'You speak the truth, madam. I counsel you and everybody around this table. Do not underestimate them,' he looked around the whole table, 'and you do not want to be on the losing side. Their retribution for your opposition will be swift and brutal.'

Gwalian now rose to her feet.

'Honoured priestess, thank you for your words of advice and caution, but I think I might make a reasonable guess at my father's response, if he were here. We are the Veneti, great Ocean sailors. Our fleet outstrips that of all other nations and tribes of Gaul and Armorica and even here in the lands of the Dewnan and in Ériu.' She guffawed in a confident way, 'We are not going to sue for peace and conciliation with these people on their terms! We will converse with them as equals. We do not want war, but we will come to terms in a way that works for all. And if they refuse, we will fight them all the way, alongside our brothers and sisters in the Dewnan!'

Again, all around the table were on their feet, led by Artur now, shouting their approval. Gwalian turned to Artur and smiled and he smiled back.

'Well said!' he declared 'I couldn't agree more!' He raised his beaker and turned to the table. 'To the Dewnan and the Veneti, brothers,' he turned back towards Gwalian, 'and sisters! Together we will defend our lands and people and confound our enemies!'

Morlain remained seated as more cheering and banging on the table followed. She looked towards the Greek trader, who remained seated also, smiling politely rather than enthusiastically at this outpouring of assertion and confidence. He alone amongst them, she recognised, realised the complete folly of their wine and mead stimulated exuberance. Then she looked towards Lancelin, who sat down before the rest and looked unusually subdued. Was he disappointed with what she had said? Had he expected her to give a rousing response like Gwalian… or was it something else? Yes, of course, the unintended consequence of his folly, which in his arrogance he would not have anticipated, was laid out now before him. Well, maybe he would learn a lesson, but then, she reflected he was the type of man who probably would not and his natural conceit no doubt would return sooner than it should.

A spit-roasted wild boar, cooked in an adjacent small room, now entered the hall and was served to the table by the hall's attendants. With flagons, goblets and beakers replenished, the evening continued with lively discussion and debate, with the majority of those seated around the table increasingly intoxicated by the wine and sense of togetherness that the roundtable engendered.

With the last of the food eaten and several more beakers of wine consumed, Gwalian stretched backwards into her seat, allowing her dress, in turn, to stretch tightly across her body, fully emphasising its contours and allowing Artur a final, inescapable, but very enjoyable view of her wholeness, beauty and, he quickly decided, perfection.

She then sat normally in her chair and stifled a yawn.

'My Lord, I feel tired; it has been a full day! My family and our attendants sleep in one of the nearby roundhouses. I will retire soon, but I look forward to talking to you more in the morning. How well do you know Ker Tamara? I would be very pleased to show you around.'

'Please, Gwalian, may I call you that? Call me Artur. I may have visited in my childhood, but I do not recall it. I would be very pleased to be shown around.'

She smiled gently back at him.

'Good and, yes, you may call me Gwalian, and I shall call you Artur.'

She stared at him for a moment, as if expecting him to say more. Instead, he just smiled back before allowing his gaze to wander around the table. Several conversations continued, but the Company and others were already looking weary or asleep at their place, a combination of tiredness and the wine causing them to fade quickly as the evening concluded.

As he looked towards Morlain, her conversation ended and she turned to him, holding his gaze for a moment before rising to her feet and saying, 'Lady Gwalian, I will spend the night with Cantassa and her acolytes. Thank you for your hospitality. No doubt we will talk again soon.'

They both watched her leave and as the doors of the hall closed behind her, Artur turned towards Gwalian. 'We met earlier. She has much to say, is clear of her opinion and seems desirous of directing my men and me in a course of action of her choosing.'

'Yes,' she smiled again at Artur, 'she has a very clear view on what path we should follow. She and my father have had several strong arguments recently as their opinions have differed. Do not underestimate her, Artur; she is clever. My father is a strong and clever man too and I am very proud to be his daughter, but occasionally, even I feel he argues with her simply because he does not like it that a woman half his age is as clever as he is and is not afraid to stand up and give her opinion clearly and strongly.'

'Hmm, maybe, but I think her caution was challenged strongly tonight, and from what you have said, your father would have led that challenge had he been here. She will go away tonight and consider that I am sure and realise that others also feel strongly about what is the correct course of action.'

She looked back at him in a way that he could not quite read – a smile that had something else within it. 'Yes, I'm sure you are right, but she will rest now and no doubt Cantassa and her acolytes will help her to relax.' Her eyes widened slightly as she said, 'And she will return tomorrow, or in the days to come, with renewed purpose.' Gwalian paused again before saying, 'She is on our side, Artur, even if we don't always agree with her.'

She reached for her goblet and drank the remaining small amount of wine within it, before placing it back with purpose on the table.

'But now I am tired and will retire. Will you and your men be happy to sleep in here? The fire will keep you all warm for a good part of the night, I think, and the hall servants will stoke it again at first light. I see our visitor has already chosen a spot nearer to the warmth!'

She looked across to Gyras, rolled up in a blanket close to the fire, and laughed before rising and bowing gently to Artur. He, in turn, jumped to his feet.

'Yes, yes, we will be fine, of course.' He continued eagerly, 'We will talk more in the morning.'

She smiled warmly back at him.

'Goodnight.'

***

Morlain lay on her front on a large feather mattress with her head turned to its right on a pillow of soft leather filled with duck down. Beside her, with her head turned towards the high priestess, lay Cantassa, priestess of the house. Both had their eyes closed as the acolytes rubbed warm soothing oils, infused with lavender, rose and chamomile into their backs and shoulders. A late evening fire at the centre of the room cast lazy shadows across the conical roof of the roundhouse, occasionally lighting their increasingly relaxed and still faces, which was interrupted only by the odd wince as the acolytes surrounding them found a tender spot, on the shoulder or back.

Morlain was in need of it more. An exhausting day, both in the saddle and in debate, had taken its toll, even for a young woman in her prime. So as soon as she was in the house, away from watching eyes, and her need for performance and presentation was over, she had collapsed. Cantassa, friend and confidant had immediately called for assistance to support the high priestess to the large bed at the far end of the house. Older than Morlain by about three or four winters, the priestess of the house had been her friend and informal advisor from a very early age, providing not only good guidance, but also laughter and intimacy when the strain of her vocation needed soothing.

The young acolytes had washed the extensive dust of the day from her body and then laid her gently on her front before selecting a mixture of balms and oils to relax and prepare her for sleep, providing the recuperation she needed from the exertions of the day. Cantassa, who was never one to miss a good massage, had joined her on the bed to take advantage of both the relaxing oils and tender, restorative hands. She was also there to provide a listening ear and supportive voice to her friend at the end of what had clearly been a difficult day.

'He seemed a bit dismissive of my support. That is what I don't understand. Even newly returned from exile, he must understand our danger... he said as much at Menitriel.' Morlain spoke quietly; her eyes still closed, as the oil and manipulative fingers stretched and soothed her body.

'Morlain, my dear, you are so sensible and, of course, in many ways wise beyond your years, so why would you think that this would be easy?'

Cantassa exhaled gently in contentment at a particularly satisfying application of pressure below her right shoulder blade.

'You have been blessed, my dear; many follow your lead, crave your advice and look to your skills. They love you for your wisdom and your kindness. However, they have had many moons, many seasons with you while he has been away for the formative years of his childhood and forgotten much, so do not be surprised by his reluctance to be intimate after only a day of conversation. I might venture it is unreasonable to expect it.'

'Maybe,' Morlain replied, pausing to consider while she shifted slightly to allow further attention to the lower left side of her back. 'He seems much taken with Gwalian, though. How can I gain his attention, talk to him, if he only has eyes for her?'

'You can't, not straight away; you must be patient, wait for your chance. It will come. I have nothing against Gwalian; she is strong and determined, like her father, and she is, we must acknowledge, a fine-looking woman who has turned many heads before, but she does not have your insight, your knowledge and skills. She cannot see as we can see. Wait and watch, Morlain. It is only the beginning. Your life's work starts in earnest today, but it will not finish today.' She paused for a moment, 'He will also, of course, come to realise that there is more than one fine-looking woman in this world who wants to help him achieve his destiny.'

She opened her eyes and smiled softly at Morlain, who lay looking back at her, but with her thoughts elsewhere. Morlain looked into her friend's eyes, registering her final comment and laughed softly.

'I have advantages, Cantassa, but I think she is the prettier one.'

'Dearest, I disagree and you and I have kept each other warm for all these years; but if he is the one for you, you must also be gentle with him. Do not seek to dominate him straight away, be too commanding or too assured of the correct path to take. If he is his father's son, you know he will resent that, even if he is also his blessed mother's son. I know that trouble and conflict quickly approach, but they are not here yet. Build his trust gradually. You and he will be the stronger for it in the end, I am convinced of it... and only when that is achieved can I contemplate properly giving you up to him.'

The acolytes completed the massage, collected their oil bowls and stood back from the bed, before giving a gentle bow and retreating into the dark of the opposite side of the house.

Cantassa raised herself on to her right arm and allowed her long blonde hair, arranged around her head to enable the massage, to tumble down across the top half of her body.

'Sweetest, it is late and there is much to do in the morning. No more discussion now; let us pull the covers over us and rest,' she leant down as she said this and kissed Morlain gently on her lips and then on her forehead as she turned onto her back. The fire had all but died away now and the house was quiet as the two friends drew close, keeping warm underneath the covers. Morlain returned the kiss and softly caressed her friend, who held her close, their bodies gently touching each other. For a moment, Cantassa released her embrace. Morlain lay back down on the bed, and within an instant, fell into a deep and restful sleep.

the lord of the crossing

The boat pulled through the inflow of Enyam before the oars that propelled it rose on instruction and its prow touched gently on the wooden jetty running along the riverbank. The boat had no cargo, except its human passengers. Against a strong current, it was not possible to row a heavily-laden boat upstream, beyond the tidal reaches, for most of the year. The inland port below the citadel of Ker Tamara was, therefore, a collection and loading point to take goods to Ictis, downstream. Here, above the furthest reaches of Ocean's momentum and penetration, Tamara remained constrained and powerful, cutting through the land, creating narrow, low gorges and wriggling like a giant serpent, constantly changing direction from her source on a remote empty heathland.

At the inland port, the Path of Ronan traverses Tamara, the first crossing, bestowed by Orsa in the ancient days, who was sent down by the Mother Bear to tell of the bounty of Mamm Norves, a sacred and strategic crossing that gave both control and profit from the flow of goods downstream. The Veneti colony controlled these shipments and defended Tamara as a route way to Ocean and from incursion and attack.

There was a light breeze, and in the early spring sunshine, she was full, but benign, flowing gently, making the job of the rowers a comparatively easy one. In winter, after sustained rain or melting snows, her strength of flow reached such a peak that nothing could row against her. Then, everything stopped. The boats were secured and the people of the Nanmeur retreated to their houses, kept their fires well fed and waited for the waters to subside.

As the boat touched the landing stage, the front man jumped from to the jetty with rope in hand and swiftly wound it around a post that rose above the cut timber walkway. He ran parallel to the boat and caught the thrown rear-holding rope. As he hauled the rear end towards the bank, others jumped ashore and helped secure the boat.

In the middle of the boat, Aodren, Lord of the Veneti and the Crossing, stood watching impassively as the crew did their work. Once secured, they all stood back and allowed him to step from the boat to the bank followed by his small retinue. Winoc, standing anxiously on the bankside, came forward to meet him.

'My Lord, we are glad of your return. I hope you found resolution at the silver mines?'

'Winoc, yes – thank you. Although only temporary, I think. We have sent them away for now, but they will be back, I am sure.'

A moment of weariness appeared to overcome him and Winoc paused before continuing. 'The young Pryns of the Dewnan has arrived, as anticipated. Lady Gwalian hosted him and his Company last evening and this morning she will show him Menluit and Ker Tamara. He is aware that you had a pressing need yesterday, as you instructed.'

'Good, Winoc. Thank you.'

Aodren cut in as his steward drew breath. His poise now fully recovered, he was eager to make up for his lost evening.

'I will walk up the hill to Ker Tamara; no doubt I will find them all up there. Where have we stationed his men? They can pitch tents, of course, in the pasture lands below Pendre and the trev.'

'My Lord, I think…'

Winoc, faltering and nervous of imparting the news of the actual size of the Company, did not have the chance to say more. Aodren had climbed the ladder that gave access to the top of the bank and disappeared beyond it, followed by his retinue.

He walked quickly through the trees and along the path that ran beside the river, which was surrounded by the first signs of spring and suffused in a pungent carpet of wild garlic. After a short distance, it gave way to an open area at the base of the hill of Ker Tamara. Here, there were riverside houses and buildings associated with the port, holding pens and storage for goods for onward transportation, all built on slightly higher ground away from Tamara and her immediate narrow floodplain. Now, however, Aodren turned away from the port and at a great pace, with his followers struggling to keep up, as he walked up the hill towards the ancient river fort of Ker Tamara.

Winoc watched him go, sighed and followed after them, preparing himself for the inevitable reaction.

***

Morlain sat against the base of the tree. Had he seen her? She thought not; it was too far for him, even though he had looked in her direction. If she had stood, he might have recognised her, but not if she sat like this.

She had prepared for this since her elevation to high priestess. It was part of the legacy she had received and the promise as a young acolyte she had made to his mother, before that fateful day. She had instigated his return, worked with her fellow priestesses to ensure that he arrived safely. Yet here she was watching him covertly across the gap that divided Cantassa's house from Menluit, rather than talking to him and planning for the challenges ahead.

It all felt a bit deflating.

Cantassa was right, of course; to expect everything to be right on their first meeting was unrealistic. She had just expected, because they had known each other in childhood, although he now claimed to have forgotten, that he would be easier to talk to, more ready to talk to her. That was all.

Now he turned away from her and sat down, clearly deep in thought. As she watched on, considering how to reach out to him, engage him, Gwalian walked down from the trev towards him. As she approached, he turned around and jumped up to greet her.

Wrapped in each other's presence, neither of them noticed Morlain stand up and walk back to the house.

***

He knew she was watching him.

Artur had seen her fleetingly as he walked down from Pendre. Even though he could not see her face, she had appeared to duck down as he looked towards her. He knew it was her, even at this distance. It might have been a chance observation while she was out for some morning air, but even here she was trying to control – and what was the purpose of her watching him?

Did she have everything planned? He knew his attitude towards her was irrational. He was the King of the Dewnan's heir and she was the high priestess; he should talk to her as she had suggested at their meeting at Menitriel. He sat down and gazed across the grazing pasture that surrounded Menluit. Elowen and Morlain had spoken of the importance of his return and he wanted to discuss that more, and prove to his father that he was worthy of his title. He knew that she wanted to help him to do that and Maedoc, Lancelin, and even Gwalian, had spoken well of her.

As that name entered his thoughts, she came flooding back; Gwalian, beautiful and engaging. His stomach tightened and he smiled. What did she think of him? If she had no feelings towards him, was she simply being polite and performing her duty? If so, Artur was unsure what he would do. He frowned as he gazed and a shadow passed across his thoughts.

A noise behind him made him turn suddenly.

There she was. More beautiful and enhanced if that was possible – in her figure and her looks by the morning's crisp, clear light. For a moment, she stood looking down at him; her dress of the previous evening replaced by a sleeveless woollen top and linen trousers that fitted tightly to her legs and leather sandals. Was this normal? Did she look this good every day, or was it just for him? He wanted to turn round, jump up and embrace her, kiss her and release the passion that he felt building within him, a glorious life-enhancing release as he felt the warmth of her body next to him and the moisture of her lips on his. Oh, if only!

No, wait, he was getting ahead of himself. Had she noticed; could she sense his thoughts? He blushed slightly. This wave of emotion was engulfing him and he was only just swimming. He must maintain control.

'Artur, I am sorry; I have disturbed your thoughts. I will leave you and wait for you back at my father's hall.'

She turned to go, but he jumped up instantly.

'No, in fact,' he said, pausing while his eyes wandered a little nervously, 'it was you I was thinking of.'

'Were you, that's nice,' she paused also before continuing brightly, 'and I was thinking of you. I have come to look for you. If we are to have our tour, we should get started. You see, I have come dressed for walking and climbing. My father will return soon and take all of your attention. Shall we go and enjoy our morning while we can? Have you had breakfast?'

'Yes, I took meat and fruit before I came out.' He looked intently into her eyes. 'I would like to understand more of Menluit and Ker Tamara, and I look forward to meeting Lord Aodren.'

'If all is resolved at the mines, he will quickly return, and I anticipate our paths will cross at Ker Tamara. Winoc has gone ahead to meet him from his boat.'

They walked back up the path, side by side, nearly touching but not quite. His arm agitated in anticipation, the closest part of his body to this incredible force of attraction that walked alongside him. He looked again across the fields trying to maintain his composure. It was hard. He would tell her, but not yet. How would she respond? He did not know and he must not look foolish – not to her.

As they walked, Artur noticed, towards the bottom of the field, what appeared to be a large hole in the ground, surrounded by stakes and fencing, presumably to keep the sheep out.

'Gwalian, what is that large hole in the field? What is its purpose?'

'It is a mine. There are many alongside Tamara and the lands that surround her. The Veneti first came to Nanmeur to work the mines and trade the metals that we found. They are a significant source of wealth for us and, of course, for your father. The grey and silver metal first found on the surface and in the govers are what gave Menluit its name.'

Artur stopped and looked down towards the mine.

'We have opened up many mines,' she continued, 'and sourced copper, tin and silver all along Tamara. There is a ready market in Armorica and in the lands beyond and for which, it seems, the men of the Curiosolitae are increasingly ready to try to make a claim.'

Gwalian turned and looked at him with a mildly sardonic smile.

'If the Greek is genuine, then he and my father will no doubt want to talk about metals for his customers. Until the troubles, traders from across Gaul visited regularly, interested in dealing with our supply.'

She looked with him down to the mine.

'That dig is new and there are more established ones you will see further along. There is an established silver mine on the far side of the trev and larger mines further down Tamara. It is at one of these that my father felt compelled to attend yesterday to remove the Curiosolitae men who had presumed to take control and our trade. They say they are now the preeminent tribe of Armorica and therefore deserve a share at least of the return from the mines of Tamara. But we have precedence here and my father will not give that up easily.'

She raised her eyebrows in conclusion before turning back up the hill. 'Come on,' she called over her shoulder. 'I talk of Tamara. Let's go and have a look at her.'

They passed through the gates and walked up through the trev to Pendre. A number of the Company sat outside. Several called to the hall, and others came out as Artur and Gwalian approached, including Kea. He was supportive and saw himself as an intermediary between the Prince and his Company, and sensed that Artur shared a common cause with him – a father to prove wrong and a reputation to build. He stepped forward and spoke for a number of them.

'Good morning, Pryns Artur, Lady Gwalian. It is a bright morning and we feel the need for action, to begin our quest properly. What are your first instructions?'

Artur had intended to spend an enjoyable morning with Gwalian, alone, but no, of course, they had all fought their way to this place and a plan of action was now required. It was Gwalian, however, who spoke first.

'Pryns Artur, may I suggest that you and your immediate followers come with me now to the quay? From there, we can take boats downstream to Ker Tamara, where we will almost certainly meet my father.'

Artur's eyes gently widened as he smiled back at her. He turned to the half-assembled Company.

'A good idea. Kea, can you gather the rheidyrs and follow us? Lancelin will know the way, I'm sure.'

Artur and Gwalian walked on to the far side of the settlement and a small gate in the earthwork bank. More hidden than the main gate, it opened out on to a steep decline and a zigzag path that descended the bank with a slightly less precipitous gradient. With breakfast completed, people were now coming and going regularly through the gate, despite it being more concealed. After they had passed through and were out of the way of the continuing traffic, Artur paused and took in his first proper view of Tamara.

She wound languidly around the base of the hill below, flowing from left to right. She then bore left slightly out of his line of vision, before reappearing again under high cliffs; then she swung right again and slipped out of his sight into a low gorge, cut by her in the land. At the start of the gorge, on high points on either side, people were discernible, dark shapes moving before defensive banks. This, then, must be the twin forts – Ker Tamara on the near bank and Dynas Dowr Tewl on the far.

As they walked down the path, the continuous flow of people meant that others passed them going up the hill. The path, as it descended, crossed several terraces cut into the hillside, with sentries posted along the length of the hill. As they descended, Artur looked across the river. A little further downstream on the opposite bank, smoke rose from the roundhouses. Surrounding them were small fields, some with crops and some with livestock grazing in them.

'There is much more to the settlement than I expected,' he said.

'Yes, everything comes together here; boats, produce and goods for sale – and warriors.' She turned quickly and smiled at him as she led the way down the path.

In front of them, numerous small boats milled around midstream, waiting for their turn to approach the quay at the foot of the path. Some carried goods, supplies for the trev, or bundles of produce and cloth. Others were water taxis carrying people from the small round across the river or upstream from the twin forts.

'It is really one large inland port from here to the wharves at Ker Tamara,' she said, 'and we transport everything that we can by water. The boatmen serve my father and they will transport anything they feel their boat can carry, up and down the river. The road brings heavy goods to the crossing around the bend of the river over there, but many other, lighter goods and a lot of different people travel both up and downstream between the crossing, Ker Tamara and Menluit.'

Engrossed in the view and description, neither of them noticed the boatmen of the riverboats, freighters and taxis look downstream, begin to pull harder and withdraw. Through their midst came a larger boat with multiple oars, and in it is prow stood Aodren.

Impatient of the meeting, he had reached Ker Tamara swiftly, only to find his daughter and guest not there. Instantly, he had called for his boat to take him from its mooring to a small jetty under the cliff of Ker Tamara. He had, meanwhile, descended even steeper steps from the promontory of the fort to wait testily while the boat set out again to meet him. The rowers, having worked against the current from the silver mine, had their heads bowed now as they approached Menluit quay, pulling hard to manoeuvre the boat. Aodren, confident in his position, stood impervious to the movement around him and, instead, peered ahead, looking for some sign of his daughter.

Then he saw her, distinctive, confident, as she strode onto the quay. Behind her was a young man, painfully young from this distance, but then had they not all become painfully young? Was it not a sign of his age? The briefest of sighs passed his lips before he dismissed the thought from his mind and prepared himself for the fast-approaching landing stage.

'Artur, it is my father. He has returned sooner than I thought.'

Gwalian stood straight and looked downstream confidently towards her approaching father. The hustle and bustle ceased, for the moment at least, as people moved back, ready to acknowledge the returning Lord as he passed by on his business. Artur, uncertain of the protocol, stood just behind Gwalian and watched as the boat and its prominent individual approached. Here, he could sense real deference and felt it too, despite his own position, towards an older man who commanded respect from those around him. Artur watched and noted how Aodren fixed his gaze, stood straight and held his head confidently. He expected this deference and all must wait for him to disembark, say what he had to say, issue his direction and then move on before they could continue with the rest of their day.

The oarsmen and coxswain were working hard as the boat closed on the quay, and the Prince took in his first proper view of the Veneti lord. His long, dark hair and matching long moustache had distinctive grey flecks in it, and his intense dark eyes looked back at Artur now, assessing him, forming his own first opinions. He was of average height, not as tall as the Prince, but stocky, well-built and, Artur guessed, at least forty winters old. Many began to show signs of decline by their fortieth year, but for Aodren it was clear that his age simply served to increase his presence and command of all those around him.

The ropeman in the bow quickly leapt ashore to fend off and prevent the boat from striking the stage. Using his rope to bring the craft to a halt, he tied it off on a wooden bollard. Father and daughter now stared intently at each other. Aodren only deviating to look confidently and questioningly at the Prince. With the boat secured, he stepped ashore.

'Father, we did not expect you so early, or we would have been at Ker Tamara to meet you.'

Winoc and the others in the boat came ashore. The steward looked worried.

'Daughter, do not concern yourself; the spring rain so far has been light this year. Tamara is gentle in her flow and passage is easier. We came more speedily than anticipated.'

Now he switched his attention to Artur, but Gwalian, who was quick to respond, spoke again.

'Father, this is Pryns Artur of the Dewnan.'

Before she could say more, Aodren asked, 'Is it? Do you speak for yourself, young man?'

'My Lord, I am Artur O'Dhearg ap Mawgan, Pryns of the Dewnan, and I am very glad to meet you at last.'

'Good, and I am Aodren, of the Veneti, Lord of the Crossing. Have confidence in the days ahead Pryns Artur, be assertive. War is coming, and if we do not wish to yield to Roman bullying, we will need all of the confidence we can muster before much longer.'

His face was stern for a moment, then relaxed slightly and his eyes softened.

'I am pleased to meet you too. Although you may not remember it, we have met before, when you were very young in your father's hall. The fighting force you bring with you is very welcome.'

Winoc, unseen by Aodren, shuffled his feet and looked down, coughing nervously.

As they spoke these initial words of greeting, other voices, unaware of the meeting, grew louder as they approached... male voices, laughing as they descended to the quay.

Lancelin and Tinos, men of Nanmeur, were in the lead, followed by Kea, Drustan, Silyen and Gawen. At the back, Casvelyn, Nouran and Gourgy seemed in deep conversation. Lancelin and Tinos, recognising Aodren as he stared firmly back at them, one eyebrow raised, came to a quick stop at the start of the stage.

Artur spoke quickly. 'Lord Aodren, this is my Company, rheidyrs drawn from across the lands of the Dewnan to support the coming battle. Already, we have had a skirmish with Belgae, maybe Durotrages warriors that attacked us, penetrating deep into our lands. We dealt with them and now stand ready to fight alongside you, against our common enemies.'

'Have you? Then you, at least, will see the threat of the Estrenyons and join with me in marvelling that your father does nothing about it and refuses to acknowledge the threat.'

As he spoke, a sternness returned to his face. Although he continued to speak to Artur, he seemed to give equal attention to Lancelin.

'I had heard, of course, you were gathering men to you, to take the fight to the Belgae and soon, perhaps, to the Roman aggressor. The Veneti stand for the same. We are masters of the sea and a trading nation. We will not yield to any threat without a fight.'

He looked directly now towards Lancelin, who was surrounded silently by the Company. Even the bluntness of Gourgy and Nouran was subdued by the confident and commanding Veneti chieftain, assured in his superiority.

'Tell me, Pryns Artur, how many men did Lancelin bring to your Company?'

Artur hesitated, uncertain at the reason for the question, while Lancelin, all his humour now lost, stood apprehensively and clearly anticipated what was coming next.

'He and his gille joined the Company but, unfortunately, his gille was killed in the skirmish with the Belgae. Lancelin fought bravely and took the fight to the intruders. Why do you ask?'

Aodren stared at the young man of the valley.

'Shall we just say that your father's call came at a fortuitous moment and Lancelin here did not need to be asked twice to rally to its call for support?'

'Father...' The swift rise of Aodren's hand silenced Gwalian, before he turned back to the Prince and his face relaxed into a half smile.

'Come, let us walk up the path to Pendre and we shall say no more about it, particularly if he has fought bravely on your behalf.'

Artur looked quickly at Gwalian, but she looked away from him. He quickly turned back and walked off the stage to catch up with Aodren. The Company, Gwalian, Winoc and the rest of Aodren's retinue followed behind.

'I am told that you have come through Ocean's mightiest storm. You are lucky to be here!'

'I am, I believe. Only my coxswain and I survived, our boat was cast upon the rocks close to Ker Kammel. Good men who had rowed to within sight of land were lost. It grieves me to think of them so close to safety and yet helpless as they went into the water.'

'Hmm, the loss of comrades is always saddening.'

As they climbed the path, there was a short pause before Aodren spoke again.

'Bad luck also that the worst storm on the Mor Pretani in living memory coincided with your crossing, don't you think?' He looked sideways as he strode assuredly forward. 'You had no sense of other forces at work I presume?'

Artur glanced quickly at him as he worked hard to keep up alongside the older man.

'Are you suggesting that the storm was created because of my crossing? Elowen, the priestess, said that the spirits of the sea demanded a high price for my safe return, a sacrifice. Do you believe that too?'

'Yes, I heard about the old priestess.' He stopped and turned to the Prince, and in a moment of sudden candour, said, 'I don't know what I believe really, but can it be right that your father sits there and does nothing, while Belgae raiding parties penetrate deep into his lands, and refuses to join with me in taking the attack to the Estrenyons, and won't even contemplate joining with me in preparing to meet the Roman threat? We hear often of the glory of the Pretan and the Dewnan, the Acheans and the Dewnan, why not Veneti and Dewnan? I mean, it's worth a try, is it not? It is getting to the point where neither of us has anything to lose.'

He looked searchingly into Artur's eyes.

'He is a shadow of the man I knew when your mother was alive, and I know that still, even now, he grieves her loss. She would have made any man proud to be her companion, but, even so, something is not right. We face threats from the Estrenyon and an even bigger Roman storm, but there is also a threat from within. At the very least, it is induced inertia, but maybe... maybe it is something more sinister than that; collusion with our enemies and an undue influence over your father. Keep your eyes open, Pryns Artur; the threat to our safety, to our way of life comes from many different directions.'

For a moment, he continued to look into Artur's eyes before turning and marching on up the path, saying as he went, 'Be assured, whatever is at work, you can rely on the support of the Veneti and my own commitment to defend the lands of the Dewnan, my brothers and sisters across the Mor Pretani, and our common Pretan culture and way of life. Whatever it takes.'

The rest of the group came up the path behind him now and Artur watched Kea, Drustan and Gawen, in particular, as they looked expectantly back at him but, without saying anything, he turned and followed in pursuit of Aodren.

'Lord Aodren, thank you for your support. My men are also committed to working with you to take the fight to the enemy. We will fight strongly together, I think.'

'Yes, I am sure we will, but we should not in any way underestimate the force that we confront. The Romans are different to those that have threatened us before; strong, organised. It will take great guile and courage to stop them and even more determination to keep them at bay. I am told that once crossed, they become even greater adversaries. Our ability on Ocean is where we must seek our advantage.'

They were nearing the top of the path again now and all parted before them, just as had happened as at the quay, and the gate ahead also cleared for them to pass through. The rest of the Company were right behind them now, and Artur could hear Nouran – out of the gaze of the Veneti chieftain and restored to his acerbic self – complaining to anyone who would listen.

'Is this some sort o' trainin exercise? Joke, laugh, walk down, cold stare; turn aroun', route march back! Unconventional, you gotta admit… and what 'ave ee bin up to, young Lancelin? Uze seem quite accomplished in rubbin folks up the wrong way, I 'ave to say…'

Artur heard no more as he passed through the gate and back into the trev. Aodren strode towards the hall, stopped and turned towards the pastureland. Maedoc, who had seen them enter the gate, approached them now with most of the gilles and retainers behind him.

'Pryns Artur, where is your force, your men? Have they not camped in the trev lands?'

Winoc nervously stood forward. 'My Lord, it seems, at least, I have been trying to tell you since you landed at Ker Tamara.'

Aodren looked sharply towards his steward. 'Tell me what? No, let me guess, that I have been denied again the assistance that I have sought?'

The intensity of his look caused the steward to hesitate in his reply and the Prince, recognising immediately the misconception stepped forward and said, 'Lord Aodren, these are my men, rheidyr and gille. We come to fight with you against whatever foe we face and with courage and determination. I think that we will add much to the coming battle.'

'Do you? Good, I am glad you do.'

He did not disguise his incredulity.

'At least you have the naivety and optimism of youth on your side and, no doubt, you and the brave Lancelin and all your other followers will meet an honourable death, but it is not enough, nowhere near enough! What are you, forty men at most? Surely, this is your father's idea of a joke. Do you know that I have men deployed the length of Tamara to Ocean's mouth!'

He paused for a moment, before turning to Artur with a look bordering on contempt.

'Do you have any idea of the size of the Roman force? No, of course, you do not. You will have heard little of this in Demetae of blessed isolation! They have countless warriors at their command, in numbers that dwarf even my force and contain a number of men I cannot even count. No matter how valorous your fight, they would make short work of you, before marching on as if you had never even been there.'

He began to walk towards Pendre.

'Lord Aodren, my father, has said we are the initial force. More will be provided, if needed.'

Aodren called back, 'Really, do you believe that?' He stopped and turned. 'You have been with him. Only when a Roman spear is stuck into his belly or his lands overrun by the Estrenyons will he act. Then it will be long past too late and the Pretani, Veneti and Dewnan will be no more, because he and others like him refused to stand up for what we believe in and fight to protect our families, our homes and our livelihoods against destructive and wilful aggression.'

Now he spoke to Winoc.

'Where is the Priestess? She promised me much more than this. What has she to say now?'

***

The Prince looked at those around him. The banter of the previous evening and the walk up the hill from the river had gone, replaced by grim expressions.

'We knew it would be hard. It is going to be hard. In my father's hall, on our journey here, we have heard nothing different. We have already fought together in the middle of our land in a skirmish that we should not have had to fight and we will stand up to our enemies again soon. Who will join me in attending this Lord of the Veneti in his hall? Let us enter Pendre and begin to prove to him that in us, he has the very best of the Dewnan, each of us the equal of many men added to his fighting force!'

He walked towards the hall and turned to face them. No one said anything and then, just as his look of steely determination was about to fail, Gwalian said, 'I will come with you. I am no warrior, but I can wield a sword and flex my bow for what I believe in!'

She stood upright, proud before him, taking and holding his attention as she offered her support.

'My father is passionate. A proud Veneti who has laboured hard to make this colony work and does not want to see it all cheaply surrendered to some foreign invader, and given away through a failure to respond. Come, you and I, with our friends, comrades, let us talk to him, and convince him that our contribution will be strong.'

'It is not long since we met and yet, in you, I feel a kindred spirit. Yes! Let us go to him, tell him of our desire for the fight and our belief in each other.'

Kea stepped forward quickly now, breaking the brief intensity of their exchange.

'Artur, we are all in this for the opportunity. We know there are long struggles ahead, but it is a little early to be abandoning our quest. Let us talk to Aodren and, as we say in the Kernovi, "Gans a'gas nei sav!" We stand with you!'

The Prince, flanked by Gwalian and Kea, now looked again at the rest of the Company. Gourgy stood out with his wry and expansive grin, amused by the exchange between Artur and Gwalian.

'Aye, young'un, we've barely begun! I came on this trip to fight Romins and let 'em feel the power of my sword arm! I'll not be goin' 'ome until Ize bin satisfied! Bring em on. I'll take thirty of 'em before they take me down!'

There were nods and 'ayes!' from others in the group. Finally, Drustan spoke for all.

'Cousin, we want to get on, prepare and plan our approach. Take us to Pendre. Let us hear what he has to say; maybe he has fresh news from Porth Ictis and across the Mor Pretani on how we can take the fight to our enemies. That is what we are here for; that is our mission.'

Artur held the gaze of Drustan for a moment before saying to them all, 'Come to Pendre. We have much to discuss.'

The brightness of the late morning streamed into the interior of the hall through the double doors. At the far end, Aodren stood with his back to them at the large roundtable that the Company had eaten at the previous evening. Sensing their approach, he turned to face them.

'Lord Aodren, we understand the scale of the task ahead because others, such as you, who know much more, have told us about it. We are here to help and believe we will add greatly to your forces. We will fight with you, wherever that may lead. So we have come to ask how we can prepare for the challenges ahead.'

Gwalian stood alongside Artur, and Aodren sternly looked at his daughter in a quizzical way, but she was ready for him and returned his stare with assuredness. After a few moments, he smiled affectionately and reverted to the Prince.

'Pryns Artur, these are difficult days and the days ahead will only become more difficult. The stark realities of the Roman advance and the irritating prodding and probing of the Belgae and their hired brigands lead me to speak candidly. However, despite your smallness in numbers, your help is welcome and, no doubt, there are fine warriors within your Company who will withstand many a lesser assailant.

'My son, Ewen ap Aodren, has recently crossed RunHoul to harry the Estrenyons and double-talking Durotrages. His company, a small force also, are battle hardened. They have campaigned tirelessly against Durotrages and Belgae incursions, doing enough to keep them occupied and gathering goods for trade across the Mor Pretani. He will return to Nanmeur by the wax of Loor Skovarnek. When he returns, we will decide on our next move. A refreshed force sent back to challenge the incursions on our borders or, instead, prepare to join the fight in Armorica.

'I expect word from across the Mor Pretani very soon. Rome will not leave the lands of the Pretani, the descendants of Venetia alone. We have too much, are too powerful, and this man Caesar seems only interested in making gains for himself and his men. They will not leave us alone.'

He took a sip from a previously unnoticed beaker of wine, before continuing.

'Prepare, young Pryns. Prepare for war. Use the days well between now and Loor Skovarnek; learn to fight together, understand and trust each other implicitly. You will need that soon. Prepare your boat. My men will transport you down the river to Porth Ictis, where we moor our larger boats. Choose one and again learn how to work together with Ocean. Prepare Pryns Artur!'

He sought to make eye contact around the Company as he finished his response, and they all stared determinedly back at him. His face lightened slightly as his look fell once more upon Gwalian.

'Daughter, I assume you are here in moral support rather than as a recruit to this warrior company?'

'Father, I am here to support Pryns Artur and his men and show solidarity with their cause. I do not anticipate at present the need to join the Company as a warrior, but as you know, I can hold my own with my sword arm and bow and arrow should the need arise; and who here fully understands what we may yet be called upon to do in support of our friends? Not I, but if I need to take up arms to defend this Company, then I will do so.'

Plain-faced she looked back at him.

He chuckled, with pride and pleasure beaming out from him. 'Daughter, I do not doubt it, but I hope that it will not come to that; and yet, it might. We all need to prepare for what may soon be required of us.'

Others in the hall had listened to the conversation and now Aodren addressed them all.

'Let us all come together at sundown for a meal and more discussion. I am hopeful the Lady Morlain will join us. Pryns Artur, you and your Company are most welcome. We will talk again later, but for now, I must attend to other business.'

***

Sira Howl slipped languidly towards the horizon when Morlain and Steren Uskis passed again through the gates of Menluit. Despite the fading light, trev life was all around her; the clink-clink of hammer on anvil, the shouts of children as they played and the startled cries of unseen hens, alarmed by a disturbance, real or perceived, that sent them scurrying.

Behind her, the ewes in the pasturelands called to their lambs, who were nearly young sheep now, and a male blackbird above perched atop one of the vertical posts of a nearby roundhouse, calling to its mate as they built their nest for the coming season.

In one of the roundhouses, a baby cried, and sitting in front of the nearest house was one of the older women, preparing vegetables for the pot. She looked up and briefly showed a toothy grin before returning to her task. The air was almost still and the cooking fires of the roundhouses rose perpendicularly into the darkening sky.

An early owl hooted in the woods beyond the trev. All was peace and calm, a normal spring evening, like so many before.

She dismounted and, for a moment, looked around her. Here, encapsulated, was everything she held dear: the sights and sounds of the community, the developing green of the valley, which was in the full exuberance of life reborn, with trees showing early leaf and the flowers of path and hedgerow now poking through. Just as it had always been, and no Roman, Belgae or other aggressor would change it; on that, she was determined.

Three shouting children burst out from the roundhouse, jostling and rattling the vegetable pot as they ran towards her, the scolding of the old woman following after them. As they passed her, they called, 'Hello, my Lady!' and ran on down the hill.

Her reverie disturbed, she smiled to herself and continued towards Aodren's hall.

As she approached, she saw Maedoc sat on a bench by the main doors, sharpening his sword and several others by the look of it, all arranged and resting on the bench beside him. He looked up as she came near to him.

'My Lady, I had hoped it would not be long before we saw you again.'

'Good friend, I think you knew it wouldn't be. How has your day been? You are busy, I see.'

'Yes,' he looked sombrely as she sat down next to him on the bench. 'There is much talk of war and battles and more raiding Belgae. It pays to be prepared, so I am sharpening swords and knives for the Pryns and me before our supper is served.'

'Maedoc, do not look so glum! What of the Pryns? Has he had an illuminating day?'

'My Lady, Lord Aodren has returned and added further emphasis to the challenges ahead. He has also made his dismay at the size of our Company very clear, that he thinks it inadequate, and that the King is in some way mocking him, although the Pryns and Lady Gwalian have stood together and sought to persuade him otherwise.'

Did Maedoc perceive the faint flicker in her eye as he said these last words? She continued quickly and strongly. 'Hmm and yet those of us fully involved know that it is a substantial achievement and it's progress in itself for the King to do this at all and propose the forming of the Company. For him to send the massed bands of the Dewnan to war for a threat he refuses to fully accept, is unrealistic and perhaps Aodren should recognise that.'

Maedoc stared ahead in concentration, listening to what she said. He looked back at her and in a hushed but more urgent voice, 'So, what of Armorica, my Lady, the land of Venetia and Thurien? Will the King just abandon it? Leave it to its fate? Surely, the Romans have only one intention.'

'Yes, you are right and either he is indifferent to their fate or he calculates that it is better to protect what he has than to throw all his resource into fighting a battle he and the Veneti almost certainly will not win. Certainly, those around him urge him to think this. The Romans, he thinks, will not cross the Mor Pretani. For them, it is a step into the unknown and will, therefore, be contained within Armorica and Gaul. Also, flushed with what they think is their success at conjuring the tempest for your crossing from Demetae, some around him have convinced him that if the Romans do attempt to cross the Mor Pretani, Ocean's fury will consume them, although they do not tell him that explicitly. It is folly, of course, but he will not listen to me or your Elowen or the likes of Aodren, who he considers a guest in his land. He also thinks all of whom should be more respectful of the King's views.'

She looked him in the eye now, with raised eyebrows, before concluding, 'Fortunately, Aodren pays no attention to this and prepares to make his contribution to the battle, which is one of the few flickers of hope we have that all may not yet be lost.'

She rose and stood before him as he looked up at her.

'Anyway, it is Aodren, of course, that I come to see. Is he in the hall?'

'Yes, conversing with the Pryns and others. I am nearly done here. I will join you soon.'

Aodren, at the head of the roundtable, looked up as she crossed the open floor.

'I expected you much sooner, Lady Morlain, given the arrival of Pryns Artur and his Company, of which you talked so positively about through recent moons.'

'Lord Aodren, I was here only yesterday and was uncertain of when you would return today. I have been busy, as I am sure you have too, but now here I am ready to reflect on fresh news and talk of plans for the coming moons and our preparation for the fight ahead, now that the Pryns and Company are with us.'

All of the Company and Aodren's immediate followers were gathered around the table listening to the conversation and anticipating more discussion.

'Very well,' Aodren continued, 'food will be served very soon. Please take your seats: the Pryns and his rheidyrs, as our guests at the roundtable; Lady Morlain, of course; Winoc; Callard; Loan, please join my daughter and I. Everybody else, please use the longer tables on either side. Mead and wine will be served first.'

As he turned aside, he noticed a face that he did not recognise.

'Who is that man, Pryns Artur, one of your Company? He is well dressed. I thought you had introduced me to all your rheidyrs?'

Gwalian answered first.

'Father, forgive me, with the events of the day, I had forgotten about him, although he has made no attempt to introduce himself to you and I do not believe I have seen him since early this morning. His name is Gyras, a trader, he says, from the Greek city of Massalia and here with Lord Judikael's endorsement.'

The Prince quickly turned towards Aodren.

'The fault is mine. He joined my Company on the road near to here. He said he was looking for you and opportunities for trade. He showed us a token, a symbol of your kinsman Judikael, that convinced your men of his genuineness and so we brought him here. Gwalian is right, though, we have heard very little from him today and I am surprised he has not introduced himself.'

Aodren stared back at Artur before turning in the direction of the Greek and saying, 'You.' Several turned towards him, but Aodren ignored them and tried once again to get the merchant's attention, 'No you, Gyras, is it? He who seeks trade with me and the Veneti of Menluit? We have not been introduced; state your business and then join us at the roundtable.'

Gyras stepped cautiously forward. 'Lord Aodren, I have enjoyed the spring afternoon, wandering the woods behind the trev. I anticipated that you would be busy with the Prince and, therefore, I determined to wait until this evening to introduce myself. I am Gyras of Massalia. It is my honour to meet you and I hope to serve you at last. I met Lord Judikael about one moon ago at Gwened in search of silver, tin and other goods in traded return for my own offerings. There is very little that I cannot find if there are particular items that you seek. I supply wine, silks and spices and many other goods, gathered from the lands that surround the Mesogeios, the Middle Sea, and lands much further away, Asia, Arabia, Nanda, Magadha and beyond.'

He paused for a moment, conscious that the eyes of the room were upon him.

'I was graciously received by the Lady Gwalian last evening and now, once we have eaten, I hope we can discuss in more detail how I may be able to build new links for this colony with my many customers across Gaul, in Massalia, and across Italy and Hispania.'

Aodren looked sternly towards him and held the Greek's gaze, before replying, 'It will be a number of years, I think, before your connections in Gaul are able to trade again, after the misery and destruction of the last few years. When they do, they will no longer be proud Gauls or Celts but, instead, subsumed under Roman control, paying tribute collectively and individually to the all-controlling empire, lost forever as an independent tribe or nation. As for Massalia, Italy and Hispania, I have heard of these places, but I have never been there. I have met traders from Massalia and even Hispania before, but never a man of Italy. I suspect, before much longer, it will be my misfortune to meet far more of such men.'

Unsure of whether he believed the Greek, he decided to be provocative.

'Tell me, do you come directly from the Roman general or one of his lesser generals, perhaps this Crassus who seeks to impose his control upon us? Do you have a very good reason, other than Lord Judikael's recommendation, why I should believe your claim that you have managed to pass the Roman army and cross the Mor Pretani? We have seen none of your fellow traders here for many moons, save those from Armorica. Are you an agent for the Curiosolitae perhaps, and part of their plan to undermine and overwhelm the Veneti?'

'My Lord Aodren, I come here with a genuine desire for trade and deal making. We spoke of the Romans and Gaul last evening and yes, I have encountered many Romans in my life and supplied goods and materials to many of them and, no doubt, when I return to Massalia, I will meet many more of them, but I have come here to trade.'

Morlain spoke next.

'Lord Aodren, I think as you do; we should treat all unexpected visitors, certainly those from beyond Armorica, with suspicion. Why be here now, with the Roman legions at your tail, ready to pounce and destroy once more? No successful trader that I know puts himself in harm's way unless he has no other choice.'

The Prince felt the need to speak and recover his position after forgetting about the Greek.

'My Lord I-I think… it is my belief that we should treat this man with care. I say we detain him now. Do we expect more word from Armorica? Let us hear more from across the Mor Pretani first and then decide how to deal with him.'

Imperceptibly, Gwalian squeezed Artur's leg in encouragement under the table, unseen by the rest, apart from her all-seeing father. Artur turned to her and the briefest of smiles passed between them before she swiftly followed the Prince.

'Father, I knew you would share my caution. The Pryns is right; this man cannot leave. If he is on some form of reconnaissance journey for the Roman general, if they have designs on Armorica, who is to say they are not interested in other parts of the ancient Pretani lands?'

Gyras listening with mounting alarm to the conversation and gripped his chair increasingly tightly as Gwalian's assessment summed up his reason for being there. Agitated, he cut in as she had finished speaking.

'Lord Aodren, I am a man of trade, not of subterfuge or war. There are many in the lands that I have spoken of who know that I am here, including your own kinsman. They anticipate my return and the opportunities I will bring with me to purchase the merchandise and materials I will trade on your behalf to them. If I do not return, that opportunity will be lost and may not return for many moons. I have taken great risks to be here, it is true, but I have come in pursuit of trade.'

'Gyras of Massalia, you will come to no harm while you are here, I can assure you of that, but you will not leave until I have heard more from my homeland. I have just returned from expelling the increasingly belligerent and bold men of the Curiosolitae. They seek trade, our trade! Perhaps you are their man from the Middle Sea, their agent from the warm lands, or maybe you work for a Roman general. I do not know, and therefore you will stay with us until I know more. Then, at the end of it all, if, as you say, we all come out of it unscathed, and if you are who you say you are, you will have my heartfelt apologies. Furthermore, I will send you off with the best goods that we can trade and ensure that you create the best impression with the contacts that wait for your return. If you are genuine, you have nothing to fear except a more extended visit than you had planned.'

He then looked away from the Greek and around the table.

'My friends, eat and drink and let us talk of other matters, at least for this evening. Then, when we have refreshed ourselves fully, may I ask Lady Morlain for a story perhaps, in honour of the Pryns and his Company? Remind us of the origins of this place and of the first Lord of the Crossing?'

Morlain looked plain-faced at the Veneti lord. In spite of the regular robust engagements between them, she liked him. Nothing, she had come to see, would ever prevent him, or them, from feasting and drinking. Not even if the whole Roman army was camped outside the gates of Menluit.

***

Ronan and the King of the Bears

As Menitriel grew in stature, King Ronan, ever mindful of the revered Venetia and his father's words, continued to look towards the distant hills where Sira Howl rose each day and imagined the lands beyond them.

One morning he, his councillors and leading warriors came together on the ramparts of the citadel. Together they surveyed the mighty wood that covered the valley floor as far as they could see until the far hills rose in the distance. The King spoke to them all as they looked across the sylvan vastness.

"Menitriel stands tall, a beacon to all around, and here, on the ramparts of our mighty fortress each morning, we give reverence to Sira Howl and his returning light; but now we must go further. Only the fables of the Dewnan tell us what lies beyond the Great Wood. The stories tell of temples in the landscape, drowned lands, cold seas and dark forests, beyond which the Estrenyons lurk; and yet, the Dewnan say, no one has entered the wood and returned. This is the challenge for the Pretan! I will lead an expedition to those far distant hills. Come, who will join me?'

Many of them hesitated, full of silent trepidation, afeared of the spirits that lurked amongst the trees.

Again, Ronan said, "I am not afraid, come, which of you will join me?"

Still they hesitated and then, just as Ronan began to despair of his warriors, Iwen, the youngest, said, 'I will come with you, my Lord. It is true, I am afraid of what the Great Wood may hold, but you led us here with your wisdom and courage and Sira Howl is our light and our guidance, so I will follow you now, although I do not know where it will lead me.'

Shamed by the bravery of the youngest and least experienced among them, the others committed themselves to the quest and very soon set out from the citadel. As they descended the hill of Menitriel into the trees, the going was good, at first. Sira Howl was high in the sky, the trees were well-spaced and the riding was comfortable. They saw birds, deer, and heard the snuffle and rustle of boar in the thicket and undergrowth as the light dwindled. Sira Howl descended beyond Menitriel and they followed the paths created by the deer or some other animal and went towards the far-distant hills, from where they trusted he would rise again the following morning.

Ahead, two badgers ran onto the path, stood and stared at them and then turned and scuttled off down the path into the growing darkness. The light faded quickly, and as it did so, the trees got thicker and taller. The canopy now hid the sky, diminishing further the dwindling light. Silence fell and it seemed as if all around them listened to their progress. Suddenly, there was a cough and then a groan and growl, followed by a piercing scream, shuffling and the sound of breaking twigs. The rheidyrs held firmly to their reins with one hand and their sword hilt with the other. Occasionally, sparkles of light appeared and then, as the Company looked nervously towards them, snapped shut or disappeared amongst the trees. Was it light? Were there people living in the wood, after all, an ancient people, or did something else, the spirits of the wood, watch them and lure them, waiting for their chance.

Ronan, seeing the increasing terror on the face of rheidyr and horse alike, decided it was best to make camp and continue their journey in the morning. They lit campfires and sat closely together. None wanted to admit their fear, but all longed for morning and the return of Sira Howl and his redeeming light. In the distance, the howling of wolves added to their sense of trepidation in this dark and fearsome place. As the fire dwindled, the warriors drew even closer together.

Ronan spoke to them all. 'Do not be afraid, we go towards Sira Howl. He will return and find us sitting here, waiting patiently, ready to continue our quest. Let us stoke the fire now and we will take it in turns to keep watch.'

As he finished speaking, a new deep and loud voice, grumbling and mumbling in the darkness, spoke from beyond the nearest trees. All jumped up, alarmed, and the horses neighed loudly in fright. The warriors backed towards each other, while Ronan stood before them, peering into the darkness, looking towards where the voice had come from.

'What is this – grrrr? Who has entered my domain without my permission? Is it you, Ronan, leader of men, as has been foretold? Do you dare to bring man-fire into the land of Orsa? Show yourself, now! I am coming towards you and I am coming very quickly. Make ready for my arrival and be very AFRAID!'

The warriors trembled but stood firm, looking towards the voice and standing behind the King as the rushing and the rustling *of leaves and branches and an increasingly heavy thud of swift footfall pounded towards them. Terror was in their eyes as they looked at each other and shook with fear. It was the spirit of the Great Wood and it was going to consume them!*

'Prepare yourselves; be ready to stand firm!' Ronan instructed. 'Spirit of the night, come from the darkness! Do not talk from where we cannot see you. I am indeed Ronan, show yourself, whether you be creature, spectre or man!'

Suddenly, in front of him, branches and leaves crashed apart and a very large brown bear reared up onto its back legs, and spreading its front paws wide, roared.

'I am no Man! I am a bear and son of the great Mother Bear in the sky. To her, one day, I will return, but now I am real, here, amongst the trees and living things of the Earth Mother. I have anticipated your coming, the inheritance as foretold, but do not command me, man-creature, in my domain, grrrr! Talk with reverence before me. I have the power to inspire, but also to vanquish. I am warrior, leader and defender. I am Orsa, Master of the Great Wood and Lord of the Crossing, sent down to guide the children of Mamm Norves. You are surrounded and you will do as I tell you!

The hall sat riveted as Morlain moved quickly around, expanding her arms, puffing up her long hair and contorting her face, eyes opening wide and growling intermittently as she created the great bear before them, bringing life and drama to her delivery. Even Artur smiled warmly, engrossed in the story and impressed with her ability to tell it. She, in turn, while telling the story to the hall, seemed to direct her attention to him, telling a story within a story that was only for him.

The bear swiped Ronan's sword from his hand and the King backed quickly away from the reach of his swinging paws. Two badgers, barking their support, one behind each leg, peered out from behind the bear as it towered above them.

'Kneel before me, intruder and wood burner! Brogh, warden of the woodland edge, has followed you from the moment you entered our sacred land and we have waited for you, because from here there is no escape, unless I allow it. Tell me quickly, why should I be merciful, even if you are the chosen one?

Ronan dropped to his knees and the warriors, trembling violently and not daring to look at the bear, all followed his lead.

With his eyes fixed on Orsa's,' Ronan replied, 'Great King of the Wood, Son of the Great Mother Bear in the sky that watches over us for Mamm Norves, we did not know that we had trespassed, but now that we see your magnificence, our only action is to kneel before you in reverence! I am Ronan of the Pretan, son of Thurien and Lord of Menitriel, as you have stated, and these are my followers. We seek passage through your lands, with your permission, to reach the hills on the far side of the wood.'

Orsa dropped down to all four legs and walked slowly around the warriors as they knelt, poking his snout at them, sniffing and smelling them, grumbling and growling as he went.

'Hmm, grrr, yes, I knew you would come. Many have tried to pass through these woods, but it is Ronan I have waited for; still, I do not trust you, you smell dangerous. I came to the Earth to inspire and guide and yet, I know that one day your people will betray me. You have built a land of men on the great hill beyond, which Sira Howl fades, taking down my trees and using them for your purposes. GRRR! Is that why you are here? Is this how it begins? Have you come for the large trees, the great trees at the centre of my lands? Are you trespasser, thief and destroyer?' His agitation built rapidly. 'You have lit fires. Is this to aid your purpose? Do you intend to use them to burn the wood? Grrr. I think that my brothers, sisters and I will deal with you now, in spite of the prophecy. I see through you "King Ronan". You are not King here, I am and will remove you and your followers. I sense your purpose is bad.'

All of the warriors instinctively took their hand to their sword hilts and some of them stood up. Many eyes stared back at them now, surrounding them in the gloom. Snouts followed by angry faces began to appear. There were many more bears than they had thought, and there was no escape. The end that they had feared at the beginning seemed about to be realised.

Ronan acted quickly.

'Do not touch your sword hilts,' he commanded. 'King Orsa, we come in peace and not to take trees. We have lit fires, but with branches that have fallen and are old and dead, and only to keep us warm and so that we can see in the darkness. We are men, you understand, and not as fortunate as bears, we do not have thick coats of hair to keep us warm and we cannot see in the dark, and so we must light fires, but in doing this we will harm no living tree.

Come now, Great King of the wood, let us talk, you and I, to each other, King to King. We can reach an agreement, I am sure, that will bring honour and benefit to us both.'

Orsa studied the King, wriggling his snout as he considered Ronan's words.

'What do you propose, "King Ronan"? How might we live alongside each other? How will you prove worthy of the prophecy, if I relent and allow you to live?'

'Great King, let us build a road that passes through your lands from our lands to the far distant hills. It will provide safe passage for my people, but in return, we will not stray from this road, except by your permission. I give you my word and bind my descendants upon the light, warmth and continuing beneficence of Sira Howl to continue this agreement.'

'How will you ensure this? Grrr. How do I know, Ronan, that I can trust all of your people?'

'In this, I will build stations along the length of the road, where my people may pause and rest on their journey. From these stations, which will be special places at natural clearings in the canopy from where we can see the light of Sira Howl, we will guard the road and ensure that none stray where they should not into the lands of Orsa, King of the Great Wood and Lord of the Crossing. We will plant new trees here, nurture and revere the woods. The sacred road that we will build, respecting Orsa and his people heading towards Sira Howl, we will call Sawkerdh – or "safe passage".'

Orsa rose again to his full height, but now spoke into the gloom, addressing the eyes that shone around the clearing.

'Hmm, GRRR! What do we think brothers and sisters? Is this man worthy of our trust?'

Grumbles, roars and growls came back and the discussion and debate that followed continued until the fire had faded to embers, with none of the warriors daring to stoke it with any more logs, fallen or not. Eventually, King Orsa spoke to Ronan again in the gloom.

'We accept your proposal, Ronan, King of Men. We are ready to live alongside you and your people, to work together. It is the prophecy, but if you stray from your word, we will make you pay and we will always be watching you.'

Ronan walked forward and bowed before him. 'Mighty King Orsa, thank you for your generosity. You will always be a symbol *of strength and wisdom for our people, inspiring us to great things, and I give you my word that you will not regret it.'*

'Growl – make sure that I do not. Now, rest, all of you, you are under my protection and in the morning I will guide you to Tamara, mighty flowing priestess of the land, and the crossing that divides this wood. A special place that is sacred to all creatures. I will show you how to cross and then I will send you on your way.

In the morning, with the first rays of Sira Howl's radiance spreading through the trees, Ronan and his company rose and gave thanks for his continuing presence and guidance. When they had finished, they saw Orsa and the other bears approaching through the wood.

'King Ronan, bring your men; Tamara is not far, follow me now.

They followed the Great Bear through the trees. After a while, they descended a hill into a small, shallow gorge that she had cut into the land and, a little further on, heard the gushing and flowing of her waters and came to a riverbank. They walked along the bank a short way to where an acolyte river joined the priestess of the land.

Orsa said, 'Here, where Tamara cuts the land and Enyam comes to serve her, there are places where it is shallow in different seasons and it is possible to cross easily to the other side. Occasionally, my kin and I come and fish for salmon and other fish. But you are welcome to pass this way also, with your road.'

'Where will you fish if our road passes through here?' asked Ronan.

The bear appeared to chortle. 'There are many places where we can feed from her beneficence.'

Ronan nodded his acknowledgement and Orsa stood back a little and said, 'King Ronan, gather your followers and cross Tamara here. Her waters will bless you and give you new purpose. Then go towards Sira Howl and soon you will come to your far distant hills, and remember – this crossing is sacred, where the spirits of our ancestors and we, the living, mingle and where the stars in the heavens watch over you. Revere it now and forever. It will shape and guide your people until the end of their days.'

Silence fell, save the flow and bubble of Tamara as the bear held Ronan and the whole Company in the intensity of his gaze.

Then Orsa turned away, saying as he did so, 'For now, I bid you farewell and I wish you good journey!'

The Company stood and watched the bears go. When they had disappeared into the trees, Ronan turned to his men and said, 'Henceforth, Orsa will inspire us and will be a symbol of great strength and wisdom for our people. Onward now to our destination, follow me!'

a pair of brown eyes

At the wax of Loor Tevyans

Gwalian walked along a deer path beside Enyam, a tributary of Tamara. Sira Howl shone his morning light through the trees and the path cut its way through bushes of hornbeam and blackthorn resplendent with white blossom and interspersed with dogwood, wild cherry and young crab apple trees with pink and white flowers and recently unfurled leaves. Running down to the water's edge was a thick and pungent carpet of wild garlic mixed with wood violets, anemones and primrose. The loud whistle of a nuthatch caused her to look up to the branch where it stood proudly alert, looking back at her.

Her concentration, though, was not on the early growth of spring, but instead on the noise of conversation and laughter, mixed with the sounds of splashing water coming from a little way ahead.

As she drew closer, something made her stop. Instead of walking confidently into the middle of the conversation, as she normally would, she walked down the bank and cautiously moved forward to view the unfolding scene, hidden from those ahead by a blackthorn tumbling to the water.

Enyam was no more than three or four men wide at her greatest width and the height of a grown man deep at any point along her entire length, and occasionally, at points such as here, meandered gently, creating a deep pool suitable for bathing and short burst swimming.

Gwalian smiled as she looked on. The Company were learning to swim and, thinking they were in a secluded location, had discarded all of their clothing for this first lesson. The Prince stood fully naked, giving instructions on a gravel spur that jutted out from the bank into the river. Without making a sound and being very careful to ensure she was unseen, Gwalian settled down to watch. His voice, loud so that they could all hear, carried easily to her.

'Swimming saves lives. Never again will I lose good comrades for a lack of this ability. We will learn first without the burden of clothing and then practise in clothing.'

Gwalian watched, intrigued and increasingly enjoying herself as Artur gingerly picked his way, bootless, into the river, negotiating stones and obstacles on the riverbed, before it was deep enough for him to swim. It was clearly very cold, and as she watched, the temperature caused pertness in his alert and toned upper body. There was strength in his arms and in the tautness of his stomach and chest muscles. Her eyes widened slightly and she breathed in deeply and exhaled slowly as she watched, and her eyes wandered down to his body to his round firm, muscular upper thighs and his ample manhood. Involuntarily, she licked her lips as, with a loud splash, he was in and swimming across the pool to where Maedoc had already begun to demonstrate the stroke and how they should use their arms.

As she watched, there was a sudden pattering on her head as small gravel stones and dried seed casings from the previous summer showered down on her. She spun around. Above her, the blackthorn bush rustled and there were the sounds of clothes ruffling and feet moving accompanied by a muted deep giggle. She could see no one, but someone had seen her. Slowly, carefully, so as not to give away her presence, she turned back to the swimming lesson, and as she did so, Lancelin walked quickly and confidently down from the bank to the gravel spur.

'Where have you been?' Kea shouted sternly from the water, still distrustful of an apparently indulged son and irritated by the disrespect that he seemed to show to the Prince in his delayed arrival. The man of the Kernovi attempted to disguise his agitation with banter. 'We fight together, we freeze together, our bollocks drop off together, it is a contract we have made and we don't want any shirkers, Lancelin. No doubt you will tell us that you can swim and do not feel it worth your while to share our pain.'

As Kea was talking, Lancelin sat on the spur, removing his boots. He jumped up now and began to remove his clothing. His darker skin distinguished him from those in the water, where a mass of white and pink were the prevailing colour. A thin mat of dark hair spread across his chest, matching the tight dark curls on his head.

'Not at all Kea, I am always ready to share your pain. I can swim, as it happens, and swim well, but that does not mean I think it beneath me to help teach you lesser mortals the basics that might, one of these days, save your miserable little lives!'

Kea, plain-faced, regarded him from the water as Lancelin placed his upper garments next to his boots. The man from the valley bent over, his back muscles taut, and removed his trousers and leggings, revealing a further light covering of body hair, beginning on his lower back and descending to a 'v' shape before disappearing between two firm, and in the fresh morning air, goose-pimpled buttocks. On both arms, intricate tattoos came down from shoulder to wrist, while on his lower legs, just above his ankles, further tattoos showed a similar design of intricate curls, dragonheads and flourishing lines that wrapped around and flowed down the centre of his foot, towards his toes.

Gwalian looked on. He was handsome and strong and he knew it. For a moment, she savoured all that she saw and forgot his deceit and betrayal.

'Pryns Artur, I am sorry that I am late. My father detained me this morning for an important discussion'. His eyes shot quickly to Kea and then back to the Prince. 'I have come as quickly as I could.'

The Prince nodded his acknowledgement, before congratulating Ambros on his first successful swim. Lancelin, meanwhile, turned in the direction of Gwalian, gave a brief, mischievous smile and then, with no hesitation, walked confidently into the river and dived into the pool.

Unseen by the Company, Gwalian, mortified, looked on. Would he always let her down? She had to move. She knew him too well. He would not be able to resist uncovering her for very much longer and she certainly did not want the Prince or his men to know that she had been there. Quietly, she withdrew back up the bank and walked deeper into the woods but close enough still to hear them.

It had to be now, she had decided. Artur liked her, she knew that he had made little attempt to conceal it, but it had to move quickly now. War was coming, her father had said so, and after Lancelin's betrayal, she needed an anchor, a close companion to move forward with in the difficult days ahead. It was not too

214

much to ask and she liked Artur too; he was handsome and strong and he listened to her, found her interesting and did not diminish her with his own self-obsession and ego. The High Priestess seemed very interested in him too. She watched his every move and her interest clearly went beyond the provision of extra fighting men promised to her father. There was something else at work, something deeper, and so she needed to act quickly before her advantage was lost.

After a while, she came to a spread of slightly fading short, stubby woodland daffodils, mixed with early bluebells. At the far edge of the carpet of flowers was a cluster of early purple orchids with their distinctive cone-shaped deep-pink flowers. Quickly, she picked one bluebell and orchid, trimmed the stalk of each plant and left just enough green to insert them between the pin and the brooch of her dress, allowing the flowers to spread upwards towards her left shoulder. Once satisfied that its position was in the way that she wanted it, she turned and walked back towards Enyam.

Artur, who had dressed first in his loose baggy trousers, leather boots and undershirt, saw her approach and, smiling broadly, walked towards her.

'Hello! I thought you were at Pendre today. It is good to see you.'

'It is good to see you too. You have been in the water, I see. Quite cold, I imagine!'

'Yes!' he laughed as he spoke, 'very. We have not been in long, but it is important that we learn to swim if we are to cross Ocean again.'

'Hmm, very sensible,' she couldn't resist peering over his shoulder, 'and are you making progress?'

'A little…'

He caught her gaze over his shoulder and noticed the vibrant pink and blue flowers spread on her own shoulder, emphasising her effervescence and confidence. Their eyes met and Sira Howl's morning light sparkled out from her as she smiled gently, intimately, back at his young hopeful face.

'You probably shouldn't go much further. Some of the hardier souls of the Company are still in the water, with no clothes on.'

'Really, how intriguing!'

215

Her eyes widened as she looked at him and then strained again to look over his shoulder. She could see several of the Company on the bank, but the sound of splashing was still coming from the river.

'Are you finished here? Can you walk with me? There is much to see in these woods and for you to explore.'

Her eyes widened slightly as she looked at him again. 'I would enjoy being your guide. Or do you have other plans for the Company?'

He was very ready to accept and to change whatever he had been planning to do. 'Yes, a walk. Wait here a moment, I will get the rest of my clothes and my sword.'

He ran back to the bank.

'The lady Gwalian has come and would like to discuss some things with me. I will see you all later, back at Pendre, for our close combat practice.'

He bent down to pick up his remaining clothes, sword and belt, before turning and quickly walking away again.

For a moment, there was silence amongst the Company as they all looked at each other. Several raised eyebrows met wry grins before Drustan elevated himself to the position of command and took charge of the morning's exercise.

'Come on, I think we have chilled ourselves enough. Let's head back to Pendre. I'm famished, let's go and seek out some refreshment.'

Lancelin, the last one in, was also the last to leave the pool. Sombre now, his bravado subdued, he pushed slowly through the water to follow the others out. It was only a small mistake, or at least he thought so. Why had she taken it so badly? He still could not understand it.

***

Gwalian was walking slowly away, deeper into the woods, when Artur caught up with her.

'I'm glad you came today. I would have missed you if I hadn't seen you.'

She laughed, 'Yes, you would!'

His smile faded slightly and he focused on the ground, deep in thought as he spoke. 'I could have said that better. Would you believe me if I said that I feel nervous when we speak?'

'I cannot think why. We are good friends now.'

'Yes, yes we are.'

He walked closely beside her now, his body agitated. Their arms touched and she stopped and turned to look at him, her eyes, enquiring and smiling.

He said, 'I cannot wait any longer! I have to tell you that I think you are beautiful and how special, wonderful, it is when I am with you.'

He turned at the sound of further shouts, splashes and laughter.

'I have a challenge to face and a feeling of affinity with my Company grows each day,' he looked back, 'but that does not compare in any way to the pleasure that I get from seeing you, listening to you, talking to you. If I am nervous, well, it is because I so much want to get it right, in the hope that, eventually, you might feel the same way about me too.'

His appealing eyes looked towards her, seeking the response he wanted.

She smiled and said, 'Come on, I have something to show you. I think you will like it, but we will need to walk a little bit further into the woods and cross Enyam and, as we go, I think you might have to tell me that bit again about how beautiful I am!'

Her smile turned to a grin and she held out her hand. Relieved, he walked towards her and took it. It felt good to hold it! She, in turn, gripped his hand firmly; there were no uncertainties or tentative steps here. The elegance of her strong, slender body alongside his began to produce an additional pulse within him. Gwalian felt the current of his body in close proximity to hers and the strength of his hand that was wrapped up in her own. It was not an overwhelming strength, but firm and confident. It excited her. He was interested in her, everything about her and was boyishly handsome. Gently and almost involuntarily, she squeezed his hand as they walked. Where would this lead them? She did not know, but her plan for the morning had been made stronger by this unexpected turn of events.

Quickly, they came again to Enyam and the flat stones placed across her, forming a bridge.

'This is the only way to cross without getting wet.'

On the far side, the path rose steeply until the ground levelled. Ahead, amongst the trees, Artur could see a small hut, square and built with axe split, half-moon timber. It had a door and, unusually, windows, each with its own set of shutters. A gentle spiral of smoke came from a hole in the apex of the thatched hip roof.

'What do you think?' she asked excitedly. 'It is my special place, which my father built for me when I was a child. I come here in spring and summer mainly, to gather flowers and for peace and solitude.'

The house spoke for her, original and different.

'It is a very interesting design. I like it!'

'Good, come and look inside.'

As she walked through the door, she said over her shoulder, 'Berlewan has come to prepare refreshments for us.'

He acknowledged her attendant and took in the room. He saw that this was more than just a hut in the woods; it had chairs, a table, a bed and a cooking area where Berlewan was now stirring warm liquid refreshment in a small cauldron over the fire.

'Often, during Golowan, Medh and Barlys, I stay overnight, with Berlewan, of course, and my father's guards not far away at their watch posts along the river. But I still have a sense of being alone, of having escaped to my own special place.

On the wall behind her, above the bed, hung a hunting horn and, beside it, a large bow and quiver of arrows.

'Whose is the bow?'

'Mine! All Veneti children learn the bow and arrow in the ancient tradition, as we are descendants of those first archers that crossed Ocean with mother Venetia.'

'But surely, the bow is bigger than you!'

She saw the look of incredulity in his face and read its meaning. 'It is a full-sized bow. While Berlewan finishes preparing, let's go outside and see who can fly an arrow the furthest!'

The warmth of her smile remained, but now it had a tint of determination, and despite his infatuation, he was not going to ignore the challenge. 'Let's do that.'

Smiling, she took the bow, quiver, and with a raised of her eyebrows to Berlewan, followed him out of the door.

'Do you have much experience of archery?'

'I can use the bow and arrow.'

'Good, you go first then. Name your tree and strike it firmly at shoulder height.'

She seemed confident, but surely, he must have the greater experience?

No matter how handsome and otherwise appealing they are, she thought, all men have that arrogance, that immediate assumption that they will be better.

Artur held the bow with his left hand and stretched his fingers before taking the string with his right hand. Tall as he was, the bow stood alongside him at a similar height. Back in Demetae, where he had learnt how to hold and fire the arrow, the bows were plain, ugly almost, and made of elm, but strong and effective. This bow was different. It was made of yew, strong but lighter and more elegant in the sweep of its curve. The inner edge of the bow stave or belly felt round and smooth to the grip, accentuated by evident regular care.

Artur vaguely indicated a tree in the middle distance, positioned his arrow, held his left hand steady, drew back the hemp string and fired. The arrow whistled between the trees and struck a trunk firm and true at about shoulder height in the area that he had indicated.

'Not bad!' she said, and opened her eyes wider before saying, 'you clearly have used a bow before. Right, now it is my turn.'

She took the bow from him, while he sat down on the stump of a tree behind her to give Gwalian the room that he assumed she needed. She selected an arrow, began to prepare and he immediately noticed her dexterity and how her whole body moved in support of her actions when she placed the arrow. Standing on tiptoes first, creating an arc as her slender frame bent forward across the bow, she lifted it upwards and then moved backwards in the receding arc. Her feet returned fully to the ground, now holding the arrow firmly in place. Despite her slender frame, her legs were powerful and strong and as she moved, her small firm bottom pushed determinedly within her dress as both bow and body lifted as one. In contrast to Artur, once she was upright, she held her string arm steady and, instead, bent her whole body, taut, into the action of stretching the bow gripped in her left hand. The strength of her arms was clear as the bow stave contorted to its maximum extent.

The arrow shot from the bow without any form of warning and flew through slender gaps between the trees, striking her target true at shoulder height, ten good paces beyond the tree where Artur's arrow rested. There was no argument, he had lost this first round. Several rounds followed and he put all his effort into reaching further with each arrow, but she won every contest. Her technique was superior to his. Her commitment to this particular skill exceeded his.

After the fifth set of arrows, Gwalian looked across to Artur. He took his defeat well. Her brother, Lancelin and others would not have reacted in this way and, instead, sought any reason for their defeat other than the fact that she, at this at least, was better than them. She liked that about him. Despite his boyish nervousness, he was strong, content and confident in the man he was, or at least he appeared so; and if someone, man or women, was better at any one thing, he was happy to admit it – and praise that person's ability.

'Maybe I should have told you at the start that I come here often and practice regularly and have been doing so for many years.'

He guffawed. 'It shows! Your technique is distinctive and effective. Perhaps, later, you could help me to improve mine. I have never seen a bow fired in that way before, it is different. The Company and I can learn from it, I am sure, perhaps to our advantage in battles to come.'

'I would be very pleased to do that. I'm sorry if I have misled you though.'

'Please! I have thoroughly enjoyed our archery and I could watch you all day firing arrows…' For a moment, his voice faded away and their eyes met. Something stirred within him, desire and a tautness within his stomach as it rose and fell with a steady rhythm, before he continued half-heartedly, '…and learn from your technique.'

Even as he tried to mask his thoughts, he gave them away. Maybe he was too honest, but it was endearing and a genuine desire for him built within her. He did things that she would do; appeared to see things as she would see them and his humility, mixed with strength when required, drew her even more closely to him. Her pulse was quickening. She smiled again and took a deep breath. 'Come on, Berlewan has had to go back to Pendre, but she has left us our refreshments. We will get the arrows later.'

Inside the hut, Gwalian ladled two beakers full of the warm tonic, handed a beaker to Artur and stood before him in front of one of the windows. He took a step back and a large gulp and licked his lips. He was thirsty and it felt good in his mouth. She responded to his bold intake of tonic by doing the same. Her eyes fixed on his, and she rolled her tongue around her lips, in a slower and more considered way than him, enjoying the sparkle and pulse of the liquid as it passed into her body.

Artur said, 'Hmm, this is good, just what I needed.'

He took another full mouthful. Again, she did the same and now a movement in the clouds or the tree cover allowed Sira Howl to stream his light through the window. A gentle breath of wind lifted her dark brown hair and created a surrounding intensity of light that matched the warmth of her face and the smile of pleasure that was produced by the soft caress of this unexpected wind. Her dress was sufficiently translucent to suggest the line of her body underneath and a hint of what it would look like if she was not wearing it.

Artur breathed in deeply and quickly, put his beaker down, walked over to her, took her hands with great purpose and said, 'May I kiss you?'

The mix of tenderness, with his sudden but welcome bold decision sent a pulse of intense pleasure through her. Her strong legs wavered. She gripped his hands tightly, lent forward and their lips touched lightly. He stood firm; he knew how to take command, holding her steady and enjoying the intimacy of her soft touch and gentle, moist, quickly repeated kisses. Suddenly, he stopped, looked intensely into her eyes, almost as if he was convincing himself that this was really happening before their lips came together again. Now he held her waist and drew her strongly towards him, she gasped as his chest, full of active, alert muscles, rubbed firmly against her and her arms for a moment spread out from her. Her breasts gently rubbed his torso and she reached up and held his head firmly in her hands, working her fingers through his hair. He could have carried on and on, savouring every part of those wonderful and glorious lips and the friction and excitement generated by the rub of her body, but he needed to breathe.

'Gwalian, I adore you, you know that, don't you? You are so beautiful! When I should be concentrating, listening to what your father says, I am not! I am looking at you and thinking of you. It is as if you have completely consumed me and all I want is to be part of you, with you, to talk and listen to you. It is so intense it hurts!'

'Stop!' she exclaimed, 'Why are you talking to me? You should be kissing me. Why stop now, when our passion was building so well? You have much to learn, I think, but kiss me more, handsome Pryns. I have watched you too and my affection for you builds with each day, but please, we should not waste this moment with unnecessary words! Drink more and then come to the bed, kiss me again and show me your affection!'

He stared intently into her eyes, nodding his head, turned, found his beaker and finished off the last of the liquid. He licked his lips and turned back, held out his hand and led her to the bed in the corner of the room. She drank the last of her tonic, and while trying to place it back, dropped the beaker as he pulled her more firmly towards him. Now he did not hesitate and held her firmly around the waist, gently caressing the upper part of her bottom with his lower fingers.

As their mouths came together again, firmly and determinedly, their lips wrapped around each other, exploring, conveying passion and desire, and she began to tug at his baggy undershirt. It came free from his leggings with ease. Her hands reached under and touched gently the bare skin of his upper body. It was all she had anticipated, taut and tense with pleasure. She held his back and gently stroked her hand up and down the middle of his chest, stretching up to continue the kiss.

She could feel the firmness of his desire in his leggings and she stretched up again and gently rubbed against him with the lower part of her body as she whispered in his ear. 'Take off your shirt. I want to see your wonderful body, it feels so strong!'

With his shirt removed, he wrapped her in his bare arms and his natural warmth transfused through her. The kiss rejoined. Now they were breathing heavily and murmurs of pleasure passed between them. Then, she stretched up again.

'Now, can you reach over to the buttons on the back of my dress? Yes, that's it. Undo them!'

As he did so, clumsily, she softly kissed his cheek and held him close to her. When he had finished she undid the leather tie belt around her midriff, stepped back, allowed the dress to drop to the floor and stepped out of it. She wore the simplest of undergarments. Her body shape was clear through it; her slender strong frame and well-shaped, rounded breasts gently sloped to the alert and large brown nipples that were showing clearly through the cloth. Her ruffled hair and her eyes, warm and deep, looking back at him, confirmed her desire. The agitation of his body, the power of his emotion and his all-consuming focus on her drove her forward. Never had she felt such yearning so close to her, and all for her! Now his hands ran up, down, all over her body and she, in turn, caressed as they kissed, squeezing his firm, pert buttocks, and pulling the lower half of his body even tighter to hers.

Suddenly, she stopped and stood back.

'Do you dare?'

'Do I dare?'

'All of our clothes off and come and kiss me again on the bed.'

'I dare!'

His leggings were off in an instant and her undergarment came over her head. For a moment, they stood and admired each other and yes, she was just as beautiful naked as he had imagined and he handsome and strong beneath it all, as she knew he would be, and with his total desire prominent and clear before her. They looked into each other's eyes and smiled and then, simultaneously, both laughed. She took his hand and gently pulled him towards her. The rub of skin and body as each held the other sent a fresh pulse of fervour and desire through them and into each other's arms as they fell, entwined, onto the bed.

***

Andras's horse took several steps sideways as the Princess shuffled irritably in the saddle.

'Zethar, are you sure this is where we are to meet? No matter how remote, I am nervous of discovery. He must come quickly and our agreement must be swift.'

Anogin had replied to Zethar's appeal for his return. If the Dumnoni "prynces" wanted his support, she must meet him away from the main routes in a remote place where they could strike a deal in private. He had identified the place and sent a guide to meet Andras, Zethar and two loyal male followers. These were bodyguards who would betray nothing of what they had seen. They had set out early, met the guide and ridden to this wild and windblown heath.

'My lady, this man has been sent to guide us. I am sure it is the right place. We must wait for Anogin to arrive.'

With the light fading, a horse and rider began to appear on the track, coming towards them out of the descending darkness. As he rode up to them, he looked sternly at the waiting group as if inspecting them, assessing the bodyguards and asserting his authority over the two women, in particular. He was a giant of a man who ignored Andras and showed no form of deference to her highborn position. His address was brief and to the point.

'Zethar, I come as requested. What do you require?'

'Lord Anogin, brave and noble warrior of the Belgae, may I introduce Prynces Andras, heir to the throne of the Dewnan.'

Anogin frowned and looked grimly across to Andras. He did not speak or offer any other form of acknowledgement or greeting to her. Zethar, aware of his temper, paused for a moment, waiting to see if he would say anything before hurriedly continuing.

'As you are aware my lady Andras's illegitimate brother, the bastard son of the old witch queen, begotten we believe from one of the many entanglements of late-night intimacy, common amongst the witches and their acolytes, has returned. Her father, old fool that he is, believes the boy is his son and has seen fit to equip him with sufficient support that, if it's not checked, could offer the potential for momentum to build. The current witch queen guides matters secretly and plots his elevation to leader of our people. He is an offspring of their order, manipulable and as warped and twisted as the rest of them. We must stop them both and remove them if we are to prevent a reversal of our hopes and intentions. We have both come to this place to request your support and commission you, secretly, to attack the Veneti colony, seek out the bastard Artur and the witch Morlain, and then kill them both and all who stand to defend them.'

He sat back in his saddle appraising the two women. His contempt was palpable, for Andras, in particular. Zethar, who was both experienced in and wary of his temper, continued nervously.

'We bring gold so that you may cross back to the Durotrages and recruit a sufficient force of men to undertake this task.'

'Humph,' he scoffed. 'I will take your gold, but will have no trouble recruiting men of the Durotrages. Veneti scum come frequently to the villages along the far bank of the Axe and take anyone they find – men, women and children – for their slave ships and fight all who stand in their way. No, it will be easy to recruit a force of motivated men. Hand over the gold and, before I ride, tell me: what else do you offer if I achieve what you ask for?'

Not knowing him as Zethar did, Andras spoke next, confident for a few brief moments of her superior position, unaware of his quickness to temper and worse if challenged.

'Lord Anogin, Zethar speaks well of you, but before we talk of a further offer, tell me, how confident can I be that you will deal with Artur and his Company when you could not before?'

Quickly his horse was alongside hers. He towered over her, grabbed her arm and pulled her towards him. The guards drew their swords, then, looking contemptuously around him, he threw the arm away again and sat up straight in his saddle.

'Listen, so-called prynces, I am here to take your gold and ensure that you make a binding promise for my reward when I remove this false pryns, offspring of the wicked and heretical order of witches and their bedraggled throwback to the Pretan sun idolatry. Gradually, my people are moving across this land, cleansing, removing sorcery and magic; and when I have done this for you, this is what you will do to reward me. Ensure that your father acknowledges me, that the rights of trade at the river crossing are mine and that my friends in the Curiosolitae have control of Tamara and Ictis. He will order the removal of the Veneti pirates and send a force of warriors to round up all we have not killed, ready for transport and sale in the market at Alet. When this is done, you will come to me and honour Anogin as Lord of the Crossing.' He grabbed her arm again. 'Do you understand me!'

She held up her other hand to stop any thought by her retainers of responding to his aggression, although both seemed reluctant to confront this large and powerful man.

'I understand you, and if you achieve this for me, I will do that for you.'

He laughed.

'I am not doing it for you. I am doing it because I want to do it. You will do my bidding because if you do not follow my instructions, I will make it clear to all that you instigated this. You, who sought to undermine your father's orders – another woman in this lax and insipid kingdom who has ideas well above her position. Then I will approach your father. You will be mine and all that is yours will be mine. I will be his heir and you will obey me in everything that I command. Women do not lead men. It is wrong, unnatural and disgusting. This land is in ruin through the folly of weak men who allow the witches' cult to persist and interfere in the affairs of men. The Belgae and our allies will rule the Dumnoni, and a proper order will come – and you "prynces" will do all that I command in pursuit of that inevitable end. Now, give me the gold and I will begin this task.'

Andras, tense and shaking, nodded to one of the guards, who handed over the gold.

Anogin, snatched the bags from him, fixed them to his saddle and made ready to depart. 'Do not let me down "lady Andras" or betray my purpose, because if you do you will regret it.'

His horse turned, sensing departure. Anogin turned the animal back and sneered, 'And there was I thinking it would be more difficult to deal with a prynces famous for her magical powers. Where are they now? No, you are as weak as all your sex and your tribe of feeble miscreants. You need me, a man of the Belgae, to achieve your end, but you have got more than you bargained for and I will hold you to the bargain we have set.'

For a moment, he held her firmly in his glare, then turned the horse and galloped off into the night.

***

'Madam, you must come quickly! Your father looks for you and the Pryns. Messengers have come from Gwened. He calls for you and Pryns Artur and grows angry. He has sent me to find you. Please come now!'

At first, they did not hear her.

'Madam, forgive me! I have to disturb you; I dare not return without you and do not want your father to find you here. Please, tell me you have heard me and will come quickly now!'

Days had passed since the competition with the arrows and their first embrace. Since then, each afternoon after combat practice found them here, engrossed and oblivious; but Loor Tevyans now completed his final phase, and with it, as yet unperceived by them, their brief and passionate encounter was beginning to change.

Gwalian breathed in deeply and rose above Artur. Smiling back at him for a moment, she got up from the bed.

'Berlewan, I have heard you, thank you. Wait for us at the stepping stones. We will come right away.'

'Madam, the messengers bring news of great urgency. Please hurry.'

'We will be right along Berlewan, wait for us at Enyam.'

They both understood the importance of the message and yet, as she stood naked, talking through the door, he gazed at her luxuriant brown hair and the smooth curve of her back down to that wonderful, perfectly formed bottom. He did not move from the bed; and as she turned back to him, surveying his glistening, alert body, ready for anything, she desired. Her eyes gestured towards him and she said, 'I don't care if the Romans are rowing up Tamara at this very moment. We cannot waste that!' and with that conspiratorial smile that would get him to do anything, asked, 'How quick can you be?'

***

Loor Tevyans had risen early and begun to climb, determined to make the most of his last zenith for another year. Bright and thin, he edged half revealed above the treeline while Sira Howl, with a softer, decreasing glow, dipped serenely below the horizon. Beneath this transit, between heavenly King and Gille,

Artur and Gwalian belatedly hurried across the open ground in front of Pendre, Lord Aodren's hall at Menluit.

Artur pushed one of the large entrance doors open and allowed Gwalian to go ahead of him. A strong smell of sweat and odour, mixed with wood smoke, greeted them. Grimy faces half-revealed in the dim light of the hall turned to face them now, before parting to create a way through for the Prince and Gwalian to pass.

'At last, you are here! Come and sit next to me, Pryns Artur. Daughter, we have important news from Gwened. I awaited your arrival before sharing it with everyone.' His stern face looked from one to the other. 'I would not have waited much longer.'

As they seated themselves, Aodren said quietly but firmly to them, 'This is a matter of great urgency, as you must have suspected. I am sure Berlewan made that clear and so I am disappointed it has taken this long to get here from your hideaway. Yes, do not look so surprised, I know where you have been. Priorities, daughter, my Lord Pryns, priorities, you need to get yours in order.'

A final glare and then, before either could respond, he turned away to address the room.

All of the Company had places and Artur could see raised eyebrows and knowing glances looking back at him as he glanced around the table. Something deep within him made him look to Morlain, hoping subconsciously perhaps for encouragement. She looked impassively back at him, not at Gwalian, just him, and the slightest movement of her eye showed her displeasure.

Aodren spoke beside him.

'Blaez and Tanet bring urgent news from Armorica and from King Mael himself. As we have expected, but not desired, the Roman general wants more of us than we are prepared to give. A day of reckoning approaches for us all.'

He spoke directly to the emissaries.

'My friends, you have crossed the Mor Pretani quickly, aided by a favourable wind, demonstrating, I hope, the support of Ocean's spirits, which surely we need right now. Come, share your news.'

Blaez stood and purposefully looked around the hall, at the anxious faces that stared back at him, concerned.

'The Romans have commandeered and built a fleet of ships at the mouth of the Liger. Our spies tell us they will send it against us by the wax of the Loor Medh at the latest.'

There were gasps around the hall.

'Control, you see,' Blaez continued, 'that is what matters. They must control everything. They act as if Gaul is theirs, but still one thing bothers them; our affinity with Ocean. They desire our trade, and who knows, a bridgehead to the land of the Dewnan and the rest of the ancient Pretan inheritance. Our trade completes their conquest.'

Tanet rose and looked towards Aodren and then Morlain.

'They sent their envoys to the King, to demand a supply of corn, to maintain their legion and, they said – to "keep the peace" across Gaul.' He paused for effect and then with rising passion said, 'There will be no peace while Rome abuses our land!'

Everyone started talking at once. Some of the Company stood and started shouting across the table. Artur and Gwalian were subdued, looking grimly ahead. Kea, Gawen, Maedoc, Drustan and others within the Company stood but said nothing, looking towards the Prince, waiting for his guidance, ready to offer their support; and Morlain towards Tanet, her face giving nothing away, while Aodren rose.

'Quiet! Everyone, quiet, let them finish. Please, just give us the facts and the message from King Mael, rather than opinion and then we will discuss and agree on what action to take.'

'The facts are these, my Lord. The Roman junior general, Legate they call him, demonstrating his arrogance, sent a boy and old soldier to speak to our King and demand corn from him. Whilst these emissaries are with the King and his senior council, word comes separately, through contacts of my Lord Perig, of the Romans activity at the mouth of the Liger. There can be no doubt that, we, the heirs of Venetia, Ocean's People, are the last barrier to their complete control of Gaul and Armorica.'

As Tanet paused, Morlain sat upright at the table and spoke. 'We can all see the audacity of their approach and let us be clear, they intend provocation! Give a good price for the corn – a small investment towards a much bigger reward when they are ready; and they know we can see through them. It is what they intend, to provoke us, so that we make the first move, to which they can then respond. Well, whatever, this has been coming. Openly or covertly, their plan for total domination will not allow the Veneti fleet to be outside of their control. If we want our independence, we must fight!'

Her tousled long brown hair, with flecks of lighter brown mingled through it, surrounded and accentuated her face. Her slate blue eyes set within a soft white, downy skin stared intently at the emissaries as she finished speaking, and her lips were slightly pursed. Around her neck was a golden lunula of ancient manufacture in the shape of a half moon or perhaps the setting sun, handed down from priestess to priestess. As she spoke, the lunula captured and reflected a shaft of the last of the evening sunlight that was coming through a gap in the door and giving a glow to her face and the golden strands in her hair. She spoke with knowledge and authority, and all listened, taking assurance from her words, but the appeal of her face, golden and determined in the half-light of the hall, impressed many around the table. Artur watched quietly as she spoke, taking in her words and watching the movement of her face.

Tanet responded, 'Yes, my Lady, the fight is coming and, however it has come about, we would have reached this point anyway. They will not let us stand alone.'

Blaez looked around the table before turning first to Morlain and then Aodren and Artur. 'Come to our aid! We are all Veneti now, proud inheritors of our shared Pretan past and we must stand together or face oblivion. King Mael urges you, Aodren and all able-bodied men, to equip your ships and sail for Gwened. We need the best and fullest force that we can muster. Let us show these Romans, their Legate, and even the notorious Caesar, if he chooses to show up, what it means to face the Veneti. Fight us on Ocean if you can!'

Once again, the hall exploded into an uproar. As the shouting and jostling continued, Aodren rose slowly to his feet in grim resignation. He knew what was coming and understood the commitment he and all of them were about to make.

'Silence! Quiet, everyone, please, let us at least approach this in an organised manner!'

Nobody heard him and the din and uproar continued. Lancelin, who sat on the far side of the table, stood and produced a hunting horn from his belt, raised it to his lips and blew. The blast transcended the hubbub and silenced the room. With emphasised quick and simple movements, he took the instrument from his lips, placed it back in his belt and smiled perfunctorily at Aodren. Aodren briefly made eye contact with the young man and tilted his head in acknowledgement. He turned back to the two emissaries.

'We will, of course, respond to King Mael's call to defend our homeland, but we cannot leave immediately. We must prepare well because, make no mistake, this will be the fight of our lives. We will properly equip and leave in good order, and we must not completely abandon the colony; a place that we have all worked so hard to create. We will prepare our ships and agree who sails and who remains to protect Menluit, Ker Tamara, Dynas Dowr Tewl, Ictis and all of our mine and metal workings. You told me earlier the Curiosolitae have pledged to support the fight, but I do not believe them. If we believe that we can win and that we will return, we must protect what we have.'

For a moment, he paused, his face sober and determined.

'Tomorrow is Beltane and the fires will be sombre this year and I look for the return of my son before I can depart. If he and his men are back in the coming days, we will sail at the waning of Loor Skovarnek.'

He turned now to his right.

'Pryns Artur, what of the Dewnan? Can we count at least on you and your Company?'

Morlain's eyes widened slightly as she looked towards the Prince. Maedoc stood behind her, trying to give his best look of encouragement while the members of the Company sat up in their seats, attentive and anticipatory. As Artur rose to speak, Gwalian, sat on the other side of her father, turned to look up at him and he looked to her. The warmth of her smile of encouragement built confidence within him.

'Lord Aodren, good friends of the Veneti, you do not need to ask. We are warriors of the Dewnan, we have come to fight with you and together we will confront this Roman deceit and aggression. We too know how to handle a boat. Our sword arms will swing in your support. The Ocean People must stand and fight.' He pulled his sword from its scabbard and flourished it forward and aloft and he repeated, with as much vigour and determination as he could muster, 'We stand with you!'

The rest of the Company stood as one, as if they had been waiting for their cue to do so, unsheathed their swords and, following his lead, pointed them towards the Prince.

'Gans a'gas nei sav! With you we stand!'

Cheers broke out around the hall. People clapped and waved their fists. Gwalian led the applause and Aodren, in spite of himself, smiled broadly. As Artur put his sword away, the young man and older man clasped each other's arms tightly and for all to see, with a look of firmness on their faces.

Aodren spoke now. 'Together, we will fight for identity, distinctiveness and freedom as, since ancient days, the Veneti and the Dewnan. Let's drink to it!'

He gestured to a hall server who walked forward with a gold cup of corded decoration and with a simple handle riveted to the side. Full to the brim with mead, the cup was round bottomed, meaning that the server was compelled to hold on to it. He passed it to Aodren.

'Lady Morlain tells us this cup is linked to the legend of the Achaeans, your ancestors, if the story is true. It was brought from the warm sea and used by Ocean travellers as a symbol of togetherness between those who went into the unknown. Let us drink from it, you and I, and invoke the mighty spirits of our ancestors, as a symbol of our bond in the fight ahead.'

He took several large glugs, half emptying it and wiping his beard before passing it to Artur. The Prince took the mug and emptied it with several further glugs. Clean-shaven, he still wiped across his mouth and passed the cup back.

All in the hall now downed their mead in one or several large gulps. Cheering and shouts of encouragement broke out around them as the hall servers scurried around to top up again.

'My son, Ewen ap Aodren, will return soon and then we sail! Prepare young Pryns, all of you, prepare. They are a formidable foe. Prepare!'

Morlain had stood with everyone else looking on, and clapped too during the words of strength and encouragement. What a difference one moon could make! Artur's assuredness had grown; he looked more confident and his men were with him. They understood him and practised warfare daily, she had heard. Progress then and, maybe, she felt compelled to concede, Gwalian's influence had supported this change. Her smile faded slightly as, across the table, the two of them turned to talk to each other with words of mutual appreciation. Aodren turned to talk to others around him, and as he did so, the Prince turned from Gwalian, as she spoke to others she knew. He looked towards Morlain with a warm and engaging smile. She nodded her head lightly, encouraging and appreciative, and he, smiling again, gently nodded his head as well.

Tanet and Blaez had made their way around the table to Aodren.

'My Lord, as you know, we must return to Ictis later and depart on the early morning tide. We said we would discuss "our inheritance" before we left. King Mael is anxious that we have a plan in place for all possible outcomes.'

Aodren looked at both of them and nodded.

'Yes, let us do that. We will feast this evening, for you as our guests and in honour of our anticipated victory, but I believe that the food will not be ready for a little while yet. Let us go to one of the smaller roundhouses. I will ask others to join us.'

He gave orders for the continued serving of mead and wine for the hall guests and then touched the arm of the Prince to draw him away from his conversation with Drustan who had also come around the table.

'Pryns Artur, I would like to discuss a further matter with you in one of the roundhouses across the yard. Bring a small number of your Company with you, those responsible for the ship, in particular.'

Then he looked across the table to the Priestess.

'Lady Morlain, will you join us? There is a further matter of great importance to discuss.'

***

Gyras pulled his cloak around him and held his arms tight to his chest. Spring was everywhere, but the evenings were still cool and he was cold and annoyed as the light faded around him. How much longer would they keep him like this? He had done nothing to offend them. He had his secret purpose and given nothing away on that account. One thing was certain; if he got out of this in one piece, he would not be trading with the

Veneti again. Although, when Caesar had finished with them, he thought grimly, there would probably be no Veneti nation to trade with, and he would instead trade them, a commodity that would fetch a very good price in the markets of Agde or Massalia. He pulled his cloak firmly around him again. Despite this positive thought, he sat dispirited and irritated, looking across the houses of the settlement below him.

Although they had said nothing, his guards had seemed in a hurry to get to somewhere, to join something. They had quickly manacled his legs to this post against a roundhouse wall and walked away. He had tried to break free, but the iron chain held him securely. There had been occasional cheering and shouting, quite close by, but he had seen no one apart from a few children playing further down the village. All was quiet for the moment. The smell of wood smoke and cooking food wafted around him, and as the breeze increased, he listened to the sound of rustling leaves and creaking branches in the trees that surrounded the trev. He felt hungry and tired. The moon still provided a subdued light, but diminished now as cloud cover spread. An occasional twinkling star peeked through the last remaining gaps in the clouds, but the weather was changing. There was moisture in the air and the smell of the sea was borne on the freshening wind. A light rain began to envelop him.

This had been a fool's errand! Why come all of this way? He could have simply taken the view of the Curiosolitae sailors at Ictis. They seemed to know this land well, despite Aodren's attempts to prevent them. He could have built a report from what they had told him and then returned in one of their ships; but no, that would have been too simple for Gyras the perfectionist! He had to go all the way and now, here he was, tied to this post with no hope of escape and facing an uncertain future.

Sat underneath his cloak, he leant against the outer wall of the roundhouse. They had forgotten him, wherever they had gone and by covering himself by his cloak, he only added to his invisibility in the increasing darkness of the evening.

As his melancholy built, he became aware of voices in the roundhouse behind him. He lifted his head and turned towards the wall. There was more than one voice. Did they know he was here? It seemed not, there was no reservation. He recognised

Aodren's voice, and then the young Prince of the Dewnan said something in reply. Was that the Priestess? Then some voices he did not recognise. As quietly as he could, he drew back the cover of his cloak, sufficient to allow his left ear to rest on the outer wall. He adjusted his head slightly and then, yes, was the coating thinner here? The words came more clearly, at least in part.

'Pryns Artur, I have asked you to come away from the others,' Aodren was leading the conversation, '…your gille and Lords Drustan, Kea and Gawen… a matter we must discuss… before we depart. King Mael has… I do this.'

Gyras edged closer, trying to get his body as tight to the wall as he could. The Prince was saying something back to Aodren.

'…Maedoc is more than just my gille… as discussed… friend, adviser and… this conversation… helmsman and navigator… sent to select boat as you asked.'

Shouting burst out beyond the roundhouse and he lost the stilted thread of the conversation for a moment. By the sound of the shouts and laughter, the evening feasting and drinking was having a quicker than usual effect. Why did they drink so much alcohol? Wherever he went, Pretanike, Keltica or Gaul, they were all the same. It would surely lead to their ruin. He kept as still as possible in the hope that he would go unnoticed, but the shouting decreased and quiet returned. He laid his ear to the wall again. Actually, this was a better position. He could hear much more clearly now.

'Lord Aodren, Pryns Artur, shall we get to the point?'

The Lady Morlain's voice, confident and assertive cut into the discussion.

'There is a task of great importance that King Mael asks his Dewnan allies to undertake.'

Although he could not see them, Gyras sensed Aodren's irritation at what appeared to have been an interruption of the older man by the young woman.

'Yes… yes. Pryns Artur, what do you know of Venetia Teg?'

There was silence, perhaps, as the Prince slowly shook his head or looked to those around him to see if they knew. 'Nothing, connected to our lady Venetia, of course, I would only guess after that.'

Morlain spoke quickly. 'Artur, it is a large statue of the Mother Venetia, twice the size of a man, blessed and benign with gold covering and an inlay of jewels and precious materials, made in the years after the first Pretan landfall by the smiths amongst her devoted followers. They used some of the treasure they had brought across Ocean and it is of immense value.'

She paused for a moment.

'Few on this side of Ocean had seen gold before the arrival of the Pretan. It added such lustre and stature to these first arrivals and it has supported the many generations that have followed, the descendants of Aleman and Thurien, wherever they have gone. Even in their moment of greatest need, the Veneti will not trade the Venetia Teg, the last great remnant of that original brave journey; and Artur, however the coming battle goes, the Venetia Teg must not fall into Roman hands.'

Further down the village, a dog barked loudly. Gyras, listening so intently to the conversation, involuntarily started in reaction and lost his ear point and connection through the wall. He looked into the darkness of the evening. He had heard stories of the Pretan statue on his travels and had certainly handled many fine items of gold and silver and precious stones from across the barbarian lands. They were capable of intricacy and creating items of great beauty, but on such a scale as suggested here? He had not thought so and yet now that he knew the Priestess, he would not doubt her. What an unexpected stroke of luck to be here. They must not know that he had overheard them. He tried to find the point in the wall again.

'Do you understand what we are saying?' Aodren was speaking now. 'We go to this fight gladly and will take many a Roman scum down in the defence of our land, or consign their miserable bodies to Ocean's depths as they flounder on the rock of our fleet. But Artur, even a patriot such as I can see that no Gallic, Celtic or Ocean tribe has stopped them so far. We must concede that the fight may yet go badly and if it does they must not take the Venetia Teg. That is King Mael's request; come to our aid and fight bravely in our defence, but if we are overwhelmed, ensure that your Company remains able to make its escape and bring our greatest treasure to Nanmeur and the land of the Dewnan.'

As he listened intently, sniffing interrupted Gyras's concentration. The bark of the dog was sudden, loud and beside his other ear. Startled, he fell backwards, jarring his leg against the manacle chain. Cursing and unthinking, he lashed out and now the dog barked and growled as well. There were voices coming towards him. He lay prostrate on the ground with the dog on top of him. The voices were next to him, the dog was pulled away and his cloak yanked off him.

'Hey, what are you doing?'

'What am I doing? Abandoned here, soaked by this wretched drizzle and mauled by your dog! That's what I'm doing!'

Others appeared from out of the gloom and then ambling around the roundhouse came one of his guards, clearly a little drunk, and said something to the man who had challenged him. He, in turn, nodded and walked away, dragging the dog behind him.

The other guard also appeared now. One of them undid the chain and they both dragged Gyras to his feet and escorted him towards the main hall and the developing feast. As he passed the roundhouse door, he looked towards it and there, standing, watching him was Morlain. He quickly looked ahead, but he knew that she continued to watch as his guards escorted him away.

***

The hall servants brought in the first of the evening's food to the round high table of Pendre, and then the tables that clustered around it. All were alive with conversation, eating and drinking. As they entered, Maedoc drew Prince Artur aside.

'My Lord, Artur, I have been thinking about the boat that we will use to cross to Armorica. Following our discussion with Lord Aodren, I must speak with you.'

'Maedoc, yes, of course. It will be slightly quieter over there.'

They walked to a corner of the hall where the cloaks, shields and spears were stored.

The older man turned to the Prince.

'I have been to Ictis, as you instructed. The Veneti build fine and upright boats, but still I am concerned. As directed by you and Lord Aodren, I have chosen our boat from the fleet. It will easily carry us all across the Mor Pretani. Although smaller than the other boats, it is of similar construction and strong. I am sure it will allow us to carry the Venetia Teg, should we need to.'

'Maedoc, you know I meant what I said to Aodren earlier and have said previously, on all matters relating to the boat, you are our lead. We will follow whatever you advise.'

'I know, but I need to know that you are happy with this. You see, the Veneti excel in the use of the sail to power their boats. They do not use the oar.'

'I see and you think that we should have a boat with oars? It would certainly seem strange not to have a strong rowing crew and be able to use both sail and oar. Albeit it did not serve us as we might have hoped in the crossing from Demetae.'

'No, but that was an exceptional storm. Although I am sure there are many of Ocean's tempests that we must yet face, none will ever be as fierce as that one.'

For a moment, both men looked at each other, their shared, painful memory sharp in their eyes.

Maedoc continued, 'I plan to commission the shipwrights to convert the boat, under my direction, so that we can use both oar and sail. Because the boat is smaller, the crew we will have will be able to sail, but also pull the boat strongly with the deployed oars.'

'Good, and yes, I agree. Will they be able to do the work before we depart?'

'I think they will, but I will leave at first light to instruct them. Forgive me, I have already prepared the shipwrights, in anticipation that you would agree.'

The Prince smiled and nodded.

'You knew I would, and I would like to bring the Company down to Ictis as soon as possible to train with the oars and assign duties for the sailing.'

'Yes, we need to do that. The boat will be ready by the waxing half loor of Skovarnek and then we can practise thoroughly and be ready for the waning half, if that is when Lord Aodren intends to sail.'

'Good. I'm hungry, shall we go to the table?'

Maedoc looked earnestly into the younger man's eyes. 'Artur, we must have full manoeuvrability, if we need to bring the Venetia Teg back, as agreed. It worries me that they rely so much on sail and will not hear differently, Ocean's masters as they see themselves. What if there is no wind?'

'Well, I don't know. I suppose they have achieved much with the skills they have and so believe they know best. We must focus on our own approach, and you are right; if we are to get out of a tight spot and bring the Venetia Teg home, then we must have every means at our disposal to do that. But that is for tomorrow. Come, let's eat!'

***

On higher ground, approaching Tamara, a large group of travellers was on the last stage of their journey from the borders of the Dewnan lands to the crossing at the twin forts of Dynas Dowr Tewl and Ker Tamara.

The freshening breeze, coming straight at them, carried a squally, penetrating mizzle. Behind them, the sky was brighter and still clear of rain clouds. Occasionally, shafts of light shone through, defining the hill line of RunHoul, which was dominant on the horizon behind them. The main group of women, children, older boys and a few older men was struggling to maintain the pace and kept tightly packed together by a smaller group of fully-grown men, made up of warriors and guards, who were urging or herding their captives forward.

The path was rising now. Ahead in the gloom, a small but tightly-packed group of enclosed tall beach trees stood out in the landscape. The lead guard spoke to a junior, who then slowed and dropped back to the rear where most of the warrior guards were, watching their captives and keeping a close eye on what, if anything, was behind them.

'Lord Ewan, the last of the ancient stations is ahead. Shall we pause briefly to catch our breath and let the captives rest before we make the final run to Dynas Dowr Tewl?'

The reply was quiet and intended for only his fellow warrior to hear, 'Yes Arvin, but tell Menguy we will not wait long. Just enough to pass the water around and then we move on.'

The young guard acknowledged his instruction, picked up his pace and moved back towards the front of the group. As they came to the top of the hill, the second in command, Menguy, supported by several fellow guards, urged the captives in amongst the trees. The larger group of warriors at the back, who understood their roles implicitly, began to surround the captives as they all came to a stop. Several of the older captives collapsed panting on the ground.

Menguy shouted to several of his fellow warriors.

'Get the water out, use it all now. We are not stopping long and then we move on to Dynas Dowr Tewl. Nearly there now, so everyone must drink.'

Sullen, miserable and mud-smeared faces looked back at him from the captive group. Children were wide-eyed, huddled close to their mothers or older relatives, while a few, who had been separated during the raid, had crossed RunHoul alone. Theirs were frightened faces, avoiding any contact with the guards, and bereft of hope on this dank and dark evening.

Lord Ewan ap Aodren walked around the huddled mass to his second in command.

'We must not linger, Menguy. We are followed, I am sure of it, even here. Earlier, before this drizzle came on, I saw glints – armour or spears, maybe – in the sunlight, some distance back, but following us. The slaves will leave the clearest of trails, even in the dark and the wet.'

'Yes, my Lord, but there is a balance to be struck. We have come this far with our tradeable items in good condition, so we do not want to waste them now through exhaustion. A brief pause here and then mostly downhill to Dynas Dowr Tewl.'

The Veneti lord was twenty-four summers old and in his father's image. A commanding figure, nevertheless, acknowledged his second in command's sound and unquestionable logic.

The beech trees, tall and graceful above them, even in the drizzle and the heavy damp air, swayed gently in the breeze, rustling and buffeting softly. Here, birds still twittered and sang in the half-light, robins, blackbirds and above them the caw of a rook; a last conversation or call to a mate or assertion of territory before roosting. While all around them the drips of water fell from the leaves as the rain slowly penetrated the canopy.

The older man spoke to his young leader. 'I have crossed RunHoul often with you and your father and yet there is something that still excites me about the sight of these trees. We are nearly home!'

For a moment, Ewan's grim expression softened and his eyes, intense and alert all through the day, relaxed. Suddenly, he felt incredibly tired.

'Yes, they are distinctive and yet it is strange how the stories tell that originally on King Ronan's road, these were the clearings, the gaps in the great canopy of Orsa's wild wood; the stations of Sawkerdh that ran to RunHoul and all of the way to the great stone temple of Sira Howl. I have always thought that they were planted trees, protected by the local people who live around them, in honour of the once great wood and Orsa who watches over us from the sky.'

Menguy spoke then more quietly and confidentially.

'Do you suspect Durotrages are following?'

'Yes. The trev was empty of warriors or men of fighting age. Their resistance was no match for our Company. Where were their warriors? In some remote field, away hunting perhaps? They will have returned, I do not know when, but they will give pursuit. As I said, the trail will not have been hard to follow, although I am surprised they have come this far into the Dewnan lands. People who live in the disputed borderlands must expect raids and to lose people to slavery; it is the way of things. Something else drives them on, but I do not want to find out what until we are safely through the gates at Dynas Dowr Tewl.'

From this vantage point, Nanmeur, the great valley of Tamara, spread out before them all the way back to RunHoul, a vista of smaller valleys and smaller hilltops that were prominent but subservient to the massif of the distant skyline. The two men stood, silently looking back in the direction that they had come. As they did so, one final parting of the increasingly complete cloud cover shone a shaft of light onto a distant hilltop meadow and there, like a group of tiny ants moving swiftly towards a common objective, was the fleetingly glimpsed, but unmistakable movement of another warrior band. The glint of their spears and reflected light from their helmets left no doubt; and they were coming this way.

'Get them up, Menguy. Get them up! We must go. Come on! Up, up – everyone up!'

Menguy turned to the rest of the warrior guards and shouted instructions. The guards, in turn, began to push and prod at the captives. The children drew away from them and into the middle of the group and all of them, adult and child, drew back and tightly together in an unconscious, animalistic attempt to protect themselves. The Veneti began to shout and push, spreading themselves large and making angry noises as a cowherd might when moving his cattle, and slowly and reluctantly, the captive group rose and began to move out of the tree cover and on their way to Tamara and Dynas Dowr Tewl.

***

At Pendre, the feasting was over. Faces, bright and ruddy, intoxicated, smiled in the half-light from the fire; beards and moustaches, brown, blond and grey, were strewn with the remains of food and a covering of frothy white from their ale. Individuals stood to proclaim their prowess, while Marrek led a small group of Ambros, Brengy and Casvelyn in a competition of song with several of the surrounding Veneti, and in doing so, drunkenly urged the hall's two lyre players to accompany them. Conditioned by the alcohol, none seemed daunted by the challenge ahead. On the floor, the debris of the meal, meat bones, husks and shells, had been cast aside. Dogs milled around sniffing for leftovers, gnawing at the more substantial bones and growling at other dogs if they came too close.

Gyras, shackled again to an internal post while his guards joined the feast, looked on. The rain beat heavily on the roof above him. They had fed him and offered a beaker of wine. This, he reasoned, suggested that they meant him no immediate harm. His spirits, accordingly, were a little higher. Maybe there was hope yet of escape.

At the roundtable, Gwalian listened to the conversations that surrounded her. Her eyes wandered to Morlain. What had they spoken of in the meeting, away from the hall, with the messengers from Gwened? Surely, she had established now the closeness of her relationship with the Pryns. She should have been included if the Priestess was. Did her father feel perhaps that she had led the Pryns astray, blamed her for their late arrival? It bothered her. He had sat his daughter and the Pryns on either side of him, and as was surely his intention, they had not had the same chance for intimacy and conversation. She would not go to the battle, she knew that; her father would not allow it and Artur, away from her attention, had naturally focused on the fight to come.

She felt excluded and then, inexplicably, after all that had happened since the wane of the Loor Tewedh, her thoughts turned to Lancelin. On the far side of the table, he sat, looking at her, smiling, gently, enquiringly. Did he know her best of all, as childhood friends? Could he read her mind and understand her likely thought pattern? Maybe, but she had not forgiven him, and she could never trust him properly again.

Her father interrupted her thoughts as he now addressed all at the table.

'We have talked of battle and fight enough, more of that in the morning. Tonight, I must return downriver for essential business at Ictis. Before I go, who is sober enough to give us a story or a song for the evening? Something that will inspire us.'

Before anyone could speak, Gwalian rose to her feet and said confidently to him, 'Father, I will sing *The Ballad of Ronan and Ailla*, a story of hope restored.'

Gwalian lifted her head to the hall and her voice, soft and mournful at first, began. The two lyre players left the singing competition and walked around the table to accompany her. The hall quietened and all turned to the central roundtable. They knew the sweetness of Gwalian's voice and hushed those around them who still spoke or persisted with some point they were making.

Aodren looked at her with narrow eyes. He understood her and her likely purpose, but he could not deny her in the middle of this gathering.

Artur, with only a vague memory of the song, smiled warmly and encouragingly back at her.

Morlain, expressionless, watched on.

***

The Ballad of Ronan and Ailla

On hilltop high, she stood forlorn
Grim light in eastern sky
Her friendship was betrayed and
All chance of life gone by

Driving wind and drenching rain
Raised from the Ocean green
Contrived to taunt the morning and
All that might have been

Her broken heart, distraught and
Little hope now to recover
From her warrior's lusty gaze
His dalliance with another

Green swathe in the valley
Across the ancient wood
She called for hope restored
Strong, valiant and good

Sira Howl, hearing sad lament
Shone hope, to restore
Bright behind and above her
Light renewed once more

Spears glint amongst the trees
And in the valley seen
Bright, new, the Pretan lord
Emerged from the green

King Ronan and his Company
Safe passage Orsa gave
Sang to their deliverance, and
Rode forth together brave

Ascending to the summit, he
First beheld her there,

Brilliant, pure, her face
So bright and fair

You are beautiful, said he, and
Had I known you were here
Much sooner would I have journeyed
Despite our sylvan fear

Signifying great beauty
Long will last your fame
For all the Pretan people
Blessed will be your name

Hope restored, she smiled again
So radiant was that smile!
My Lord, my name is Ailla
Stay now, with me a while

Ailla my name is Ronan and
I will never leave you
I have found my life companion
To you I will be true

We will build a life together
Lead the Pretan kind
Upon these and yonder hills
In face of all we find

Towards the Sira Howl
Will always be our aim
But with you, dearest Ailla
My heart will now remain

Forth they led the Pretan
A new song in their hearts
Towards the mighty Father and
The wisdom He imparts

Che Raid of Che Durotrages

Through the dank and the mist, the river fort loomed ahead of them. Captors and captives, sodden and exhausted, slowed their pace and Tamara was audible below as they approached the gates of Dynas Dowr Tewl.

Menguy was first to the gate and banged firmly on it, hailing the guards. There was no reply. He banged again.

'Up there! Open up. Lord Ewan and Company are returned. Come on, open the gate!'

Ewan had come up quickly from the back.

'Can we force it open?'

The captives stooped, their breath short and stomachs rising and falling rapidly, as the rain ran down their faces and dripped off them. Most of them did not look up and some, supported by others, just managed to stand. Some of the older ones, the most wearied of all, had collapsed on the mud-churned ground, coughing and retching loudly.

A voice, agitated and nervous, finally answered from the other side. 'My Lord, it is very late. We had not expected you.'

Slowly the gate began to move, but it was clear that those opening it were struggling.

'Push… get that gate open!'

The gate swung, knocking those who pulled it to the ground, and Ewan marched through with Menguy. The fort and its enclosure was half the size of Ker Tamara and smaller again than Menluit, housing six extended families, a garrison, farmers, boatmen and cargo handlers on this side of Tamara. It seemed eerily quiet, however, even at this point in the night.

'You!'

Ewan pointed to the nearest gate-puller, getting to his feet and dusting himself down. He recognised him, but couldn't recall his name. 'Where is everyone, what has happened to the garrison?'

The young guard's face looked nervous. 'My Lord, most are at Menluit. My Lord Aodren entertains messengers from Armorica. They come in search of aid against the Roman threat,' he hesitated and his eyes fell to the ground, 'we think.' He looked up again, 'The whole valley talks of it. Lord Ewan, forgive us, only a few of us remain to keep the watch while others rest.'

Ewan shook his head as he glared back at the guard. Then he turned quickly to Menguy. 'It's no good – we can't store them here; we have to cross Tamara.'

Menguy looked back through the gate to where several of the captives were visible in the gloom, staring vacantly ahead, heads rocking backwards and forwards.

'I am not sure they will all make it.'

'They have to make it. It is downhill and I'd rather lose a few than all of them. If we linger here with this handful of freshmen, I fear that is exactly what will happen.'

He turned back to the guard.

'You had better wake up the others. We are being followed, yes, followed! I don't know who they are, Belgae or Durotrages, but they are on our trail and they will be here soon. You will be our first line of defence. I hope, for your sake, you will be ready.'

He turned and marched back out of the gate.

'Everyone up, come on, get them up. We cross Tamara. We cannot stay here. Dynas Dowr Tewl has been shamefully abandoned it seems. We move on!'

The older ones did not move and were already asleep. The younger ones around them were pushing, urging them to wake up, but some did not hear.

'Drag them if you have to. Get the stronger ones to help you. We leave nothing behind!'

Pushed, prodded and kicked back to life, the captives moved and eventually got to their feet for the descent to the river.

***

The hall was quiet now. Aodren had departed to catch a boat downriver with the Veneti messengers soon after Gwalian's ballad. Belatedly, he had asked his daughter to join him for his day of exchange and discussion at Ictis. Lancelin had gone also on another of his short journeys, a "call from his father" as the rest of the Company now referred to it with eyebrows raised. What was he doing really?

Morlain and the women of the hall had also retired for the night; Morlain back to Marghros. For a while, the drinking, talking and occasional songs of a very different kind had continued, but now with the night nearly over, loud snoring was the dominant noise of the room. Artur, Maedoc, Kea, Drustan and Silyan remained awake. If they had been drunk earlier, they had drunk themselves sober. Gawen stood behind them. Not a drinker of wine or mead, he had remained sober all night, quietly watching the proceedings and being supportive when called for. Now, he gripped his bow and manipulated oil, of his own mixing, into his tall bow to maintain its flexibility and power. Along with the others, he listened as the Prince spoke.

'We move to Ictis in the next few days to prepare. Maedoc has taken steps to adapt our boat. We will row and sail and be prepared for all weather.'

Drustan yawned expansively before saying tiredly, 'Cousin, the Veneti are highly-able sailors, they will not wait while we row to keep up.'

'Nor should they, cousin, but we will not rely on our oars only. We will sail also and Maedoc is as good a sailor and navigator as any I know. We will hold our own, but also maintain our flexibility. If there is no wind, they will not sail; but we will row. We go to Ictis to practise our rowing.'

The others nodded their heads, agreeing with the Prince in a functional way. It had been a long night.

Suddenly, the door at the end of the hall swung open and several men entered, quickly followed by several more. Artur and those around him rose quickly and drew their swords, but instead of challenging them, the leader of the newcomers took two large metal serving plates and began to bang them together loudly.

'Wake up, come on, wake up! We are under attack, you lazy drunken arseholes. Where's the garrison? Come on!'

He started kicking those most solidly asleep, while those with him started grabbing and shaking others as they marched down the hall.

'Who are you? And what is your business here? Put your swords away! At least someone's awake, I suppose. Have you come from Armorica? Where is my father?'

Artur took a step out from the rest.

'I am Artur O'Dhearg ap Mawgan, Pryns of the Dewnan and these are some of my Company. We come to fight the Roman threat in support of our Veneti kin. Who are you?'

The young man stopped in front of him, and changing his mood completely, laughed loudly, 'Are you really? The Dewnan, agreeing to a fight, voluntarily, and not waiting until they have no other option? What strange events are these? Has the priestess entranced you?'

He paused for effect for a moment.

'I am Ewan ap Aodren, returned from defending your lands against the Estrenyons with my Company, fighting battles and sourcing produce to keep this port alive and your father's revenues intact.'

He paused again to frame a scornful stare.

'Whoever you are, where is my father?'

Artur had returned his sword to its scabbard, but gripped the hilt firmly now, nonetheless, and could sense the others around him bristling with irritation at the dismissiveness of the Venetian. As none of them was a man of Nanmeur, they had not met Ewan ap Aodren before.

'He has gone with the messengers from Armorica to Ictis. He will return tomorrow evening.'

'Very well, then we must get these good-for-nothing drunken bags of shit up. Despite our best efforts, an incursion force follows us, probably Belgae, maybe Durotrages. Soon, they will attack, I am sure. So let us see, Pryns Artur what you and your Company are made of.'

Before the Prince could respond, Ewan had turned away and was giving instructions. 'Sound the alarm; wake the whole trev up, everyone up. We need every man.'

He began banging the plates again and gradually men began to stir. Artur and the rest woke up the other Dewnans and the

Prince addressed them quickly in a close-packed huddle just outside the hall doors.

'We have only just met, but I do not like the tone of Ewan ap Aodren. We are the fighting Dewnan. Already, we have seen off Belgae and maybe it is the same group back again. I hope so; their leader and I have unfinished business.'

As they rose and clasped each other's arms, another man ran past and shouted into the hall, 'Lord Ewan! There are flames and smoke at Dynas Dowr Tewl. You must come quickly – they are here!'

Ewan came running out of the building, followed by a number of others. 'To the boats, it's the quickest way. To the upper quay at Ker Tamara, they must not cross the Tamara. Follow me!'

Through the gate and down to Menluit Quay they went, shields slung across their backs, held firm by one hand with leather strap and sword hilts gripped tightly with the other. After the overnight rain, the steps were wet and slippery and the quicker Veneti, familiar with the safer footings, jostled the Dewnans, more cautious on the steep descent, as they urged them forward and pushed past in their haste to the fight. The late daffodils around them, bright and clean after the rain, were caught in the draught of the warrior's passing and bobbed and saluted them as they went on their way.

Below, in the early morning light, a multitude of small craft, capable of carrying six or maybe seven warriors, piloted by boatmen of the port, converged on the quay ready to transport them downstream. On the far bank, the lower ground retained a dampness in the air and the chill of the now clearing skies of early morning gave rise to mist, which partly concealed the roundhouses and small farms that surrounded them.

After she left the quay, Tamara meandered first sharply to the left, and then more leisurely to the right in a grand sweep. On the far bend, the mist mixed with smoke that drifted down from Dynas Dowr Tewl. Flames flickered on the heights, and then a glint and another – swords catching the building flame and morning light as the first defence against the attack continued. Then, there was someone running, followed by a group of warriors; their swords shimmered as they gave chase, caught and hacked their victim to the ground.

On to the quay, Maedoc and the other gilles were in the lead for the Dewnans, calling for boats. The boatmen, familiar with the Company now, were quick to respond and soon took them out into Tamara's flow. As they swung around the left meander, the river cliff of Ker Tamara rose up above them and, through the small wisps of lingering mist, the figures of men were just discernible, running along wooded paths towards the fight.

Ahead, Ewan was shouting and gesticulating to the boats around him; and as he did so, his advance guard pulled towards a landing point. The cliffs receded now as the river bent to the right and an increasing area of lower ground spread out into a narrow floodplain. Men were on the bank, taking shields from their backs and drawing swords. The Dewnan boats slowed as the boatmen worked to hold their craft in the flow of the river, waiting their turn to bring them alongside the first downstream jetty of the port. Metal on metal and the cries and screams of women and children could be heard further downstream.

The Dewnan boats came alongside and Artur and Maedoc leapt ashore, followed by the rest of the Company. Ewan and the Veneti did not stop to wait or plan their collective deployment. Artur, however, signalled to the Company and they gathered around him.

'Keep close together. We have practised our tight formation, our arrow-shaped attack so let us stay disciplined. Listen for my direction; we do not know what is up ahead. Come on!'

There were shouts of approval and toothy grins from those around him, and they turned and moved forward along the bank. The Prince led from the front, flanked by Drustan and Kea, Maedoc and Gawen, while the rest of the Company, hampered by the narrowness of the path and increasing stacked goods, crops, timber and corralled cattle, fell in behind them.

Quickly, they came to the fight. The attackers' advance guard, the bridgehead, was already across, others were crossing and sword arms swung as the Veneti came upon them. Bodies lay on the ground, port workers lost in a valiant attempt to hold the crossers back. Veneti shields smashed into the attackers who protected the bridgehead, a shield wall thirty men wide in the shape of a crescent moon, and faces shuddered and distorted as wood and metal crunched against chest, jaw and cheek. Swords slashed and cut deep into arms, probing gaps above the shield wall and then below, as shields rose to protect against an overarm lunge being thrust deep into any unprotected belly or leg. Cries of pain and anger filled the air and still, unseen, the screams and cries of women and children mixed strongly with the developing battle. Artur glanced at Maedoc who, with a grim and irritated expression, acknowledged he heard it too.

With only the briefest pause to judge the best point of entering the melee, the Prince led the Company into the fight. The sound of metal on metal rang out and the dull thud of sword striking shield. As the attackers became defenders, some leaned over the shield wall and used their swords in a combination of wild swings and stabbing motions. At the front of the fight were Nouran and Gourgy, exaggeratedly turning one way and then the other, posturing, laughing and joking as they looked for gaps in the shield wall.

'Ow's that in yer fleshy girt legs you crappy Estrenyon scum? Does it 'urt yet? Show us yerr balls, if uze got any, and we'll 'ack em off!'

They were not quite quick enough, however, to dodge the concerted poking and flailing of the defender's swords. Blades cut through their clothing and upper shield arms. Blood seeped through the material of their jerkins, down their arms and across the grip of their shield hands. In response, the men of RunIsca growled deeply, building to a loud roar of anger as they hacked and cut at the shield wall and, with sheer force of will, supported by the rest of the Dewnan around them, began to push it back. More gaps appeared. The Dewnans plunged their swords through, finding targets, sinking their swords into exposed flesh and striking hard bone as the bridgehead stumbled backwards. Several fell, impaled by a Dewnan thrust or falling over their injured comrades.

Now the Veneti joined the Dewnan. Ewan in the lead with his immediate retinue around him, pushing through the Dewnan, knocking several off balance in their need to be seen at the front of the main push.

Not expecting to have their focus interrupted from behind, the Dewnan paused for long enough to slow the overall push of the attack and bring it to a halt. Artur and others at the front, sensing withdrawal around them, drew back also. The attackers regained their footing, and although they were much closer to the edge of the bank, the shield wall closed again and prepared to stand firm. A gap opened between attacker and defender as Dewnan and Veneti fell back, and all recognised that, briefly, the fight was suspended.

Ewan surveyed Artur with a cold hard stare. 'Coordination, my Lord Prince, is vital if we are to prevail. Impetuous actions will serve no one. We will lead with battle-hardened warriors. Prepare your men and I will issue further instructions. We will soon have these scum pushed back.'

'Lord Ewan, we would have consigned them to Tamara by now if you had not halted the attack with your pushing and shoving. What were you trying...'

As he spoke, Ewan turned away and began talking to the Veneti around him.

The Prince took a long deep breath, shook his head and looked sternly towards the Veneti lord. Gourgy, gripping his injured arm, spoke for them all under his breath.

'Trumped up fucker! We 'ad em there and my mate Nouran's 'ad is arm chopped for his pain. Now we'z gon'ave t'start all over again!'

His sword drawn, Casvelyn, closest to Artur as they had fallen back, took a step towards Ewan's turned back. The Prince held his shoulder.

'We'll sort him out later. Everybody back together. Come on, we can do it again!'

As he issued his rallying cry, Ewan turned back towards them.

'Veneti, Dewnan, to me. They are Belgae, Belgae scum. Let's skewer the bastards!'

Artur stood back and turned to the Dewnans.

'Alright, let's see what our Veneti lord's made of!'

With Ewan several paces in the lead, the Veneti barged past the Dewnans, who stood and watched them go. As he approached the shield wall, Ewan turned. There was triumph on his face to be back at the front of the charge. He raised his arms and urged his men, Dewnan included, to the fight. As he did so a shield in the wall rose, tilted and swung at his head with full force, striking him clean across his face. Skin and hair distorted, his nose bent sharply to the left as blood splattered out. He crumpled and toppled backwards as the oncoming Veneti, swiftly followed by the Dewnans, swarmed around him.

Behind the shield wall, there was ironic laughter.

'Tosspot! Who goes charging at a shield wall on their own?'

'They're all daft wankers an' inbreds! Come on, lads. Stand firm, there's more where that came from.'

Artur, with a clear view, took control of the situation. 'Men of the Veneti. Menguy, is it? Cover for your Lord. Take the right. Maedoc, Briec, Tremaine, Tinos, Ryol, help me carry Lord Ewan back to a safer position. Drustan, take the rest of the Dewnans to the left.'

Three on either side, they carried Ewan back and away from the fight. As they laid him on the ground, with the din, furore and shout of battle continuing behind them, the pounding of hooves drew near, and there was Morlain astride Steren Uskis. Swiftly, she came upon them and dismounted.

'Artur, I came as soon as I heard. Belgae again I am told?'

'So I believe.'

The screams of the women and children went on, and across the river, others now shouted. The cows were thoroughly agitated and a growing crescendo of mooing added to the rising pitch of the din. She turned and looked both ways along the bank, taking in all that she saw.

'What has happened to Lord Ewan?'

'Struck by a shield in the charge. He is lifeless and yet I think he still lives.'

She bent down and examined his head before standing back up again.

'He lives, and yet he is not with us. Perhaps he speaks with the Underworld, bargains for his life and a return to this world. Many would assume him dead, but he is not; it is not decided. He is lucky. He has a chance. Cover him over and ensure he is warm; I cannot be certain, but I think that he will wake soon.'

'Good, I must get back to the fight. The rest of you, come on.'

'Artur,' she said urgently, 'something is not right. They are not all warriors. Those on the far bank are farmers, I would guess. No doubt, Lord Ewan has brought a quota of slaves back with him from his reconnaissance for the market at Ictis. I caught sight of them in the pen as I rode through the trees. That is the screaming you can hear.'

Her eyes stared intently at him, searching for a reaction, but he just nodded his head, looking in the general direction of the screaming.

'The slaves may be the loved ones of those farmers, snatched from some distant trev when the farmers were conveniently not around – and now, somehow, they have become linked with the Belgae war party trying to establish a foothold on this side of Tamara.'

'Hmm, so first we repel the Belgae and then get to the bottom of what is going on here. Morlain, I must to the fight.'

'You must.'

She drew her sword with a flourish as fine as any he had seen. Although shieldless, she stood ready for the battle.

'I do hope you were not thinking that it would be me who stood guard over Lord Ewan? Detail two of your men and then join me!'

And she was gone, two hands on her sword hilt, poised and ready for the first strike as she strode to the fight.

***

Gyras lifted his head from underneath his cloak. As the drunken tumult had finally faded, sleep had overwhelmed him. Awake now, he cautiously raised himself to look around. The hall was empty. He sat up and considered his position. Where had they all gone?

The manacle rubbed and chaffed painfully on his leg as he moved around. Briefly, he considered it, before grabbing hold of the iron links and pulling with increasing jerks, trying to move the post or remove the iron tether from the post, but both held firm. He could get his fingers between the leg and the iron. Would the manacle come apart? His wrist and face muscles stretched taut as he gripped and pulled as hard as he could, but the lock held firm. Whatever else he thought of them, they knew their ironwork.

Crouched first on one knee, the knee of the manacled leg, he tried to push his unshackled leg and foot into the ground in order to raise himself, but the manacled leg made this task harder than he thought. He pushed and was up, but his legs, weak from too much sitting, collapsed underneath him and he fell forward on to the earthen floor with a muffled cry while the manacle cut and jarred again at his ankle. He closed his eyes. It was hopeless. He was destined to die in this godforsaken wet, miserable shithole, tied to this post.

He opened his eyes again, head sideways on the floor, and became aware of something metallic on the floor underneath the nearest table. He raised his head slightly – a coin maybe? The barbarians had little use for them, unless they were markers of favour, like the one he had carried from the Veneti. What was it? He got himself up on to his arm and began to shuffle around on his side in the semicircle that the manacle and chain allowed. He reached out as he came into line with the glinting object. It was something small and metal, and he extended as far as he could, stretching, reaching under the bench by the table. He breathed out; it was no good – it was still half an arm away, under the table itself. He needed something to extend his arm.

Then he saw it, only a little further way around on his semicircle; a short animal bone, stripped clean by man and dog and discarded on the floor. He shuffled around, grabbed the bone and shuffled back. If he could just reach out, with the bone at the very tips of his fingers... Got it! He dragged the metal object to within his reach and threw the bone away. Was it? It was! He held a small iron key in his fingers.

'Please be the right key,' he said aloud. Pulling himself out from under the bench, he raised himself up into a sitting position and lent forward towards the manacle. He inserted the key and the manacle split in two.

Slowly, he stood and then bent to rub his bruised ankle. Somehow, in some way, he would make them pay for this. Now, however, he had to get away. Not by the river as he had originally intended, there was too big a risk of being seen. No, he would go by the road and walk so that he could conceal himself quickly whenever the need arose. He needed to find somewhere to hide now, away from their trev, rest his ankle for a little while and then be on his way, picking up the coins he had buried for safekeeping on the way up and head for the port. It had been half a day's ride up, so a day's walk back perhaps, and then he would look for a Curiosolitae boat to get him back to Gaul and to Caesar. He had much to report.

***

'The bridgehead stands firm, Heer Anogin. They have a foothold that the inbreds are finding it difficult to overcome.'

'Good, and the farmers?'

'They will not cross, despite the call of their kin. I am not sure what they expect to happen, unless they take the fight to the Veneti scum, but then we have carried them this far.'

'They will cross. They are our diversion. They will break out from our bridgehead and take the swords of the Dumnoni and their Armorican interlopers while we establish our position and remove the old witch queen's runt and the heretic sorceress. Let me past; I will move these farmers. If they do not cross the river, they will all regret it.'

A foot taller than all around him, and broad in build to match, Anogin stood out. He now revealed himself more openly to those on the other bank. Artur, concentrating on the fight in front of him, caught sight of him out of the corner of his eye. Others noticed him too, remembering him, distinctive from the fight in the woods.

He strode over to the Durotrages farmers. One of them, an elder of the community, stepped forward to meet him.

'My Lord, none of us are warriors, we cannot swim, and there are spirits in the water. Crossings are sacred places, and we hesitate to cross unless it is safe to do so, and the spirits have had their offering. It is always our custom to do this.'

Anogin shook his head. 'Your women, old folk and children seemed to have crossed safely? My men fight on the far bank in your cause. Are you the weakest part of your degenerate tribe? It is not good enough. This is a Durotrages raid and yet the Belgae do all the work. You will all cross this river and you will do it right now.'

He shook his head again, drew his sword, turned away and then turned back again and drove his sword straight through the heart of the Durotrages elder.

'There, I make sacrifice to the gods, spirits and whatever else your simple mind thinks lurks in the water.'

He looked to the rest of the group.

'If the rest of you don't want to suffer the same fate, you will cross this river and help my men to take the battle forward.'

Anogin withdrew his sword. The Durotrages elder, eyes wide-open, stared back at him, before convulsive coughing and the retching of blood consumed him. Staggering backwards, he turned to the rest of the farmer group. Stumbling forward towards them, he tried to say something. He reached out and then fell flat on his face in the mud, blood seeping out of his back where the sword had gone through.

Some of the younger men from the Durotrages group drew their swords now, shaken from their indecisiveness and stepped forward, ready to take action against the Belgae giant. The Belgae around Anogin, with grim, angry faces and growls of challenge and sneer, stepped forward ready to respond.

'Come on then, farmer boys. We'll try to pretend we're scared!'

Cidric, one of the Durotrages, nervous but braver than the rest, moved forward from the group and half-turned to face them, watching the Belgae as he did so.

'Wait… not now.'

He turned and stared firmly at Anogin.

'We cannot fight Belgae and Veneti today. Across the river, follow me. There are no arrows flying and the Belgae will consume the slavers. Come, if we are to see our women and children again, we must go to the fight.'

The rest, uncertain what to do, and in a state of shock at the killing of their elder, were ready to follow any firm direction. Anogin, eyes cold, calculating and unflinching, watched Cedric and the rest of them as they went past. When the last of the farmers had passed, he turned to the bulk of the Belgae still on this side of the river.

'Right, we follow behind, push them along and make sure none of them diverts from the crossing. Kill any that do – and remember: when we are across, the Dumnoni prynsling is mine. To the crossing!'

***

The wall of shields stood firm and the Dewnan and Veneti, breathing heavily, stepped back from the fight to consider their next move.

Morlain's arms were red with exertion, and with sweat on her brow, she watched the opposite bank, where the bulk of the Belgae force and the farmers, if that was what they were, seemed to be preparing to cross. Artur stood next to her and all rested briefly around them while the shield wall hurled abuse. Shouting came across the water and they knew this was the pause before the main encounter to come.

Morlain turned to the Prince. 'Artur, do you know the tall man in the midst of the group on the far bank? He has just killed one of the farmers. He looks at you, watches you.'

He could see Anogin clearly now, instead of occasional glimpses between the trees. Breathing deeply and purposefully, he said, 'We have met before. He was with the Belgae that we encountered on our journey from Ker Kammel to Menluit. I have unfinished business with him.'

'You sound apprehensive. Does something concern you?'

'Well, he is very big, bigger than I thought he was in the woods.'

'Yes,' she smiled in solidarity with him. 'He is large. Perhaps we can take him on together. He looks at me too; I feel sure he means to kill us both.'

'I will fight him alone.'

As if he had heard, Anogin turned and looked straight at him.

Artur breathed deeply again. 'Morlain, I am sure that is the man who killed my mother.'

Her tiredness vanished and she stood up beside him. 'Really, are you sure? So that is why he continually follows your movements? I wonder if others have told him about you. If so, he will know you were also in the tent on that awful day and he missed you. Is that why they are here? He also has unfinished business then. It is not about the slaves, even though they have dragged the farmers along with them. It is about you and, maybe, about me.'

She turned towards him.

'Artur. I do not know everything, but I have endeavoured to find out what I can. That man detests our way of life. He does not represent Kings or even Romans, but is a rogue force instead, driving others through fear to support him or corralling the equally wicked around him. He is a bully and a coward.'

She looked at him determinedly, her face suddenly distraught with passion, and said, 'Artur, he must not succeed. Our whole plan, the defence of our land and our tradition, is here and now, the first of the great battles with the enemy. He is like a sickness, working away from inside, returning, infiltrating our collective body, a poison in our lands. We are the last of the great Pretani, heirs of the Acheans, the last great hope to defend all that we hold dear, against Belgae, Romans and all other incursions. He intends to kill us, stop us, snuff us out, and not because it is all part of some great plan by an invading army, but because he does not like us. He will kill anyone who disagrees with him because of his intolerance and meanness of spirit. It all makes sense. Why would such a large group follow a bunch of prospective slaves this far into Dewnan lands? Slaving is a mean and tawdry way to make a living, but it happens; they take some of ours, we take some of theirs. Miserable for those involved, but not something that normally provokes a response anywhere near as large as this. No, it is a mask for something else, something far more momentous, threatening and it will not, cannot succeed. Come on, let's take him on and take him out. If we do, the rest will falter, certainly the farmers, I am sure.'

How she knew so much, so suddenly, and had made the connections, he could not say; but her passion and determination cut deep into his soul and he felt unintentionally struck by her desire. She gripped her sword hilt hard and raised it up ready to fight. As she did so, a freshening breeze blew through the trees. It caught her tousled hair, spreading it buoyantly behind her, backlit by the dappled light of the morning sun, rising steadily, vanquishing all trace of overnight mist. Despite all of that, his chance had arrived and he was determined to take it.

'Morlain, this is my fight and I will take him down. He will not escape again!'

The men on the far bank were crossing the river and, as they turned to face the bridgehead, the shield wall burst open, Durotrages farmers and the vanguard of the Belgae warriors, who intermingled with them, charged out, shouting abuse at the Dewnans and Veneti in front of them. Once all the farmers were across, the rest of the Belgae, far more confident in the water, streamed over behind them.

Drustan, Kea, Gawen and Menguy roused the men, shouting instructions. The Belgae moved swiftly, urging the Durotrages forward and preparing to engage the upcoming Dewnan and Veneti. They smashed into each other and now there was no push and slow attrition in front of the shield wall, just open combat. Several of the farmers fell quickly to the front swords of the Dewnan and Veneti, but it wasn't just farmers who were in the charge. The battle-hardened Belgae started to take men down. Brengy's gille fell and then Brengy, fighting alongside him. A sword cut across his legs, and he fell to his knees. He tried to get up but the cut had paralysed his legs. Casvelyn, seeing his friend in trouble, tried to get across. He took one of the farmers down with a similar cut to the leg as he attempted to reach Brengy, but it was too late. A sharp oncoming Belgae sword separated his head from his body as he knelt. Blood cascaded into the air from the place where Brengy's head had been and his body, still kneeling, twitched jerkily in its death spasm. Casvelyn roared with anger, chopping and slashing, aiming for any of the Belgae he could reach. He ran the first oncoming Belgae through the midriff with his sword, blood spraying the ground around them. Other Belgae surrounded him now. Their greater numbers allowed for three or four Belgae or Durotrages to each defending Dewnan and Veneti. At first, as the Estrenyons streamed across the river, it looked desperate. Casvelyn disappeared into a press of hacking swords and stamping feet; and then, the press parted and he lay on his front, head distorted sideways, eyes cold and exaggeratedly wide, with the mud tinged red all around him.

Enraged, Drustan, Kea and Menguy nevertheless kept order, shouting and organising, shaping the defenders into a more organised group. Nouran, Gourgy, Silyen and Gawen led the combat, holding back the advance. It was too tight here for bow and arrow and so Gawen swung his sword with the rest of them, determined to avenge his kinsmen's deaths. Artur and Morlain, separated from the rest by a wedge of attackers, held a smaller group of Belgae at bay. It was clear the wedge was no accident and the Belgae in front of them cajoled the others around them, deliberately trying to contain the attack on the rest of the Dewnan and Veneti and isolate Artur and Morlain, waiting for others to cross. Maedoc tried to force his way across, but the Belgae's strongest and most determined fighters were engaged in this and he could not get through.

Then, Anogin strode up onto the bank. One of the last to cross, the Belgae giant came with confidence and fixed determination. He had come to seize control and complete his self-appointed task, begun ten summers before, to bring an end to the moribund "Ocean" peoples and their heretical ways. He would remove this last remaining enclave, this final point of resistance to the correct and proper order.

Flanked by two Belgae warriors, who had waited for his crossing, they ignored the main battle and made straight for Artur and Morlain, while those who had initially engaged them fell back. Anogin gripped his sword with intent – a blackened blade with a crossguard and pommel of silver. The sword matched his stature and he swung it freely now as Artur stood firm, agitated but ready to meet him.

'At last,' he sneered, 'we meet again, whelp of the Witch Queen.'

His booming voice rose in volume for maximum effect. He spoke the common tongue, but with a harsher accent and inflection in his words; the accent of the Estrenyon.

'You know me! I am the man who killed your mother, the infamous bitch and faded shadow wraith from the land of the setting sun, halfway to the underworld and an affront to the proper order. No good came from her perverted ways and ten summers you have lived longer than you should have done. I have come to correct my error!'

As he spoke these final words, he broke into a run, sweeping his sword up into the air, and with a roar, brought it down with great force. It all happened so quickly. Artur only just got out of the way. He staggered back, falling and as he did so. To the left of Anogin, he could see Maedoc and the other Dewnans beyond the Belgae fighters, parrying, clashing sword with sword, trying desperately to remove the barrier that prevented them coming to his aid. To Anogin's right, Morlain held off a determined cut and thrust from his two supports. It was hard work, but she held her own.

'That's it, runtling; look around for the other inbreds, but they won't help you now because I'm going to kill you, and when I have killed you, I will kill them. I shall particularly enjoy skewering the sorceress, just as much as I enjoyed dispatching your mother. There is only one way to remove an evil infection. Cut it out!'

He came again, sword aloft, his stride pounding the ground towards the prostrate Prince. He had to get up, get out of the way. Again, just before the sword fell, he rolled to the right. Getting to his feet, Artur created enough space to turn and, standing now, breathing heavily, prepared to engage. He raised his sword and advanced.

'Yes, I know you. How could I forget your repugnant Belgae face? You are vile, Estrenyon. You have no place in the lands of the Golden Pretani! My mother fought you hard that day and would have had you, but you called on all your miserable sidekicks to overwhelm her, like the weakling you really are. To do the deed that you could not do on your own. Come on then, let's see if you've got it in you!'

Artur lunged, Anogin angered by the Prince's challenge, parried it with force to the right and the clash of the swords sang. First, a deep metallic note as Anogin's heavier blade pushed the Prince's lighter sword aside from its base, but then, as Artur recovered, lighter, higher notes as weapon met weapon in a sustained exchange. Artur felt his height disadvantage as Anogin didn't seem to move, despite his best efforts. Instead, with a manic grin and wide staring eyes, Anogin parried the Prince's attacks with seeming ease.

'Try hard, witch's spawn. Soon you will tire, and then I will kill you!'

He moved forward again, but it was no sudden run – instead, a slow and determined stride. The sheer weight of his presence gradually pushed Artur back behind Morlain and towards Tamara. For a moment, one of her attackers took his eye off her as Anogin passed. It was all she needed. She leapt aside with lightning speed, out of the reach of the second Belgae, and plunged her sword deep into the first Belgae's upper left leg. He cried out in excruciating pain as the blade cut through soft skin, taut muscle and grazed his bone. She locked her eyes firmly on his and held firm before withdrawing the blade and standing back. He stumbled, arms spread wide, dropping his sword before collapsing, incapacitated, blood gushing down and across his knee.

The second Belgae wavered for a moment as she advanced. This, he knew from all the stories, was the wicked witch who, like a great gorging worm, ate into men's minds, controlling and manipulating them for her own evil and perverted purposes. He had to stand firm. He met her first confident assault strongly and quickly, the sound of sword on sword resumed. He was grunting with determination and she breathed heavily, but neither now wavered in their concentration.

The battle raged behind them, but the bulk of the Belgae force still held back the Dewnans and Veneti, and continued to isolate Artur and Morlain in their struggle.

The Prince was gradually being overwhelmed. The brute force of the giant was too much for him. He was on the edge of the bank now.

'One step from oblivion, little pryns, and soon all of this will be mine! Come on! Give it up, accept your fate and let me put you out of your misery. Consign yourself to the death and miserable end that is yours with my sword deep in your pathetic little belly. Let me stick it in and twist it to ensure that the job is properly finished. Not long now. NARGGH!'

His sudden leap forward caused Artur to stagger and fall backwards down the steep bank to Tamara. Anogin's roar of delight, manic eyes and twisted grin followed him as his back and head struck rock and pebble. He lay prostrate, helpless on the ground while Anogin prepared to leap for the kill; but then a female voice, clear and determined, caused the giant Belgae to pause.

'Anogin, I know you, who you are and what you are about.'

She breathed heavily as she challenged him.

'Fight me first – or are you scared that a woman will overwhelm you? Show you for what you really are: a coward who cannot fight unless it is all set up for him. We are better than you and all of your Belgae henchmen. We are the defenders of a great and glorious people and we are going nowhere. Come on, fight me, if you can!'

He turned slowly around and there she stood, dress ruffled and face muddied, but her eyes alive with resolution. Behind her, one Belgae on his knees, his head bowed in a state of semi-unconsciousness and the other, blood gushing from a deep wound in his torso, slumped against a tree.

'Come on, it's you and me now. Let us see if you really are the big man I've heard about.'

It was her calm insistence that incensed him and he turned now to face her, bristling with agitation, but even in the height of his chauvinism, he could not ignore that she had already dispatched two of his best fighters. He approached slowly, considering his best line of attack.

'Yes, little witch bitch, let us fight while the prynsling sleeps. I have come to destroy you both. The men of this land lost their way years ago when they allowed manipulative harpies like you to weaken their souls with your song of delinquency and sap their strength in this sad peripheral half-world. Down there is the little pryns, your last great hope, broken and ready for dispatch.'

His eyes flickered darkly and his blackened teeth showed through as he leered at her.

'Yes! You see I know things too – and I know your name, Morlain.'

She came straight at him. 'The whole valley knows my name!'

Her swing was surprisingly strong and he felt the force of it reverberate through his sword as he parried it to the left. She stepped away from him and paced back and forth in front of him, her sword poised.

'Are you going to make a move, or must I come to you again?'

Morlain thrust towards his right leg and he responded more convincingly, parried the attack to the right and followed quickly with a cutting swing. Quickly, she recovered, and bending her body, swung back to the left halting it with a loud clang. Rapidly now, swing met swing and the reverberating clash of the swords rang out again. A fight, alone, pivotal to it all while the rest of the battle raged on around them.

Artur pulled himself up. His leg and back felt bruised and stiff, but he had to get back up. He lifted his sword but left his shield. Using several wind-toppled large tree branches that lay across the bank, he clambered upwards.

As he came over the top, Morlain caught his eye for a moment, and as she did so, said loud and clear, 'Pryns Artur, just winded I see. Good to have you back. He weakens. Soon he will be ours!'

While the Prince struggled to get up onto the bank, Anogin thrust forward again, his anger growing at his inability to overwhelm her easily. She was tired, but she had fought hard. Suddenly, he was finding it hard work.

'I will have you, bitch, because I can fight longer than you can. I am a man and a warrior and you are some dirty little backwoods whore.'

She gritted her teeth and came even more strongly at him. Anogin stepped backwards and, as he did so, a protruding tree root hidden in the undergrowth caught his foot and knocked him off balance. He tottered sideways. She lunged towards him, her blade aimed straight at his midriff, but as she did so, he pushed with his legs and, instead, managed to stumble backwards and quickly re-establish his footing.

Committed to the thrust of her sword, she staggered forward but managed to stand up and turn to face Anogin as he came at her. He swung his sword with strength and purpose. Just able to duck, the sword missed her head, but as she bent, Anogin came past and raised his sword into the air, brought his elbows together and thrust them down into her back. She gave a small cry of intense pain as she slipped and fell flat on her face in the mud and undergrowth. Her sword fell out of her hand and, for a moment, she did not move.

Anogin, empowered by her pain and agony, roared manically.

Morlain was crawling, trying to stand, but she had sprained her ankle and could not get up. His lust for blood, his sense of impending triumph, overwhelmed him. He ran around to the side and kicked Morlain firmly in her ribs. Her body convulsed and she coughed and exhaled violently, her head falling forwards again into the mud. She tried to get up and he kicked her again, laughing viciously. Now he stepped back, gripped his sword firmly with both hands and raised it high, ready to slash at her head, decapitate her as she crawled feebly, desperately along the ground, grasping at clumps of grass, small branches, anything in her desperation to get away from his boot and the cut of his sword.

Then, he paused.

'I will cut out the disease, evil witch. It is the end of your order and the Atrebates and the Belgae will conquer all!'

They were the last proper words he said. Artur, his strength restored in response to Morlain's plight, sprang across the ground between them. The Belgae giant, absorbed in his obsession to remove his opponent in as brutal a manner he could manage, and the fame and renown it would bring him in the Belgae lands, briefly, fatally, forgot his instinct for self-preservation. The Prince came at him at an angle and thrust deep into his ribcage, breaking bone and gouging blood and flesh as it went. He held firm and then twisted the blade as the eyes of the giant met his.

'You will not harm her any more. I have waited for you and this moment, to avenge the evil that you inflicted on this land and I will not allow you to do it again. You are finished now! Here is where we turn the tide, as my mother intended.'

He thrust harder and, with all the strength he could summon, he pushed against Anogin, and as the giant staggered backwards, withdrew his sword, twisting it again.

The Belgae, however, stood firm, his head shaking, twitching – perhaps in disbelief, perhaps in one last act of defiance. This was not supposed to happen. The gods had chosen him to cleanse the land of evil and restore the proper order; but today, evil triumphed. Even in his final moments, his total disdain for them filled his body. His mission was failing, but others would come one day soon, and it was his dying wish that the witch realm of the Dumnoni would fall.

His lips curled slowly in a sneer of contempt as his head shook. He swung his great sword and, ponderously, made to charge at Artur. Their swords clashed and then, as Anogin raised his sword high to swipe, Artur stepped to the side and thrust forward again into his pelvis, before quickly withdrawing the blade as the Belgae emitted a sigh of resignation, his mouth wide open, blood seeping out of each corner. His arms and sword, like a tree branch slowly splitting from its trunk, lowered in front of him. Still he managed to maintain the sneer and curled lips, but now he could not move his legs. His eyes roamed erratically, trying to fix the Prince with a determined stare, his lips tinged red with the blood that was oozing from his mouth. He was trying to say something. Whatever it was, it was unintelligible. He had lost control. Life was slipping away. His knees buckled and he lurched forward. With one final defiant look, he crashed to the ground at Artur's feet, his head striking rock and distorting. He tried to move it, his body shuddered and then, there was no more movement. He was dead.

Now the Dewnan and the Veneti fought hard! Led by Drustan, Kea and Menguy, they drove determinedly at the remaining Belgae, aiming to reach the Prince and the stricken Morlain. Quickly Artur ran to her.

'I am alright, I am alright; bruised and battered, but I will live and nothing is broken, I think. Go back to the fight. There is work still to do. Your men… the Company need you.'

He looked tenderly down towards her, his face full of concern.

'You are more hurt than you admit. Let me help you, at least to move you away from the fight. Come on, let me help you up.'

She turned her head and looked up to him, her eyes moist and half closed with pain and exhaustion.

'Maybe I could do with a hand to get me to my feet. I think I have sprained my ankle.'

The noise of the battle raged behind them, but the Dewnan and the Veneti ensured that the Belgae were fully occupied, allowing Artur to get Morlain away from the main part of the fight. She leant on his shoulder as she hobbled towards the riverbank.

'You saved my life,' she breathed heavily. 'Thank you. I think he meant to remove my head from my body.'

Suddenly, her whole body convulsed and her mouth coughed violently, retching both blood and bile. He held her as best he could. She stood upright, winced as she put too much weight on her swollen ankle, swallowed, and with eyes half closed, said, 'I need to rest. Please, help me to get to those trees. Honestly, I will be all right. It looks worse than it is. It's just that he kicked me very hard.' After all that he had heard and seen, he was surprised to feel her sudden anguish and a sob. 'And it will take a little while to recover.'

'Morlain, your bravery saved my life. I should be thanking you.' They had reached the trees. 'Sit, here, away from the battle. Now we will take the fight to them. Rest and I will return.'

'Good.' A pale smile passed across her lips as she looked up at him. 'Now go, finish the job, and take care.'

***

Two boats, full of Veneti warriors crossed Enyam's inflow and approached the first upstream jetty of the port. As the oarsmen held the boats in midstream, Lancelin stood in the prow of the first and gave instructions to the second.

'Moor on the far bank and follow the path to the crossing, cut off any who try to escape.'

Lancelin's boat pulled across to the jetty and he and Gwalian jumped ashore, he with his sword drawn and she with her bow firmly gripped. Lancelin called to the rest. 'We'll skirt along the bank, away from the pens and storage yard, and take them by surprise. Come on!'

They came upon the fight as Artur approached the rear of the Belgae line, engaged with the Dewnan and Veneti in front of them.

'Give it up, men of the Belgae; your leader is dead, your cause is lost and I still stand!'

Nouran's voice rose above the rest. 'Ee's right, scum bags. Yer big lummock of a leader is done for, skewered like the fat pig ee was. Cut and run while uze can, if I were you!'

Yet still the Belgae fought hard. Giving in was not part of their plan.

Then an arrow whizzed past Artur's head and embedded itself in the back of one of the closest Belgae. He fell instantly, then another – precise, deadly in its accuracy – brought a second Belgae down. The Prince turned to see the Veneti reinforcements emerge from behind the tree that Morlain sat in front of, roaring their battle cries, led by Lancelin, sword drawn. Alongside him was Gwalian, preparing a third arrow.

The new arrivals unnerved the Belgae. Those nearest the crossing began to falter in their resolve. Others fell to the attack that came at them from both sides now and their heads faltered, looking nervously from side to side. The flank closest to the crossing collapsed and the Belgae force, stumbling and frantically pushing, turned, panicked and ran. Water splashed everywhere as they fled and tried to get back across the river away from the tightening grip of the twin-sided attack, which had forced them into the narrow space the crossing afforded. Then, more shouting and battle cries as the fleeing Belgae met the oncoming Veneti contingent on the far bank. A small group, who had remained on the far side, managed to get away, but the rest quickly engaged with the oncoming rush of the Veneti men as they ran down the far bank and splashed into the water. There was real panic now – they had nowhere to go. Pushed back, they collided with the rest of the Belgae force trying to cross. Quickly, the river filled with bodies and blood-smattered warriors. There was no escape. With the Belgae now heavily outnumbered, the Dewnan and the Veneti closed in for the kill. For the Dewnan, it meant vengeance for the deaths of Casvelyn and Brengy and the hurt to Morlain.

Tamara deepened as the overnight rain washed down through the low hills and farmland of Nanmeur. Some of the injured Belgae lost their footing and fell into the increasing flow of water downstream of the crossing. Unable to get up and swim, they screamed for help but to no avail. The battle roared around them as they drowned noisily but unheeded, as the Dewnan and the Veneti stuck to their task. Finally, when the slaughter was nearly complete, the last of the Belgae threw away their swords and held their hands up in surrender. Just six remained, standing tall. Artur, at the forefront of the push from the port side bank, held his sword high to halt the fighting.

'Bring them back across, everyone to the port side. Victory is ours!'

All around cheered and splashed their way across, past bodies that still floated in the shallows. Some of the Veneti, those that had recently arrived, looked to Lancelin. He, in return, raised his eyebrows ironically and nodded, almost imperceptibly, but Artur saw it. He was pleased for the reinforcements and yet, for reasons he wasn't sure of, felt resentful of Lancelin's presence. He said nothing.

As he and the Company approached the bank, Gwalian was smiling as she came forward to greet him. Lancelin was quickly at her side.

'Pryns Artur, it was fortunate that we arrived when we did, it seems. Gwalian and I came as quickly as we could.'

Was it a statement of fact or was he trying to say something else, a hidden meaning? Artur looked sternly from one to the other and Gwalian's smile faded.

'I thank you both. We have fought hard today and lost good friends. We were overcoming the Belgae force, but your arrival certainly speeded our victory.'

The Company, with help from the Veneti, dragged the six Belgae prisoners ashore. Their grim faces contemplated the Prince. Several sneered at him, but none uttered a word as they awaited his decision on their fate.

First, though, he spoke again to Gwalian. 'Your brother, Lord Ewan, has returned. His men have fought bravely here today, but he was hurt early in the battle. He lies now, guarded by Tremaine and his gille, beyond the trees over there. I think you should go to him and see how he recovers.'

He smiled palely at her obvious concern at news of Ewan. She felt unsettled. Something had changed since she had seen him at Pendre the previous evening – a feeling between them, a bond, if not lost, had diminished at least. She was unsure why, but turned to walk towards where Ewan lay and Lancelin said, 'We have come upriver together. I will accompany you, provide assistance if I can.'

Artur turned and looked at Drustan, Kea and Gawen for a moment. They stared grimly back at him, an understanding built between them; his inner circle with Nouran, Gourgy and Maedoc. They knew what he was thinking. Only in the heat of a battle would any of them trust Lancelin.

Maedoc, standing close behind him said quietly, 'My Lord, We need to consider how we will deal with the prisoners. Will you excuse me while I tend to the Lady Morlain?'

Artur snapped out of his brooding and turned to his friend. 'Yes, of course, Maedoc. Can you help her, if she can walk? We will meet at the slave pen.'

Artur turned back to the mass of the Dewnan and the Veneti.

'Menguy, will you and your men deal with the bodies please. Build a pyre on the far bank, away from the port and well away from the path to Dynas Dowr Tewl.'

Menguy also stared grimly back at the Prince, did he suspect that something was about to happen? Maybe, but if he did, he said nothing.

'Pryns Artur, I will take all of the Veneti men, if that is agreeable to you. There are many bodies to gather and to retrieve from the river. And your fallen comrades?'

Gawen stepped forward. 'Pryns Artur, they are my kin. We travelled together. I will build a pyre for all three at the entrance to the port, upstream from here, where we landed earlier.'

The Prince, sombre and with suppressed anger in his voice as he looked along the line of battered, bloodied and bruised prisoners, continued: 'Gawen, that is fitting, but do not light the funeral fire until we join you, once we have dealt with our prisoners. We will honour Casvelyn, Brengy and his gille and their bravery together. Tinos, Ryol, will you join Gawen and help to build the pyre?'

Silyen, Drustan, Ambros, Marrek, Nouran, Gourgy, Kea, Briec, gilles and attendants – and the Belgae prisoners – were all that now remained, waiting for what the Prince would say next.

'Right, bring the prisoners and follow me.'

The Dewnan outnumbered the Belgae about four to one as they firmly held each of the captives and forcibly manhandled and dragged them through the trees. Following the Prince, and in the direction of the main goods-holding part of the port, they walked towards the slave pen.

As they came through the trees, they saw Morlain, supported by Maedoc, coming along a path that converged with theirs in the open area, in front of the slaves. Ahead, a small group of men with their swords drawn ready for confrontation, stood between the approaching Dewnan and the main gate to the pen.

Gourgy was the first to respond. 'Why! I thought we'd cleaned all 'em scumbags up. Let us at 'em. We'll soon sort 'em.'

He and the others around him drew their swords and made ready to engage, but Artur raised his hand to stop them and called to the man at the front of the armed group. 'Have we not had enough death and killing for one day? What do you want? You are not Belgae; what is your fight with us?'

Cidric stood forward. He did not sheath his sword but lowered it as he replied. The other Durotrages looked angrily at the captured Belgae.

'Lord, my name is Cidric and I speak for us all. We are Durotrages and we do not want to fight, only to take our wives, children and our old folk and go home. The bastard Veneti took them. They are the scourge of our lands and raid our homes while we work in the fields. They put all who cannot defend themselves in chains, drag them across country and lock them in their pen, not caring who lives and who dies from exhaustion.'

He paused for a moment, never taking his eyes from Artur.

'Then, those deceiving scumbags,' he gestured towards the Belgae, 'convinced us that they would help us to recover our people, but they actually wanted an expendable human shield to take the full force of your defence as they tried to cross the river. Many of our kin now lay slain in your woods and would still be alive, to till the fields and manage beasts, if the bastard Veneti had just left us alone.'

Artur nodded, considering Cidric's words.

'Cidric, we too have no fight with you. Instead, at the wain of Loor Skovarnek, we must take our real fight across the Mor Pretani to the Roman aggressor and defend our Pretan heritage and way of life. It is a heritage we share, I think, and we have stood together before against these wretched Estrenyon warlords and their followers.' He gestured to the prisoners, 'Brothers in arms, fighting together and manning the great line of forts that spread across your lands.'

Cidric was nodding his head now. He had heard the stories too.

Artur continued, 'Those days will come again! We will spread the Pretani way across all of the land as before, and so there is no sense in fighting against each other now. Go Cidric. Take your people with you and go back to your homes. We will not fight you or prevent you.'

He stood aside and gestured for the Dewnans to part for them to pass through.

He could hear disquiet amongst the Company. Drustan said quietly into his ear. 'Cousin, is this wise? They are not our property to give away.'

Artur turned to him. 'They are not anyone's property, but innocent farmers and their families, plucked from their trev and fields as they worked. The Durotrages are allies of the Dewnan, not slaves for barter and sale.'

He looked forcibly at his cousin who nodded and stood back.

Artur, as an afterthought said, 'And Drustan, as the Durotrages come out, replace them with the Belgae and secure them with the chains in the pen.'

Cidric and the Durotrages fighters looked nervously around them, surprised by the decision. Words passed with those in the pen. Artur looked to them, impatient for action, aware of the need to move quickly while his word and his authority still held all around him.

'Come on, let's go! When they have secured these Belgae scum in the pen, some of my men, Ambros, Marrek, Nouran and Gourgy and their gilles and retainers, will go with you two days back along the road to your land to assist your safe passage, but you must move with as much speed as possible now, even with your old folk. We have a battle to go to.'

Cidric and the others turned and opened the pen. The chains were undone using the key, which had been hung out of reach of the incarcerated, and those within began to pass quickly through the gate. As they gathered, ready to move off, Artur allowed himself a glance towards Morlain. She was waiting for him. Her head gave the slightest of inclinations, telling him what he needed to know. She agreed with his decision.

'Pryns Artur, we will not forget this.' Cidric stood before him. 'It is said that King Gawell favours a Belgae alliance and has been bought by them. He believes in a new way; but some of us still hold to the old alliances, built in kinship and with blood. We will ensure that others know that the bond between Durotrages and Dewnan is still alive in the ancient land of Orsa!'

'Cidric, I would like to think so, but now, Ambros and Marrek will lead the way and Nouran and Gourgy will defend the rear. Be vigilant. You may need to fight again before you reach your homes. Go with as much speed as you can muster and get as far as you can. The members of my Company that go with you must be back by dusk four days from now.'

Gourgy approached the Prince next as the last of the Belgae prisoners was secured. 'Not sure oi'm right pleased at playin' nurse to a bunch o'farmers, old folk and kids; 'ope yer not thinkin o'leavin without us, young Pryns.'

Artur spoke quietly but persuasively. 'Of course not. You and Nouran are two of our strongest fighters. Ambros and Marrek know the road up and over RunHoul, but some of the Belgae escaped. I need you to look out for them as you protect the Durotrages; take them out if you can, but do not abandon the farmers… and Gourgy, I want you back in four days. We need to practice our rowing.'

He opened his eyes a little wider and smiled, and Gourgy's toothy grin came back, 'Right yer are.'

Quickly now, the Durotrages pulled together, and marshalled by the supporting Dewnans, began to file along the path towards the crossing. As they went, there was suddenly a cry from behind the Prince as he and the others stood watching the Durotrages depart.

'Stop, fools! Who has let the slaves go? Was the gate not secured? Why are you not stopping them?'

Artur looked to Morlain. His eyes said that he had thought this might happen; maybe, even hoped that it would. He turned and Ewan, highly agitated, hobbled – supported by Lancelin and Gwalian – towards them. Her face appealed to Artur, but he did not look at her and instead looked coldly at her brother.

'Lord Ewan, I gave the order to free the captives.'

'How dare you, you had no right, who are you?' He had regained consciousness, but maybe not yet all of his memory. He turned to his two supports in turn. 'Sister, is this the boy you have spoken of? Mawgan's son? I hope he is not as careless with you as he is with my property. How does he hope to gain my approval for your union with actions like this? Lancelin, where are the men you brought upstream? Go and find them now and round up these slaves. Where is Menguy?'

The departing Durotrages and Dewnan had halted at this outburst. The Prince turned to them now. 'On you go, Gourgy and Nouran. You have a job to do. Go.'

Drustan clearly didn't agree and others looked nervous. Letting slaves go was unusual, and the Veneti were their allies, surely? Artur glanced again towards Morlain and Maedoc and they at least gave no doubt of their solidarity. He turned back. Lancelin had not moved. If he had attempted to follow the Veneti lord's command, Artur had decided that he would have to leave the Company immediately. He might even have tried to stop him with his sword.

Lancelin spoke next with a patient smile. 'Pryns Artur, the terms of your father's agreement say that the Veneti are at liberty to trade in whatever goods they gather and bring to this port. Should we not respect that? We are, after all, soon to cross to Armorica together and better to go without disagreement?'

'Were you there when my father made the agreement?'

'I'm sorry?'

'Were you in the hall when my father made the agreement? It is a simple enough question.'

'Well, no, obviously I...'

'No, so do not interpret my father's words on my behalf. These people will go back to their homes from where they should not have been taken and we will go and fight the Romans.'

The departing Durotrages began to disappear from view in amongst the trees.

'Where is Menguy, Menguy!'

Ewan, exasperated, looked angrily at Artur. 'We, the Veneti,' he paused for effect, 'have defended your lands and your interests for years while you and your father did nothing. We defend against pirates and prevent incursion by the Belgae, who would readily take this land and all its mineral wealth if they could, and this is how you repay us?'

'The Veneti have been good friends to the Dewnan and played an important part in defending our land and, of course, our arrangement has been mutually beneficial. Lord Ewan, your ill-considered actions brought these Belgae here. Men of my Company, good men, have died defending against an attack that need not have happened. Your men fought hard and bravely too, but it all need not have happened, and to lead the Belgae on to us was foolish and reckless. We will not take slaves from old friends and potential allies. That is my decision. I would suggest that you rest now and recover properly from your injury, while

I must go and honour those who gave their lives to recover your mistake.'

'Pryns of the Dewnan you may be, but I will make you pay for your insolence! My father and I have the power here.'

He broke from the support of Gwalian and Lancelin and made to draw his sword. Artur's hand went to his hilt and Kea and Drustan drew their swords. They had no need, Ewan, still light-headed strode forward only to fall involuntarily to his knees. Gwalian, with a look of hurt and anger towards Artur – a cutting edge to her face that he had not seen before – rushed forward and attempted to haul him back to his feet.

'Brother, stand up, come away. You must fully recover before you attempt anything strenuous.'

Artur moved forward to help, chastened by her look of reproach and concerned now that he had been too forthright to a still injured man.

'Get away! I don't need your help. I will not forget this. Lancelin, help me!'

Artur stepped back and looked on sternly while Lancelin helped Ewan to his feet and they turned and walked away.

Gwalian, visibly shaking with anger at the treatment of her brother, came forward and spoke quietly but firmly to Artur. 'Much has changed, my Lord, since only yesterday evening. We rushed back to help you, gathering support as we came, but it seems you, in some way, resent that and now, you wish also to denigrate my brother and the house of Aodren for going about our lawful business. We who have defended your lands and fought bravely when none others would.'

She paused for a moment and there was contempt in her eyes, so recently full of passion and desire.

'And yet, perhaps we should comfort ourselves. If this is how you treat your friends, I fear for your enemies. I have seen a new side to you today, Artur ap Mawgan, and I don't like you as much as I thought I did.'

She turned and walked away, and as his adrenaline decreased with the confrontation over, doubt began to creep into Artur's mind. It was hard to stay angry with her. It was Lancelin, with that smug supercilious countenance and delusional sense of his own importance! He did not care for Ewan either, and no matter how well both of them had defended the Dewnan lands, he could not see when he would ever fight with passion and determination beside them, as he might alongside Drustan, Kea or Gawen. Lancelin's attentions to Gwalian irritated him and there was something between them, but what? She had never said. No one had.

Morlain saw his reaction to Gwalian's rebuke, and with Maedoc's help, walked over to him.

'If it was good, don't throw it away. You are very different already to the man I met at Menitriel; confident and assertive in a way that maybe even I would not have expected so soon. You have fought a hard-won battle today and you and your men have grown to know each other, but we all know there has been another positive influence on you. Don't lose that to petulance and quick reactions – on both your parts!'

As she turned away, her chest was clearly still in a lot of pain. She appeared to be trying to whistle, but no sound came out. 'Maedoc, it is no good. I can't do it, can you?'

He lifted his head and blew a sound through his mouth, two notes, higher, then lower and, through the trees, Steren Uskis trotted confidently towards them.

She nuzzled his head and seemed to say something to him before turning back to Artur.

'I must go to Marghros and Dynas Kazak now and rest properly. I am exhausted. There is much to do and I must take all steps to recover quickly. Could you and Maedoc help me on to Steren Uskis? He will take me home.'

Once on his back, she turned and briefly spoke again.

'We will meet again soon.'

With that, the horse turned and trotted away towards the path to Ker Tamara. Artur watched her leave for a moment before turning to Maedoc.

'And now we will honour our dead.'

***

This Sacred Land – *end of the first part …*

Read on

This Sacred Land Part 2: The Fight for Freedom

With the Belgae defeated, and the Durotrages given their freedom, Artur casts his eyes across the sea to the ever-gathering shadows of war. Around him, there is disharmony and discord, with friends having fallen or turned against him. Before him, there is an army more powerful, and more vicious, than any the world has ever seen.

Can he make a stand where so many have fallen? Can he defy a great tide that is set to wash the Dewnan from their lands?

There is little chance for them in battle, and no choice but to fight, so he does the only thing he can do…

Gathering his Company, he joins the Veneti warriors in crossing the Mor Pretani. Whether he is ready yet or not, he has to put aside the suffering of his childhood so that he can confront Caesar's forces and save his people.

Even with Morlain's blade and Lancelin's guidance, it might not be enough. Even with his men's undying loyalty and the Sword of Menluit in his hand, it might not be enough. But they will stand and they will inspire the legends that will follow and, if this is to be the last page of their story, so be it. For it will be a story well told. A story to inspire. The story of the Dewnan.

connect with
tim bagshaw

Find out more about the Chronicles of the Dewnan and the author, Tim Bagshaw, at: www.inthelandofthedewnan.com

Printed in Great Britain
by Amazon